Pirate Cinema

Pirate Cinema

Cory Doctorow

TOR
TEEN

A Tom Doherty Associates Book
New York

PIRATE CINEMA

Copyright © 2012 by Cory Doctorow

Edited by Patrick Nielsen Hayden

A Tor Teen Book
Published by Tom Doherty Associates, LLC
175 Fifth Avenue
New York, NY 10010

www.tor-forge.com

Tor® is a registered trademark of Tom Doherty Associates, LLC.

ISBN 978-0-7653-2908-0 (hardcover)
ISBN 978-1-4299-4318-5 (e-book)

First Edition: October 2012

Printed in the United States of America

0 9 8 7 6 5 4 3 2 1

For Walt Disney:
remix artist, driven weirdo, public domain enthusiast

Acknowledgments

The initial inspiration for this book came from the actual Pirate Cinema movement all over the world, and I thank them most sincerely for letting me rip, mix, and burn their real-world awesomeness. Thanks also to Vodo.com's Jamie King, my go-to guy for help with the squatting bits. Simon Bradshaw was indispensable when it came to getting the legals right. Sarah Hodgson was a big help with the northerness, and Jo Roach was the all-time champ when it came to improving my dialect. As always, my mother, Roz Doctorow, was a stellar proofer and subeditor—I only wish I'd inherited more of her detail orientation.

Thank you to the United Kingdom, my adopted country, for making me an Official British Person in 2011. Thank you to the MPs who stood up to the dreadful Digital Economy Act, especially the indefatigable Tom Watson, who defied the three-line whip from the Labour Party. A backwards thanks to the corporatist lickspittles in Parliament and the Lords whose cowardice and corruption inspired this book. You know who you are, and so do the rest of us. We won't forget it, either. Betting against the Internet in the twenty-first century is felony stupidity, and I will personally see to it that this gross dereliction of duty dogs what's left of your political careers, forever.

Thanks to the copyfighters who stood up so brilliantly to SOPA, PIPA, and ACTA in 2012 and made me feel, for a moment, like some of my book was coming true.

Finally, thanks as always to my favorite British people: my wife, Alice, and my daughter, Poesy, who put up with all manner of bad behaviour on the way to this book's completion.

Pirate Cinema

Prologue

I will never forget the day my family got cut off from the Internet. I was hiding in my room as I usually did after school let out, holed up with a laptop I'd bought thirdhand and that I nursed to health with parts from here and there and a lot of cursing and sweat.

But that day, my little lappie was humming along, and I was humming with it, because I was about to take away Scot Colford's virginity.

You know Scot Colford, of course. They've been watching him on telly and at the cinema since my mum was a girl, and he'd been dead for a year at that point. But dead or not, I was still going to take poor little Scoty's virginity, and I was going to use Monalisa Fiore-Oglethorpe to do it.

You probably didn't know that Scot and Monalisa did a love scene together, did you? It was over fifty years ago, when they were both teen heartthrobs, and they were costars in a genuinely terrible straight-to-net film called *No Hope,* about a pair of clean-cut youngsters who fall in love despite their class differences. It was a real weeper, and the supporting appearances in roles as dad, mum, best mate, pastor, teacher, etc, were so forgettable that they could probably be used as treatment for erasing traumatic memories.

But Scot and Monalisa, they had *chemistry* (and truth be told, Monalisa had *geography,* too—hills and valleys and that). They smoldered at each other the way only teenagers can, juicy with hormones and gagging to get their newly hairy bits into play. Adults like to pretend that sex is something that begins at eighteen, but Romeo and Juliet were, like, *thirteen.*

Here's something else about Scot and Monalisa: they both used body doubles for other roles around then (Scot didn't want to get his knob out in a 3D production of *Equus,* while Monalisa was paranoid about the spots on her back and demanded a double for her role in *Bikini Trouble in Little Blackpool*). Those body doubles—Dan Cohen and Alana Dinova—were in *another* film, even dumber than *Bikini Trouble,* called *Summer Heat.* And in *Summer Heat,* they got their hairy bits into *serious* play.

I'd known about the /No Hope/*Equus*/*Bikini Trouble*/*Summer Heat* situation for, like, a year, and had always thought it'd be fun to edit together a little creative virginity-losing scene between Scot and Monalisa, since they were both clearly yearning for it back then (and who knows, maybe they slipped away from their chaperones for a little hide-the-chipolata in an empty trailer!).

But what got me into motion was the accidental discovery that both Scot and Monalisa had done another job together, ten years earlier, when they were *six*—an advert for a birthday-party service in which they chased each other around a suburban middle-class yard with squirt guns, faces covered in cake and ice cream. I found this lovely, lovely bit of video on a torrent tracker out of somewhere in Eastern Europe (Google Translate wouldn't touch it because it was on the piracy list, but RogueTrans said it was written in Ukrainian, but it also couldn't get about half the words, so who can say?).

It was this bit of commercial toss that moved me to cut the scene. You see, now I had the missing ingredient, the thing that took my mashup from something trite and obvious to something genuinely *moving*—a flashback to happier, carefree times, before all the hairy bits got hairy, before the smoldering began in earnest. The fact that the commercial footage was way way down-rez from the other stuff actually made it *better,* because it would look like it came from an earlier era, a kind of home-film shaky-cam feel that I bumped up using a video-effects app I found on

yet another dodgy site, this one from Tajikistan or Kyrgyzstan—
one of the stans, anyroad.

So there I was, in my broom-closet of a bedroom, headphones
screwed in tight against the barking of the dogs next door in the
Albertsons' flat, wrists aching from some truly epic mousing,
homework alerts piling up around the edge of my screen, when
the Knock came at the door.

It was definitely a capital-K Knock, the kind of knock they
Foley in for police flicks, with a lot of ominous reverb that cuts
off sharply, *whang, whang, whang*. The thunder of authority on two
legs. It even penetrated my headphones, shook all the way down
to my balls with the premonition of something awful about to
come. I slipped the headphones around my neck, hit the panic-
button key combo that put my lappie into paranoid lockdown,
unmounting the encrypted disks and rebooting into a sanitized
OS that had a bunch of plausible homework assignments and some
innocent messages to my mates (all randomly generated). I assumed that this would work. Hoped it would, anyway. I could
edit video like a demon and follow instructions I found on the net
as well as anyone, but I confess that I barely knew what all this
crypto stuff was, hardly understood how computers themselves
worked. Back then, anyway.

I crept out into the hallway and peeked around the corner as
my mum answered the door.

"Can I help you?"

"Mrs. McCauley?"

"Yes?"

"I'm Lawrence Foxton, a Police Community Support Officer here on the estate. I don't think we've met before, have we?"

Police Community Support Officers: a fake copper. A volun-
teer policeman who gets to lord his tiny, ridiculous crumb of
power over his neighbors, giving orders, enforcing curfews, dragging you off to the real cops for punishment if you refuse to obey
him. *I* knew Larry Foxton because I'd escaped his clutches any

number of times, scarpering from the deserted rec with my pals before he could catch up, puffing along under his anti-stab vest and laden belt filled with Taser, pepper spray, and plastic handcuff straps.

"I don't think so, Mr. Foxton." Mum had the hard tone in her voice she used when she thought me or Cora were winding her up, a no-nonsense voice that demanded that you get to the point.

"Well, I'm sorry to have to meet you under these circumstances. I'm afraid that I'm here to notify you that your Internet access is being terminated, effective"—he made a show of looking at the faceplate of his police-issue ruggedized mobile—"now. Your address has been used to breach copyright through several acts of illegal downloading. You have been notified of these acts on two separate occasions. The penalty for a third offense is a one-year suspension of network access. You have the right to an appeal. If you choose to appeal, you must present yourself in person at the Bradford magistrates' court in the next forty-eight hours." He hefted a little thermal printer clipped to his belt, tore off a strip of paper, and handed it to her. "Bring this." His tone grew even more official and phony: "Do you understand and consent to this?" He turned his chest to face Mum, ostentatiously putting her right in the path of the CCTV in his hat brim and over his breast pocket.

Mum sagged in the doorframe and reached her hand out to steady herself. Her knees buckled the way they did so often, ever since she'd started getting her pains and had to quit her job. "You're joking," she said. "You can't be serious—"

"Thank you," he said. "Have a nice day." He turned on his heel and walked away, little clicking steps like a toy dog, receding into the distance as Mum stood in the doorway, holding the curl of thermal paper, legs shaking.

And that was how we lost our Internet.

"Anthony!" she called. "Anthony!" she called again.
Dad, holed up in the bedroom, didn't say anything.

"*Anthony!*"

"Hold on, will you? The bloody phone's not working and I'm going to get docked—"

She wobbled down the hall and flung open the bedroom door. "Anthony, they've shut off the Internet!"

I ducked back into my room and cowered, contemplating the magnitude of the vat of shit I had just fallen into. My stupid, *stupid* obsession with a dead film star had just destroyed my family.

I could hear them shouting through the thin wall. No words, just tones. Mum nearly in tears, Dad going from incomprehension to disbelief to murderous rage.

"*Trent!*"

It was like the scene in *Man in the Cellar,* the bowel-looseningly frightening Scot slasher film. Scot's in the closet, and the murderer has just done in Scot's brother and escaped from the garage where they'd trapped him, and is howling in fury as he thunders down the hallway, and Scot is in that closet, rasping breath and eyes so wide they're nearly all whites, and the moment stretches like hot gum on a pavement—

"*Trent!*"

The door to my room banged open so hard that it sent a pile of books tumbling off my shelf. One of them bounced off my cheekbone, sending me reeling back, head cracking against the tiny, grimy window. I wrapped my head in my hands and pushed myself back into the corner.

Dad's big hands grabbed me. He'd been a scrapper when he was my age, a legendary fighter well known to the Bradford coppers. In the years since he'd taken accent training and got his job working the phone, he'd got a bit fat and lost half a step, but in my mind's eye, I still only came up to his knee. He pulled my hands away from my face and pinned them at my sides and looked into my eyes.

I'd thought he was angry, and he was, a bit, but when I looked into those eyes, I saw that what I had mistaken for anger was really *terror.* He was even more scared than I was. Scared that without the net, his job was gone. Scared that without the net, Mum couldn't sign on every week and get her benefits. Without the net, my sister Cora wouldn't be able to do her schoolwork.

"Trent," he said, his chest heaving. "Trent, what have you done?" There were tears in his eyes.

I tried to find the words. *We all do it,* I wanted to say. *You do it,* I wanted to say. *I had to do it,* I wanted to say. But what came out, when I opened my mouth, was nothing. Dad's hands tightened on my arms and for a moment, I was sure he was going to beat the hell out of me, really beat me, like you saw some of the other dads do on the estate. But then he let go of me and turned round and stormed out of the flat. Mum stood in the door to my room, sagging hard against the doorframe, eyes rimmed with red, mouth pulled down in sorrow and pain. I opened my mouth again, but again, no words came out.

I was sixteen. I didn't have the words to explain why I'd downloaded and kept downloading. Why making the film that was in my head was such an all-consuming obsession. I'd read stories of the great directors—Hitchcock, Lucas, Smith—and how they worked their arses off, ruined their health, ruined their family lives, just to get that film out of their head and onto the screen. In my mind, I was one of them, someone who *had* to get this bloody film out of my skull, like, I was filled with holy fire and it would burn me up if I didn't send it somewhere.

That had all seemed proper noble and exciting and heroic right up to the point that the fake copper turned up at the flat and took away my family's Internet and ruined our lives. After that, it seemed like a stupid, childish, selfish whim.

I didn't come home that night. I sulked around the estate, half-hoping that Mum and Dad would come find me, half-hoping they wouldn't. I couldn't stand the thought of facing them again. First I went and sat under the slide in the playground, where it was all stubs from spliffs and dried-out, crumbly dog turds. Then it got cold, so I went to the community center and paid my pound to get in and hid out in the back of the room, watching kids play snooker and table tennis with unseeing eyes. When they shut that down for the night, I tried to get into a couple of pubs, the kind of all-night places where they weren't so picky about checking ID, but they weren't keen on having obviously underage kids taking up valuable space and not ordering things, and so I ended up wandering the streets of Bradford, the ring-road where the wasted boys and girls howled at one another in a grim parody of merriment, swilling alco-pops and getting into pointless, sloppy fights.

I'd spent my whole life in Bradford, and in broad daylight I felt like the whole city was my manor, no corner of it I didn't know, but in the yellow streetlight and sickly moonglow, I felt like an utter stranger. A scared and very small and defenseless stranger.

In the end, I curled up on a bench in Peel Park, hidden under a rattly newspaper, and slept for what felt like ten seconds before a PCSO woke me up with a rough shake and a bright light in my eyes and sent me back to wander the streets. It was coming on dawn then, and I had a deep chill in my bones, and a drip of snot that replaced itself on the tip of my nose every time I wiped it off on my sleeve. I felt like a proper ruin and misery-guts when I finally dragged my arse back home, stuck my key in the lock, and waited for the estate's ancient and cantankerous network to let me into our house.

I tiptoed through the sitting room, headed for my room and my soft and wondrous bed. I was nearly to my door when someone hissed at me from the sofa, making me jump so high I nearly fell over, I whirled and found my sister sitting there. Cora was two years younger than me, and, unlike me, she was brilliant at school, a right square. She brought home test papers covered in checkmarks and smiley faces, and her teachers often asked her to work with thick students to help them get their grades up. I had shown her how to use my edit-suite when she was only ten, and she was nearly as good an editor as I was. Her homework videos were the stuff of legend.

At thirteen years old, Cora had been a slightly podgy and

awkward girl who dressed like a little kid in shirts that advertised her favorite little bands. But now she was fourteen, and overnight she'd turned into some kind of actual teenaged girl with round soft bits where you'd expect them, and new clothes that she and her mates made on the youth center's sewing machines from the stuff they had in their closets. She always had some boy or another mooching around after her, spotty specimens who practically dripped hormones on her. It roused some kind of odd brotherly sentiment in me that I hadn't realized was there. By which I mean, I wanted to pound them and tell them that I'd break their legs if they didn't stay away from my baby sister.

In private Cora usually treated me with a kind of big-bro reverence that she'd had when we were little kids, when I was the older one who could do no wrong. In public, of course, I wasn't nearly cool enough to acknowledge, but that was all right, I could understand that. That morning, there was no reverence in her expression; rather, she seethed with loathing.

"Arsehole," she said, spitting the word out under her breath.

"Cora—" I said, holding my hands up, my arms feeling like they were hung with lead weights. "Listen—"

"Forget it," she said in the same savage, hissing whisper. "I don't care. You could have at least been smart, used a proxy, cracked someone else's wireless." She was right. The neighbors had changed their WiFi password and my favorite proxies had all been blocked by the Great Firewall, and I'd been too lazy to disguise my tracks. "*Now* what am I supposed to do? How am I supposed to do my homework? I've got GCSEs soon; what am I supposed to do, study at the library?" Cora revised every moment she had, odd hours of the morning before the house was awake, late at night after she'd come back from babysitting. Our nearest library closed at 5:30 and was only open four days a week thanks to the latest round of budget cuts.

"I know," I said. "I know. I'll just—" I waved my hands. I'd got that far a hundred times in the night, *I'd just*— Just what? Just apologize to Universal Pictures and Warner Brothers? Call the main switchboard and ask to speak to the head copyright enforcer and grovel for my family's Internet connection? It was ridiculous. Some corporate mucker in California didn't give a rat's arse about my family or its Internet access.

"You won't do shit," she said. She stood up and marched to her room. Before she closed the door, she turned and skewered me on her glare: "Ever."

I left home two weeks later.

It wasn't the disappointed looks from my old man, the increasing desperation of the whispered conversations he had with Mum whenever finances came up, or the hateful filthies from my adoring little sister.

No, it was the film.

Specifically, it was the fact that I *still wanted to make my film*. There's only so much moping in your room that you can do, and eventually I found myself firing up my lappie and turning back to my intricate editing project that had been so rudely interrupted. Before long, I was absolutely engrossed in deflowering Scot Colford. And moments after *that*, I realized that I needed some more footage to finish the project—a scene from later in *Bikini Trouble* when Monalisa was eating an ice-cream cone with a sultry, smoldering look that would have been perfect for the post-shag moment. Reflexively, I lit up my downloader and made ready to go a-hunting for Monalisa's ice-cream scene.

Of course, it didn't work. The network wasn't there anymore. As the error message popped up on my screen, all my misery and guilt pressed back in on me. It was like some gigantic weight pressing on my chest and shoulders and face, smothering me, making me feel like the lowest, most awful person on the planet. It literally felt like I was strangling on my own awful emotions, and I sat there, wishing that I could die.

I scrunched my eyes up as tight as I could and whispered the words over and over in my mind: *want to die, want to die*. If wishing could make you pop your clogs, I would have dropped dead right there in my bedroom, and there they'd have found me, slumped over my keyboard, eyes closed, awful whirling brain finally silent. Then they'd have forgiven me, and they could go back to the council and ask to have the net reconnected and Dad could get his job back and Mum could get her benefits again and poor Cora would be able to graduate with top marks and go on to Oxford or Cambridge, where all the clever clogs and brain-boxes went to meet up with all the other future leaders of Britain.

I'd been low before, but never low like that. Never wishing with every cell in my body to die. I found that I'd been holding my breath, and I gasped in and finally realized that even if I didn't die, I couldn't go on living like that. I knew what I had to do.

I had almost a hundred quid saved up in a hollow book I'd made from a copy of *Dracula* that the local library had thrown away. I'd sliced out a rectangle from the center of each page by hand with our sharpest kitchen knife, then glued the edges together and left it under one of the legs of my bed for two days so that you couldn't tell from either side that there was anything tricky about it. I took it out and pulled my school bag from under the bed and carefully folded three pairs of clean pants, a spare pair of jeans, a warm hoodie, my toothbrush and the stuff I put on my spots, a spool of dental floss, and a little sewing kit Cora had given me one birthday along with a sweet little note about learning to sew my own bloody shirt buttons. It was amazing how easy it was to pack all this. Somewhere in the back of my mind, I'd always known, I think, that I'd have to pack a small bag and just go. Some part of my subconscious was honest enough with itself to know that I had no place among polite society.

Or maybe I was just another teenaged dramatist, caught up in my own tragedy. Either way, it was clear that my guilty conscience was happy to shut its gob and quit its whining so long as I was in motion and headed for my destiny.

No one noticed me go. Dinner had come and gone, and, as usual, I'd stayed away from the family through it, sneaking out after all the dishes had been cleared away to poach something from the cupboard. Mum was gamely still cooking dinners, though increasingly they consisted of whatever was on deepest discount at Iceland or something from the local church soup kitchen. She'd brought home an entire case of lethally salted ramen noodles in bright Cambodian packaging and kept trying to dress them up with slices of boiled eggs or bits of cheapest mince formed into halfhearted, fatty meatballs.

If they missed me at dinner, they never let on. I'd boil a cup of water and make plain noodles in my room and wash the cup and put it on the draining board while they watched telly in the sitting room. Cora rarely made it to dinner, too, but she wasn't hiding in her room; she was over at some mate's place, scrounging free Internet through a dodgy network bridge (none of the family's devices had network cards registered to work on the estate network, so the only way to get online was to install illegal software on a friend's machine and cable it to ours and pray that the net-gods didn't figure out what we were up to).

And so no one heard me go as I snuck out the door and headed for the bus station. I stopped at a newsagent's by the station and bought a new pay-as-you-go SIM for cash, chucking the old one in three different bins after slicing it up with the tough little scissors from the sewing kit. Then I bought a coach ticket to London Victoria terminal. I knew Victoria a bit, from a school trip once, and a family visit the summer before. I remembered it as bustling and humming and huge and exciting, and that was the image I had in my head as I settled into my seat, next to an old woman with a sniffle and a prim copy of the Bible that she read with a finger that traced the lines as she moved her lips and whispered the words.

The coach had a slow wireless link and there were outlets under the seats. I plugged in my lappie and got on the wireless, using a prepaid Visa card I'd bought from the same newsagent's shop, having given my favorite nom de guerre, *Cecil B. DeVil*. It's a tribute to Cecil B. DeMille, a great and awful director, the first superstar director, a man who's name was once synonymous with film itself. The trip to London flew by as I lost myself in deflowering poor old Scot, grabbing my missing footage through a proxy in Tehran that wasn't too fussed about copyright (though it was a lot pickier about porn sites and anything likely to cause offense to your average mullah).

By the time the coach pulled into Victoria, my scene was *perfect*. I mean *perfect* with blinking lights and a joyful tune P-E-R-F-E-C-T. All two minutes, twenty-five seconds' worth. I didn't have time to upload it to any of the YouTubes before the coach stopped, but that was okay. It would keep. I had a warm glow throughout my body, like I'd just drunk some thick hot chocolate on a day when the air was so cold the bogeys froze in your nose.

I floated off the coach and into Victoria Station.

And came crashing back down to Earth.

The last time I'd been in the station, it had been filled with morning commuters rushing about, kids in school blazers and caps shouting and running, a few stern bobbies looking on with their ridiculous, enormous helmets that always made me think of a huge, looming cock, one that bristled with little lenses that stared around in all directions at once.

But as we pulled in, a little after 9:00 P.M. on a Wednesday, rain shitting down around us in fat, dirty drops, Victoria Station was a very different place. It was nearly empty, and the people that were there seemed a lot . . . grimmer. They had proper moody faces on, the ones that weren't openly hostile, like the beardie weirdie in an old raincoat who shot me a look of pure hatred and mouthed something angry at me. The coppers didn't look friendly and ridiculous—they were flinty-eyed and suspicious, and as I passed two of them, they followed me with their gaze and the tilt of their bodies.

And I stood there in that high-ceilinged concourse, surrounded by the mutters and farts of the night people and the night trains, and realized that I hadn't the slightest bloody idea what to do next.

————

What to do next. I wandered around the station a bit, bought myself a hot chocolate (it didn't make the warm feeling come back), stared aimlessly at my phone. What I *should* have done, I knew, was buy a ticket *back* home and get back on a bus and forget this whole business. But that's not what I did.

Instead, I set off for London. *Real* London. Roaring, nighttime London, as I'd seen it in a thousand films and TV shows and Internet vids, the London where glittering people and glittering lights passed one another as black cabs snuffled through the streets chased by handsome boys and beautiful girls on bikes or scooters. *That* London.

I started in Leicester Square. My phone's map thought it knew a pretty good way of getting there in twenty-minutes walk, but it wanted me to walk on all the main roads where the passing cars on the rainy tarmac made so much noise I couldn't even hear myself think. So I took myself on my own route, on the cobbeldy, wobbeldy side streets and alleys that looked like they had in the time of King Edward and Queen Victoria, except for the strange growths of satellite dishes rudely bolted to their sides, all facing the same direction, like a crowd of round idiot faces all baffled by the same distant phenomenon in the night sky.

Just then, in the narrow, wet streets with my springy-soled boots bounding me down the pavement, the London-beat shushing through the nearby main roads, and everything I owned on my back—it felt like the opening credits of a film. The film of Trent McCauley's life, starring Trent McCauley as Trent McCauley, with special guest stars Trent McCauley and Trent McCauley, and maybe a surprise cameo from Scot Colford as the worshipful sidekick. And then the big opening shot, wending my way up a dingy road between Trafalgar Square and into Leicester Square in full tilt.

Every light was lit. Every square meter of ground had at least four people standing on it, and nearly everyone was either laughing, smoking a gigantic spliff, shouting drunkenly, or holding a signboard advertising something dubious, cheap, and urgent. Some were doing all these things. The men were dressed like gangsters out of a film. The women looked like soft-core porn stars or run-way models, with lots of wet fabric clinging to curves that would have put Monalisa to shame.

I stood at the edge of it for a moment, like a swimmer about to jump into a pool. Then, I jumped.

I just pushed my way in, bouncing back and forth like a rubber ball in a room that was all corners and trampolines. Someone handed me a spliff—an older guy with eyes like a baboon's arse, horny fingernails yellow and thick—and I sucked up a double lungful of fragrant skunk, the crackle of the paper somehow loud over the sound of a million conversations and raindrops. The end was soggy with the slobber of any number of strangers and I passed it on to a pair of girls in glittering pink bowler hats and angel wings, wearing huge "Hen Night" badges to one side of their deep cleavage. One kissed me on the cheek, drunken fumes and a bit of tongue, and I reeled away, drunk on glorious! London!

A film kicked out and spilled eight hundred more people into the night, holding huge cups of fizzy drink, wafting the smells of aftershave and perfume into the evenings. The tramps descended on them like flies, and they scattered coins like royalty before peasants. They were all talking films, films, films. The marquee said they'd been to see *That Time We All Got Stupid and How Much Fun It Was, Wasn't It?* (the latest and most extreme example of the ridiculous trend to extralong film titles). I'd heard good things about it, downloaded the first twenty minutes after it played the festival circuit last year, and would have given anything to fall in alongside of those chattering people and join the chatter.

But it was a wet night, and they were hurrying for the road, hurrying to get in cabs and get out of the wet, and the next show let in, and soon the square was nearly empty—just tramps, coppers, men with signboards . . . and me.

The opening credits had run, the big first scene had concluded, the camera was zooming in on our hero, and he was about to do something heroic and decisive, something that would take him on his first step to destiny.

Only I had no bloody clue what that step might be.

I didn't sleep at all that night. I made my way to Soho, where the clubs were still heaving and disgorging happy people, and I hung about on their periphery until 3:00 A.M. I ducked into a few all-night cafés to use the toilet and get warm, pretending to be part of larger groups so that no one asked me to buy anything. Then the Soho crowds fell away. I knew that somewhere in London there were all-night parties going on, but I had no idea how to find them. Without the crowds for camouflage, I felt like I was wearing a neon sign that read I AM NEW IN TOWN, UNDERAGE, CARRYING CASH, PHYSICALLY DEFENSELESS, AND EASILY TRICKED. PLEASE TAKE ADVANTAGE OF ME.

As I walked the streets, faces leered out of the dark at me, hissing offers of drugs or sex, or just hissing, "Come here, come here, see what I've got." I didn't want to see what they had. To be totally honest, I wanted my mum.

Finally, the sun came up, and morning joggers and dog-walkers began to appear on the pavements. Bleary-eyed dads pushed past me with prams that let out the cries of sleepless babies. I had a legless, drunken feeling as I walked down Oxford Street, heading west with the sun rising behind me and my shadow stretching before me as long as a pipe-cleaner man.

I found myself in Hyde Park at the Marble Arch end, and now there were more joggers, and cyclists, and little kids kicking around a football wearing trackies and shorts and puffing out clouds of condensation in the frigid morning. I sat down on the sidelines in the damp grass next to a little group of wary parents and watched the ball roll from kid to kid, listened to the happy sounds as they knackered themselves out. The sun got higher and warmed my face, and I made a pillow of my jacket and my pack and leaned back and let my eyes close and the warmth dry out the long night. My mind was whirling a thousand miles per hour, trying to figure out where I'd go and what I'd do now that I'd come to the big city. But sleep wouldn't be put off by panic, and my tired, tired body insisted on rest, and before I knew it, I'd gone to sleep.

It was a wonderful, sweet-scented sleep, broken up with the sounds of happy people passing by and playing, dogs barking and chasing balls, kids messing around in the grass, buses and taxis belching in the distance. And when I woke, I just lay there basking in the wonder and beauty of it all. I was in London, I was young, I was no longer a danger to my family. I was on the adventure of my life. It was all going to be all right.

And that's when I noticed that someone had stolen my rucksack out from under my head while I slept, taking my laptop, my spare clothes, my toothbrush—everything.

Chapter 1

ALONE NO MORE/THE JAMMIE DODGERS/
POSH DIGS/ABSTRACTION OF ELECTRICITY

My "adventure" wasn't much fun after that. I was smart enough to find a shelter for runaways run by a church in Shoreditch, and I checked myself in that night, lying and saying I was eighteen. I was worried that they'd send me home if I said I was sixteen. I'm pretty sure the old dear behind the counter knew that I was lying, but she didn't seem to mind. She had a strong Yorkshire accent that managed to be stern and affectionate at the same time.

My bedfellows in the shelter—all boys, girls were kept in a separate place—ranged from terrifying to terrified. Some were proper hard men, all gangster talk about knives and beatings and that. Some were even younger looking than me, with haunted eyes and quick flinches whenever anyone spoke too loud. We slept eight to a room, in bunk beds that were barely wide enough to contain my skinny shoulders, and the next day, another old dear let me pick out some clothes and a backpack from mountains of donated stuff. The clothes were actually pretty good. Better, in fact, than the clothes I'd arrived in London wearing; Bradford was a good five years behind the bleeding edge of fashion you saw on the streets of Shoreditch, so these last-year's castoffs were smarter than anything I'd ever owned.

They fed me a tasteless but filling breakfast of oatmeal and greasy bacon that sat in my stomach like a rock after they kicked me out into the streets. It was 8:00 A.M. and everyone was marching for the tube to go to work, or queuing up for the buses, and it seemed like I was the only one with nowhere to go. I still had about forty pounds in my pocket, but that wouldn't go very far in the posh coffee bars of Shoreditch, where even a black coffee cost three quid. And I didn't have a laptop anymore (every time

I thought of my lost video, never to be uploaded to a YouTube, gone forever, my heart cramped up in my chest).

I watched the people streaming down into Old Street Station, clattering down the stairs, dodging the men trying to hand them free newspapers (I got one of each to read later), and stepping around the tramps who rattled their cups at them, striving to puncture the goggled, headphoned solitude and impinge upon their consciousness. They were largely unsuccessful.

I thought dismally that I would probably have to join them soon. I had never had a real job and I didn't think the nice people with the posh film companies in Soho were looking to hire a plucky, underage video editor with a thick northern accent and someone else's clothes on his back. How the bloody hell did all those tramps earn a living? Hundreds of people had gone by and not a one of them had given a penny, as far as I could tell.

Then, without warning, they scattered, melting into the crowds and vanishing into the streets. A moment later, a flock of Community Support Police Officers in bright yellow high-visibility vests swaggered out of each of the station's exits, each swiveling slowly so that the cameras around their bodies got a good look at the street.

I sighed and slumped. Begging was hard enough to contemplate. But begging *and* being on the run from the cops all the time? It was too miserable to even think about.

The PCSOs disappeared into the distance, ducking into the Starbucks or getting on buses, and the tramps trickled back from their hidey holes. A new lad stationed himself at the bottom of the stairwell where I was standing, a huge grin plastered on his face, framed by a three-day beard that was somehow rakish instead of sad. He had a sign drawn on a large sheet of white cardboard, with several things glued or duct-taped to it: a box of Kleenex, a pump-handled hand-sanitizer, a tray of breath-mints with a little single-serving lever that dropped one into your hand. Above them was written, in big, friendly graffiti letters, FREE TISSUE/SANITIZER/MINTS—HELP THE HOMELESS—FANKS,

GUV!, and next to that, a cup that rattled from all the pound coins in it.

As commuters pelted out of the station and headed for the stairs, they'd stop and read his sign, laugh, drop a pound in his cup, take a squirt of sanitizer or a Kleenex or a mint (he'd urge them to do it; it seemed they were in danger of passing by without helping themselves), laugh again, and head upstairs.

I thought I was being subtle and nearly invisible, skulking at the top of the stairwell and watching, but at the next break in the commuter traffic, he looked square at me and gave me a "Come here" gesture. Caught, I made my way to him. He stuck his hand out.

"Jem Dodger," he said. "Gentleman of leisure and lover of fine food and laughter. Pleased to make your acquaintance, guv." He said it in a broad, comic cockney accent and even tugged at an invisible cap brim as he said it. I laughed.

"Trent McCauley," I said. I tried to think of something as cool as "gentleman of leisure" to add, but all I came up with was "Cinema aficionado and inveterate pirate," which sounded a lot better in my head than it did in the London air, but he smiled back at me.

"Trent," he said. "Saw you at the shelter last night. Let me guess. First night, yeah?"

"In the shelter? Yeah."

"In the *world*, son. Forgive me for saying so, but you have the look of someone who's just got off a bus from the arse-end of East Shitshire with a hat full of dreams, a pocketful of hope, and a head full of grape jelly. Have I got that right?"

I felt a little jet of resentment, but I had to concede the point. "Technically I've been here for *two* days," I said. "Last night was my first night in the shelter."

He winked. "Spent the first night wandering the glittering streets of London, didn't ya?"

I shook my head. "You certainly seem to know a lot about me."

"Mate," he said, and he lost the cockney accent and came across pure north, like he'd been raised on the next estate. "I *am* you. I *was* you, anyway. A few years ago. Now I'm the Jammie Dodger, Prince of the London Byways, Count of the Canalsides, Squire of the Squat, and so on and so on."

Another train had come in, and more people were coming out of the station. He shooed me off to one side and began his smiling come-ons to the new arrivals. A minute later, he'd collected another twelve quid and he waved me back over.

"Now, Master McCauley, you may be wondering why I called you over here."

I found his chirpy mode of speech impossible to resist, so I went with it. "Indeed I am, Mr. Dodger. Wondering that very thing, I was."

He nodded encouragement, pleased that I was going along with the wheeze. "Right. Well, you saw all the other sorry sods holding up signs in this station, I take it?"

I nodded.

"None of 'em is making a penny. None of 'em know *how* to make a penny. That's cos most of the people who end up here get here because something awful's gone wrong with them and they don't have the cunning and fortitude to roll with it. Mostly, people end up holding a sign and shaking a cup because someone's done them over terribly—raped them, beat them up, given them awful head-drugs—and they don't have the education, skills or sanity to work out how to do any better.

"Now, me, I'm here because I am a gentleman of leisure, as I believe I have informed you already. Whatever happened in my past, I was clever and quick and tricksy enough to deal with it. So when I landed up holding a sign in a tube station hoping for the average Londoner to open his wallet and his heart to buy me supper, I didn't just find any old sheet of brown cardboard box, scrawl a pathetic message on it, and hope for the best.

"No. I went out and bought all different kinds of cards—bright yellow, pink, blue, plain white—and tested each one. See?" He reached into the back pocket of his jeans and drew out a small, worn notebook. He opened it to the first page and stuck it under my nose. It was headed "Colors: (HELP THE HOMELESS)" and there were two columns running its length, one listing different colored cardboards, the other showing different amounts.

"Look at that, would you? See how poorly brown performs? It's the bottom of the barrel. People just don't want to open their wallets to a man holding a sign that looks like it was made out of an old cardboard box. You'd think they would, right? Appearance of deserving thrift an' all? But they don't. They like practically any color *except* brown. And the best one, well, it's good old white." He rattled his sign. "Lots of contrast, looks clean. I buy a new one every day down at the art supply shop in Shoreditch High Street. The punters like a man what takes pride in his sign."

Another tubeload of passengers came up, and he shooed me off again, making another twentysome pounds in just a few minutes. "Now, as to wording, just have a look." He showed me the subsequent pages of his book. Each had a different header: HOMELESS—HELP. HUNGRY—HELP. HELP THE HUNGRY. HELP THE HOMELESS. DESPERATE. DESPERATE—HELP. "What I noticed was, people really *respond* to a call for action. It's not enough to say, 'homeless, miserable, starving' and so on. You need to cap it off with a request of some kind, so they know what you're after. 'Help the Homeless' outperforms everything else I've tried. Simple, to the point."

He flipped more pages, and now I was looking at charts showing all the different things he'd given away with his signboard, and the combinations he'd tried. "You gave away *liverwurst*?" I stared at the page.

"Well, no," he said. "But I tried. Turns out no one wants to accept a cracker and liver-paste from a tramp in a tube station." He shrugged. "It wasn't a great idea. I ended up eating liverwurst for three days. But it didn't cost me much to try and fail. If you want to double your success rate, triple your failure rate. That's what I always say. And sometimes, you've just got to be crazy about it. Every time I go into a shop, I'm on the lookout for something else I can do. See this?" He held up a tiny screwdriver. "Eyeglass tightener. You wait until sunglasses season, I'm going to be *minted*. 'Free DIY Spectacle Repair. Help the Homeless.'"

"Why are you telling me all this?"

He shrugged again. "I tell anyone who'll listen, to be honest. Breaks my heart to see those poor sods going hungry. And you seemed like you were fresh off the boat, like you probably needed a little help."

"So you think I should go make a sign like yours?"

He nodded. "Why not? But this is just a way to get a little ready cash when I need it." He carefully rolled up the signboard, emptying his cup into his front pocket, which bulged from the serious weight of an unthinkable quantity of pound and two-pound coins. "Come on, I'll buy you a coffee."

He walked us past the Starbucks and up Old Street to Shoreditch High Street, then down a small alley, to a tiny espresso stand set in the doorway of an office building. The man who ran it was ancient, with arthritic, knobby fingers and knuckles like walnuts. He accepted two pound coins from Jem and set about making us two lattes, pulling the espresso shots from a tarnished machine that looked even older than he did. The espresso ran out of the basket and into the paper cup in a golden stream, and he frothed the milk with a kind of even, unconscious swirling gesture, then combined the two with a steady hand. He handed them to us, wordlessly, then shooed us off.

"Fyodor makes the best espresso in east London," Jem said, as he brought his cup to his lips and sipped. He closed his eyes for a second, then swallowed and opened them, wiping at the foam on his lip with the back of his hand. "Had his own shop years ago, went into retirement, got bored, set up that stand. Likes to keep his hand in. Practically no one knows about him. He's kind of a secret. So don't go telling all your mates, all right? Once *Vice* gets wind of that place, it'll be mobbed with awful Shoreditch fashion victims. I've seen it happen. Fyodor wouldn't be able to take it. It'd kill him. Promise me."

"I promise." I was really starting to enjoy his overblown, dramatic way of speaking. "On my life I doth swear it," I said. I didn't mention that the only coffee I'd ever drunk was Nescafé.

"You're overdoing it," he said. "You were doing okay until you got to 'doth.'"

"Noted," I said. Personally, I liked "doth."

"Here's the thing," he said. "Most of the poor bastards who end up on the street never really think it through. It's not a surprise, really. Like I said, people usually get here as the result of some awful trauma, and once they're on the road, it's hard to catch your breath and get some perspective. So nothing against them, but there's a smart way to be homeless and a dumb way. Do you want to learn about the smart way?"

I had a pang of suspicion just then. I didn't know this person. I hadn't even noticed him in the shelter (but then, I'd spent my time there trying not to inadvertently provoke any of the boys with eye contact, especially the ones talking about their knives and fights). Everything I knew about being homeless I'd learned from lurid *Daily Mail* cover stories about poor tramps and runaway kids who'd been cut up, fouled, and left in pieces in rubbish bins all over England.

One word kept going round my head: "Groomer." Supposedly, there was an army of groomers out there, men and women and even kids who tried to get vulnerable teens (like me, I suppose) to involve themselves with some dirty, ghastly pedophile scheme. These, too, featured prominently in the screaming headlines of the *Daily Mail* and the *Sun,* and we had an annual mandatory lecture on "network safety" that was all about these characters. I didn't really believe in them, of course. Trying to find random kids to abuse on the net made about as much sense as calling random phone numbers until you got a child of your preferred age and sex and asking if she or he wanted to come over and touch your monkey.

I'd pointed this out once in class, right after the teacher finished showing us a slide that showed that practically every kid that was abused was abused by a family member, a teacher or some other trusted adult. "Doesn't that slide mean that we should be spending all our time worrying about you, not some stranger on the net?" I'd got a week's detention.

But it's one thing to be brave and sensible in class; another thing to be ever-so-smart and brave as you're standing on a London street with less than thirty quid to your name, a runaway in a strange city with some smart-arse offering to show you the ropes.

"You're not going to cut me up and leave me in a lot of rubbish bins all over England are you?" I said.

He shook his head. "No, too messy. I'm more the cement-block-around-the-ankles-heave-ho-into-the-Thames sort. The eels'll skeltonize you inside of a month. I'll take your teeth so they can't do the dental records thing."

"I confess that I don't know what to say to that."

He slapped me on the shoulder. "Don't be daft, son. Look, I promise I won't take you inside any secluded potential murder sites. This is the Jammie Dodger's tour of London, admission free. It's better than the Ripper tour, better than one of them blue disk walking tours, better than a pub crawl. When you're done with the Jammie Dodger tour, you've got knowledge you can use. What say you, stout fellow?"

"You're overdoing it," I said. "You were doing okay until you got to 'stout fellow.'"

"It's a fair cop," he said. "Come on."

Our first stop was a Waitrose grocery store in the Barbican. It was a huge place, oozing poshness out into the street. Mums with high-tech push-chairs and well-preserved oldies cruised in and out, along with the occasional sharp-dressed man in a suit. Jem led me through the front door and told me to get a shopping cart. I did, noting that it had a working checkout screen on it—all the ones back home were perpetually broken.

As I pushed it over to him in the produce section, one of the security guards—cheap suit, bad hair, conspicuous earphone—detached himself from the wall and drifted over to us. He hung back short of actually approaching us, but made no secret of the fact that he was watching us. Jem didn't seem to mind. He walked us straight into the fruit section, where there were ranks of carefully groomed berries and succulent delights from around the world, the packages cleverly displaying each to its best effect. I'd never seen fruit like this: it was like hyper-fruit, like the fruit from films. The carton of blackberries didn't have a single squashed or otherwise odd-shaped one. The strawberries were so perfect they looked like they'd been cast from PVC.

Jem picked up one of each and waved it at the cart so that one of its thousands of optical sensors could identify it and add the total to a screen set into the handle. I boggled. The strawberries alone cost twelve pounds! The handle suggested some clotted cream and buns to go with them. It offered to e-mail me a recipe for strawberry shortcake. I merely goggled at the price. Jem didn't mind. He gaily capered through the store, getting some rare pig-gallbladder pâte ("An English Heritage Offal Classic") for fifteen pounds; a Meltingly Lovely Chocolate Fondant (twelve pounds for a bare mouthful); hunnerwurst-style tofu wieners (six pounds); Swiss Luxury Bircher Museli (twenty-two pounds! For a tiny bag of breakfast cereal!). The screen between my hands on the handle stood at over two hundred pounds before he drew up short, a dramatic and pensive finger on his chin.

I had a sinking feeling. He was going to steal something. I knew that he was going to steal something. Of *course* he was going to steal something—everyone knew it. The other shoppers knew it. The security guard certainly knew it. There were hundreds of cameras on the shopping cart to make it easier to scan your groceries, each one no larger than a match-head. I didn't care how experienced and sophisticated this guy was, he was about to get us both arrested.

But then he patted down his pockets, then said, in a showy voice, "Dearie me, forgot my wallet." He took the cart out of my hands and wheeled it to the security guard. "Take this, would you, mate?"

And then he left so quickly I almost didn't catch up with him. He was giggling maniacally. I grabbed his shoulder. "What the hell was that all about?" I said.

He shook my hand off. "Easy there, old son. Watch and learn." He led me around the back of the shop, where two big skips—what they called "Dumpsters" in American films—sat, covered in safety warnings and looking slightly scary. Without pausing, Jem flipped up the lid of the first one. He peered inside. A funky, slightly off smell wafted to me, like the crisper drawer of a fridge where a cucumber's been forgot for too long.

"Here we go," he said. "Go get us some of those boxes, yeah?" There were stacks of flattened cardboard boxes beside the skips. I brought a bale over to him and he wrestled them free of the steel strap that tied them tight. "Assemble a couple of them," he said.

I did as bade, and he began to hand me out neatly wrapped food packages, a near item-for-item repeat of the stuff we'd found in the store. Some of it had a little moisture on it or something slimy, but that was all on the wrapping, not on the food.

"Why is all this in the bin?" I asked as I packed it into the box.

"All past the sell-by date," he said.

"You mean it's spoiled?" I'd filled an entire box and was working on another one. I gagged a little at the thought of eating rotting food from the garbage, and I was pretty sure that was what Jem had in mind.

"Naw," he said, his voice echoing weirdly off the steel walls of the skip. "The manufacturers print sell-by dates on the packages because they don't want to get sued if someone eats bad food, so they're very conservative. And of course no one will buy anything that's past its sell-by date at a store. But if you think about it logically, there's no magic event that happens at midnight on sell-by day that makes the cheese go off." He handed me a neatly wrapped package of presliced Jarlsberg cheese. "I mean, cheese is basically spoiled milk already. Yogurt, too!"

He moved on to the next skip, carefully closing the lid. "Ooh!" he said, and handed me a case of gourmet chocolate bars, still sealed. One side of it had been squashed. "Probably fell off the stock-shelf or got squished in shipping. Those are bloody good, too—I like the ones with chili in."

"Ooh," he said again. "Bring me boxes, will you? More boxes." I went and wrestled another set of cardboard flats off the pile and slipped them out of their band. Jem vaulted the skip's edge and held a hand out. I gave him a box, listened to the sound of things being moved about inside. Then his hand came out again, and I passed him another box. Then another. "Come see," he said, and I stood on tiptoe to peer over the edge.

Jem had used the boxes to make a sort of corridor through the food and other rubbish, like a miner's tunnel, and he was turning over the skip's contents, and he was building a tower of tins in one corner of it. "I was hoping for this," he said. "Oh, yes." He stacked more tins. I peered at the labels. GOURMET COCONUT MILK, the nearest one read. REINDEER MEAT, another read. FILIPINO SARDINES. REFRIED BEANS.

"What's all that?"

"That," he said, "is the remains of Global Tradewinds, Ltd. They used to tin the best gourmet delicacies from around the world and sell 'em here. But they went bust last month and all the Waitroses have been taking them off the shelves. I knew I'd find a skip full of their stuff if I waited long enough!" He rubbed his hands together.

"We're not going to carry all that stuff out of here?" I said. There were dozens of tins.

"We certainly are," he said. "Christ, mate, you can't seriously think that I'd let this haul go to waste? It'd be a sin. Come on, more boxes." He snapped his fingers.

Shaking my head, I went and got more boxes. He tossed me a roll of packing tape. "Tape up the bottoms—they're not going to hold together just from folding, not with all this weight."

"Where the hell are you going to keep all this junk?" I said. When I'd started boxing up food, I had a vision of feasting on it, maybe putting the rest in my backpack for a day or two. But this was a month's worth of food, easy.

"Oh, we're not going to keep it, no fear."

In the end, there were eight big boxes full of food, which was about six more than we could easily carry.

"No worries," he said. "Just form a bucket brigade." Which is exactly what we did. I piled up seven boxes and Jem took one down to the end of the block. I picked up another box and walked toward him while he walked back to me. When we met, I gave him the box and he turned on his heel and walked back to the far end, stacking the box on top of the one he'd just put down. Meanwhile, I'd turned round and gone back to my pile, scooping another box. It was a very efficient way of doing things, since neither of us were ever sitting around idle, waiting for the other.

I worried briefly about someone stealing one of the boxes off the piles while they were unattended, but then I realized how stupid that was. These were boxes of rubbish, after all. We'd got them for free out of a skip. We could always find another skip if we needed to.

We moved the boxes one entire block in just a few minutes and regrouped. I was a bit winded and sweaty. Jem grinned and windmilled his arms. "Better than joining a gym," he said. "Only ten more roads that way!"

I groaned. "Where are we taking these bloody things?"

He was already moving, hauling another box down the pavement. "Back to the station," he called over his shoulder.

When we got to Old Street Station, he straightaway went up to two of the tramps, an elderly couple wearing heavy coats (too heavy for the weather) and guarding bundle-buggies full of junk and clothes. They didn't smell very good, but then again, neither did I at that point, 'cos I'd forgot to pack deodorant in my runaway go-bag.

"Morning Lucy; morning, Fred," Jem said, dropping a box at their feet. "You all right?"

"Can't complain," the old lady said. When I looked closer, I saw that she wasn't as old as all that, but she was prematurely aged, made leathery by the streets. She was missing teeth, but she still had a sunny smile. "Who's the new boy, Jem?"

"Training up an apprentice," he said. "This is Trent. Trent, these are my friends Lucy and Fred." I shook their rough, old hands. Lucy's grip was so frail it was like holding a butterfly. Fred grunted and didn't look me in the eye. He had something wrong with him, I could see that now, that weird, inexplicable wrongness that you could sense when you were around someone who was sick in the head somehow. He didn't seem dangerous— just a bit simple. Or shy. "Brought you some grub," Jem said, and kicked his box.

Lucy clapped and said, "You are such a good boy, Jem." She got down on her creaky knees and opened the box, began to carefully paw through the contents, pulling out a few tins, some of the fruit and veg. She exclaimed over a wheel of cheddar and looked up at Jem with a question in her eyes.

"Go on, go on," he said. "Much as you like. There's more where that came from."

In the end, the two of them relieved us of an entire boxful of food. As they squirreled it away in their bundle-buggies, I felt something enormous and good and warm swell up in my chest. It was the feeling of having done something good. Something really, really good—helping people who needed it.

They thanked us loads and we moved on through the station.

"Do they know that the food comes from a skip?" I asked quietly.

Jem shrugged. "Probably. They never asked."

"Haven't you taken them to see all the stuff in the skips?"

He snorted. "Fred and Lucy are two of the broken people I was telling you about. Tried to help 'em with their signs, tried to help 'em learn how to get better food, a decent squat. But it's like talking to a wall. Lucy spent a year in hospital before she ended up out here. Her old man really beat her badly. And Fred . . . Well, you could see that Fred's not all there." He shrugged again. "Not everyone's able to help themselves." He socked me in the shoulder. "Lucky thing there's us, hey?"

We came to another tramp, this one much younger and skinny, like the drug addicts I'd seen around the bus station in Bradford. His hands shook as he picked out his tins, and he muttered to himself, but he couldn't thank us enough and shook my hand with both of his.

One by one, we covered the station exits and the tramps at each one. Jem never tried to keep anyone from taking too much, nor did he keep back the best stuff for himself. By the time we were done, we were down to a single box of food, mostly the odd tinned foreign delicacies. These were the heaviest items in the haul, of course.

"Come on, then," he said. "Let's have a picnic." We walked out of the station and down the road a little way and turned into the gates of a beautiful old cemetery.

"Bunhill," he said. "Originally 'Bone Hill.' It was a plague pit, you see." The graveyard was a good meter higher than the pavement in front of it. "Masses of people killed in the plagues, all shoveled under the dirt. Brings up the grass a treat, as you can see." He gestured at the rolling lawns to one side of the ancient, mossy, fenced-in headstones. "Nonconformist cemetery," he went on, leading me deeper. "Unconsecrated ground. Lots of interesting folks buried here. You got your writers: like John Bunyan who wrote *Pilgrim's Progress.* You got your philosophers, like

Thomas Hardy. And some real maths geniuses, like old Thomas Bayes—" He pointed to a low, mossy tomb. "He invented a branch of statistics that got built into every spam filter, a couple hundred years after they buried him."

He sat down on a bench. It was after midday now, and only a few people were eating lunch around us, none close enough to overhear us. "It's a grand life as a gentleman adventurer," he said. "Nothing to do all day but pluck choice morsels out of the bin and read the signboards the local historical society puts up in the graveyard."

He produced a tin-opener from his coat pocket and dug through the box. "Here," he said. "You like Mexican refried beans?"

"You mean like from Taco Bell?"

He shook his head. "Nothing at all like Taco Bell. Much better than that rubbish." Rummaging further in his pockets, he found a small glass bottle of Tabasco sauce. He opened the beans, sprinkled the hot sauce on them, and mashed it in with a bamboo fork he extracted from a neat nylon pouch. He took out another and handed it to me. "Eat," he said. "We're on a culinary tour of the world!"

It wasn't the best meal I've ever eaten, but it was the oddest and the most entertaining. Jem narrated the contents of each tin like the announcer on a cooking show. The stodgy breakfast gruel had finally dissolved in my stomach, leaving me starving hungry, and the unfamiliar flavors went a long way toward filling the gaps. When we were done, there were only two or three tins left, which Jem offered to me. I took a tin of bamboo shoots in freshwater and left the other two for him.

He stood and stretched his arms over his head then bent down to touch his toes, straightened, and twisted from side to side. "Right then," he said. "Basic lessons are over. What have you learned, pupil mine?"

I stood and stretched, too. My muscles, already sore from carrying all the food, had cooled and stiffened while we ate, and

I groaned as they reluctantly stretched out. "Erm," I said. "Okay, no brown signs." He nodded. "Don't trust sell-by dates." He nodded again. "Skips are good eating." He nodded. "Well," I said. "That's pretty cool."

"You're forgetting the most important lesson," he said. He shook his head. "And you were doing so well."

I racked my brains. "I don't know," I said. "What is it?"

"You have to come up with it on your own," he said. "Now, what are you going to do next?"

I shrugged. "I guess I'll make a sign. I'll find a pitch that's not too close to you, of course. Don't want to cut into your business."

"I'm not bothered. But beyond that, what are you going to do? Where will you sleep tonight?"

"Back at the shelter, I suppose. Beats sleeping in a doorway."

He nodded. "It's better than a doorway, true. But there's better places. Me, I've had my eye on a lovely pub out in Bow. All boarded up, no one's been in for months. Looks cozy, too. Want to come have a look at it with me?"

"You're going to break in?"

"No," he said. "That's illegal. Going to *walk* in. Front door's off its hinges." He tsked. "Vandals. What is this world coming to?"

"It's not illegal to walk in?"

"Squatter's rights, mate," he said. "I'm going to occupy that derelict structure and beautify it, thus elevating the general timbre of the neighborhood. I'm a force for social good."

"But will you get arrested?'

"It's *not illegal*," he said. "Don't worry, mate. You don't have to come, if you don't want to. I just don't like that shelter. It's all right for people who can't do any better, but I always worry that there's someone more desperate than me who can't get a bed 'cos I'm there.

"Plus those old pubs are just lovely—hardwood floors, brass fittings, old wainscoting. Estate agent's dream. Just the tile on the outside is enough to break your heart."

He stuck out his hand. "Nice to have met you, son. I expect we'll run into each other again soon enough."

"Wait!" I said. "I didn't say I wouldn't come!"

"So come, then!"

We caught a 55 bus from Old Street. He paid my fare, handing over a clatter of pound coins from his jingling pocket. We went upstairs to the upper deck and found a seat, right up front, by the huge picture window.

"The London channel," he said, gesturing at the window and the streets of London whizzing past us. "In high def. Nothing like it. Love this place."

We passed through the streets of Shoreditch and into Bow, which was a lot wilder and less rich. Mixed in among the posh shops were old family shops, bookies, seedy discount shops, and plenty of boarded-up storefronts. The people were a mix of young trendies like you'd see in Shoreditch, old people tottering down the road carrying their shopping, women in Muslim veils with kids in tow, Africans in bright colors chatting away as they walked the streets. It felt a lot more like Bradford, with all the Indians and Pakistanis, than it did like London.

We went deeper into Bow, through a few housing estates, past some tower-blocks that were taller than any apartment building I'd ever seen, some of them boarded up all the way to the sky. This was a lot less nice than the high-street we'd just passed down, proper rough. Like home. But it didn't make me homesick.

"This is us," Jem said, pressing the STOP REQUEST button on the pole by the seat. There was almost no one else left on the bus, and we wobbled down the steps as it braked at a bus stop where all the glass had been broken out, and recently, judging by the glittering cubes of safety glass carpeting the pavement as we got off.

We crunched over the glass and I heard a hoot—like an owl, but I was pretty sure it had come from a human throat—from off in the distance. There was an answering whistle.

"Drugs lookouts," Jem said. "They think we might be customers. Don't worry, they won't bother us once they see we're not here for sugar. Just keep walking."

He set off across an empty lot that was littered with an old mattress, pieces of cars, shopping carts, and blowing, decomposing plastic bags. Across the lot stood a solitary brick building, three stories tall. The side facing us had a ghost staircase—the brick supports for a stairwell that once ran up that wall when it was part of the building next door. Looking around, I could see more ghosts: rectangular stone shapes set into the earth, the old foundations for a row of buildings that had once stood here. The pub—for that's what it was—was the last building standing, the sole survivor of an entire road that had succumbed to the wrecker's ball.

As we drew nearer, Jem stopped and put his hands on his hips. "Beautiful, innit? Wait'll you see inside. An absolute tip, but it'll scrub up lovely."

We crossed to the building, and Jem entered without stopping. I followed, and my nose was assaulted with the reek of old piss and booze and smoke and shite. It was not a good smell. I gagged a bit, then switched to breathing through my mouth.

Jem, meanwhile, had shucked his backpack and dug out some paper painter's masks. He slipped one over his head and handed the other to me. "Here," he said, a bit muffled. "We'll take care of the smell soon enough, no worries. But first we have to do something about this door."

He produced a hiker's headlamp from his bag and fitted it to his head, switching it on and sending a white beam slicing through the dusty, funky air. He shut the door with a bang, and his torch became the only source of light in the shuttered pub, save for a few chinks around the boards on the windows. I felt a moment's fear. *This is where he cuts me up and chucks me in a bin.* But he didn't show any interest in cutting me up. Instead, he was peering at the lock. He fitted a screwdriver to it and began to remove the mechanism. I could see that it was bent and broken by some ancient vandal.

"Bloody screws have rusted into place," he muttered, dipping into his bag for a small plastic bottle with a long, thin nozzle. He dripped liquid onto the screws. "Penetrating oil," he said. "That'll loosen 'em up."

"Jem," I said, "what the hell are you doing?"

"Changing the locks. Got to establish my residency if I'm going to claim this place for my own." He reapplied the screwdriver to the door.

"You what?" I said. "You're going to claim this place? How do you think you'll do that?"

"With one of these," he said, and he handed me a folded sheet of paper. I unfolded it in the dark, then held it in the light of his torch so that I could read it.

LEGAL WARNING
Section 6 Criminal Law Act 1977
As amended by Criminal Justice and Public Order Act
1994
TAKE NOTICE
THAT we live in this property, it is our home, and we
intend to stay here.
THAT at all times there is at least one person in this
property.
THAT any entry or attempt to enter into this property
without our permission is a criminal offense as any one
of us who is in physical possession is opposed to entry
without our permission
THAT if you attempt to enter by violence or by
threatening violence we will prosecute you. You may
receive a sentence of up to six months imprisonment
and/or a fine of up to £5,000.
THAT if you want to get us out you will have to issue
a claim in the County Court or in the High Court, or
produce to us a written statement or certificate in terms
of S.12A Criminal Law Act, 1977 (as inserted by

Criminal Justice and Public Order Act, 1994).

THAT it is an offence under S.12A (8) Criminal Law
Act 1977 (as amended) to knowingly make a false
statement to obtain a written statement for the purposes
of S.12A. A person guilty of such an offense may
receive a sentence of up to six months imprisonment
and/or a fine of up to £5,000.

> Signed
> The Occupiers

I tried to get my head around the note. "What the hell is
this?" I said.

He grunted as he twisted the screwdriver and I heard the
screw he was working on rasp and begin to turn. "What's it look
like?"

"It looks," I said carefully, "like you're claiming that you now
own this pub."

He finished the screw he was working on and went to work
on the next one. "That's about right," he said. "Squatter's rights."

"You said that before. What's a squatter's right?"

"Well, you know. When buildings are left derelict, like this
one, the landlord gone and no one taking care of it, it's a, you
know, a blight on the neighborhood. Attracts drug users, prostitutes, gangs. Becomes an eyesore. After World War Two there
were loads of these buildings, just sitting there vacant, dragging
everything around them down. So families that couldn't afford
housing just moved into them. It's not a crime, it's a civil viola-
tion. You can't get arrested for it, so don't worry about that. The
worst they can do is force you to move out, and to do that, they
need a court order. That can take months, if not years."

"Sounds like you've done this before." It seemed too good to
be true. I had no idea what a multistory pub was worth, but it
had to be hundreds of thousands of pounds. Could we really just
move in and take it over?

"Yeah," he said. "I don't sleep in shelters if I can help it. I'm between squats at the moment, but not for long. Sleeping in shelters." He shrugged, the lighting bouncing around the room. "Well, it's not for me, like I said."

He had the lock off now, and he withdrew a heavy new lock from his bag, lined it up with the screw holes in the door to make sure it'd fit, then filled the holes with some kind of putty and set to screwing in his lock. "That should do it for now," he said. "Once that liquid wood sets, that lock won't budge. They'll have to angle-grind it off. Later, I'll put in a few deadbolts."

"Jem," I said. "What the hell are you doing?"

"I'm establishing a squat," he said. "Try to keep up, will you? I'm going to clean out this place, put that notice in the window, move in some beds and that, get the electricity and gas working, and I am going to live here for as long as I can. Remember what I was telling you about there being a better way to be homeless? This is it."

I swallowed. "And what am I doing here?"

"There's loads of room," he said. "And it's hard to do this alone. You've got to keep someone on the premises at all times, to tell them to bugger off if they turn up wanting to repossess the place. They can't enter the place so long as there's someone home, not without a warrant. Oh, sure, I could leave the radio on and hope that that fooled 'em but—"

He was going a mile a minute. I suddenly realized that he was even more nervous than I was. He'd had this place scouted out and all ready to move into, but he couldn't take it over until he found a confederate—me. Someone had to stay home while he was out getting food and that.

"You want me to move in here? Jem—"

He held up both hands. "Look, the worst thing, the absolutely *worst* thing, right? The worst thing that could happen is that they get a court order and evict us and we're back at the shelter. Back where you started. It might take a day, it might take *years*. In the meantime, what else have you got to do? Do you really want to spend the rest of your life sleeping eight to a room?

Look, son, this is the chance to become a gentleman of leisure instead of, you know, a *tramp*. Don't you want that? 'Course you do. *Of course you do!*"

I took a step back into the dark of the stinking, shuttered pub. "Look, mate," I said. "It all sounds nice, but this is really fast—"

He stood up and dusted his hands on his thighs. "Yeah, okay, fair enough. But you wouldn't have come along if I'd told you you were going to end up living in a squat, right? I wanted you to *see* the place before you made up your mind. Just look at this place, son, just look at it! Think of the potential! We'll get big comfy sofas, clean up the kitchen and get the water going, stick up a Freeview antenna, find some WiFi to nick, it'll be a bloody palace. A bloody *palace*! Just think about what it could be like! We'll get some wood polish and bring up the wainscoting and those old snugs, shine up the chrome in the kitchen. We could have dinner parties! Christ, you should see the fridge and walk-in deep-freeze they've got in there—we could store a year's worth of food and still have room."

I teetered on the edge between my anxiety and his infectious excitement. "I don't understand," I said. "How is it possible that this won't get us banged up? Aren't we trespassing?"

He shook his head. "Not until there's a court order. Until then, we're brave homesteaders on the wooly outer edges of property law. It's a lovely place to be, mate. Places like this, it's in the public interest for us to occupy 'em. The cops might show up, but so long as you don't let 'em in and you know what to tell them, they won't do anything except make noises. Come on, what do you say? You want to be a streetkid or do you want to be an adventurer?"

I looked around the reeking and dark pub. Now that my eyes were adjusting to the dim, I could see all the battered furnishings lurking in the shadows. It had once been a lovely place, I could see that. Nice tile work. Old wooden floors and snugs and benches. A long wooden bar with stumps where stools had been torn loose, and a broken back-mirror. I remembered how big the building had been from the outside, all the extra rooms and I wanted to explore them all, map them like a level in a game, find all their treasures and get them put to rights.

"All right," I said. "Deal. For now, anyway. But you got to promise me you won't get me arrested or cut me up and leave me in rubbish bins all over Bow."

He crossed his heart. "Promise. I told you I was a brick-around-the-ankles man, didn't I?"

Once he had the locks on the door—three of them, including two deadbolts that had to be slowly and painfully screwed into the jamb and door with long, sharp steel screws, a wrist-breaking task that took both of us an hour in turns—he drew a letter out of his bag, in a sealed envelope with a first-class stamp.

"Right," he said. "This letter is addressed to me, at this address: The Three Crows pub, Bow. I'm going to nip out and find a post-box and put it in the mail. That'll get us started on proof that we live here, which'll be handy when and if the law shows up. I'll also get us some dinner. You all right with pizza?"

I was well impressed. "You've done this before."

"Never on my own, always as part of someone else's gang. But yeah, once or twice. I tell you, squatting is for kings, shelters are for tramps. Once you decide to be a king, there's no going back. So, pizza?"

My stomach leapt at the word *pizza*. "As the Buddha said in the kebab shop, 'make me one with everything.'"

He snorted and left, calling out, "Lock up and don't let anyone in until I get back, right?"

"Right!" I called into the closing door. He'd left me with his head torch, and I strapped it on. I'd expected it to be quiet in the pub once he'd gone, but it was alive with spooky old building sounds: creaks and mysterious skittering sounds of rats in the walls. Let's not mess about: the place was stitching me up. In my head, the clittering of mouse claws over unseen boards was the scrabbling of the local drugs lookouts—the ones we'd heard calling to one another as we made our way to the pub—clawing their way in through secret loose boards. And those creaking boards—that was some monstrous, leathery old tramp who made this place his den, holed up in some dank corner where he was now rousing himself, getting ready to cut up and eat the interlopers who'd intruded on his territory.

I have an overactive imagination. At least I'm man enough to know it. I mean, part of me knew that there was no one else in this rotten tooth of a building. And I'd spent the morning meeting and feeding a whole gang of tramps and even they had been polite, friendly, and more scared of me (and their own shadows) than I was of them. So I resettled the headlamp on my forehead and slowly began to explore the pub, making a conscious effort to keep my breathing even and my shoulders from tightening up around my ears.

Tell you what, though: there are better ways to explore a spooky abandoned building than with a headlamp. The narrow beam of light jiggles like crazy every time you move your head the slightest, teensiest bit. The beam of light that passes right in front of your face means that you have zero peripheral vision. Every time you bounce the beam off something reflective and blind yourself, it creates a swarm of squirming green after-burns that look *exactly* like the hands of phantoms rising out of the walls, about to strangle you. It is the perfect re-creation of every zombie film you've ever seen where the hero's breath rasps in and out as he walks carefully through the halls of some blood-spattered military base, waiting for a pack of growling undead biters to boil out of a doorway and tear him to gobbets and ooze.

There's only one thing worse: turning off the lamp.

I started off slow and careful, bent on convincing myself that I wasn't half-mad with fear. There was a large kitchen which did have a huge walk-in deep-freezer, which smelt a bit off, but not totally rancid. The pipes rattled and groaned when I turned on the taps, but then the water began to flow, first in irregular bursts of brown, rusty stuff and then in a good, steady gush of clear London

tap water, the river Thames as filtered through twenty million
people's kidneys, processed, dumped back into the Thames, filtered, and sent back to those thirsty kidneys. It's the bloody circle
of life. Reassuring.

By now, I had a genuine case of the heebie-jeebies, and I had
an idea that maybe some of the upstairs windows hadn't been
quite boarded up so there might be some rooms with the light of
day shining through them and chasing away the bogeymen. So
I found the staircase, which creaked like one of the Foley stages
they use for horror-film sound effects, and made my noisy way
up to the first floor. I didn't hang around long. Not only was it
pitch-black, it also smelled even worse than the ground floor.
Someone had lived here and left behind a room filled with dried-
out turds and the ammonia reek of old, soaked-in piss.

You want to hear something funny? Once I'd got past my
total disgust, I felt a landlord's resentment at this abuse of "my"
home. Some interloper had installed himself here and done this
awful thing to *my* beloved home. Never mind that he'd been
there first, that I hadn't known this place existed before that
afternoon, and that I had pretty much broken in and claimed it as
my own. I *deserved* this place, I was going to take care of it in a way
that the animal that had crapped all over the floor could never
understand.

Yeah, it's odd how quickly I went from squatter to owner in
my head. But on the other hand, I remember the first time I
mixed down my own edit of a Scot Colford clip and watched it
spread all over the net, and how much I'd felt like that clip was
mine, even though I'd taken it from someone else without asking.
It's a funny old world, as the grannie in *Home, Home on the Strange*
(Scot's first and best rom-com) used to say.

Up on the second floor, things were just as dark, but less
awful. There was wax on the floor where someone had burned
candles, and I kicked over a few stubs. There was a pretty horrible
mattress and a litter of lager-tins in what looked like an old
office—the local estate kids' romantic getaway, I supposed—and

another room stacked high with chairs and tables, all chipped and wobbly looking. I filed that away for future reference.

On the third and top story, I found some rooms whose windows were not boarded up. These let in a weak, grayish twilight, but it was a huge relief after the pitchy dark of the rooms below. I thought I'd wait there for Jem to return. How long could it take to post a letter and get a pizza? Though, from what I'd seen of Jem, I wouldn't have been surprised if his way of posting a letter involved breaking into the central sorting office, stealing a stamp, then reverse-pickpocketing it into a letter-carrier's bag.

The third floor was a huge, open space: dusty and grimy, but mostly free from any sign of human habitation. It was ringed with windows on all its walls, and I could imagine that it'd be a lovely penthouse someday when we'd finished doing up the place. But for now, I was more interested in the fact that the western windows were unboarded. I switched off the headlamp and examined them. They were filthy, but they looked like they might open up, letting in even more light. I yanked the painted iron handles and pushed and tugged and grunted and rattled them until they squealed to life in a shower of dried paint and fossilized mouse turds and rust-colored dust. Slowly, painfully, I cranked the windows wide open, flooding the room with London's own dirty gray light. The fresh air was incredible, cooling and reassuring, as was the light in the room. With its help, I noted a box of candles and a stack of chairs in one corner.

I looked out the window at the bleak housing estate. It looked like a bomb site: blasted flat and partially ruined, with rotting brickwork and railings hanging free. Loads of the flats looked to be completely deserted, with their windows boarded up. We'd had some like that back on my estate in Bradford: places where the roof had caved in or the pipes had burst and the council had decided just to leave them empty instead of finding the money to fix them up. I didn't know much about how things were run, but I knew that the council didn't have any money and was always cutting something or other to make ends meet.

If you made a biopic of my life to that point, you could call it *Not Enough Money* and hire someone to write a jaunty theme song called *He's Skint (Yes, 'e is)*. It'd be a box-office smash.

So this bomb site was pretty familiar to me. And it looked like Jem might be the first person I'd ever met who didn't have a problem being broke. He seemed to have figured out how to live without cash, which was a pretty neat trick.

I peered out the window again, looking for Jem. I didn't see him (did he go to Italy for the damned pizza?), but I did spot the drugs lookouts he was talking about before. Just kids, they were, eight or nine years old, playing idle games or chatting on the balconies of the estate, sitting in doorways eating crisps, doing things that were pretty kidlike. But whenever someone new came onto the estate, they started up with their birdcalls, sending them echoing off the high towers.

They began to coo and call and I thought *That must be Jem. About bloody time.* But when I looked out, it wasn't Jem: it was a huge, shambling man with long dreads and a black duffel bag that he hauled as if it weighed a ton. He was wearing scuffed boots, greasy blue-jeans, a beaten wind-cheater—he looked like a tramp. Or maybe a killer who hunted tramps and dismembered them and carried them around in a duffel bag.

And he was headed straight for the pub.

I mean, it wasn't like there was anywhere else he could be headed for. The pub stood alone in the wasted field, like the lone tooth in a bleached skull. The man bounced when he walked, dreads shaking, arm penduluming back and forth with that weighty bag.

My first thought was that this was some kind of goon sent by the owner to beat the hell out of me and toss me out. But there was no way that the landlord could know what we were up to. Jem hadn't even put up the sign yet.

Then I thought he must be a dealer, alerted by the lookout. Maybe one of these loose floorboards disguised a secret stash with millions in sugar or smack or something even more exotic—a cache of guns?

Then I thought he might just be someone who had got here before us, someone who lived here and did such a good job of covering up for himself when he was out that I couldn't find his nest.

Then I stopped thinking because he was standing at the door, thudding rhythmically with a meaty fist, making the whole building shake. My guts squirmed with terror. I thought I'd been afraid before, but that was the nameless, almost delicious fear of something in the dark. Now I had the very pointed, very specific terror of a giant, rough-looking bloke hammering at my door. I didn't know what to do.

Seemingly of their own accord, my feet propelled me back downstairs into the pub's main room, where my headlamp was the only light. It made sense, right? After all, when someone knocks at the door, you answer it.

He was still thudding at it, but then he stopped.

"Open up, come on!" he shouted in a rough voice. "Haven't got all bloody night."

I cowered in one of the snugs.

"Jem, damn it, it's me, open the goddamned door!"

He knew Jem's name. That was odd.

"Jem's not home," I said in my bravest voice, but it came out like a terrified squeak.

There was silence from the other side of the door.

"What do you mean he's not home? I just crossed the whole bloody city. Jem, is that you? Look, mate, I don't want to play silly buggers. Open the damned door, or—"

My balls shrank back up against my abdominal cavity. It was a curious sensation, and not pleasant.

"It's not Jem. He should be back soon. Sorry," I squeaked.

"Look, I'm the spark, all right? Jem asked me to come round

and get you switched on. I've got loads of other things I could be doing, so if you want to sit in the dark, that's up to you. Your choice." A spark—an electrician! Jem hadn't mentioned this, but he *had* said something about getting the electricity switched on. I'd assumed he'd meant convincing the power company to switch us on, but that wasn't really Jem's style, was it?

Cautiously, I made my way to the door and shot all the bolts and turned the lock.

The man loomed over me, at least six foot six, with red-rimmed eyes. He wasn't white and he wasn't black—but he wasn't Indian or Pakistani, either. He smelled of machine oil and sweet ganja, and his free hand was big and knuckly and spotted with oil. He pushed past me without saying a word and strode boldly into the middle of the pub.

He sniffed disapprovingly. "Doesn't half pong, does it? My advice: scatter some fresh coffee grounds right away, that covers practically everfing. But I bet this place has a evil great extractor fan in the kitchen, you run that for a couple days and you'll get it smelling better." He turned to face me. "You'll be wanting to close that door, Sunshine. Never know what sort of villains are lurking around in bad old east London."

I closed the door. I was still wearing my headlamp, and its beam showed my shaking hands as I worked the locks.

"I'm Dodger," he said as he clicked on a big torch and wandered behind the bar with it, shining it underneath the counter. "The spark." He stood up and headed for the kitchen. "You ain't seen the mains-junction for this place, have you?"

"No," I managed, still squeaking. "I'm Trent," I said. "I'm Jem's friend."

"That's nice," he said. He was in the kitchen now, and I could hear him moving things, looking behind things. "Lucky you."

"It's got to be in the cellar," he said. "Where's the door?"

"I don't know," I said. "I just got here."

"Never mind, found it. Come here, Jem's friend." He was

kneeling in the middle of the kitchen floor, torch in one hand, the other gripping the ring of a trapdoor set into the floor. I accidentally blinded him with my light and he let go of the ring and shielded his face. "Careful, right? Christ, those headlamps are utter toss." He handed me his torch, heavy with all the batteries in it. "Shine that where I'm working, and not in my eyes. Douse that ridiculous thing on your noggin."

I did as bid, and watched in fascination as he hauled and strained at the ring, lifting the trapdoor and letting it fall open with an ear-shattering crash. A ladder descended into the darkness of a cellar. "Okay," he said, "mission accomplished, time for a break." He fished in his pocket and brought out a packet of rolling papers and a baggie of something—weed, as it turned out, strong enough to break the stink of the pub as soon as he opened the bag. "Let's improve the air quality, right? Hold the light, that's a good lad." He laid the paper on the thigh of his jeans, smoothed it out, then pulled out another and carefully joined it to the first, making a double-wide paper. He sprinkled a mammoth helping of weed into the center of the paper and then quickly skinned up a spliff so neat it looked as if it might be factory made. He twisted the ends, stuck it in his mouth and struck a match on the floor and lit it.

He toked heavily and let out a huge cloud of fragrant smoke. "Want some?" he said, holding out the joint and streaming more smoke out of his nostrils.

Like one of those kids in an advert about the dangers of peer pressure, I took it and smoked it. As I inhaled, my mind was filled with paranoid fantasies about all the things the grass might be laced with: horse tranquilizers, rat poison, exotic hallucinogens, synthetic heroin. But it tasted and went down like the weed I'd smoked every now and again at school. I took one more sip of smoke, careful not to get the paper soggy, and passed it back.

He took another gigantic toke, then one more. He passed it back to me. I didn't seem to be feeling any effects, so I drew in a deep double-lungful, handed it back, then took it again once he'd done with it. We'd smoked it halfway down and he waved at me and croaked, "Keep it, mate, gotta do some work." I still wasn't feeling it, which was weird, because normally I was the first one to get all silly when there was a spliff going around. Shrugging, I toked some more and held the lamp while he went down the rickety ladder. I felt pretty cool, I must say, all edgy and "street," smoking this geezer's spliff in a pitch-dark squat. Just a few days before I'd been a lad from the provinces and now here I was in the great metropolis, doing crime, cutting capers, and hanging out with new mates who called themselves things like "Dodger."

It was *epic.*

Dodger was down in the cellar, and he called to me to shift the light over to the panel he'd found. He scratched his chin meditatively as he contemplated it, and I noticed that the beam of light I was shining was flickering a little, and swirling a little around the edges. Maybe it was dust in the air. Dodger wasn't complaining, so I didn't say anything.

Working with the same neat efficiency he'd applied to skinning up the spliff, Dodger started to take tools out of his bag. First, some kind of big meter with a pair of alligator leads he touched to different contacts on the board, working with precise, small movements. Then he nodded to himself and drew out a toolbelt that he slung around his waist, taking from it a bunch of screwdrivers and working on the plate with them in turn until the entire junction box came free of the sweating, rough brick wall. Now he brought out a spool of wire and snipped off a meter-long length, stripping the ends. He went back to work with the screwdrivers, and I squinted to see what he was working on.

Eugh," he exclaimed, and reached a gloved hand into the space behind the junction box and withdrew a handful of dry, papery, furry things. "Mummified mice," he called. "Little bastards had a chew of the wires and got a surprise. Lucky thing I spotted 'em before I got the juice back on—dry as they are, I wouldn't have been surprised if they went up in flames like old leaves."

He dropped the mummified rodents to the dirt floor of the

cellar and went back to work, grunting to himself and calling on me to shift the light this way or that. There was something funny about his voice, a weird quality imparted to it by the dead space of the cellar or something, and I snorted a small giggle.

"Right," he said, "one for the money, two for the show, three to get ready, aaand . . ." He snapped a huge switch and the lights all through the pub blazed to light. "*Go cat go!*" I fumbled the torch and squinted against the sudden light. Then there was a loud *pop* and the pub was plunged back into darkness. I smelled a bonfire smell of melted plastic.

"Right," Dodger said again. "Right. That's how it's going to be, hey? Get that light back on me, mate, this one's going to need some major work."

I groped for the torch, which had stayed on when I dropped it, and discovered that I couldn't maintain my balance. I toppled onto the filthy floor, narrowly missing a headfirst plummet down the trapdoor and ladder. I sat up gingerly, head swimming, and found the lamp. "I think," I said, around a thick tongue. "I think maybe I smoked a little too much. Just a little . . ." I trailed off. My hands felt like they were encased in boxing gloves, and I could barely feel my face, and it was all brilliantly hilarious.

Dodger made a rude noise. "Christ, you're not half a little nancy, are you? Thought you northerners were supposed to be hard as bricks. Just sit there and hold the light, will you?"

I did, and three more times, Dodger switched on the mains and three more times there was a loud crack, smoke, and sudden darkness. The third time, there was even a little fire in the wiring, which he snuffed out with a small chemical extinguisher. This fire seemed to indicate that the job was much bigger than he'd suspected and he went to work in earnest, using a wrecker's bar to knock loose several bricks and dig deeper into the conduit that led into the cellar.

The weed pressed on my arms and legs like lead weights and I found my head drooping to my chest, my eyelids closing of their own accord. I dozed off and on in a slow, giddy, stoned stupor.

The lights blazed on and popped out in an irregular rhythm as Dodger made his erratic progress, each event rousing me momentarily. I was woken up properly by Dodger thumping on the sole of my shoe with the handle of his screwdriver, reaching up from the cellar, shouting, "Oi! Oi! Get the door, son!"

I blinked my eyes and listened. Someone was clattering at the door in a jaunty *rat-a-tat-a-tat,* using something metallic like a key ring to beat out an uptempo ditty.

I walked to the door on feet that felt like they'd grown three sizes, trying to shake the weed off my mind and limbs.

"Who is it?" I shouted.

"Prince Charles," Jem said. "I've come to give you a royal medal for service to England. Open the damned door, son!"

I worked the locks with stupid fingers and swung open the door. It was full dark outside, which made the interior fluorescent tube lights seem as bright as the sun. Jem stepped back, nearly dropping the pizza boxes he was holding before him. "Sorry," he said. "Had some business to attend to. Took a little longer than I thought. Looks like Dodger found the place okay, though?" He jerked his head at the lights and handed me the pizza boxes. They wafted out a smell as intoxicating as any perfume, cheesy and greasy and salty and hot and my mouth flooded with so much saliva I nearly dribbled it down my front.

"You didn't tell me anyone was coming over," I said, hearing a note of accusation in my voice. I wanted to say, *He scared me to death. Thought he was here to murder me!* But I also wanted to be, you know, hard and street and that.

Jem snorted and shut and bolted the door, shucked out of his oversize parka and draped it over a chair. Without it, he was as skinny as a broomstick, arms like toothpicks and legs like pipestems. "Said I was sorry, didn't I? I thought I'd be back before Dodger showed. You don't need to be scared of him, old bean, he's a pussycat, Dodger is."

"I heard that," Dodger shouted from the kitchen. "Don't make me beat you like the dog you are, Jem." He stepped into the pub and looked around, wrinkling his nose again. "Christ, the pong in this place just keeps coming at you in waves, like. That's a *textured* stench."

Jem waved his hand. "We'll take care of that soon enough. Meantime, I got some coffee."

Dodger nodded. "Yeah, that'll do for a start, give it here."

Jem unzipped his backpack and handed over a paper sack of coffee grounds. Dodger popped it open, breaking the vacuum seal with a hiss and the smell of coffee was dark and warm at once, cutting through the piss and must smell. Dodger poured some out in his hand and sprinkled it around the pub, paying special attention to the corners and the baseboards. While he did this, Jem opened up his pizza boxes, wiped down his fingers with some sani-towels, and started to tease the slices apart, dripping gooey cheese.

He offered me a wipe and I realized how grimy my hands were, like I'd been arm-deep up a cow's arse or worse, and I fastidiously scrubbed all around, up to my elbows and under my fingernails. Jem eventually plucked the wipe out of my fingers—it was in tatters. "You've been smoking Dodger's weed," he said.

I nodded.

"Does funny things to you, that stuff. Smoke enough of it, you come out like Dodger. No one wants that." Dodger, finished with the coffee-sprinkling, balled up the empty sack and tossed it at Jem's head, beaning him right on the bonce.

Jem pointed at the cooling pizzas. One was covered in mushrooms, peppers, and sweet corn. The other had pepperoni, mince beef, shrimp, and anchovies. Normally I hated both sweet corn *and* anchovies, but between the weed and the odd events of the day, I felt like I could try anything that night.

I tried the veggie slice first and found the sweet-corn made it just perfect, an almost-crunchy texture in the niblets that made the pizza especially great to chew. It was bursting with tangy tomato and garlic and spices—I could taste oregano and basil, and lots more I couldn't place. It was the best-tasting thing I'd ever eaten, because I was eating it as part of an adventure. Then I tried a meat slice and that was *even better*, the salty anchovy and its fishy flavor rich as a good soup and perfect in a million ways. I was a normal English teenager and I'd grown up eating pizza all my life, but I'd never eaten pizza like that.

"Where the hell did you get this?" I said. "It's–It's–It's *insane*."

Jem grinned around his own slice. "Good, innit? Place I know, they use a wood-fired oven, make their own dough. I'd sooner starve than eat Domino's. Save up for this stuff. It ain't cheap, but this is a special occasion."

Dodger rolled a slice into a tube and popped it into his mouth like a spring roll. He chewed it voraciously and swallowed hugely. "My nipples explode with delight!" he shouted, making us all dissolve in stupid giggles.

From there, it became a contest to see who could say the most ridiculous thing about the pizza. I tried, "I will marry this pizza and make it my queen!" and Jem topped it with "You are the pizza that launched a thousand sheeps!"

Before long, the food was gone and we'd picked the last strings of cheese off the greasy cardboard. I was feeling more myself now, and when Jem pulled out three tins of lager from his bag, I passed on it and washed out an unbroken pint glass and filled it with tap water, which tasted amazing, even though there was a metallic flavor from the old pipes behind it. I hadn't realized how thirsty I was.

Jem and Dodger drank the beer slowly, talking about people I didn't know in other squats. From what I could work out, they had lived together somewhere else, but Jem had left—maybe after a fight with the other squatters—and ended up in the shelter, and that's how I'd met him. It sounded like this had all happened quite awhile ago, and the sting had gone out of the old arguments.

Neither of them seemed to mind that I wasn't joining in with the conversation, so I got myself another glass of water and explored the pub again, this time with the lights on. Most of the lights had burned out or were missing their bulbs, but it was still bright enough to see, and without the crazy horror-show

headlamp, it was all a lot less sinister. It was also a lot less promising: there were missing floorboards in some of the rooms
(how narrowly had I missed breaking my leg?) and the stairs
were sagging and splintering.

Still, I could see what the place would look like after a lot of
paint and sanding, after cleaning and polishing and stuff. The pub
had seen a lot of wear over the years, but it had been built with
love, out of solid brick and wood, and it had been well maintained
before it got all rundown and knackered.

I sat down in one of the little second-story rooms, propped
up against one of the walls, and tried to imagine what it would be
like with bookcases and a desk and a big edit suite with some giant screens here. And then, for the second time that day, I dropped
off sitting up, with my chin on my chest.

That was my first day in the Zeroday, as we called our pub
home. Over the next two weeks, Jem and I foraged for food,
scrounged furniture, did some tube-station begging, and applied
ourselves vigorously to painting, sanding, and refurbishing the
Zeroday from roof to cellar.

Jem had a lot of friends who'd drop in, and it became clear
that some of them were planning on staying. I didn't mind at
first—they were mostly older than us, and they knew a lot about
sanding and painting and getting the plumbing unstuck. It's hard
to say no to someone who's willing to help you scoop up ancient
tramp turds and carry them off to a distant skip for disposal. Besides, having all these people around meant that Jem and I could
venture out together without leaving the pub unguarded, and this
was a massive plus.

But some of them were a bit dodgy. There was Ryan, an older
guy who always wanted the first pick of the food we brought
home from flash grocery skips, and took the best stuff and put it
in his own bag, but never helped get the food or bring it home.
He liked to stay up late drinking and smoking endless fags that

filled the pub room with thick smoke, and then he'd complain about the noise when we got up in the morning.

Some of the little 'uns were just as bad: Sally had run away from Glasgow and hated everything about London. She claimed to be seventeen, but I thought she was probably more like fifteen. She moaned about the air, the weather, the food, the accents, the boys, the girls, the mobile reception, all of it. When she first showed up—she came to our housewarming party, a week after we moved in, along with a whole crew of people who knew people who knew Jem—I was a bit excited. She was very pretty, pale and round-faced, with big brown eyes, and I liked her accent. But by the time we finished dinner, I was ready to throttle her. And of course, she was one of the ones who kept showing up to stay at ours, hogging the sofas or even taking over one or another of our beds without asking. Then she'd get up in the morning and complain about the water pressure and the grime in the shower. Jem got fed up with this and he met her on her way into the bathroom one day with an old toothbrush and a bottle of tile-cleaner and told her it was her turn to clean the shower. She didn't speak to either of us for a week, which was just fine with me.

"Come on, Sunshine," Jem said to me one morning as I wandered into the big pub room in search of coffee. Jem had set up a coffee filter in a kind of sock that hung from a wooden stand. He brewed lethally strong coffee, using beans he bought without complaint from his espresso wizard Fyodor, paying four times what the local Co-Op asked for beans.

I accepted a cup with a nod of silent thanks and sipped it, closing my eyes while the caffeine found its way into my bloodstream and began to kick some arse.

"What's on your agenda today, then?" he said.

I shrugged. "Not much to do round here," I said. "What I really want to do is get back to work with the net, but . . ." I spread my hands. "No lappie, right?"

Truth be told, I'd deliberately avoided getting a new computer or borrowing someone else's. Whenever I thought about getting online, two awful feelings crashed in on the thought: first, that my mum and dad would have found a computer at the community center and filled my inboxes with pissed-off messages about me running away, and second, that I had lost my wonderful virginity-stealing Scot clip. Course, the longer I waited, the angrier the messages would be, and the harder it would be for me to remember what choices I had made in the edit. I'd neatly solved both these problems by just ignoring them, and it had been working.

"Well, let's fix that, then, shall we?"

"What, do you know a skip where they chuck out old laptops?"

He pooched his lips. "Trent, you'd be amazed at what you can find in skips."

But it wasn't a skip—it was a wonderland.

We got on an eastbound bus and rode it as far as it would go, for a whole hour, out and out past where the houses started to peter out in favor of bleak, crumbly industrial estates with sagging gates and chipped brickwork. They reminded me of the old workshops and factories dotted around Bradford, long-shuttered relics with sagging and missing roofs.

We were the last ones on the bus when we finally got off. The bus stop was on a small island of pavement on the shoulder of a dual carriageway. Cars rattled and honked past. There were no people about, no shops. Jem stuck his hands on his hips. "Ready to go shopping?" he said.

"I suppose so. Where the hell are we?"

"Paradise," he said. "Come on."

He dodged across the road, vaulting the guardrail on the median. I followed, dancing around the oncoming cars. Down a winding and cracked road, we came to a low-slung warehouse with small, high windows. Jem thundered at the door with two fists.

"Hope he's home," he said.

I rolled my eyes. "You mean we came all the way out here and you don't even know if the person we're here to see is even in?" The most frustrating quirk of Jem's character was his refusal to carry a mobile phone. He might have been the last Londoner to use the red call boxes for their proper purpose (mostly, London's pay phones seemed to exist to support a thick mat of lurid cards advertising the services of prostitutes). Whenever I asked him about this, he just shrugged.

"He'll be in," Jem said. "He's almost always in." He thumped at the door again. "Aziz!" he shouted, pressing his mouth up to the crack between the double doors. "Aziz! It's Jem!" He pressed his eye to the crack. "Lights are on. He's home. No fear."

A moment later, the door rattled and swung open, revealing a potbellied Asian guy in his twenties, unshaven and rumpled in a dirty T-shirt and a pair of cutoff shorts. "Jem?" he said. "Christ, boy, when are you going to get a phone?" He turned to me. "Who's this?"

"New chum," he said. "Trent, meet Aziz the Fixer. This man knows more about computers than any ten ultranerds you'll find on Tottenham Court Road, combined. He's an artist. Aziz, this is Trent, who is in need of some new kit."

Aziz shook my hand. His fingers were long and flexible, with calloused tips that rasped on my palm. "Come in, then," he said. He turned without waiting for an answer and set off into the warehouse, leaving us to hurry after him.

The building was enormous, the size of two football pitches stitched together, with metal shelving in ranks stretching off into infinity, piled high with electronics, like the warehouse at the end of the remake of *Raiders of the Lost Ark*. It smelled of ozone, burnt plastic electrical insulation, and mouse piss (this last one being a smell I'd grown very familiar with while getting the Zeroday into shape). He led us through a maze of shelves, deeper and deeper, not saying anything, but occasionally grunting and jabbing a long finger in the direction of the shelves we passed, evidently pointing out something interesting. Jem nodded and made enthusiastic noises when he did this, so apparently he was seeing something I wasn't.

I know a fair bit about tech, if I do say so myself. Taught myself to edit, taught myself to set up dual-boots and secure proxies to dodge the snoops. But I'd never really got down into the guts of the machine, the electronics and other gubbins. They were a complete mystery to me. Being around so many dismembered and eviscerated computers made me feel like I was getting out of my depth. I liked the feeling.

"What is this place?" I said.

"Aziz's place," Jem said. Aziz looked back over his shoulder at us and grinned like a pirate. "Aziz is the best scrounger in all of bloody London. He's got the good stuff, mate."

We came to our destination, a cleared-away space with some long trestle-tables that served as workbenches, cluttered with semiassembled (or disassembled?) computers. In one corner was a big four-poster bed, unlikely as a sofa in the middle of the motorway. It was piled high with grimy pillows and bedding and even more computers. Beside it was a rolling clothes rack, the kind I'd seen in big department stores, crowded with clothes on hangers and even more clothes draped over the top.

"Right," Aziz said. "What you after? Gaming? I bet it's gaming. You look like a twitchy sod." He seemed to be enjoying himself—there was nothing threatening or hostile in his gruff bearing. I guessed that he didn't get much company and was glad to have it.

"I do video editing," I said, feeling slightly awkward about it. It was one thing to upload a mashup and *show* people how hot you were, another thing to expect them to believe it.

"Right," he said. "No problems. How much you looking to spend?"

Jem grinned. "Nuffink," he said. "Whatcha got?"

He made a fake-sour face. "Jem, boy, you're taking liberties again."

"Come off it, Aziz," he said. "You've got more junk here than you can ever flog. And haven't I found you some of your best kit?"

He made his face again. "Oh, you're a chancer. Right, okay. How's this sound, then: Twelves gigahertz, sixteen gigs of RAM, four terabyte raid, two gigs of VRAM, twenty-five-inch display?"

My jaw dropped. I was literally drooling, in danger of having dribble slosh down my chin. "That sounds pretty amazing," I stammered.

"One thing," Aziz said, "before we start. You planning on doing anything dodgy in the copyright department? No offense, but you're a mate of Jem's, so I assume you're a depraved pirate."

I looked at Jem, wondering what to make of this. He was grinning and holding up two fingers behind Aziz's back, but in a friendly way. So I said, "You got me. I'm a depraved pirate. Incorrigible." I put on a medieval, dramatic voice. "Don't blame me: blame society, for it made me the sorry soul what you see before you."

Aziz smiled broadly. "You're overdoing it. You were doing okay until you got to 'what you see before you.'"

"Everyone's a critic."

"There's a reason I ask," Aziz said. "And that's because I figure that you'd like to keep your skinny white butt out of prison."

"Good assumption."

"Right. Well, if you're going to attain that objective, you'll need to be careful about the kind of kit you use. The rubbish you buy in the high street, it's got all kinds of little snitches built in that'll finger you if you ever get nicked. So what you want is to be *highly selective* when you assemble the gear."

I shook my head. "I'm not following you," I said.

"He's talking about trusted computing," Jem said.

"Oh," I said. "That." I'd heard about TC, a little. All the bits in your computer had small, secure chips on them that users couldn't alter. Your computer and operating system could use those to know which components were installed and to make sure they weren't counterfeit. Some operating systems would refuse to use dodgy parts. But like I say, I was a video editor, not a boffin. I could google up a recipe to get my computer to do something and follow it, but it wasn't like I was paying much attention. Needed to get back to my video editing, didn't I?

"You probably think that trusted computing is there to stop you from accidentally using fake cards and that in your computer, right?" Aziz said.

"Yeah," I said. "I get the feeling you're about to tell me there's more to it."

"Top pupil," Aziz said. "Have a seat, I'm going to tell you something that might just save your arse."

I pulled a rolling chair up to Aziz's workbench. Jem waved at us. "I've heard this already. Going to go have a shufty around the shelves, all right?"

"Don't mess up my filing system," Aziz said.

Jem looked pointedly at the overflowing, madcap shelves and shook his head. "Naturally," he said. "Wouldn't dream of it."

Aziz sat down opposite me and grabbed a video card from the workbench. It was a big, fat thing, with two additional fans and a huge heat-sink. He grabbed an anglepoise lamp with a built-in magnifier and shone it on the card, lowering it so that I could peer through the lens. With the tip of a screwdriver, he pointed at a spot on the board.

"See that?" he said.

"Yeah," I said. It looked like any of the other surface-mounted components on the circuit board: flat, black, smaller than my little fingernail. I looked closer. There was something odd about it. It didn't have any markings silk-screened on it. It wasn't just soldered onto the board, either—there was something covering the places where the pins entered the board, clear and hard-looking, like it had been dipped in plastic. "Something weird about that one, yeah?"

"Oh yes," he said. "That's the Trusted Computing snitch.

It's a nice bit of engineering: triple thickness of epoxy alternating with corrosive acids that will destroy the chip if you try to remove it. Got its own little on-board processor, too, and some memory it uses to store a cryptographic certificate."

I shook my head. "Sounds like spy stuff," I said. "I had no idea."

He set the board down, pushed away the lamp. "Here's the thing no one really gets. Ten years ago, a bunch of big companies and governments decided it would be handy if computers could be redesigned to disobey their owners, keep secrets from them. If there were secrets stored in computers that owners couldn't see, you could get up to all sorts of mischief. You could make sure that computers never copied when they weren't supposed to. You could spy on peoples' private communications. You could embed hidden codes in the video and photos and network packets they made and trace them back to individual computers.

"But keeping secrets from a computer's owner is a pretty improbable idea: imagine that I wanted to sell you a chest of drawers but I wanted to fill one of the drawers with a bunch of secret papers. I could glue and nail and cement that drawer shut, but at the end of the day, once it's at your house, you're going to be able to drill it, saw it, burn it—you're going to get into that drawer!

"So we've been having this invisible arms race for the past decade, users versus manufacturers, trying to hide and recover secrets from electronics. Sometimes—a lot of the time—users win. This chip"—he gestured at the video card—"is practically impregnable to physical attack. But there's a bug in its on-board software, and if you know the bug, you can get it to barf up its secret certificate. Once you've got that, you can forge the secret numbers it embeds in the video it processes. You can get it to pretend to be a different model of card. You can get it to save video you're not supposed to be able to save.

"When a card like this is cracked, the manufacturer has to stop selling it, has to go back to the drawing board and find a way to fix the flaw. New versions of the operating systems are released that try to block using insecure cards in the future, but that doesn't work so well, since someone with a cracked card can always get it to impersonate a more secure, later model. Still, manufacturers regularly have to pitch out mountains of junk that some clever dick has worked out how to compromise."

I shook my head. "You're joking. They just throw it away because someone's figured out how to get through that stupid little chip?"

He nodded. "It's true. Weird, but true. You see, to get your gear certified for use with the big Hollywood studios' copyrights, you have to sign an agreement saying that your kit won't leak films onto the Internet. Once it does—and it *always* does—you have to fix it. But since the chip is soldered onto the board with self-destructing superglue, you can't really take it off, fix it, and put it back. So you have to bin it. Bad for the planet." He winked. "But good for us."

A light went on. "You get it all out of the bin when they chuck it?"

"Oh, I wish. No, most of this stuff gets chucked out in China and Vietnam and that. But whatever the local distributor has, I get. Which means that I've got the world's biggest supply of gear whose spy-chips are known to be hackable. This card here—" he picked it up again. It was lovely and huge, the kind of graphics card that's meant to look good in the shop, all hot colors and fans that looked like they belonged on a military hovercraft. "This card is fast as blazes. Fantastic for gaming, fantastic for cutting video and doing your own effects generation.

"And what's more, the clever people who designed it forgot to take out their testing suite before they shipped it. So there's a mountain of code in here that lets you go around the security measures, hijack the snitch-chip, and get it to give up its secrets, left over from when they were prototyping it and getting it to work. It's a dumb mistake, but you'd be surprised at how common it is. Anyway, a month ago this thing was worth eight hundred quid and now I'm finding them by the dozen in bins all over the place."

It was too weird to be true. "I don't get it: why would a store or a distributor throw it away? Wouldn't people *want* to buy a card that they can hack to do more? Wouldn't that make it more valuable?"

"Oh," he said. "Right—no, sorry, I've explained it badly. Here's what happens: you find a crack for a card and put it on the net. The entertainment bosses find out about it and have kittens. So they add something called a 'secure revocation message' to all the films and telly and that, and the next time you try to load a film or show on your box, it refuses to play, and you get an error saying that your video card is not capable of displaying this film. You take it down to the shop and they swap the card out, and the manufacturer foots the bill and chucks out your old card."

"But I thought you said you could hack the card so that they couldn't tell what model you're using?"

"Oh, *I* can do this. I can show you how to do it, too. But the average person doesn't know or care how to hack their card. So your villains and pirates and that get to go on merrily using their cards in ways that make Hollywood furious, but the punters and honest cits have their gear deactivated. It's a mad world, but there you have it."

I could remember times that Mum and Dad had had to replace their gear because of technical problems, but I'd always assumed that this was because they didn't really understand technology. Turns out it was *me* who didn't understand. Of course, everything I watched was pirated, which meant that it wasn't going to be sending any of these "revocation messages."

"Christ," I said. "Why aren't people spitting about this?"

"Plenty of people are. But it's so easy to defeat if you know what you're doing that everyone who gets angry just solves the problem and stops being angry. Like I said, it's only the honest cits who don't even know they're getting screwed who really get hurt by this."

I wondered how many snitchy secret numbers my computer had snuck into the videos I'd released. Maybe it wasn't so bad that someone had stolen my lappie. It made me feel violated and claustrophobic to think that for years I'd been practically living inside a computer that was taking orders from somewhere else, doing things behind my back that could get me in trouble.

"Right," I said. "Let's build a computer."

It didn't work at first. Using junk parts and weird, off-brand operating systems was a lot harder than just getting a machine from the library that'd been rebuilt for giveaway to local kids. But as the hours wore on, I found that I was understanding things I'd never really understood, getting under the bonnet of the machine that I used every day of my life, all day long, stripping away layers of artifice and metaphor to actually touch the bare metal and feel the electricity coursing through it.

There was something liberating about working with kit that was fundamentally worthless—stuff that had started out as rubbish. Several times, I misconnected a wire and blew out a component, making eye-watering curls of smoke and melting plastic smells. But Aziz never seemed to get upset, just took anything that looked melted and tossed it into a huge steel barrel at the end of his workbench, then got replacement parts from his infinite shelves.

"It's just junk, lad, don't sweat it."

Jem helped out, too, though he didn't know much more about computers than I did. But he had a good sense of space, and had lots of helpful suggestions for cramming all the bits and pieces we decided on into the laptop shell that Aziz had chosen for me. It was a little bigger and bulkier than I would have liked, but that meant that there was room for more gubbins inside, which meant that I could shop longer and harder for the choicest morsels to power my new deck.

Once I had all the pieces assembled and could get the computer to switch on without bursting into flames or exploding, it was time to get an operating system built and configured for it.

Aziz said, "You say you're cool with Linux, yeah?"

I nodded. There were a million operating systems that were called something like "Linux" and if you googled too deeply, you'd find massive holy wars over which ones were and weren't Linux and what we should be calling them. I didn't pay that any attention, though. I'd been dual-booting my computers into Linux since I was a little kid. Mostly it just worked—you took any old computer, stuck a Linux thumbdrive into it, turned it on, and let it do its thing. Sometimes it'd act weird and I'd have to look up some arcane incantation to type in to get it running again, so I knew that there was a lot going on under the bonnet that I wasn't anything like an expert in. But then again, I didn't know much about the hardware stuff, either, but it hadn't been as hard as I'd feared. It had just gone together, like Lego.

But the software stuff eluded me. I had built a frankencomputer of surpassing strangeness. What's more, I wanted my operating system to work in concert with illegal, compromised drivers for all the cards and components that would get them to lie about which cards they were, to leak protected video out the back doors I'd rudely hacked into them, to pretend to insert watermarks while doing no such thing. This wasn't about sticking in the drive and pressing GO.

"Want a bit of advice?" Aziz asked, round about midnight, as I cursed and rubbed my eyes and rebooted the computer for the millionth time.

I slumped. Jem was even less of a software guy than I was, and had taken over Aziz's bed, taking off his shoes and curling up and snoring loudly.

"Yeah," I said. "Advice would be good."

"Your problem is, you're trying to understand it. You need to just *do it*."

"Well, thank you, Buddha, for the zen riddle. You should

consider putting that on an inspirational poster. Maybe with a little Yoda: 'There is no try, there is only do.'"

"Oh, ungrateful child. I'm not talking in metaphor—I'm being literal. You're sitting there with all those tabs open in your browser, trying to work out every aspect of Linux microkernel messaging, binary compatibility between distributions, and look at that, you're trying to read up about compilers at the same time? Mate, you are trying to get a four-year computer science degree, on your own, in one evening. You will not succeed at this.

"It's not because you're not a smart and quick young man. I can see that you are. It's because this is impossible.

"What you're trying to do now, you're trying to learn something about as complicated as a language. You've learned one language so far, the one we're speaking in. But you didn't wait until you'd memorized all the rules of grammar and a twenty-thousand-word vocabulary before you opened your gob, did you? No, you learned to talk by saying 'goo-goo' and 'da-da' and 'I done a pee-poo.' You made mistakes, you backtracked, went down blind alleys. You mispronounced words and got the grammar wrong. But people around you understood, and when they didn't understand what you meant, you got better at that part of speech. You let the world tell you where you needed to focus your attention, and in little and big pieces you became an expert talker, fluent in English as she is spoke the world round.

"So that's what I mean when I say you need to stop trying to understand it and just do it. Look, what you trying to do with that network card?"

"Well, I googled its part number here to see why they had to stop making it. I figured, whatever it wasn't supposed to be doing, that's what I wanted it to do. It looks like the reason Cisco had to pull this one was because you can open a raw socket and change a MAC address. I don't really know what either of those things are, so I've been reading up on them over here, and that's got me reading up on IP chaining and—"

"Stop, stop! Okay. Raw sockets—that just means that you

can run programs that do their own network stuff without talking to the OS. Very useful if you want to try to, say, inject spoof traffic into a wireless network. And it's great for disguising your operating system: every OS has its own little idiosyncrasies in the way it does networks, so it's possible for someone you're talking to to tell if you're running Linux or Windows Scribble or a phone or whatever. So if there's something that won't talk to you unless you're on a locked-down phone, you can use raw sockets to pretend to be a crippled-up iPhone instead of a gloriously free frankenbox like this one.

"MAC addresses—those are the hardwired serial numbers on every card. They identify the manufacturer, model number, and so on. Get sent along with your requests. So if they seize your computer, they can pull the MAC address and look at all the logged traffic to a pirate site and put two and two together. You don't want that.

"But with the right drivers, this card can generate a new, random MAC address every couple of minutes, meaning that the logs are going to see a series of new connections from exotic strangers who've never been there before. This is what you want. That's all you need to know for now. Just follow the recipes to get the drivers configured, and look up more detail as it becomes necessary. It's not like it's hard to learn new facts about networking—just use a search engine. In the meantime, just do it."

I snorted a little laugh. Between the sleep deprivation and his enthusiasm, I was getting proper excited about it all.

From there, it went *much* faster. I learned not to worry about the parts I didn't understand, but at Aziz's urging I started a big note-file where I made a record of all the steps I was taking. This turned out to be a lifesaver: any time I got stuck or something went utterly pear-shaped, I could go back through those notes and find the place where I went wrong. All my life, my teachers had been on me to take notes, but this was the first time I ever saw the point. I decided to do this more often. Who knew that teachers were so clever?

That was when life really took off at the squat. The next week, we scouted the council estate's wireless network and got an antenna aimed at one of their access points. It was encrypted of course, and locked to registered devices so that they could keep out miscreants who'd had their network access pulled for being naughty naughty copyright pirates.

But once we had the antenna set up, it was piss-easy to get the password for the network. It was written on a sheet of paper stuck to the notice board inside the estate's leisure centre: REMEMBER: EFFECTIVE THIS MONTH, THE NETWORK PASSWORD IS CHANGING TO 'RUMPLE34PETER12ALBERT.' After all, when you need a couple thousand people to know a secret, it's hard to keep it a secret.

Once we could decrypt the network traffic we were able to use Ethereal to dump and analyze all the traffic, and we quickly built up a list of all the MAC addresses in use on the system. There were thousands of them, of course: every phone had one, every computer, every game box, every set-top box for recording telly. Armed with these, we were able to use our forbidden network cards to impersonate dozens of devices at once, hopping from one MAC address to the next.

It was all brilliant, sitting in our cozy, candlelit pub room, using our laptops, playing the latest dub-step revival music we'd pulled down from a pirate radio site, watching videos on darknet video sites, showing our screens to one another. Aziz had given me a little pocket beamer with a wireless card and we took turns grabbing it and splashing our screens on the blank wall behind the bar (we'd cleared away the broken mirror) with the projector.

Even the housemates became easier to deal with. Ryan and Sally hooked up, which was revolting, but it didn't last long, ending with a spectacular row that sent Sally home to Glasgow (finally!) and convinced Ryan that he needed some "alone time" to get over his heartbreak. With both of them gone the Zeroday's energy changed, and it became a place where there was always someone cooking something, making something, writing a story or a song. We had all the food we could eat, and we were getting along well with our neighbors, too—even the drug dealers and their lookouts dropped by to see what we were up to, and seemed to find the whole thing hilarious, mystifying, and altogether positive.

Dodger turned out to be an incredible chef, able to cook anything with anything. He prepared epic meals that I can still taste today: caramelized leeks with roasted stuffed peppers, potatoes roasted in duck fat and dripping with gravy. Then there was the day he made his own jellied eels. It turned my stomach at first, just the thought of it, but that didn't stop me from eating sixteen of them once I'd tasted them!

I never did work out what happened between Jem and Dodger and the squat they'd shared before. It was clear that they were the best of mates, though Dodger was a good five years older than us. From what I could tell though, the old squat—Dodger still lived there—had gone through some kind of purge after a blazing row over chores or something stupid like that. Dodger spent so much time at ours, I couldn't figure out why he didn't just move in. We had it pretty comfortable, with fifteen good bedrooms that we'd scrounged furniture for, a lovely front room, all the Internet we could eat.

I never got to know Dodger that well, but Jem seemed to include me when he talked about the Jammie Dodgers, which was the imaginary youth gang that we all belonged to. It was also the name of his favorite biscuit: the old classic round cookie filled with raspberry jam. I didn't like the cookies much, but I was proud to be a JD, really. It was nice to belong.

We hadn't seen Dodger for a few days. It had come on full summer, and the pub was sweltering. We still didn't dare take the shutters down off the bottom windows, but we'd pried them off the upper stories and had pointed a few fans out the windows upstairs, blowing the rising hot air out the building, sucking in fresh air from below. It made the Zeroday a little cooler, just barely livable. Like hanging about in a pizza oven an hour after the restaurant had shut.

It was three in the afternoon on a Tuesday. I was sitting in cutoff shorts and no T-shirt, staring at my laptop and trying not to think about the mountain of messages that Mum and Dad and my sister had piled up in my inbox and IM. I couldn't face opening any of them, and, of course, the longer I waited, the more angry and sad and awful it would be when I did.

Jem cocked his head. "Did you hear that?" he said. My computer's fan was working triple-time in the heat, trying to force cool air over the huge graphics card I'd wrestled into the chassis at Aziz's before it melted the whole thing to molten slag. It was proper loud, and emitted a plume of hot air that shimmered in the dim.

"Hear what?" I said. I covered the fan exhaust with a finger—it was scalding—and listened. There it was, the sound of a hundred tropical birds going mad with fear. It was the drugs lookouts, and they were in a state about something. "Maybe the coppers are raiding that sugar-shack on the eighth floor," I said. "Want to go upstairs and have a peek out the window?"

Jem didn't say anything. He'd gone pale. "Get some trousers, shoes on, let's go," he said.

I gawped at him. "Jem?" I said. "What—"

"Do it," he snapped, and pelted up the stairs, rattling doorknobs and thumping doors, shouting, "Get moving, get moving, coppers!"

It felt like I was in a dream. For the first month after we'd claimed the Zeroday for our own, I'd lived in constant fear of a knock at the door: the coppers or the landlords come to muscle us out. Jem assured me that we couldn't be arrested for squatting—it'd take a long court proceeding to get us out. But that didn't stop me worrying. According to Dodger, sometimes landlords would take the easy way out and send over some hard men with sticks or little coshes filled with pound coins that could shatter all the delicate bones in your face, your hands, your feet.

But you can't stay scared forever. I'd forgot that the Zeroday was anything except a utopian palace in Bow, our own little clubhouse. Now all the fear I'd left behind rushed back. I was so scared, I felt like I was moving in slow motion, like a nightmare of being chased. I ran up the stairs behind Jem, headed for my room. All the clothes I owned had come from charity shops or out of skips. I yanked on a pair of jeans. I had a good pair of trainers I'd bought at a charity shop, and I jammed my feet into them, and stuffed my socks into a pocket. I still had my laptop under my arm, and I turned around and legged it for the front door.

As I entered the room, I heard a thunderous knocking at the door and the baritone shout, "POLICE!" I froze to the spot. Upstairs, I could hear the sound of Jem hustling the rest of the house out the top-floor window and down the fire-stairs out back, telling them to go. The hammering grew louder.

I went back upstairs, saw Jem standing by the window, his face still pale, but composed and calm.

"Jem!" I said. "What's all the panic? You said the cops wouldn't do anything to us, just order us to appear at a hearing—"

He shook his head. "That was until this week. They've got new powers to bust us for 'abstraction of electricity.' Immediate arrest and detention. Dodger told me about it—he's gone underground. Figures that they'd like to hang him up by the thumbs."

Abstraction of electricity? "What's abstraction of—"

"Stealing power," he said. "As in, what we've been doing here for months. *Go!*"

I went out the window. Downstairs, I heard the door splinter and bang open. Jem was right behind me on the fire escape. Outside, it was a sunny summery day, hot and muggy, and the birdcalls from the drugs kids made it feel like a jungle. The fire-stairs were ancient and rusted, crusted with bird shite. I ran down them on tiptoe, noticing the patter of dry crap and dust on the ground beneath me, sure that at any moment, I'd hear a cop-voice shout, "There they are!" and the tromp of boots. But I touched down to the broken ground and looked up to check on Jem, who was vaulting down the steps five at a time, holding onto the shaking railing and swinging his body like a gymnast on a hobbyhorse. The rest of the Zeroday's crew had already gone, disappearing into the estate, keeping behind the pub and out of sight of the men at the door.

He hit the ground a moment later and hissed *"Run!"* He took off and streaked for the nearest estate tower. I took off after him. Behind us, I finally heard the shout: *"There!"* and then *"Stop!"*

Jem planted one foot, spun, changed directions and ran off at right angles, toward the distant road, across the open ground. I'd never seen him run before, barely saw him now out of the corner of my eye, but even so, I could see that he could *run,* powering up like a cartoon character.

He was leading the chase away from me. What a friend. What an idiot. Feeling like the world's biggest coward, I kept going, heading for the estate, for the door where the lock was broken, for the maze of corridors and buildings that I could disappear into.

Chapter 2

ADRIFT/A NEW HOME/A SCREENING IN THE GRAVEYARD/ THE ANARCHISTS!

Jem didn't answer my e-mails. didn't show up again at Old Street Station, didn't turn up at the skips we'd haunted. Dodger's phone was out of service—he'd either been caught or had really and properly gone underground. The rest of my housemates had melted into the afternoon and vanished as though they'd never existed.

Back to the shelter I went, feeling a proper failure, and I slept in a room with seven other boys, and I got free clothes and a rucksack from the pile, ate the stodgy meals and remembered the taste of eels and caramelized leeks, and found myself, once again, alone in the streets of London. It had been nearly six months since I'd left Bradford, and I started to ache for home, for my parents and my sister and my old mates. I made a sign like Jem's, with Kleenex and sanitizer and gum and little shoe-polish wipes, and made enough money for a bus ticket home in less than a day.

But I didn't buy a bus ticket home. I gave all the money to other tramps in the station, the really broken ones that Jem and I had always looked out for, and then I went back to the shelter.

It's not that life was easy in the shelter, but it was, you know, *automatic*. I hardly had to think at all. I'd get breakfast and dinner there, and in between, I just needed to avoid the boredom and the self-doubt that crept in around the edges, pretend that I wasn't the loneliest boy in London, that I was living the Trent McCauley story, the second act where it all got slow and sad, just before the hero found his way again.

But if there was a new way, I didn't know where it was. One day, as I sat in Bunhill Cemetery, watching the pigeons swoop around the ancient tombs—their favorite was Mary Page: IN 67

MONTHS, SHE WAS TAPD 66 TIMES – HAD TAKEN AWAY 240 GALLONS OF WATER – WITHOUT EVER REPINING AT HER CASE – OR EVER FEAR-ING THE OPERATION (I wasn't sure what this meant, but it sounded painful)—and I couldn't take it anymore. Call me a child, call me an infant, but I had to talk to me mam.

I watched my hands move as though they belonged to some-one else. They withdrew my phone, unlocked it, dialed Mum's number from memory, and pressed the phone to my ear. It was ringing.

"Hello?" The last time I'd heard that voice, it had been cold and angry and fearful. Now it sounded beaten and sad. But even so, it made my heart thump so hard that my pulse was like a drumbeat in my ears.

"Mum?" I said in a whisper so small it sounded like the voice of a toddler. First my hands, now my voice—it was like my en-tire body was declaring independence from me.

"Trent?" She sucked in air. "*Trent?*"

"Hi, Mum," I said as casually as I could. "How're you?"

"Trent, God, Trent! Are you alive? Are you okay? Are you in trouble? Jesus, Trent, where the bloody hell are you? Where have you been? Trent, damn it—" She called out, *Anthony! It's Trent!* I heard my father's startled noises getting louder.

"Look, Mum," I said. "Hang on, okay? I'm fine. I'm just fine. Missing you all like fire. But I'm fine. Healthy, doing well. Mum, I'll call again later." Calling now seemed like such a stu-pid idea. I hadn't even been smart enough to block my number. Now I'd have to get a new prepaid card. What an idiot I was.

"Trent, don't you *dare* put the phone down. You come home *immediately*, do you hear me? No, wait. Stay where you are. We'll come and get you. Trent—"

I hung up. The phone rang. I switched it off, took the cover off, took out the SIM, and slipped it in my pocket. I missed Mum and Dad and Cora, but I wasn't ready to go home. I didn't know if I'd ever be. The few seconds I'd spent on the phone had made me feel about six years old. It hadn't been pretty.

I left the graveyard, and poor Mary Page, who had never repined her case, whatever that meant.

Without realizing it, my subconscious had been scouting for a new squat. I kept catching myself staring at derelict buildings and abandoned construction sites, wondering if there was an open door around the back, wondering if the power was out. There were plenty of empty places. The economy had just fallen into the toilet again, something it had done every few years for my entire life. This one seemed worse than most, and they'd even put the old Chancellor of the Exchequer in jail, along with a couple of swanky bankers. I couldn't see that it had made any difference. There were more tramps everywhere I looked, and a lot of them had the bewildered look of mental patients who'd been turned out of closed hospitals, or the terrified look of pensioners who couldn't pay the rent.

It was strange to think that the city was filled with both homeless people *and* empty houses. You'd think that you could simply solve the problem by moving the homeless people into the houses. That was my plan, anyway. I wasn't part of the problem, you see, I was part of the bloody solution.

I was especially into old pubs. The Zeroday had been a golden find: proper spacious and with all the comforts of home, practically. I found one likely old pub in deepest Tower Hamlets, but when I checked the title registry—where all sales of property were recorded—I saw that it had been bought up the week before, and guessed (correctly, as it turned out) that they were about to start renovating the place.

After two weeks of this, more or less on a whim, I decided to ride the bus out to Bow and have a look in on the old Zeroday, see what happened to the homestead, check for clues about Jem's whereabouts. Plus, where there was one abandoned pub, there might be another. Goodness knew that Bow was in even worse economic shape than most places.

From a distance, the Zeroday looked abandoned, shutters

back up on the upper stories. The drugs lookouts took up their birdsong when I got off the bus, but soon stopped as they recognized me. I sauntered over to the pub, filled with a mix of fear and nostalgia. My heart sank when I saw the fresh padlock and hasp on the outside of the front door. But then it rose again as I neared it and saw that the lock had been neatly sawn through and replaced. I slipped it off and nudged the door.

It was déjà vu all over again. The smell of sugar and spliff and of piss and shite told me that the local drugs kids and sex trade had carried on using the place. I called out hello a few times, just in case someone was in the place, and left the door open halfway to let in some light. I found melted candles everywhere, even on "our" comfy parlor sofa, which was quite ruined, stuffing spilling out, cushions wet with something that made me want to find some hand-sanitizer.

In the kitchen, I nearly broke my neck falling into the open cellar. It was pitch dark down there, but I had an idea that maybe they'd just flipped the big cutout switch that Dodger'd installed and blacked the place out. Which meant that flipping it the other way—

I needed to come back with a torch. And some friends.

There were other kids in the shelter that I sort of got on with. A tall, lanky kid from Manchester who, it turned out, had also left home because he'd got his family kicked offline. He was another video nutter, obsessed with making dance mixes of Parliamentary debates, looping the footage so that the fat, bloated politicians in the video seemed to be lip-syncing. It was tedious and painstaking work, but I couldn't argue with the results: he'd done a mix of the Prime Minister, a smarmy, good-looking twit named Bullingham who I'd been brought up to hate on sight (his dear old grandad, Bullingham the Elder, had been a senior cabinet member in the old days when you had to look like a horrible toad to serve in a Tory government), singing a passionate rendition of a song called "Sympathy for the Devil." It was a thing of beauty, especially when he cut out the PM's body from the original frames and supered it over all this gory evangelical Christian footage of Hell from a series called *The Left Behinds* that aired on the American satellite networks at all hours of day and night. He claimed he'd got eighteen million pageviews before it had been obliterated from YouTube and added to the nuke-from-orbit list that the copyright bots kept.

Now he hosted it, along with his other creations, on ZeroKTube, which wasn't even on the Web. It was on this complicated underground system that used something called "zero knowledge." I couldn't follow it exactly, but from what Chester—as the lad from Manchester insisted on calling himself, with a grin—said, it worked something like this: you gave up some of your hard drive and network connection to ZeroKTube. Other 0KT members who had video to share encrypted their video and broke it into many pieces and stashed them on random 0KT nodes. When you wanted to watch the video, you fed a 0KT node the key for unscrambling the video, and it went around and found enough pieces to reassemble the video and there you had it. The people running individual nodes had no way of knowing what they were hosting—that was the "zero knowledge" part— and they also randomly exchanged pieces with one another, so a copyright bot could never figure out where all the pieces were. Chester showed it to me, and even though it seemed a bit slow, it was also pretty cool—the 0KT client had all the gubbins that You-Tube had: comments, ratings, related videos, all done with some fiendish magick that I couldn't hope to understand.

Chester had a street-buddy, Rabid Dog (or "Dog" or "RD"), which was a joke of a nickname, because RD was about five foot tall, podgy, with glasses and spots, and he was so shy that he couldn't really talk properly, just mumble down his shirtfront. Rabid Dog was an actual, born-and-bred Londoner, and he was only about fifteen, but had been living on the streets off and on since he was twelve and had never really gone to school. Even so, he was a complete monster for the horror films, and had an encyclopedic knowledge of them stretching back to *Nosferatu* and forward to *Spilt Entrails XVII,* which was the only subject that'd get him talking above a mutter.

Rabid Dog had got his family kicked off the net with his compulsion to rework horror films to turn them into wacky comedies, romantic comedies, torture comedies, and just plain comedies. He'd add hilarious voice-overs, manic music, and cut them just so, and you'd swear that Freddy Kruger was a great twentieth-century comedian. He liked to use OKT as well, but he wasn't content merely to make films: he made the whole package—lobby cards, posters, trailers, even fictional reviews of his imaginary films. There was an entire parallel dimension in Rabid Dog's head, one in which all the great horror schlockmeisters of history had decided instead to make extremely bloody, extremely funny comedies.

I figured that Rabid Dog and Chester were ready to learn some of the stuff that I'd got from Jem. So one day, I showed them how my sign worked and introduced them round to the oldsters at Old Street Station. The next day, we rummaged for posh nosh in the skip behind the Waitrose (always Waitrose with Jem, he said they had the best, and who was I to change his rules?), and ate it in Bunhill Cemetery, near poor old Mary Page. (Rabid Dog, a right scholar of human deformity, injury, and disease opined that she had had some kind of horrible internal cyst that had been drained of gallons of pus before she expired. What's more, he pointed this out as we were scoffing back jars of custard over slightly overripe strawberries. And he didn't mumble.)

The day after, I took the lads to the Zeroday. I'd scrounged a couple of battery-powered torches and some thick rubber gloves and safety shoes, a lucky find at a construction site that no one had been watching very closely. I put them on once we got inside, first putting on the gloves and then using my gloved hands to steady myself on the disgusting, spongy-soft sofa while I balanced on one foot and then the other, changing into the boots. I had no idea whether they'd be enough to keep me from getting turned into burnt toast by the electrical rubbish if I touched the wrong wire, but they made me feel slightly less terrified about what I was going to do.

"Hold these," I said to the lads, handing them the torches and scampering down the ladder into the cellar. It smelled dreadful. Someone—maybe several someones—had used it as a toilet, and my safety shoes squelched in a foul mixture of piss and shite and God knew what else. "Shine 'em here," I said, pointing down at the switchplate on the wall. Dodger had shown me his work after he got done with it: all the wires he'd put in neat bundles with plastic zip-straps, all running in and out of the ancient junction box with its rubber-grip handle. There were ridiculous old fuses, the kind that were a block of ceramic with two screws in the top, that you had to carefully stretch a thin piece of wire between and screw down. When the circuit overloaded, the wire literally burned up, leaving a charred stump at each screw. Dodger had kept threatening to put in a proper breaker panel, but he never got round to it, and we all got good at doing the wire thing, because the Zeroday's ancient electricals rebelled any time we tried to plug in, say, a hair dryer, a microwave, a fan, and a couple of laptops.

The lads played their lights over the switch and I saw that it was in the off position, handle up. Holding my breath, I took hold of the handle and, in one swift movement, slammed it down, jerking my hand away as soon as it was in place, as though my nervous system could outpace the leccy.

Let there be light.

The fluorescents above me flickered to life. The fridges started to hum. And above me, Rabid Dog and Chester cheered. I smiled a proper massive grin. I was home.

Putting the Zeroday in order for the second time was easier. We hauled away all the moldering furniture, installed fresh locks, unblocked some of the upper windows, and scrounged some fans to get the scorching summer air out. We scrubbed everything with bleach, found new bedding, and made ourselves at home.

It was one of those long hot summers that just seemed to get hotter. Since I'd got to London, I'd spent most of my time being gently (or roughly) rained upon, and I'd lost count of the number of times I'd wished the rain would just piss off and the sun would come out. Now it seemed like London's collective prayer for sunlight had been answered and we were getting a year's worth of searing blue skies lit with a swollen, malevolent white sun that seemed to take up half the heavens. After months of griping about the rain, we were gasping for it.

It drove the Zeroday's residents into a nocturnal existence. But that wasn't so bad. It was summer. There were all-ages clubs where kids danced all night long, pretty girls and giggles and weed and music so loud it made your ears ring all day long the next day. We'd get up at three or four in the afternoon, have a huge breakfast, shower, smoke some weed—someone always had some, and Chester swore he was going to find us some Gro-Lites and a mister and turn one of the upstairs bedrooms into a farm that would supply us with top-grade weed for the coming dark winter.

I wasn't sure about this. Having just three of us in the house, and coming and going mostly after dinnertime, meant that we were keeping a much lower profile than we'd had in the days of the Jammie Dodgers. I thought that the serious electricity that Gro-Lites wanted might tip off the landlords or the law that we were back in residence.

After breakfast, we'd jump on our lappies and start looking for a party. For this, we used Confusing Peach Of The Forest Green Beethoven, which may just be the best name of a website ever. Confusing Peach was more like an onion, with layers in layers in layers. You started off on the main message boards where they chatted about music and life and everything else. If you were cool enough—interesting, bringing good links to the conversation, making interesting vids and music—you got to play in the inner circle, where they talked about where the best parties were, which offies would sell you beer and cider without asking for ID, where you could go to get your phone unlocked so that it would play pirated music.

But it turned out that there was an even more inner circle inside the inner circle, a place where they talked about better parties, where they had better download links for music and films, where they spent a lot of time making fun of the lamers in the outer inner circle and the outer outer circle. We got to the inner-inner (for some reason, it was called "Armed Card and the Cynical April") a couple weeks after finding Confusing Peach. We didn't have much to do except post on CP, and between Chester's crazy Bullingham videos, Rabid Dog's insane horror-comedies, and some Scot stuff I awkwardly put together (I hadn't worked on Scot since the day my laptop had been nicked in Hyde Park, the day I came to London), we were hits. The inner circle opened to us only two days after we got in, and the epic parties followed immediately after. All through the hot nights, in strange warehouses, terraced houses in central London, on abandoned building sites strung with speakers and lights, we went and we danced and we smoked and we swilled booze and tried so very hard to pull the amazing girls who showed up, without a lick of success.

But we must have made a good impression, even if it wasn't good enough to convince any of the young ladies to initiate us into the mysteries of romance (I may have taken Scot's virginity in my edit suite, but sad to say that no one had returned the favor). Before long, we were in the Cynical April message boards, where the videos were funnier, the music was better, and the parties were stellar.

"Dog," I shouted, pounding on the bathroom door. "Dog, come on, mate, there's just not that much of you to get clean, you fat bastard!" He'd been in the bathroom showering for so long that I was starting to think he might be having a sneaky wank in there. He was the horniest little bastard I'd ever met, and I'd learned never to go into his bedroom without knocking unless I wanted to be scarred by the spectacle of his bulging eyes and straining arm and the mountain of crusty Kleenexes all over his floor.

The shower stopped. Rabid Dog muttered something filthy that I pretended I hadn't heard, and a second later he came out, with a towel around his waist. He'd shaved his long hair off at the start of the heat wave, and it had grown in like a duck's fuzz, making him look even younger. Now it was toffee-apple red, and the hair dye had got on his forehead and ears, making him look like he was bleeding from a scalp wound.

"Whatcha think?" he muttered, pleading silently with his eyes for me to say something nice.

"It's pretty illustrious," I said, "illustrious" being the word-du-jour on Cynical April. He smiled shyly and nodded and ran off to his room.

I quickly showered and dressed, pulling on cutoff pinstripe suit trousers and a canary-yellow banker's shirt whose collar and sleeves I'd torn off. It was a weird fashion, but I'd seen a geezer wearing nearly the same thing at a party the week before and he'd been beating off the girls with both hands. By the time I made it down to the front room, Chester was dressed and ready, too, a T-shirt that shimmered a bit like fish-scales and a kilt with a ragged hem, finished out with a pair of stompy boots so old and torn that they were practically open-toed sandals. I squinted at this, trying to understand how it could look cool, but didn't manage it. "Huh," I said.

He held up two fingers at me and jabbed them suggestively. Then he indicated my own clothes and pointedly rolled his eyes. Okay, fine, we all thought that we looked ridiculous. Why not. We were teenagers. We were *supposed* to look ridiculous.

"What's the party, then?" I said. Chester had been in charge of picking it out, and he'd been snickering to himself in anticipation all day, barring us from looking at the party listings in Cynical April.

"We're going to the cinema," he said. "And we're bringing the films."

By that time, Bunhill Cemetery was like a second home to me. I knew its tombstones, knew its pigeons and its benches and the tramps who ate dinner there and the man who mowed the huge, brown sward of turf to one side of the tombstones. When I thought about graveyards, I thought of picnic lunches, pretty secretaries eating together, mums and nannies pushing babies around in pushchairs. Not scary at all.

But then, I'd never been to West Highgate.

We snuck into the graveyard around 10:00 P.M. Chester led us around the back of its high metal fence to a place where the shrubs were thick. We pushed through the shrubs and we discovered a place where the bars had rusted through, just as the map he'd downloaded to his phone had promised.

He whispered as we picked our way through the moonlit night, moving in the shadows around crazy-kilter tombs and headstones and creepy trees gone brown and dead in the relentless heat wave. "This place got bombed all to hell in World War Two and never got put right. There's still bomb craters round here you could break a leg in. And best of all, the charity that looks after it has gone bust, so there's no security guards at night—just some cameras round the front gate."

Five minutes' worth of walking took us so deep into the graveyard that all we could see in every direction were silhouetted stones and mausoleums and broken angels and statues. The stones glowed mossy gray in the moonlight, their inscriptions worn smooth and indistinct by the years. Strange distant sounds—rustles, sighs, the tramp of feet—crawled past us on the lazy breeze.

It was as scary as hell.

Chester got lost almost immediately and began to lead us in circles through the night. Our navigation wasn't helped by our unwillingness to tread on the graves, though whether this was out of respect for the dead or fear that hands would shoot out of the old soil and grab us by the ankles, I couldn't say.

It was getting dire when a shadow detached itself from one of the crypts and ambled over to us. As it got closer, it turned into a girl, about my age, shoulder-length hair clacking softly from the beads strung in it. She was wearing knee-length shorts covered in pockets and a tactical vest with even more pockets over a white T-shirt that glowed in the moonlight.

She hooted at us like an owl and then planted her fists on her hips. "Well, lads," she said. "You certainly seem to be lost. Graveyard's shut, or didn't you see the padlock on the gate?"

I had a moment's confusion. She looked like the kind of person that showed up at Cynical April parties, but she was acting like she was the graveyard's minder or something. If I told her we were coming to a party and she represented the authorities—

"We're here for the party," Chester said, settling the question. "Where is it?"

"What party?" Her voice was stern.

"The Cynical April party," Chester said, stepping forward, showing her the map on his phone. "You know where this is?"

She snorted. "You would make a rubbish secret agent. What if I wasn't in on it, hey?"

Chester shrugged. "I saw you at the last one, down in Battersea. You were doing something interesting in the corner with a laptop that I couldn't get close enough to see. Also, you've got two tins of lager in that pocket." He tapped one bulge in her tactical vest. I hadn't noticed them, but Chester had a finely tuned booze detector.

She laughed. "Okay, got me. Yes, I can get you there. I'm Hester."

Chester stuck out his hand. "Chester. We rhyme!" As chat-up lines went, it wasn't the best I'd heard, but she laughed again and shook his hand. Me and Rabid Dog said hello and she mentioned that she'd seen some of our Cynical April videos and said nice things about me and I was glad that you couldn't tell if someone was blushing in the moonlight. Up close, she smelled amazing, like hot summer nights and fresh-crushed leaves and beer and ganja. My heart began to skip in my chest at the thought of the party we were about to find.

Hester seemed to know her way around the graveyard, even in the dark, and pretty soon we could hear the distant sounds of laughter and low music and excited conversation.

Finally, we came to a little grove of ancient, thick-trunked trees, wide-spaced, with elaborate hillocky roots. They led up to a crumbling brick wall, the back of a much larger building, some kind of gigantic mausoleum or crypt or vault, a massive depository for ex-humans and their remains.

Someone had set glow-sticks down in the roots of the trees and in some of the lower branches, filling the grove with a rainbow of chemical light. I heard cursing over my head and looked up and saw more people in the trees' upper branches, working with headlamps and muttering to themselves. Chester pointed them out and laughed and I grabbed his arm and said I wanted to know what the deal was. He'd been chortling evilly to himself the whole trip out to the graveyard, and refusing to answer any questions about the party he'd picked for us.

"Oh, mate, it's going to be *illustrious*. They've got little beamers up there, projectors, right? And they're going to show films up against that wall all night long."

"Which films?" I said. I hadn't been to the cinema all summer—between the high cost and the mandatory searches and having your phone taken off you for the whole show in case you tried to record with it, I just hadn't bothered. But there were a bunch of big, dumb blockbustery films I'd had a yen for, some of which I'd downloaded, but it just wasn't the same. When some gigantic American studio spends hundreds of millions of dollars on computer-animated robots that throw buildings at one another while telling smart-alecky macho jokes, you want to see it on a gigantic screen with hundreds of people all laughing and that. A little lappie screen won't cut it.

"Our films!" he said, and punched the air. "I submitted clips from all of us and the girl who's running it all chose them to head-line the night. Yes!" He punched the air again. "It is going to be *illustrious, illustrious, ill-bloody-us-tri-bloody-ous!* We're going to be heroes, mate." He hung a sweaty arm around my neck and put me in an affectionate headlock.

I wrestled free and found myself grinning and chortling, too. What an amazing night this was going to be!

Getting the beamers just right up in the trees was hard. More than once, the climbers had to reposition themselves, and they dropped one beamer and it shattered into a million plasticky bits, and Hester stood beneath the tree it had fallen out of and told them off with such a sharp and stinging tongue that I practically fell in love that second. She was Indian, or maybe Bangla, and in the weird light of the glow-sticks, she was absolutely gorgeous. She had a whole little army of techie girls with matching vests and shorts and they seemed to be running the show. I was trying to figure out how to introduce myself to them when someone tackled me from behind.

"Got you, you little miscreant! Off to prison for you—bread and water for the next ten years!" It was a voice I hadn't heard in so long I'd given up on hearing it again.

"Jem!" I said. "Christ, mate, get off me!"

He let me up and gave me a monster hug that nearly knocked me off my feet again. "Trent, bloody hell, what are you doing here?"

"Where have you *been*?" He was skinnier than he had been the last time I saw him, and he'd shaved the sides and back of his head, leaving behind a kind of pudding-bowl of hair. Now that I could see his face, I could also see a new scar under one eye.

"Oh," he said. He shrugged. "Wasn't as quick as I thought I was. Ended up doing a little turn at His Majesty's pleasure." It took me a minute to realize he meant that he'd been in jail. I swallowed. "Not too much time, as it turned out. All they had on me was resisting arrest, and the magistrate was kindly disposed at sentencing. Been out for weeks. But where have you been? Haven't seen you in any of the usual spots."

I rolled my eyes. "You could have just *called me* if you weren't such a stubborn git about not carrying a phone."

He reached into his shirt and drew out a little phone on a lanyard, a ridiculous toy-looking thing like you'd give to a five-year-old on his first day of kindergarten. "I came around on that. But your number's dead," he said.

I remembered chucking away my SIM after my disastrous phone call home. Durr. I was such an idiot. "Well," I said, "you could have emailed."

"No laptop. Been playing it low-tech. But where have you *been*? I've checked the shelter, Old Street, everywhere—couldn't find hide nor hair of you, son."

"Jem" I said. "I'm in the same place I've been since the day I met you: at the Zeroday."

He smacked himself in the forehead with his palm. "Like a dog returning to its vomit," he said. "Of course. And the filth haven't given you any trouble?"

"We keep a low profile," I said. "Too hot to go out during the day, anyway. Hardly anyone knows we're there."

Without warning, he gave me another enormous, bearish hug. I could smell that he was a little drunk already. "Christ, it's good to see you again!"

"Where are *you* living?" I asked.

"Oh," he said. "Here and there. Staying on sofas. The shelter, when I can't find a sofa. You know how it goes."

"Well," I said. "My mate Chester's been kipping in your room, but I'm sure he'd move. Or there are plenty of other rooms. It's just three of us in there these days."

He looked down. "That'd be lovely," he said. He put his hand out and I shook it. "It's a deal."

So I introduced him round to Chester and Rabid Dog, who'd both heard all about him and seemed glad enough to meet him, though Chester was more interested in Hester and trying to be helpful to her, and Rabid Dog, well, it was impossible to say what Dog was thinking at any given moment, what with all the mumbling. But I didn't give a toss: I had my best pal back, I had my new pals, it was a hot night, there were films, there was beer, there were girls, there was a moon in the sky and I wasn't in bloody Bradford. What else could I ask for?

By the time they started the films, there must have been fifty kids in the trees and bushes. Some were already dancing, some were passing round cartons of fried chicken or enormous boxes of sweets. Loads were smoking interesting substances and more than one was willing to share with me. The night had taken all the sting out of the superheated day, leaving behind a not-warm/ not-cool breeze that seemed to crackle with the excitement we were all feeling.

One of the girls running the films climbed down out of a tree I was leaning against and nodded to me, then looked more closely. "You're the Scot guy, yeah?"

Feeling a massive surge of pride, I looked down at my toes, and said, quietly, "Yeah."

"Nice stuff," she said. She stuck her hand out. I shook it. It was sticky with sap from the tree branch she'd been clinging to, and strong, but her hand was slender and girly in a way that made me go all melty inside. Look, it was summer, I was sixteen, and anytime I let my mind wander, it wandered over to thoughts of girls, food, and parties. Every girl I met, I fell a bit in love with. Every time one of them talked to me, I felt like I'd scored a point in some enormous and incredibly important game that I didn't quite understand but madly wanted to win.

"Thanks," I said, and managed not to stammer, quaver, or

squeak. Another point. "I'm—" I was about to say "Trent," but instead I said, "Cecil." Everyone else had a funny street name— why the hell did I have to be boring old Trent forever? "Cecil B. DeVil."

She laughed. She had a little bow-shaped mouth and a little dimple in her chin and a mohican that she'd pulled back into a ponytail. Her skinny arms were ropy with fine muscle. "I'm 26," she said.

She didn't look any older than I was. I must have looked skeptical. "No, I mean my *name's* 26. As in, the number of letters in the alphabet. You can call me Twenty."

I had to admit that this was the coolest nickname I had ever heard.

"Hester pointed you out, you and your mates. She said that you made those Scot Colford films, right?"

"That was me," I said. "My mates did the others, the horror films and that Bullingham thing." I gestured vaguely into the writhing, singing, dancing, shouting mass of people.

"Yeah, those were good, but the Scot thing was genius. I love that old dead bastard. Love how he could do the most shite bit of fluff one week, then *serious drama* the next. He was a complete hack, absolutely in it for the money, but he was an artist."

I had written practically the very same words in a Media Studies report, the only paper in my entire academic career to score an A. "I couldn't agree more," I said. "So." I couldn't find more words. I was losing the game. "So. So, you're doing all this stuff with the projectors then?"

She beamed. "Innit wonderful? My idea, of course. We got the beamers from some geezer out in Okendon, guy lives in a gigantic building full of electronic rubbish—"

"Aziz!" I said.

"Yeah, that's the one. Bastard seems to know everyone. Hester met him through some squatters she knew, brought us along to get the gear. He certainly has whatever you need. From there, it was just a matter of rigging up some power supplies and a little wireless network so we wouldn't be throwing cables from tree to tree, and voilà, instant film festival. Not bad, huh?"

"It's absolutely brilliant!" I said. "Christ, what an idea! What else have you got to screen?"

"Oh, just bits and pieces, really. Mostly we went for stuff without much audio. Didn't want to rig up a full-on PA system here, might attract attention. The light'll be shielded by that hill"—she gestured—"but there's houses down the other side of the rise, and we don't want them calling in the law. So it's just wincy little speakers and video you can watch with the sound down. Your stuff was perfect for that, by the way, Scot's just so *iconic*. All in all, there's like an hour's worth of video, which we'll start showing pretty soon, before this lot's got too drunk to appreciate the art."

I shook my head. I realized that I had fallen in love in the space of five minutes. I really desperately wanted to say something cool or interesting or suave, or at least to give her my mobile number or ask her if I could take her out to an all-night place after the party. But my mouth was as dry as a talcum-powder factory in the middle of the desert.

"That's so cool," I managed. What I wanted to say was something like, *I think that this is the thing I left home to find. I think that this is the thing I was meant to do with my life. And I think you are the person I was meant to do it with.*

She looked up into the tree branches, saw something, and shouted, "No, no, not like that! Stop! *Stop!*" She shook her head vigorously and pointed a pencil torch into the branches, skewering another girl in the tactical shorts uniform who was in the middle of attaching a pocket-sized beamer to a branch with a web of elasticated tie-downs. She swore. "Girl's going to break her neck. Or my projector. In which case *I* will break her neck. 'Scuse me." She scrambled up the tree like a lumberjack, cursing all the way. I found myself standing like a cow that'd been stunned at the slaughterhouse, wobbling slightly on my feet.

Jem threw an arm around my neck, slapped the side of my face with his free hand, and said, "Come on, mate, the film's about to start. Got to get a good seat!"

I don't think I'd ever been as proud or happy as I was in the next ten minutes. The beamers all flickered to life, projecting a three-by-three grid of light squares, projected from the trees, lined up to make one huge image. That was bloody clever: the little beamers didn't have the stuff to paint a crisp, big picture. Try to get a pic as big as a film-screen and it would be washed out and blurry, even in the watery moonlight. But at close distances and small sizes, they could really shine, and that's what the girls had set up, nine synchronized projectors, each doing one little square of screen, using clever software to correct their rectangles so that everything lined up. I couldn't figure out how that worked, but then I meandered over to Twenty's control rig and saw that she had a webcam set up to watch the picture in real-time and correct the beamers as the branches blew in the wind. Now *that* was smart.

Also: I swear that I was only shoulder-surfing Twenty because I wanted to see how the trick with all the beamers was done and not, for example, because I wanted to smell her hair or watch her hands play over her keyboard or stare enraptured at the fine muscles in the backs of her arms jump as she directed the action like the conductor of an orchestra. No, those are all creepy reasons to be hanging around a lass. I only had the most honest of intentions, guv, I swear darn.

Once the screen was up and running, the buzz died off and everyone gradually turned to face the screen. Twenty had a headset on and she swung the little mic down so that she was practically kissing it. "Illustrious denizens of Armed Card and the Cynical April, I thank you for attending on behalf of the Pirate Cinema Collective, Sewing Circle and Ladies' Shooting Society. First up in the program tonight is this delightful piece of Scot Colford fannon, as directed by our own celebrated Cecil B. DeVil."

My mates cheered loudly and shouted rude things, and Twenty looked up and winked at me. I practically collapsed on the spot.

She hit a button and the video started to roll. This was my first major Scot piece since coming to London, made in the hot, anticipatory hours before we hit the parties and in the exhausted, sweaty time after we came back, as the sun was rising and I waited for the excitement to drain out of my limbs and let me sleep the day away like a vampire.

It was another piece I'd been planning in my head for years: Scot as the world's worst driver. Scot crashed eighty-three cars on-screen, *at least*. I mean, those are just the ones I know about. Sometimes it was part of an action sequence. Sometimes, it was a comedy moment. Sometimes, it was just plain weird, like the experimental tank he'd driven into a shopping mall in *Locus of Intent*. But my idea was that I could, with a little bit of creative editing, make every single one of those car crashes into a single, giant crash, with Scot behind the wheels of *all* the cars. All I'd need was exterior footage of the same cars—medium- and long-shots, where you couldn't really make out who was driving—intercut with the jumbled shaky-cam shots of the cars' interiors as Scot crashed and rattled inside, fighting the airbags, screaming in terror, fighting off a bad guy, whatever. Time it right, add some SFX, trim out some backgrounds, and voilà, the world's biggest all-Scot automotive disaster. Pure comedy.

I had done the test-edits at tiny resolution, little 640x480 vids, but once I had it all sorted, I re-rendered at full 1080p, checking it through frame-by-frame at the higher rez for little imperfections that the smaller video had hidden. I'd found plenty and patiently fixed every one, even going so far as dropping individual frames into an image editor and shaving them, pixel by pixel, into total perfection. At the time, it had seemed like a stupid exercise: you'd have to watch the video on a huge screen to spot the imperfections I was painstakingly editing. But now that it was screening on a huge piece of wall, I felt like an absolute *genius*.

I wasn't the only one. At first, the audience merely chuckled.

But as the car-crash continued and continued and continued, car after car, they began to hoot with laughter, and cheer. When it came to the closing sequence—a series of quick cuts of shaken Scot Colfords pulling themselves free of their cars and staring in horror, seemingly at one another—they shouted their delight and Rabid Dog and Chester pounded me on the back and Jem toasted me with his tin of lager and I felt one hundred feet tall, made of solid gold, and on *fire*. No embarrassment, just total, unalloyed delight. It's not a sensation English people are supposed to feel, especially northerners: you're supposed to be slightly ashamed of feeling good about your own stuff, but screw that, I was a *God*!

I glanced over to see if Twenty was, maybe, staring at me with girlish adulation. But she was scowling at her screen and mousing hard and getting everything set up for the next video, which was Chester's latest Bullingham creation, which he'd done in the style of the old Monty Python animations of Terry Gilliam, and all I remember about it was how rude it all was, in a very funny way, with Bullingham engaging in lots of improbable sex acts with barnyard animals, mostly on the receiving end. There was laughter and that, but it came from a long way off, from behind my glow of self-satisfaction. The same glow muffled the praise and laughter that accompanied Rabid Dog's horror-comedy mashup, the awesomely gory *Summer Camp IV* turned into a lighthearted comedy about wacky teenagers, the legendary blood and guts and entrails played purely for yuks.

Then the first act was over, and the screens faded and the sweetest sound you ever heard swelled: fiftysome kids clapping as hard as they could without breaking their hands, cheering and whistling until Hester shushed them all, but she was grinning, too, and I swear that was the best ten minutes of my life.

If I was editing The *Cecil B. DeVil Story*, this is where I'd insert one of those lazy montages, with me smoking a little of this, drinking a little of that, grinning confidently as I chatted up Twenty, dancing with her around the tree roots, watching the next round of films with my arm around her shoulder, getting onto a night bus with her and riding it all the way out to the Zeroday, showing her around my awesomely cool squat while she looked at me like I was the best thing she'd ever seen.

But actually, the night kind of went downhill after that. It would be hard for it not to, having attained such heights. I drank too much and ended up sitting propped against a tree, roots digging into my arse while my head swam and I tried not to puke. When I looked around to find Twenty between the second and third screenings, she was chatting with some other bloke who appeared, even in the dark, to be a hundred times cooler than me. This made me wish I was drinking yet another beer, but luckily there weren't any within an easy crawl of me and standing up was beyond me at that moment.

Some time around three in the morning, my mates poured me onto a night bus and then I *did* puke, and got us thrown off the bus, so we walked and stumbled for an hour before I declared myself sober enough to ride again, and we caught another bus, making it home just as the sun came up. We slipped into the Zeroday and Jem stretched out on the floor of my room because we hadn't figured out where he'd sleep and his old room was occupied by Chester, who, it turned out, wasn't in a mad rush to leave.

I woke up a million years later with a head like a cat-box and a mouth like the inside of a bus-station toilet. The room stank of beer-farts cooked by the long, hot day I'd slept through, turned into a kind of toxic miasma that clung to my clothes as I stumbled into the bathroom and drank water from the tap until I felt like I'd explode.

I was the last one up. Everyone else was downstairs, in the pub, and when I got there, they all looked at one another and snorted little laughs at my expense. Yes, I looked as bad as I felt. I raised two fingers and carefully jabbed them at each of my friends.

Jem pointed at the bar. "Food's up," he said. I followed his finger. Someone had laid out a tureen of fruit salad, a pot of yogurt, some toasted bagels (we froze the day-olds we scavenged, and toasted them to cover their slight staleness), a pot of cream cheese, and a bowl of hard-boiled eggs (eggs were good for days and days after their sell-by dates). My mouth filled with spit. I fell on the food, gorging myself until I'd sated a hunger I hadn't realized I'd felt. Rabid Dog made tea, and I had three cups with loads of sugar and then I blinked loads, stretched, and became a proper human again.

"Cor," I said. "Some night." I looked around at my three mates. Rabid Dog and Chester had taken the sagging sofa we'd dragged in from a skip, and Jem had seated himself as far as possible away from them, at the other end of the room. It occurred to me that while I knew Jem and I knew Dog and Chester, Dog and Chester didn't know Jem and vice-versa. Plus there was the fact that Jem had found the Zeroday, and now he was a newcomer to our happy home.

I looked back and forth between them. "Come on, lads," I said. "What's this all about? This place is effing *huge*. You're all good people. Stop looking like a bunch of cats trying to work out which one's in charge."

They pretended they didn't know what I was talking about, but they also had the good grace to look a bit embarrassed, which I took to mean that I'd got through to them.

"Some night," Rabid Dog mumbled. He had his lappie out and he turned it round so that I could see the screen, a slideshow of photos from the graveyard. Some of them were shot with a flash and had that overexposed, animal-in-the-headlamps look; the rest were shot with night filters that made everyone into sharp-edged, black-and-white ghosts whose eyes glowed without pupils. Nevertheless, I could tell even at this distance that it had been every bit as epic as I remembered. The slideshow got to a photo of Twenty and my heart went *lub-dub-lub-dub*. Even in flashed-out blinding white, she was *magisterial*, that being the new replacement for *illustrious* that had gone round at the party.

Jem snorted. "That one's trouble, boy-o," he said. "Too smart for her own good."

"What's that supposed to mean?" I felt an overprotective sear of anger at him, the kind of thing I used to get when boys came sniffing round after Cora.

He shrugged. "It was a mate of hers that brought me last night. One of those girls up in the trees. She said that your little bit of fluff there runs with a bunch of politicals, the sort who'd rather smash in a bank than go to a party. And Aziz says she's just *nuts,* full of gigantic plans."

I swallowed my anger. "None of that sounds like a problem to me," I said. "That all sounds bloody fantastic, actually." I said it as quietly and evenly as I could.

He shrugged again. "Your life," he said. "Just letting you know. And now you know. I'll say no more about it. So, it's Cecil now?"

I refused to be embarrassed about it. "Like Jem was your real name. You just picked it so you and Dodger could be the Jammie Dodgers, yeah? And Rabid Dog's mum didn't hold him up, crying and covered in afterbirth, and say, 'Oo's Mummy's lickle Rabid Dog then, hey?' And Chester from Manchester? Please. Why should I be the only one without a funny name?"

The boys were all looking at me as if I'd grown another head. I realized I'd got to my feet and started shouting somewhere in there. It must have been the hangover. Or Jem talking rubbish about Twenty.

In silence, I got some more fruit salad. Outside the locked-down, blacked-out windows of the pub, someone was shouting at someone else. Loud motorbikes roared down the street. Dogs barked. Drugs kids hooted.

"Sorry," I mumbled.

Jem bounced an empty juice box (we'd found two pallets of them, the boxes dirty from a spill into a puddle) off my head. "You're forgiven. Go get your bloody computer and email the mad cow and ask her out. Then take a shower. No, take a shower *first.*"

That broke up the tension. Dog and Chester giggled, and I

realized that Jem was right: I wanted nothing more badly than to get my lappie and see if I could find Twenty on Cynical April and try to come up with something not totally stupid to say to her.

And I did need a shower.

It took me a ridiculous amount of time to realize that I should be looking for "26" and not "twentysix" or "twenty six" in the Cynical April user directory, but once I had that down, I found myself in a deep and enduring clicktrance as I went through all of Twenty's old message-board posts, videos, and all the photos she'd appeared in. She liked to do interesting things with her hair. She had a properly fat cat. Her bedroom—in which she had photographed herself trying out many hair colors and cuts—was messy and tiny, and it had a window that looked out onto a yellow-black brick wall, the kind of thing you got all over London. Her room was full of books, mountains and teetering piles of them, and she reviewed them like crazy, mostly political books that I went cross-eyed with boredom just thinking about.

Aha! There it was: she had a part-time job at an anarchist bookstore off Brick Lane, in the middle of Banglatown, a neighborhood that was posh and run-down at the same time. It was riddled with markets, half of them tinsy and weird, selling handmade art and clothes or even rubbish that semihomeless people had rescued and set out on blankets. The other half of the markets were swank as anything, filled with expensive designer clothes and clever T-shirts for babies and that.

I'd wandered into the shop she worked at: it had *wicked* stickers, but it smelled a bit, and the books all had a slightly handmade feel, like they had come off a printer in someone's basement. It felt a bit like visiting the tinsy school library at my primary school, a sad closet full of tattered books that someone was always trying to get you to read instead of looking at the net. But my school library didn't have a beautiful, clever, incredibly cool girl working in it. If it had, I probably would have gone in more often.

It took me a minute to figure out what day of the week it was—I'd gone to bed at sunrise, and slept, and the room was shuttered in, but after looking at the clock and then making it expand to show the calendar, I worked out that this was Saturday, just before four in the afternoon. And hey, what do you know, Twenty worked afternoon shifts on Saturday at the shop: said so right there in a message board for party-planners who were trying to schedule a meeting. Another quick search and I found out that the shop closed at 5:30 P.M. on Saturdays. Which meant that I could *just* make it, if I managed to get out of the house in less than fifteen minutes, and the bus came quick. It occurred to me to try calling the shop to see if she was working and if she'd wait for me to get there, but somehow that seemed creepier than just "accidentally" wandering in a few moments before closing to "discover" that she happened to be working.

Yes, I will freely admit that this was not objectively any less creepy. That I was getting into deep stalker territory with this. That I'd only met her briefly, and that for all I knew she was seeing someone else, or was a lesbian, or just didn't fancy me.

But it was summer. I was sixteen. Girls, food, and parties. And films. That was all I cared about. And most of the time, it was either girls or food. Okay, films and food. But girls: girls most of all. It was weird. Intellectually, I knew that it wasn't such a big deal. Girls were girls, boys were boys, and I would probably start seeing a girl eventually. Everyone seemed to manage it, even the absolute losers and weirdos. But the fact was that I was *desperate,* filled with a longing for something my bones and skin seemed *absolutely certain* would be the best thing that ever happened to me, even if I couldn't say so for sure. I'd seen innumerable sex scenes on my screen—even edited one or two—and objectively, I could see that they weren't such a big deal. But there was a little man sat in the back of my skull with his fingers buried deep in my brains, and every time my thoughts strayed too far from girls, he grabbed hold of the neurons and yanked them back to the main subject.

So: fastest shower ever, brush teeth quickly, then again as I realized all the terrible things that might be festering in my gob. Dress, and then dress again as I realized how stupid I looked the first time. Speaking of first times, for the first time I wished I had some cologne, though I had no idea what good cologne smelled like. I had an idea that something like a pine tree would be good, but maybe I was thinking of the little trees you could hang up in your car to hide the stink of body odor and old McDonald's bags.

I didn't have any cologne.

"Anyone got any cologne?" I shouted down the stairs as I struggled into my shoes. The howls of laughter that rose from the pub were chased by catcalls, abuse, and filthy, lewd remarks, which I ignored. I pelted down the stairs and stood in the pub, looking at my mates.

"Where are you going?" Jem said.

"I'm going to go try and meet Twenty," I said.

"Twenty whats?" Rabid Dog said, puzzled enough that he forgot to mumble.

"The girl's name is 26," I said. "But it's 'Twenty' to her friends."

Jem started to say something sarcastic and I jabbed my finger at him. "Don't start, 'Jem'!"

"Is *that* what you were talking about last night?" Chester said. "Bloody 26! You wouldn't shut up about it. I thought you were having visions of a winning lottery number or some'at. Shoulda known."

I didn't remember any of that. Wait. No, I did. It was after the driver threw us off his bus. Which was after I threw up in it. And we were walking through somewhere—Camden? King's Cross? And I was counting to twenty-six, counting backward from twenty-six. Twenty-six, twenty-six, twenty-six. Stupid beer. If I hadn't got so drunk, I could have been talking to 26 all night, instead of making an ass out of myself in the streets of London. Stupid beer. Stupid me.

"Do I look okay?" I said.

Jem cocked his head. I thought he was going to say something else sarcastic, but he came over to me and smoothed down my collar, untucked my shirt from my trousers, did something with his fingers to my hair. "You'll do," he said. Rabid Dog and Chester were both nodding. "Proper gentleman of leisure now," Jem went on. "Don't forget that. They can smell fear. Go in there, be confident, be unafraid, be of good cheer. Listen to her, that's very important. Don't try to kiss her until you're sure she wants you to. Remember that you are both a gentleman and a gentleman of leisure. Got your whole life ahead of you, no commitments and not a worry in the world. Once she knows that, fwoar, you'll be sorted. Deffo." Jem always turned on the chirpy cheerful cockney sparrow talk when he was on a roll.

This sounded like good advice and possibly a little insulting, but I'd already had a turn at defending 26's honor and reckoned that she could probably stick up for herself anyway. And besides, I was frankly hoping to get "sorted," whatever that meant in Jem's twisted imagination. I was frankly grateful for the advice.

It took me three tries to go into the shop, and in between the tries, I stopped and breathed deeply and told myself, "Gentleman of leisure, gentleman of leisure, gentleman of leisure." Then I squared my shoulders, rescruffed my hair the way Jem had done, and wandered casually into the little shop.

She was bent over the desk, mohican floppy and in her eyes, staring at some kind of printed invoice or packing list, a pile of books before her on the counter. Even her profile was beautiful: dark liquid brown eyes, skin the color of light coffee, round nose, rosebud lips.

She looked up when I came in, started to say, "We're about to close—" and then raised her eyebrows, and said, "Oh!" She was clearly surprised, and I held my breath while I waited to discover if she was *pleasantly* surprised.

"You!" I said, trying hard to seem sincerely shocked, as though I'd just coincidentally wandered in. "Wow!"

"I'm surprised you're able to walk," she said.

God, I was such an idiot. She hated me. She'd seen me stupidly drunk and had decided I was a complete cock and now I'd followed her to work and she was going to think I was a stalker, too, oh God, oh God, oh God, say something Trent. Gentleman of leisure. "Erm." I had had over an hour on the bus and that was all I'd come up with. Erm. "Well. Yeah. Felt rank when I got up. Better now, though. Good party, huh?"

"You looked up where I worked, didn't you?"

Uulp. Idiot, idiot, idiot. "Rumbled," I said. "I, well." Gentleman of leisure. Unafraid. Full of cheer. I pasted on a smile. "I did. Cos, you know, I drank too much last night and got stupid and that, and I wanted to come here and see you again and give it another try."

She looked at her paper. "All right, that's a *little* bit creepy, but also somewhat charming and flattering. But I'm afraid your timing is awful. Got a meeting to go to right after work, which is in—" She looked at the screen on the counter. "Ten minutes."

I felt like a balloon that's had the air let out of it. She didn't hate me, but she also didn't have time for me just then. Course she didn't. I tried not to let the crushing disappointment show, but I must have failed.

"Unless," she said, "you want to come along? It's just round the corner."

"Yes!" I said, far too quickly for a cool man of leisure, but who gave a toss? "What kind of meeting is it?"

"I think you'll enjoy it," she said. She made another mark on her paper, shoved it into the stack of books, and hopped off the stool. "Come on."

The meeting was being held just down the road, in the basement room of a Turkish restaurant, the kind of place where they had hookah pipes and apple tobacco and low cushions. 26 said, "They're a good bunch—some of 'em are from the bookstore, others are from protest groups and free software groups and that.

The sort of people who're worried that they'll get done over by the Theft of Intellectual Property Bill." She said this as though I should know what it was, and I was too cool to admit that I had no idea, so I nodded my head sagely and made enthusiastic noises.

Almost everyone there was older than us by at least ten years, and some were *really* old, fifty or sixty. Lots of the blokes were older and kind of fat with beards and black T-shirts with slogans about Linux and stuff. These beardie-weirdies were the free software lot; you could spot 'em a mile off. Then there were ancient punks with old piercings and tattoos and creaky leather jackets. And there were serious, clean-cut straights in suits and that, and then a bunch of the sort you'd expect to find round Brick Lane—in their twenties, dressed in strange and fashionable stuff. Mostly white and Asian, and a couple of black people. It looked a little like someone had emptied out a couple night buses full of random people into the low-ceilinged basement.

Especially with all the DJ/dance party types, showing off their dance moves and tap-transferring their latest illegal remixes to each others' headphones. I'd always thought of music as something nice to have in a film, so I'd not paid much attention to their scene since landing up in London, but I had to admit that the things these kids could do with pop songs and computers made for some brilliant parties.

There was iced mint tea, which was *brilliant,* and someone had brought a big basket of tofu-carob biccies, which were *revolting,* but I was hungry enough to eat three of them.

"People, people," said one of the old punks. She was very tall and thin as a skeleton, and had some kind of elaborate tentacle tattoo that wrapped around her throat and coiled round her arms and her bare legs sticking out of a loose cotton sundress, disappearing into her high, scuffed Docs. "Time to start, okay?" She had a Polish accent and the air of a kindly schoolteacher, which was funny, because she looked like a warrior queen out of a post-apocalyptic action film.

We all sat down and looked over at her. 26 looked at her

with something like worship, and I wondered what it would take to get her to look at *me* that way.

"I'm Annika," she said. "Thank you all for coming. We hear that TIP is going to be introduced some time in the next month, and they're going to try to get it through with practically no debate. Which means we're going to have to be *fast* if we want to get people pissed off about it."

She took out her phone and turned on its beamer and painted a page on the back of the door to the basement room. It was dense type, but parts of it had been highlighted and blown up to be readable. It was headed THEFT OF INTELLECTUAL PROPERTY BILL and it was clear that it was some kind of boring law, written in crazy lawyer gobbledygook. I looked at the highlighted sentences: "Criminal sanctions," "commercial-scale infringement," "sentencing recommendations to be left to Business Secretary's discretion . . ." I tried to make sense of it, but I just couldn't. I felt stupid, especially as 26 seemed to get it right away, shaking her head and clenching her fists.

Annika gave us a minute to look at it. "This is a leaked draft, so we don't know how much of it will be in the bill when they introduce it, but if even a tiny amount of this is in the final, it's very bad. Look at this: Article 1(3) makes it a criminal offense to engage in 'commercial scale' infringement, even if you're not charging or making money. That means that anyone caught with more than five pirated films or twenty pirated songs can be sent to *prison*. And here, article 2(4), leaves the sentencing guidelines up to the discretion of the Business Secretary: she's not even *elected*, and she used to work for Warner Music, and she's been on record as saying that she wished we still had the *death penalty* so it could be used on pirates.

"And here, this is the best part, here down at the bottom in article 10(4)? This says that unless this results in a 70 percent reduction in copyright infringement in eighteen months, there's a whole new set of police powers that go into effect, including the right to 'remotely search' your computer, with 'limitation of liability for incidental loss of data or access.'" The people around me hissed and looked at one another. I didn't know what the hell it meant.

26 noticed my puzzlement. She pinched my cheek. "Thicko," she said. "It means that they have the right to hack your computer over the net, search your drive, and there's no penalty if they get it wrong, mess up your data, invade your privacy, whatever."

I shook my head. "That's the daftest thing—"

Everyone was talking at once. Annika held up her hands for silence. "Please, please. Yes, this is terrible. This stupid clause, this eighteen-months business, it's been in every new copyright bill for a decade, right? Every time, they say, 'If these new penalties don't work, we're going to bring in even worse ones. We don't want to, of course, heavens no, who would want to be able to put people who hurt your business in jail? What corporate lobby would ever want to be able to act as police, judge and executioner? Oh no. But if this plan doesn't work, we'll just *have to* do it. Le sigh.' It's so much rubbish. But Parliament has been giving EMI and Warner and Sony and Universal so much power for so long, they've got so used to going to parties with pop stars and getting their kiddies into the VIP screenings and behind the rope at big concerts that they don't even think about it. They just get out the rubber-stamp and vote for it.

"This time, we want to stop it. I think the time is right. People are sick to death of the piracy wars. Everyone knows someone who's been disconnected because someone in their house was accused of file-sharing. Some families are ruined by this— lose their jobs, kids fail at school—" I jolted like I'd been stuck with a Taser. 26 looked quizzically at me, but I was a million miles away, thinking of my mum and dad and poor Cora, and all the time that'd gone by without my contacting them. I knew that they were still trying to get in touch, I couldn't help but see and flinch away from the emails they sent me from the library or a neighbor's house. But every day that went past without my replying made it harder for me to think about replying the next day.

She'd said "ruined families," and I realized that yes, that's what I'd done: I'd ruined my family.

Annika was still talking and I squeezed my eyes shut to try to make the tears that had sprung up go back inside so that I wouldn't humiliate myself in front of 26. And honestly, it was also so that I could squeeze away the enormous and terrible feeling I got when I thought about my family. I could hear my pulse in my ears and my hands were shaking.

"Last time, every MP in the country got a visit from twenty constituents about the bill. They still voted for it. Of course they did, they were fully whipped."

26 leaned over and whispered, "That means their parties made them vote yes." Like she was explaining things to an idiot, I suppose, but I *was* an idiot about this stuff. And when she whispered in my ear, her hot breath tickled the hairs there and gave me an instant stiffie that I had to cross my legs to hide.

"This time, we want to get a hundred constituents to request meetings with their MPs. Ten a day, every day leading up to the vote. It's a big number: 650 MPs, 6500 activists. But we're talking about putting kids in *jail* here. I think that this will wake up even the complacent zombies who say, 'It's just the same as stealing, right?'"

Lots of people had their hands up. Annika started to call on them. Everyone had ideas about how to get normal people to show up at their MPs' surgeries with pitchforks and torches, demanding justice. I wished I had an idea, too, something that would make me seem like less of a total noob in front of 26. Then I had one, and I shot my arm straight up.

Annika called on me. I suddenly felt shy and red-faced, but I made myself talk. "So, like, when I went to copyright class at school, they told us that everyone is a copyright owner, right? Like, as soon as you write it down or save it to your hard drive or whatever, it's yours for your life and seventy years, right? So I figure, we're all copyright owners, so we could go after everyone who takes our copyrights. Like, if a film company gets your graffiti in a shot, or if an MP puts your email on her website, or whatever. So what if we sue them all? What if we put *them* in jail?"

Annika started shaking her head halfway through this. "I know that sounds like a good idea, but I'm afraid it won't work. The way the law is written, you have to show 'meaningful commercial potential' before you can ask for criminal prosecution. And in order to sue for damages, you need to be able to spend more on solicitors than they are: the law is written so that rich and powerful people can use it, but poor people and artists can't. A record company can use it to put you in jail for downloading too many songs, but if you're a performer whose record company owes you money, you can't use it to put some thieving exec in prison. They're evil, but they're not stupid: when they buy a law, they make damned sure it can't be used against them."

I felt irrationally angry at Annika. I thought I'd had a genius idea, one that would really impress Twenty, and Annika had made me look like a noob. I was a noob. I should have just kept my mouth shut. But 26 gave my hand a little pat, as if to say, *there, there,* and I felt one nanometer better.

I didn't have anything else to say after that. Everyone else seemed to know more about this stuff than I did. It turned out that one of the guys in a suit was an MP, from the Green Party, and he got up on his feet to say how much he appreciated all this, and how he knew that there were LibDem and Labour and Tory MPs who would love to vote against the whip, but they were too afraid of being thrown out of the party if they didn't cooperate. This was just too weird: I had thought that MPs got elected to represent the voters back home. How could they do that if someone else could tell them how to vote? It made me wish I'd paid more attention in school to all those civics classes.

The meeting broke up with everyone giving out email addresses to Annika, which I thought was hilarious, since she was meant to be all punk and alternative, but here she was using email like some old crumblie. I'd have thought she'd use Facebook Reloaded like everyone else, but when I asked 26 about it, she shook her head in the way that told me I was being dumb again, and said, "Facebook's all spied on. Everything you do—anyone who sets up an advertiser account can get everything, all your private info and all your friends' public info. Why do you think we use Cynical April? Anyone tries to arrange an illegal party on Facebook Reloaded, the Bill know about it before their mates do."

There we were, standing in the flood of people pushing up and down Brick Lane, elbowing past touts offering free wine with a curry from one of the dozens of Balti houses, stepping around street musicians or peddlers with blankets, stopping at food wagons or to shout at a cyclist who got too close. The sun was a bloody blob just over the roofline, and the heat was seeping away to something tolerable, and I was standing so close to 26 that I could see the stubble on her scalp and the holes up and down her ears where she'd taken her earrings out.

"Erm," I said.

"You're a real charmer, you know that?" she said. My heart dropped into my stomach and my stomach dropped out my arse and I stood there like an idiot. "Oh, come on," she said, tweaking my nose, "you don't need to be such a nutcase about this. I like you all right so far. Let's go somewhere, okay?"

I almost invited her back to the Zeroday, but that would have been too much. So I said, "I'm skint, but I know where we can get some free food."

"No five-finger discounts," she said. "I don't believe in going to jail for stupid things like stealing."

"What *do* you believe in going to jail for?"

She nodded. "Good question. I expect I'll find out soon enough."

Taking a girl to a skip for dinner makes for an odd first date, but I admit that I thought it might make me seem all dangerous and street, and besides, I really was broke. We weren't all that far from the Barbican and the Waitrose skip, but I had my sights on bigger spoils (so to speak). Over the river, Borough Market had just finished for the day. Hawkers have been selling food there since the 1200s, and it's one of the biggest food markets in the world. Most of the week, it's just wholesale, but on Saturday it opens up to the public, with endless stalls selling fine meats and cheeses, braces of exotic game like pheasant and rabbit, handmade chocolates, farmers' produce, thick sandwiches, fizzy drinks, fresh breads, and some of the finest coffee I've ever drunk. Just thinking about it made my mouth water.

But as good as it was during the day, it was even better at nighttime. That was when the stall-holders set out all the stuff that didn't sell during the day, but wouldn't last until the next Saturday market. On a Saturday night, Borough's skips were like an elephant's graveyard for slightly unlovely vegetables, mildly squashed boxes of handmade truffles, slightly stale loaves studded with walnuts or dried fruits, and wheels of cheese gone a little green around the gills. Like Jem says, cheese is just milk that's spoiled in a very specific way, and mold is part of the package. Just scrape it off and eat the rest.

We walked to Borough through a magic and sparkling night, and 26 told me all about her mates who ran the anarchist bookstore—it was called Dancing Emma's—and how much fun she had reading all the strange books they stocked. "I mean, when I started working there, I had *no idea*. I'd literally never thought about how the system worked and that. It never occurred to me to wonder why some people had stuff and other people had nothing. Why there were bosses and people who got bossed. My mum isn't very political."

"My parents don't do politics, either. Do you see your old man?"

She shook her head. "Naw," she said. "Left my mum when I was little. He's a cop, believe it or not. In Glasgow. Mum's been remarried for ages, though. Stepdad's a good bloke."

We walked a bit. I got up the courage to say, "So, why *are* there bosses? What else would we do, just let everyone do what they want?"

"That's about right. What's wrong with that?"

I started to say something, stopped. "What if someone wanted to go and do murders or commit rape?"

We walked for a while, and I snuck a peek at her. She seemed to be thinking it over. "This is hard to explain. Whenever you ask an anarchist about it, she'll usually go on and on about how most of those crimes are committed because people are poor and powerless and so on. Like, when we get rid of bosses and masters and everyone has enough, it won't matter. But I think some people are just, like, *total bastards* and I don't know exactly what you do about them. Maybe after we get rid of the state and everyone can do what they want, we'll agree on some rules, you know, some crimes that involve hurting people, and we'll all agree to enforce them." She shrugged. "You go right to the hard question, you know? I don't really have the answer. But look around London, all the crime and violence and that—it's not like having all kinds of laws and rules and jails and power is making us safe."

"Maybe we'd be a lot less safe without them," I said. I liked this kind of discussion and I didn't get much of it with Rabid Dog and Chester. My mind raced.

"Maybe. But I don't know, doesn't it seem, you know, *obvious* that at least some crime is down to the fact that there are rich bastards and poor sods? Maybe there's some nutter who'd steal even if he had plenty, but isn't most crime down to not having enough?"

I shook my head. "Maybe. But that makes it sound like poor people are bigger crims than rich ones. But we were poor, my family, and we weren't criminals. If we could get by without breaking the law—"

She laughed. "Mate, are you *serious*? You're the biggest crim I know! Or did you get a license for all those tasty clips you cut together for those videos last night?"

I laughed, too. "Right, right, okay. But I didn't make that video cos I'm *poor.*"

"Not exactly, okay. But you know that *90 percent* of the film copyrights in the whole history of the *planet* belong to five studios? And that eight companies control *85 percent* of the world's radio, TV, films, newspaper, book publishing, and Internet publishing? So if you worked for one of *those* companies, chances are that you'd be able to use all those clips you cut up. I see stuff like that all the time, stupid adverts to pimp Coke or Nike or whatever. Those companies own all our culture and they get to make anything they want with it. The rest of us have to break the law to do what they do all the time. But it's everyone's culture—that's the whole point, right? Once you put it out into the world, it's the *world's*—it's part of the stories we tell each other to make sense of life."

I'd been about one-quarter in love with 26 until this point. Now I felt like I was 75 percent of the way, and climbing. It was like she was saying something I'd always known but never been able to put into words—like she was revealing a truth that had been inside of me, waiting for her to let it out. I felt like dancing. I felt like singing. I also felt like kissing her, but that thought also made me want to throw up with nervousness, so I pushed it down.

"You're a very clever lass," I said. "Christ, that was *brilliant*."

She stopped in the middle of the pavement, and people behind us had to swerve around us, making that *tsk-huff* sound that Londoners make when you violate the Unwritten Code of Walking. I didn't care. She was smiling so much she almost lit up the whole street. "Thank you, Cecil. That means a lot, coming from you. I thought your videos were just genius. When I saw them, I thought to myself, 'Whoever made these is someone really special.' I'm glad to see that I was right."

I thought I should kiss her then. Was she waiting for me to kiss her? Her face was tilted toward mine—she was nearly as tall as me. I could smell her breath, a hint of the peppermint tea we'd drunk. I'd never kissed a girl before. What if I messed it up? What if she slapped me and never wanted to see me again? What if—

She kissed me.

In the films, they always say that you'll never forget your first kiss. In the films, your first kiss is always perfect. In the films, everyone participating in the kiss knows what to do,

In real life, my first kiss was wildly imperfect. First, there was the business of noses. Hers was small and round and adorable, like a Bollywood star on a poster. Mine was a large, no-shape English nose. Both of them tried to occupy the same space at the same time and it didn't really work out.

Then teeth. The sound your teeth make when they knock against someone else's teeth is minging, and you hear it *right in your head,* like the sound you get when you crunch an unexpected chicken bone. And it seemed that no matter where I wanted to put my teeth, she wanted to put her teeth.

And tongues! Christ, tongues! I mean, when you see them going at it in the videos, they're doing *insane* things with their tongues, making them writhe like an eelmonger's barrow. But when I tried to use a bit of tongue, I ended up licking her teeth, and then I had the realization that my tongue was in another person's *mouth,* which was nearly as weird as, say, having your hand in someone's stomach or your foot in someone's lung.

That was only the first realization that entered my head. After that, it was a nonstop monologue, something like, *Holy crap, I'm kissing her, I'm really kissing her! What should I be doing with my hands? Should I put my hands on her bum? I'd love to put my hands on her bum. I probably shouldn't put my hands on her bum. Oh, yes I should. No. Wait, why am I thinking this, should the kiss be, like, all-obliterating and occupying 300 percent of my total consciousness, transporting me to the Galaxy of the First Kiss? I wonder if this means she's my girlfriend now? I wonder if she's kissed other blokes. I bet she has. I wonder if I'm better at it than they are. I bet I'm rubbish at it. Of course I'm rubbish at it. I'm spending all my time thinking instead of kissing her. For God's sake, Trent, stop thinking and KISS. Oh, there's that tongue again. It's not exactly nice, but it's not exactly horrible, either. We're standing right here on the public pavement kissing! Everyone can see. I'm so embarrassed.*

Wait, no I'm not. I'm the bloody king of the world! See that, London, I'm KISSING! Oh shitshitshit, I just got a stiffie.

The other thing about kissing: when do you stop? I mean, if it's just your mum kissing you good night, it's easy to tell where it ends. But a kiss like this, a proper snog, where does it end? In the vids, I'd carry her into a bedroom or a closet or something. But we were in the middle of the street, on the north side of London Bridge. I didn't have any handy bedrooms or closets. Besides, my mind was still racing, going off in demented directions: *Does it matter that I'm white? Has she kissed more Asian guys or more white guys? Is she Asian? Maybe her dad is white? She doesn't look that Asian. Maybe her mum is white? Maybe she's all Asian. Maybe she's just kind of dark-skinned. Does she think I'm weird because I'm white?* I mean, this was just mad. I hadn't given two thoughts to 26's background until she kissed me—half the people I knew in Bradford had families from India or Bangladesh or Pakistan. And half of *them* were more English than I was, more into footie and the Royals and all that stuff.

And there I was, standing on the street, snogging the crap out of a girl I was falling in love with, thinking of how my neighbors in Bradford had hung out their England flags every World Cup and how no one in my English family could be arsed to watch the game. Get that? I wasn't just thinking about *football*—I was thinking of *how little I cared about football.* Stupid brain.

But at least that distracted me from the throbber in my pants, which was about to become a major embarrassment once 26 let go and I turned to face the crowd. I was going to look like someone had pitched a tent in there. Stupid cock.

Which all makes it sound like that kiss was rubbish. It wasn't.

For all that I was distracted as anything and nervous and self-conscious, I still remember every second of it, the way her lips felt on mine, the way the blood roared in my ears, the way my feet and legs tingled, the way my chest felt too tight for my thundering heart. Which must mean that for all that I was thinking a thousand miles a second, I was also paying a lot of attention to the beautiful girl in my arms.

"Whew," she said, backing off a little, but keeping her arms locked around my neck. "That was a bit of all right, wasn't it?"

I swallowed a couple times, then tried to speak. It came out in a croak: "Wow."

"Come on, then," she said, and took my hand and led me across London Bridge.

It turned out that this wasn't Twenty's first experience digging through a skip, but it was her first time looking for food.

"I usually just go after electronics. There's always someone who can use them—and now that I've met your mate Aziz, there's an even better reason to go after those skips. I figured food was more likely to be, you know, runny and stinky and awful."

It was the most mental feeling, having a conversation with Twenty after we'd snogged. I wanted to snog her again, but I also felt like I had an obligation not to just grab her and kiss her some more, like we had to go on pretending that we were still two friends on our way out for a strange dinner courtesy of the skips of Borough Market.

"It can be," I said. "But there's plenty that's really good, and it's such a pity to let it all go to waste." I took hold of a huge, smoked Italian salami. The label said it was smoked wild boar, and the paper wrapper around one end had been torn and scuffed. "You're not a vegetarian, are you?"

26 took it from me and studied it, sniffed it, and grinned. "Not tonight! Wild boar! How medieval!"

And the harvest began. There were mountains of food to choose from, and we set aside the choicest morsels for our enjoyment, making a pile that, in the end, was more than we could hope to eat. Still, we took it all up in a couple of cartons we found behind one of the skips and set off again.

"We'll give the extra to tramps," I said, and sure enough,

before we'd reached London Bridge again, we'd already given away all of the surplus and tucked the rest into our rucksacks.

I chanced another look at Twenty as we climbed onto a bus and walked up the stairs to the upper deck. She was grinning ear to ear, and I remembered how I'd felt when Jem had taken me to Waitrose skip for the first time. Like there was a secret world I was being admitted to: like someone had just taken me through the back of a wardrobe into Narnia.

"I liked your idea," she said as the streets whizzed past us. "About doing all the MPs and record execs and that for piracy? I thought that would be lovely, a really cool bit of theater."

"Annika said it wouldn't work," I said, but inside I was glowing with pride.

"Oh," she said, waving her hands. "I don't think any of it is going to *work*. They've been at this for *years*. Every time the bastards from the film and record companies buy a new law, we all get out into the streets, make a lot of noise, call our MPs, go to their offices, write expert analysis of why this won't work, and then they pass it anyway. Parliament's not there to represent the people, or even the country. Parliament's there to represent the rich and powerful—the bosses and the rulers. We're just the inconvenient little *voters* and you and I aren't even *that* for a couple years. What's more, once they put you in jail, you don't get a vote, so the more of us they lock away, the fewer of us there are to vote against them."

"That's depressing," I said. "What a load of B.S."

Then she kissed me again, not for very long, just a peck on the lips that still got my heart pounding again. "Don't be so down. This just means that we're going to have to, you know, dismantle Parliament to get any justice. Which, when you think about it, is a *lot* more fun than writing letters to your MP."

Chapter 3

FAMILY/FEELING USELESS/A SCANDAL IN PARLIAMENT/
A SCANDAL AT HOME/WAR!

One morning, I woke up and realized that I was *home*. The Zero-day was quiet—it was only two in the afternoon and I was the first out of bed—and as I padded downstairs in a dressing gown that I'd found in a charity shop for a pound, I saw the signs of my new family all around me. Jem was a pretty fair artist, and he'd taken to decorating our walls with gigantic, detailed charcoal murals, working late into the night, drawing whatever struck his fancy, blending scenes of London's streets into elaborate anatomical studies he copied out of books into caricatures of us and the people we brought home, me with my nose huge and my teeth crooked and snarled; Dog with his spots swollen and multiplied all over his face; Chester so horsey that he had pointy ears and a tail. Most of all, he caricatured himself: scrawny, rat-faced, knock-kneed, grinning an idiot's grin with a dribble of spit rolling off his chin, clutching a piece of charcoal, and drawing himself into existence.

We'd got tired of getting splinters from the floor and had gone on a painting binge, with Chester leading the work—he'd helped out his dad, who was a builder, back home. We sanded and painted the floor a royal blue and it was as smooth as tile under my bare feet. The dishes were drying in the clean rack beside the sink, and I picked up my favorite coffee cup—it was a miniature beer stein, studded with elaborate spikes and axes, an advertisement for some fantasy RPG, and we'd found eight hundred of them in a skip one night—and made coffee in Jem's sock-dripper, just the way he'd shown me. The fridge was full, the sofa had a Cecil-shaped dent in it that I settled into with a sigh, and the room still smelled faintly of oregano and garlic from the epic spaghetti sauce we'd all made the night before.

I heard another person's footsteps on the stairs and turned to see Twenty picking her way down them, dressed in one of my long T-shirts and a pair of my boxers and looking so incredibly sexy I felt like my tongue was going to unroll from my mouth across the floor like a cartoon wolf.

"COFFEE," she said, and took my cup from me and started to slurp noisily at it.

"Good morning, beautiful," I said, sticking my face up the shirt's hem and kissing her little tummy. She squealed and pushed my head away and gave me a kiss that tasted of sleep and warm and everything good in my world. She sat down beside me and picked up her lappie and opened the lid, rubbed her finger over the fingerprint reader until it recognized her. "What's happening in the world?"

I shrugged. "Dunno—only been up for five minutes myself." She snuggled into me and began to poke at the computer. And there and then, cuddling the woman I loved, in the pub I'd made over with my own hands and with the help of mates who were the best friends I'd ever had, I realized that this was the family I'd always dreamed of finding. This was the home I'd always dreamed of living in. This was the life I'd always wished I had. I was as lucky as a lucky thing.

And pretty much as soon as that feeling had filled me up like a balloon and sailed me up the ceiling, I remembered my parents and my sister and the life I'd left behind, and the balloon deflated, sending me crashing to the ground. I made a small noise in the back of my throat, like a kitten that's been separated from its mum, and 26 looked into my face.

"What is it?" she said. "Christ, you look like your best friend just died."

I shook my head and tried for a smile. "It's nothing, love, don't worry about it."

She tapped me lightly on the nose, hard enough to make me blink. "Don't give me that, Cec. Something's got you looking like you're ready to blow your brains out, and when you're that miserable, it's not just your business—it's the business of everyone who cares about you. I.e., me. Talk."

I looked away, but she turned my head so that I was looking into her bottomless brown eyes. "It's nothing. It's just." I really wanted to look away, but she wouldn't let me. "Okay, I miss me mam. Happy?"

She tsked. "Boys are such idiots. Of course you miss your family—how long has it been since you saw them?"

I did the maths in my head. "Ten months," I said. Then I thought again. "Hey, I'm turning seventeen next month!"

"We'll bake you a cake. Now, how long has it been since you called 'em?"

I shook my head. "I haven't, not really. Once, but only for a few minutes. Didn't work out so well." I'd told Twenty about how I came to leave Bradford, of course, but I hadn't told her much else about my family. I didn't like to talk about them, because talking about them led to thinking about them and thinking about them led to misery.

She glared. "That's terrible! How could you go that long without even *calling*? Your mum and dad must be beside themselves with worry! For all they know, you're lying dead in a ditch or being forced to peddle your pretty arse in a dungeon in Soho." She got up from the sofa and faced me, hands on her hips. "I know you, boyo. You're not a bastard. It can't feel good to be this rotten to your parents. You owe it to yourself to call them up."

I spread my hands with helplessness. "I know you're right, but how can I do it? It's been so long? What do I say?"

"You say *sorry,* idiot boy. Then you say *I love you* and *I'm alive and doing fine.* Do you think it's going to get any easier if you keep on procrastinating? Call them. Now."

"But," I said, and stopped. I was fishing for an excuse—any

excuse. "If I call them from my mobile, they'll have my number and they'll trace me. I'm only sixteen still; one call to the cops and I'll be dragged back home."

She rolled her eyes with the eloquent mastery of a teenaged girl. "Tell me you can't think of a way of making a call without having it traced back to you."

I grimaced. She had me there. There were only about twenty free Internet phone services. Most of them were blocked by the Great Firewall of Britain, but I'd been routing around the censorwall since before my testicles dropped. "Fine," I said. "I'll do it later."

"What, when all your mates are awake and around and embarrassing you? The hell you will. There's no time like the present, boyo."

So I found a headset and wiped it clean and screwed it into my ear and paired it up with my lappie and dialed Mum's number. It rang four times and bumped to voice mail, and I breathed a huge sigh of relief as I disconnected the phone. "No answer," I said. "I'll try again later."

"Don't tell me your whole family shares one phone? Are you from the past or something?"

"You're too damned clever for your own good, 26. Fine, fine." I called Dad's number. Four rings and . . . voice mail. "No answer," I said cheerfully. "Let's get some breakfast—"

"What about your sister, what's her name, Nora?"

"Cora," I said. "You really paid attention when I told you about my family, didn't you?"

"I always pay attention," she said. "That way, I can tell when you're lying to me, or yourself. I pay attention to *everything*. It's my superpower."

I dialed Cora's number with a heavy heart, then held my breath as the phone rang: once, twice, three times—

"Hello?"

"Cora?"

"Who is this?" Her voice sounded thick, like she'd been

sleeping. But it was the middle of the afternoon. I'd figured on her being at school. It was a Wednesday, after all. The school jammed all pupils' phones (though teachers and heads got special handsets that worked through the jammers).

"Cora, it's me." I didn't want to say my real name. It's silly, but I hadn't introduced myself to 26 as Trent yet. It's not like it was a big secret—I'm sure my roommates had grassed on me— but I felt weird being anyone apart from Cecil in front of her.

"*Trent?*"

"Yeah." There was silence. "So, how are you?"

"Holy shit, I can't *believe* it! Trent, where the hell have you *been*? Mum and Dad think you're dead or something!"

"No," I said. "I'm alive. I'm doing fine. You can tell them that." There was stunned silence from the phone. "So," I said. "So. How are you, then?"

She snorted. "Oh, we're all bloody wonderful here in old Bradford. Dad's still out of work, Mum's still fighting to get her benefits without queuing up at the Jobcentre, and I've just failed three of my subjects."

It was like an icicle through the heart. I wanted to throw the laptop across the room. Instead, I took a deep breath and squeezed my hands into fists and then let them go. "How could you be failing in school, Cor? You're a supergenius."

"It's just hard, okay? How many days could I skip breakfast to study at the library? How was I supposed to do my assignments late at night when the library was shut? Besides, who the hell cares? It's not as though I'm going to go to my deathbed whispering, 'If I'd only got better marks in GCSE Geography.'"

The icicle twisted. I used to say that line about deathbeds every time I brought home a failing grade. My little sister had learned well from my example.

"Say something," she said.

"I—" I closed my eyes. "Cora, you need to do better in school. You've got too much brains to be failing. I know it's hard but—"

She interrupted me. "Oh, shut up your stupid hypocritical noise. You've got no *idea* how hard it is. As soon as things got bad, you buggered off to wherever you're hiding out. Don't you be lecturing me about my life. You're swanning around the world having adventures and I'm stuck—"

She broke up and I could hear that she was crying. I didn't know what to say. I looked with helpless anger at 26, who'd made me make this call. Her expression was full of sympathy and that softened me, made my anger turn to misery so that I thought I might start crying, too.

"I'm really sorry, Cora," I said. "You're right, one hundred percent right. It's all my fault. I've got no call to lecture you on your behavior, not when I'm so far away."

"Where *are* you, Trent? We're all so worried about you. It's all Mum and Dad talk about, when they're not getting at me about my schoolwork or shouting at each other about money."

"I'm—" I shut my mouth. "I'm not ready to tell you that, yet. I'm sorry, Cora. I just can't take the risk. But how about if I give you a phone number where you can leave me a message?" As I talked, I went to a free voice-mail service and signed up for an account, using a dodgy browser plugin that automatically generated a fake name and address in France, along with a one-time fake email that it signed up for using the same details. A few seconds later, I had a phone number in Ghana.

"You're a suspicious sod," she said. "Fine, give me the number."

I read it to her. "Get a calling card from a newsagent to call it, otherwise it'll be a fortune. I'll check it once a day and get back to you, all right?"

She sighed. "It's good to hear your voice again, Trent."

I smiled. "It's good to hear yours, too, Cora. I've missed you. All of you. Where are Mum and Dad, anyway?"

"Oh, they're at school. The head wanted to 'have a word with them' about me. I'm apparently on the slippery slope straight to hell."

I groaned. This was clearly all my fault.

"Oh, stop it," she said. "You messed us over when you got the net cut off, but *they* cut the net. It's not as though you committed a murder. Hell, Tisha's brother's in jail for murder and *he* gets to use the Internet! He's doing a degree in social work through the Open University. They're the bullies and the bastards. You're just an idiot." She paused. "And we miss you."

Tears were leaking out of my eyes and running down my cheeks. I was embarrassed to be crying in front of 26, but I couldn't stop. I swallowed snot and tears, snuffled up a breath. "I miss you, too, Cora. All of you. But especially you. Call me, okay?"

She made a small, crying noise of her own that I took for assent and I disconnected.

I glared at 26, furious at her for making me go through that ordeal. But she put her arms around me and pushed my head against her neck and shoulder and made a "shh, shh," sound that went straight to the back of my brain and I felt like I was five years old again, with a skinned knee, being comforted by a teacher as I bawled my eyes out. I couldn't stop. I didn't *want* to stop. It was like my brain had been filled with poison and pus, and it was finally all running out. I let it go.

The thing Cora said to me—*They cut off the net. They're the bullies and the bastards*—resonated in my skull for the rest of the day. Who were *they*? I hadn't really thought about the people who got the laws passed that had changed my life forever—not the bigwigs at the film and record companies nor the MPs who showed up and voted to mess over even more of the voters who lived in their districts.

When I tried to picture them, my image of them got all tangled up with all those educational copyright videos they'd made us watch in school, where big stars came on and told us how awful we all were to download their stuff without paying for it, and then they'd trot out some working stiffs—a spark, a make-up artist, a set builder—who'd drone on about how hard he worked all day and how he needed to feed his kids. We'd just laugh at these—the ancient, exquisitely preserved rock star we saw getting out of a limo crying poverty; the workers who claimed that we were taking food out of their kids' mouths by remixing videos or sharing music, when every kid I knew spent every penny he could find on music as well as downloading more for free.

But now I tried to imagine the men who bought and sold MPs like they were pop songs, who put laws into production like they were summer blockbusters, and got to specify exactly what they'd like the statute book to say about the people they didn't like. I realized that somewhere out there, there were gleaming office towers filled with posh, well-padded execs who went around in limos and black cabs, who lived in big houses and whose kids had all the money in the world, and these men had decided to ruin my family for the sake of a few extra pennies. There were actual human beings who were answerable for the misery and suffering of God knew how many people all around the world—rich bastards who thought that they alone should own our culture, that they should be able to punish you for making art without their permission.

"What are you thinking about?" 26 said. She was sitting in the pub's snug, laptop before her, earpiece screwed in. She'd been on the phone and email all day to Annika, planning some kind of big event for the next day, when they were hoping that people from all over the country would descend on their MPs' offices to complain about the Theft of Intellectual Property Bill. All kinds of groups had joined in, and volunteers were contacting long lists of members and supporters to see if they'd commit to going out. I couldn't join in, of course: I wasn't on the voter's roll. I didn't, technically, exist. Technically, the Zeroday was an abandoned building and no one lived there.

"I'm thinking about how all this work you're doing, it's all because some rich bastards want to get richer."

Chester made a little tooting noise like he was blowing a bugle and Jem began to hum some revolutionary anthem I vaguely recognized—that French song, the one that they used in the advert for the new Renault scooters. Even Rabid Dog rolled his eyes. They were okay about 26 coming by—she was good company—but they hated it when I talked politics. They seemed to think I was only interested in it because 26 was. Mostly, I think they were jealous that I had a girlfriend.

Twenty ignored them, as usual. "Well, yeah. 'Course."

"So why don't we do something to *them*? Why are we mucking around with Members of Parliament, if they're not the ones who make the laws, not really? Why not go straight to the source? It's like we're trying to fix a leaky faucet by plastering the ceiling below it—why don't we just stop the drip?"

She laughed. "What did you have in mind, assassination? I think you'd probably get into more trouble than you could handle if you tried it, boyo."

I shook my head. "I don't know what I have in mind, but it just seems like such a waste of effort. These horrible wretches are sat in their penthouses, making the rest of us miserable, and they go off when they're done, go to some big house in the country. They get to eat in posh restaurants while we literally eat rubbish from skips—"

"What the hell's wrong with rubbish from skips?" Jem said, all mock-affronted.

I waved him off. "Nothing's wrong, Jem. You're the Sir Jamie Oliver of eating garbage, all right? But you get my point—they make us suffer and what do we do? We ask people nicely to go to their MPs' offices and beg to have them debate a law that will put their kids in jail for downloading a film."

"Well, what do you propose?" Chester said.

I was pacing now, and I thumped my hand against the door. "I don't know, okay? Maybe—I don't know, maybe you should make videos of these fat bastards eating babies for a change, instead of picking on Bullingham all the time."

Chester shook his head. "Wouldn't work, mate. No one knows who these people are. No one would recognize them.

When I animate Bullingham eating babies and squishing puppies beneath his toned, spotty, hairy buttocks, it's, you know, it's *commentary*. No one has to ask, 'Who's the geezer with the babies in his gob, then?' Wouldn't work with some anonymous corporate stooge."

I thumped the door again. "Fine. So let's make them famous! We'll follow them with cameras, go through their rubbish bins and post their embarrassing love letters, steal their kids' phones and expose all the music *they* take for free."

"They'd do you for harassment."

I glared at all of them. "Fine," I said. "Fine. Do nothing then. And when your mates start going to prison and you can't get any friends together for a protest movement because they're all banged up, you'll see I was right."

I sat down on the sofa, as far from Rabid Dog as I could. He still wasn't speaking much when Twenty was around, though he'd got better at talking when it was just the boys. There was an uncomfortable silence. I stared at my bare feet.

Jem cleared his throat. "So," he said. "So, I've got news, if you're interested."

Chester said, "I am interested in your news, good sire," in an artificial voice.

"Well, I've been nosing around the town hall," he said. "The title registry. Trying to figure out who actually owns this firetrap. After the way they ran us out the last time, I thought it must be some Russian mobster or something. But that ain't it at all. You will never guess who our landlord is."

Chester said, "Um, is it Sir David Beckham?"

"Nope."

"The Archbishop of Canterbury?"

"Nope."

"Mickey Mouse?"

"Nope."

"Just tell us who it is," I snapped. I wasn't in the mood for playfulness.

"Only the bloody Bow Council! They ended up assuming the title for this place when the faceless corporate entity that bought it up declared bankruptcy and vanished up their own arseholes. They owned heaps of property all around here, and owed millions to the banks, so when they vanished, it was the banks sitting on all this stuff, and they auctioned it off, and the council bought it. So basically, this is a *public* building."

I was interested in spite of myself. "So it was the council that sent those goons in after us last time?" Somehow I figured that the local government would be gentler in its approach.

"I wondered about that, too. But I found the minutes of a council meeting where they approved hiring this anti-squatter firm with the unimaginative name of SecuriCorp to get rid of scum like us. They're notorious, SecuriCorp, hire a lot of crazy thugs, properly brutal. They've got a whole business model built on being savage pricks."

I shook my head. "Well, then, I suppose it's only a matter of time until they show up again."

He laughed. "That's where you're wrong, chum. I did some more digging and looked up the Meter Point Administration Service. That tells you who supplies the electricity to the place. Our Authorized Energy Provider is Virgin Gas and Electric. So yesterday, I rang up their customer service line and introduced myself as the new tenant on these premises and asked to have a pay-as-you-go box fitted. They're doing the job this week."

I shook my head. "You *what*?"

"It's brilliant, don't worry. They'll fit the mains box, and then we'll have to go buy top-ups on a card at the newsagent's. It's just a few pounds a week. But once we're paying for our power, we're not guilty of Abstraction of Electricity anymore. And that means they can't use SecuriCorp against us. Which means that they're going to have to get rid of us the hard way." He bowed in his seat. "You may applaud now."

Chester and Rabid Dog clapped enthusiastically, and I joined in with them. It *was* a clever little hack. Thinking of it only made me more miserable. Everyone else had a way to solve their problems.

Me, I was just useless.

The day of action on the Theft of IP Bill went off even better than Annika and her mates had planned. In Bow and other East London districts, the average MP heard from *150* voters who showed up to explain why TIP was a bad idea. 26 dragged me out to the meeting with her MP, in Kensal Rise, a part of London I'd never been to before. It was a weird place, half posh and half rundown, with long streets of identical houses that ran all the way to the horizon.

Her MP's surgery was in a storefront between a florist and a dinky café that was rammed with mums with babies. I was nervous as we rocked up, and more nervous still when a bored security guard made us empty our pockets, marched us through a metal detector, and demanded to see our IDs.

26 was cool as a cuke. "You can't make us show ID to see our MP. It's the law: 'It is unlawful to place any condition on the ability of a lawful resident of an electoral district to communicate with his Member of Parliament, Councillor, or other representative.'"

The security guard furrowed his brow like he was experiencing enlightenment (or taking a particularly difficult crap). 26 took a deep breath and prepared to throw more facts at him, but a voice called out from behind him, through an open door: "It's all right, James. I would recognize Ms. Kahn's voice at a hundred yards on a busy street. Do come in, dear."

It was a woman's voice, moderately affectionate, middle-aged. It belonged to a moderately affectionate, middle-aged woman sitting on a sofa in a small office crammed with bookcases, papers, little kids' pictures, and letters tacked to a huge notice-board, and a pair of huge, battered laser printers that looked like they should be at Aziz's place. She stood up as we walked in, bangles on her wrist tinkling as she shook 26's hand.

"Nice to see you again, dear. It's been a busy day, as I'm sure you know. Who's your gentleman friend?"

I had worn clean jeans and a T-shirt without anything rude written on it for the occasion, which was properly formal by Zeroday standards. Still, I felt as out of place as a fart in a palace.

"This is Cecil," Twenty said. "He's been helping out with the organizing." It was true—I had spent a good twenty hours that week tweeting, emailing, calling, and messaging people from the mailing list, wheedling them to show up at their MPs' surgeries. I could rattle off ten reasons you should do it, three things you should stress with your MP, and five things you mustn't do without pausing for breath. It had made me feel a little less useless, but not much.

"Pleased to meet you, Cecil. I'm Letitia Clarke-Gifford, MP for Brent. Well, the two of you can certainly be very proud of yourselves. I've been seeing your army of supporters in lots of ten today, and I don't think I'll be able to get through them all even if I work through supper. From what I can tell, it's the same all over the country. I expect it's making *quite* an impression. A lot of my colleagues in Parliament like to use a rule of thumb that says a personal visit from a voter means that a hundred voters probably feel the same way. Even the very safest seats are in trouble when a thousand or more people are on your case about an issue."

26 beamed. "I can't believe the turnout—it's *amazing*!"

I blurted out, "So, will it work?"

Both turned to look at me. 26 looked irritated. The MP looked thoughtful.

"I'll tell you straight up, I'm not positive it will. It breaks my heart to say it, because your lot have clearly played by the rules and done everything you're supposed to do. When voters across the country are against legislation, when no one except a few big companies are *for* it, it just shouldn't become law.

"But the sad fact is that this is going to a three-whip vote."

That jogged my memory, back to something Annika had

said. "You mean if they don't vote in favor of it, they get kicked out of their own party?"

She nodded. "It may not sound like much to you, but you don't get to be an MP unless you've spent your whole life working in and for your party. All your friends will be in the party, your whole identity. It's a miniature death penalty. Now, if *all* of the MPs in caucus defied the whip, I don't think the party would cut them loose. But no MP can be really *sure* that her colleagues will vote for conscience, and no one wants to be the only one to stand up for a principle. They're all thinking to themselves, 'Hum, well, I'll hold my nose and vote for this today, and that means that I'll get to stay in Parliament and have the chance to do good for my constituents the next time.' They call that 'realpolitik'—which is a fancy way of saying, 'I've got no choice, so I'll pretend that it doesn't bother me.'"

I looked at 26. It seemed like the MP was just saying what I'd been saying all week long: there was no point in playing along with the politics game, because the other side got to make the rules. Twenty's rosebud mouth was pinched and angry.

"Why wouldn't the party let them vote the way the people want them to? It just doesn't make any sense."

Clarke-Gifford shrugged. "Lots of reasons. The entertainment industry's always been big here. Exporting our culture is part of the old imperial tradition: we used to own half the world, some MPs think we might end up owning half the world's screens.

"Plus there's the fact that the members and the party bigwigs get courted heavily by all these famous people. They get to go to the best parties in the country. Their kids go on holidays with popstars' kids in exotic places. They go to premieres and get to go on the red carpet alongside of people who are literally legends, get their pictures in the papers next to film stars that every one of their voters idolize.

"When their good friends from the industry tell them that downloading is exactly like theft, they're inclined to believe them. After all, don't you believe the things that your mates tell you?"

"So we shouldn't have even bothered?" 26 looked like she might cry. I quietly slipped my hand into hers.

"No, no. No! It's not a wasted effort. If you lose this round, you can go back to your supporters and say, 'see, see how big the stitch-up is?' And they can go to *their* mates and say, 'Look, hundreds and thousands of people asked their MPs to do the right thing, but big business forced them into voting against the public interest. Don't you think you'd better get involved?' Little by little, your numbers will grow, until they can't afford to ignore you any longer. And in the meantime, there are *some* parties that let members vote their conscience, sometimes—our party, and the Greens; the LibDems, too."

I tried to imagine explaining to my parents why they should rise up and shout in the streets about this. After all, this was the issue that had cost them their jobs, their benefits, their daughter's education—their son! But I couldn't imagine it. Mum could barely walk, let alone march down the road. And Dad? He'd be too busy trying to find a way to pay for dinner to join the revolution.

I looked at 26 again. She seemed to have got a little cheer and hope out of the MP, so I kept my gob shut.

Clarke-Gifford was also looking at 26, maybe thinking that she'd given her a little too much reality. "Besides, maybe I'm wrong," she said, unconvincingly. "Maybe with all the support you lot have got today, the party won't dare whip the vote in case they have a rebellion in Parliament. After all, Labour doesn't want to be the party that votes for it if the Conservatives vote against it—or vice-versa."

26 smiled bravely (and beautifully, I might add), and said, "That's a really good point. If one party goes with us, it'll make the other one look really bad. That's something we could talk to Annika about. I still want you to meet her, Letitia—you'd get on so well."

The MP smiled. "Well, I'm having my annual constituency garden party next month. Why don't you bring her around then? There'll be little sandwiches with the crusts cut off and everything. Bring your young man, too. Now, if you'll excuse me, it sounds like there's a new group of constituents in the front room waiting to tell me how terribly important it is that I vote against a tremendously important piece of legislation."

We passed them on the way out, a group of ten people, clutching paper notes for their meeting with their MP. 26 quizzed them on how they came to be there and whether they'd ever done something like this before. It turned out that they were a church reading circle, and four of the members had had their Internet cut off so they'd come out. And no, they'd never come out for something like this before, but enough was enough.

As we walked away down the street, 26's arm around my waist, my arm around her shoulders, I thought, *What if they give up hope because the vote goes the wrong way? What had Annika said? "Eventually so many of us will be offline or in jail that there won't be anyone left to organize."* But 26 was warm under my arm, and she'd promised to introduce me to her mum and dad, which meant that I was going to learn her real name at last—the visit to the MP's office had given me a surname, *Kahn,* but her real first name remained a tantalizing mystery. I'd asked her what it was on that first night together, and she'd confessed to *Sally,* but she later swore it was *Deborah, Sita,* and *Craniosacral.* She'd answer to anything I called her, and all her friends called her Twenty or 26, and I enjoyed the mystery, but I was looking forward to puncturing it. And thinking about finding out her real name distracted me from feeling nervous about meeting her family. I had met loads of my friends' parents before, but never my *girlfriend's* parents. I had recurring panics when I thought about shaking the hand of the mother of the girl that I'd had sex with the night before.

Oh, didn't I mention? Yes. We were having sex. *Lots of it.* And it was wicked. It didn't happen until the third time she stayed over—we snogged and stuff, but I kept stopping short. Eventually, she asked me why I wasn't trying to shag her and I hemmed and hawed and confessed that I'd never done it before.

She gave me a big, sloppy kiss, said, "I'll be gentle," and stripped off. Since then, we'd been at it like rabbits. Disgusting. Drove my flatmates around the bend with our carrying on and grunting and that.

Yeah, I was pretty made up about all of it. But I had this nightmarish daydream in which I shook her mother's hand and blurted, "Very pleased to meet you, ma'am. It's really lovely, having it off with your precious daughter."

"Nervous about meeting my parents?" Twenty said.

"Naw," I lied.

They lived in one of the terraced Victorian row houses with a little garden out front. Twenty pointed out the stumps of an iron fence that had once surrounded the garden: "During World War Two, everyone pulled up their steel fencing and that to make into battleships. But there wasn't any good way to recycle the metal so the government just dumped it all into the English Channel."

"I did not know that," I said. "Um. Look, are we going to go meet your mum and dad?"

She laughed and gave my arse a swat. "Calm down, boyo. You'll do fine. It's not fashionable to say it, but my parents are actually quite cool."

You know how houses have smells that their owners never seem to notice? 26's house smelled *great*. Like the cedar chips they'd spread on the paths in the public parks every spring, mixed with something like lemon peel and wet stone.

The place had wooden floors and wooden steps leading up to an upper story, coathooks and framed antique maps, and books.

Thousands of books.

They teetered in stacks on the stairs and in the hallway. Shelves ran the length of the corridor, just about head-height, packed with a double row of books, some turned sideways to fit in the cramped space. They were in a state of perfect (and rather glorious) higgeldy-piggeldy, leather-bound antiques next to cheap paperbacks, horizontal stacks of oversized art books and a boxed encyclopedia serving as a little side table, its top littered with keys, packets of Kleenex, rolled pairs of gloves, umbrellas, and, of course, more books.

26 waved a hand at them. "My parents are readers," she said.

"I can see that."

She turned and called up the stairs, "Oh, parents! I'm home! I've brought a boy!"

A woman's voice called down, "The prodigal daughter! I was on the verge of turning your bedroom into a shrine for my dear, departed offspring!"

26 rolled her eyes, but she was smiling. "I'll just be in the kitchen, eating all your food, all right?"

I followed her down the short hallway, past a sitting room— more books, a comfy sofa and chair, a small telly covered in dust— and into an airy kitchen that led into a glass conservatory that showed a small back garden planted with rows of vegetables and wildflowers.

She went straight to the fridge and began pulling out stuff—a tall glass pitcher of what looked like iced tea or apple juice (it turned out to be iced mint tea, and delicious, too), half a rhubarb-strawberry pie, a small cheeseboard under a glass bell. She handed it to me and I balanced it on the parts of the kitchen table that weren't buried in reading material. 26 jerked a thumb over her shoulder: "Glasses in that cupboard and cutlery in the drawer underneath it."

I fetched them down, and she cut us both generous slices of pie and thick slices of Red Leicester cheese, and poured out two tall glasses of tea. I sat down and she plunked herself in my lap. At that moment, I heard footsteps on the stairs. "Get off," I whispered, horrified at the thought of meeting her mum with her on my lap.

She waggled her eyebrows at me. "Why?"

"Come on," I said. "Don't do this."

She winked at me, and said, "She'll love you," and leapt off my lap just as her mum came into the kitchen.

She was a tall Indian lady with bobbed hair shot with gray, smile lines bracketing a mouth that was just like 26's. She wore a pretty sundress that left her muscular arms bare, and her bare feet showed long toes with nails painted electric blue.

26 pointed at her toes: "Love them!" she said, and gave her mum a full body hug that I knew well (it was her specialty). "Mum, this is Cecil, the boy who's been kidnapping me to East London all summer. Cecil, this is my mum, Amrita."

I stood up awkwardly and shook her hand. "Very pleased to meet you, Mrs. Kahn," I said, aware that my hands were dripping with sudden, clammy sweat.

She gave me a quick up-and-down look and I was glad I'd dressed up a little for the MP meeting. "Nice to meet you, too, Cecil. I see that 26 has got you something to eat already." I looked at Twenty—her *mum* had called her *26*!—and saw that she was grinning smugly.

"It's delicious," I said. I was on good-manners autopilot.

"So, tell me how your big meeting went," she said, settling in on another chair after moving its stack of books to the top of the pile on the next chair. She leaned across the table and used 26's fork to nick a large bite of her pie, then made to get another one, but 26 slapped her wrist. Both were smiling, though.

"Letitia said it was all a waste of time," 26 said. "The vote is fixed."

"I can't believe that's what she really said," her mum said. She looked at me.

"Well," I said, "not exactly. But she did say that she thought it would be hard for other politicians to vote our way because their parties would punish them."

Her mum winced. "Yes, I was worried about that, too." She sighed. "I'm sorry, darling. You never can tell. Maybe getting people worked up about this will pay off later, with a bigger movement—"

"That's what Letitia said," 26 said snappishly. "Fine. I get it, it's fine."

Her mum nodded and pointedly looked at me. "Where do you go to school, Cecil?" she said.

Erm. I looked at my hands. "I don't, really," I said. "Well. It's like—"

26 said, "Cecil left home because he got his family cut off from the Internet by downloading too much."

Her eyes widened. "Oh," she said. "I'm sorry to hear that. Where are you living now?"

"With friends," I said. It was true, as far as it went, but I knew I was blushing. Technically, I was homeless. Well, *technically* I was a squatter, which was worse than homeless in some ways. 26's house wasn't posh, and it was obvious that her parents weren't rich, but they weren't the same kind of people as my family. The books, the funny toenails, how *young* her mum looked—it made me realize what people were talking about when they talked about "class." I had to make a proper effort to stop myself squirming.

"Where's Dad?" 26 said, changing the subject without much subtlety.

"He's down the cellar, messing about in his lab."

"Is he a scientist?" I said. I had a vision of a white-coated, German-accented superbrain, and felt even more inadequate.

They both laughed though. "No," her mum said. "He brews beer. He's mad about it. He hardly drinks the stuff, but he loves to make it. I think he just enjoys all the toys and gadgets."

"Want to see?" 26 said.

"Erm, sure," I said.

Once her mum was out of the room, 26 whispered, "He's not my real dad, not biologically. But I think of him as my father."

We descended the cellar stairs and came into a low room with a cement floor, the walls lined with tables and shelves containing enormous glass bottles, buckets, siphons, and charts hand-annotated with fat greasepencil. Her dad was bent over a huge glass bottle filled with murky liquid. He was wearing blue jeans and a green smock, and what I could see of his hair was wiry, short, and gray.

"Dad," 26 said, "I've got someone I'd like you to meet."

He straightened and turned around. I was surprised. Mentally, I'd figured that 26 was mixed-race, so when I saw that her mum was Indian, I assumed her dad was white, but he was Indian, too. And then I remembered that he was her stepfather. I decided that I was absolutely rubbish at predicting peoples' racial backgrounds and resolved to do less of it from then on.

He was as kind as her mum, but he had ferocious concentration lines in his high forehead and a groove between his eyes you could lose a ten-p piece in. He blinked at us for a moment, then smiled.

"Dad, this is Cecil. Cecil, this is my dad, Roshan."

He nodded appraisingly at me. I had a paranoid moment, thinking that he was about to ask me something like, "What makes you think that you're allowed to have sex with my daughter?" But what he actually said was, "Could you give me a hand with something?"

26 tsked. "*Dad*, I didn't bring Cecil over so that you could turn him into a human forklift."

He shushed her. "It's only that I need to get this"—he pointed at a waist-high glass bottle of brownish-black beer—"onto that table."

I was glad to be useful. "Of course!" I said, and went over to the bottle and squatted in front of it, taking hold of the neck and the bottom. He took the other side.

One, two, three!"

We lifted. It was like trying to budge a house. The bottle must have weighed thirty-five stone. I strained, and so did he, his face going purple and a vein standing out in his lined forehead. We groaned and the bottle rose. We got it up to waist-height and staggered two steps to the table and put it down with a *clunk*. I mashed my fingers a bit and I yanked them free and squeezed my hand between my thighs.

"You all right?" he gasped. He was rubbing his biceps.

"Yeah," I said. "Didn't think we were going to make it."

26 clucked her tongue again. "Dad, that was very naughty. You could have given yourself a heart attack."

"Small sacrifice for art," he said, and thumped the bottle, his wedding ring making it ring like a bell. "This is licorice stout," he said. "With some Valerian root. It's a muscle relaxant. It's an experiment."

"Mum says you're going to need to serve it over a dropcloth. She calls it incontinence in a glass."

"She's probably right, but it's coming up a treat. Wait a tick." He rummaged in a crate and pulled out a plastic pump. He fitted it over the bottle's neck and worked it vigorously, holding a chipped teacup under its spout. It gurgled, then trickled a stream of the dark beer into his cup. He passed it to me.

"Try a sip," he said. "It's not quite ready, but I'm really liking where it's headed."

I sniffed at it, a bit suspicious. It smelled . . . earthy. Like fresh-turned soil—though I couldn't tell you where I'd smelled fresh-turned soil!—or wet stone (I realized that this was where the wet-stone smell I'd noticed when we came into the house must have come from). It was so dark it looked like a black mirror. I tasted it. It was only slightly fizzy, and it was sour in that way that beer or rye bread are, and there were about twenty different flavors behind it, including a strong black licorice flavor that was improbably delicious and sharp inside that big, round earthy taste.

"Fwoar," I said, and took another sip. Twenty's dad grinned as though I'd just paid him the highest of compliments.

He pumped another cup and passed it to 26, then one for himself. He held out his cup and we all clinked glasses and sipped some more.

"Hardly any alcohol in it, yet," he said. "I'm going to try to make it very weak, four percent or so. The Valerian will pack a righteous bloody kick."

"What's Valerian?" I asked.

Twenty said, "It's a herb. A sedative. I take it when I get my cramps, knocks me flat on my arse."

"You're going to put it in beer?" I sniffed at the cup again. The dregs were swirling around the bottom, thick with gritty sediment.

He waggled his eyebrows and made his fingers dance. "Just a bit. A smidge. I'm thinking, 'Dr Dutta's All-Purpose Wintertime Licorice Sleepytime Brew.' Going to make labels and everything. It will be brilliant on dark, awful winter nights, put your lights out like a switch."

Twenty slurped the rest of hers back. "Dad's bonkers, but it's mostly a harmless kind of crazy. And when he's not making beer, he's a pretty fair barrister."

He held his hands at his breastbone and made a funny little bow. I found myself really liking him. And his beer.

"What are you two up to?"

"I was going to take him round the neighborhood, show him some of my favorite places."

He nodded. "Will you stay for dinner? I was going to grill some steak. And tofu wieners for Little Miss Veggiepants over there."

"Dad," she said. "I haven't been a vegetarian for *months*."

He rolled his eyes. "Who can keep track? Meat for everyone, then. Okay with you, Cecil?"

"Sure," I said, again, not wanting to seem rude, but wondering if 26 would mind. How long did she want me hanging around her parents? How long until I said or did something that embarrassed her and made them hate me and forbid her to see me?

"*You're* not a veggiepants, are you?"

"No sir," I said seriously. "I'll eat anything that doesn't eat me first." I had to stop myself explaining that I normally lived on a diet of rubbish harvested from skips.

"Good man," he said. He kissed 26 on the top of her head. "Bring him back by seven o'clock and I'll have supper on the table."

She grabbed my hand and dragged me upstairs. "Come on," she said, squeezing my hand. "I'll show you my room."

She slammed the door behind us as soon as we got into her room—a bit bigger than my room back in Bradford, but every bit as crowded with papers, posters, a litter of memory sticks and keys and semifunctional beamers, along with a load of climbing gear and ropes hanging from hooks rudely screwed into the plaster.

She swept a pile of clothes off the single bed and pushed me down on it, then climbed on top and began to kiss me. "Still fancy me now that you've met my insane parental units?" she whispered in my ear.

I squeezed her bum. " 'Course!" I said. "They're brilliant, you know. Really nice. I thought they'd hate me on sight."

"Naw," she said. "Compared to my last boyfriend, you're the catch of the century."

I pulled my face away from hers. "You've never talked about him. Who was he?"

She shrugged. "A major tosser, as it turns out. Not one of the highlights of my life and times. Caught him fondling my so-called best mate behind the school one day. I forgave him, but then I caught him snooping around my computer, reading my private stuff. That was unforgivable. So I put him out with the rubbish."

Of course, I had a thousand daft questions, like "Did he shag better than me?" and "Was he white, too?" and "Was he smarter than me?" and "Was his thing bigger than mine?" and "Was he posh?" and so on. But as stupid as my undermind was, the stuff up front had the good sense to only say, "Well, there you go. Sounds like an idiot. But I'm glad to have someone to make me look good."

She kissed me again. "Let's go see my stomping grounds."

The Kensal Green Cemetery was even bigger than Highgate—like a city for the dead, surrounded by a crumbling wall that had been patchily repaired, the outside road lined with shops selling headstones and statues of angels and that.

26 took me in through a gap in the wall hidden by tall shrubs that smelled of dog piss, which led into a field of knee-high wild grasses growing around crazy-tilted headstones whose names had been worn away by wind and rain and the passing of years.

"Isn't it magic?" she said as we meandered through the stones, warm earth smells in our noses, preceded by the scampering sounds of small animals haring off through the grass to get out of our way. "It's where I got the idea for the screening in Highgate. I'd *really* love to do one here, next. We could get a pretty big crowd into the more remote bits of the place. I'd love to do the screenings every week, or maybe every fortnight. Get a big audience. That one in Highgate was like, the high point of my life."

I wished yet again that I hadn't spent most of it getting so rat arsed. From what Rabid Dog and the others said, it had been absolutely, epically magisterial. "Yeah," I said. "It was pretty stupendous."

"But if we did it that often, we'd be sure to get rumbled."

"Not if we changed locations. It wouldn't always have to be cemeteries. They're not going to be any good once autumn rolls in and it starts pissing down with rain practically every night. But there's loads of indoor places you could do it, too—Jem's always scouting spots for squats, he can't help himself. Lots of boarded-up warehouses type of thing. And then there's underground; saw a little urban infiltration video from these absolute nutters who go running around in the old Victorian sewers. Some of them, they're like castle dining halls. The Victorians were mad for grandeur. Can you imagine how fantastically cool it would be to lead a load of people in wellies down some damp tunnel and into a huge brick vault with popcorn and seats and a big screen?"

"Magisterial," she said.

One thing led to another—specifically, 26 led me deeper into the graveyard's secluded secret places—and before long we sat in the lee of a stone mausoleum, soft moss beneath us, snogging like a pair of crazed ferrets. Eventually, 26 checked her phone and announced that we were about to be late for dinner and we ran through the now-closed graveyard, ducking back through the same crumbled section of wall.

Dinner was delicious and, after a few minutes, very friendly. Her dad was really funny, and had loads of stories about mad judges and dodgy clients. Her mum was more reserved—and clearly a bit put off by the idea of her daughter having a boyfriend—but she warmed and even let me help with the washing up, which turned into something of a party as 26 turned on some music from her phone and pitched in to help, too, and soon we were dancing and singing around the kitchen.

When I kissed her good night at the door—a brief one, as her parents were in the front room, reading in sight of the picture windows that overlooked the doorway—she whispered, "You done good," in my ear. The words stayed with me on the long tube journey home, and they had me smiling all the way.

If you care about any of this stuff, you already know what happened with the Theft of Intellectual Property Bill: in the end, only thirty-nine MPs bothered to turn up for the vote. That left 611 absent without leave. I guess they were all having a lovely lie-in with the newspapers and a cup of tea. At first, I thought that only thirty-nine attendees meant that we'd won—I'd googled up the rules for Parliament and it said that you needed at least forty for a vote.

I was cheering about this on a Cynical April board when some clever bastard pointed out that the Speaker of the House—the bloke who kept order and handed out the biscuits at teatime— also counted, bringing the total up to forty. The independent and Green candidates all voted against it, and so did many of the Lib-Dems, but twenty-one Labour, Conservative, and Liberal Democrat MPs voted in favor of it, and it passed, with only fifty-five minutes' debate.

The office of every MP who took the day off work was flooded with calls from angry voters, but as Annika pointed out, they didn't really have to worry, most of them, since there wasn't anyone to vote for in their district who would have come out against the bill, not with their party's whips out and enforcing order.

Within a week of the law coming into effect, they had their first arrest. Jimmy Preston, the kid they took away, had some kind of mental problems—autistic spectrum, they said on the BBC—and he didn't go out much. But he'd collected 450,000 songs on his hard drive through endless, tedious, tireless hours of downloading. From what anyone could tell, he didn't even listen to them: he just liked cataloging them, correcting their metadata, organizing them. I recognized the motivation, having spent many comforting evenings tidying up and sorting out my multi-terabyte collection of interesting video clips (many of which I'd never even watched, but wanted to have handy in case they were needed for one of my projects). He had collected most of them before the law came into effect, but TIP also made it a crime to possess the files.

Six months later, the sentencing judge gave him five years in prison, the last year adult prison after he turned twenty-one—because the Crown showed that his collection was valued at over *twenty million* pounds!—and the media was filled with pictures of this scared-eyed seventeen-year-old kid in a bad-fitting suit, his teary parents hovering over his shoulder, faces pulled into anguished masks.

But he didn't serve five years. They found him hanging from the light fixture in his cell two weeks later. His cellmates claimed they hadn't noticed him climbing up on the steel toilet with a rope made from a twisted shirt around his neck, hadn't noticed as he kicked and choked and gurgled out his last breath. The rumor was that his body was covered in bruises from the beatings he'd received from the other prisoners. Jimmy didn't deal well with prison. We all got to know his name then—until then, they'd kept it a secret because he was a minor—and he went from being Mr. X to Dead Jimmy.

By that time, there were already fifteen more up before judges around the country. Most were kids. In each case, the Crown argued that the size of their collections qualified them for adult treatment after their twenty-first birthdays. In five more cases, the judge agreed. All were found guilty. Of course they were guilty. The law had been written to *make them guilty*.

It wasn't just kids, either. Every day, there was news about video- and file-hosting services shutting down. One, a site that had never been much for pirate clips, just mostly videos that people took while they were out playing and that, posted this notice to its front door:

> After eight years of serving Britain's amateur videographers, filmmakers, and communities, UKTube is shutting its doors. As you no doubt know, Parliament passed the Theft of Intellectual Property Act earlier this month, and with it, created a whole new realm of liability and risk for anyone who allows the public to host content online.
>
> According to our solicitors, we now have to pay a copyright specialist to examine each and every video you upload to make sure it doesn't infringe on copyright *before* we make it live. The cheapest of these specialists comes at about £200/hour, and it takes about an hour to examine a ten-minute video.
>
> Now, we get an average of fourteen hours' worth of video uploaded *every minute*. Do the maths: in order to stay on the right side of the law, we'd have to spend £16,800 *a minute* in legal fees. Even if there were that many solicitors available—and there aren't!—we only

turn over about £4,000 a day. We'd go bankrupt in ten
minutes at that rate.

We don't know if Parliament intended to shut
down this site and all the others like it, or whether this
side effect is just depraved indifference on their part.
What we do know is that this site has *never* been a
haven for piracy. We have a dedicated, round-the-
clock team of specialists devoted to investigating
copyright complaints and removing offending material
as quickly as possible. We're industry leaders at it, and
we spend a large amount of our operating budget on
this.

But it didn't get us anywhere. Bending over to help
the big film companies police their copyrights cost us a
fortune, and they thanked us by detonating a legal
suicide bomb in the middle of our offices. You hear a
lot of talk about terrorism these days. That word gets
thrown around a lot. But a terrorist is someone who
attacks innocent civilians to make a point. We'll leave it
to you to decide whether it applies here.

In the meantime, we've shut our doors. The
hundred-plus Britons who worked for us are now
looking for jobs. We've set up a page here where you
can review their CVs if you're hiring. We vouch for all
of them.

We struggled with the problem of what to do with
all the video you've entrusted to us over the years. In
the end, we decided to send a set of our backups to the
Internet Archive, archive.org, which has a new server
array in Iceland, where—for the time being—the laws
are more sensible than they are here. The kind people at
archive.org are working hard to bring it online, and
once it is, you'll be able to download your creations
again. Sorry to say that we're not sure when that will
happen, though.

And that's it. We're done.

Wait.

We're not quite done.

We have a message for the bullies from the big film studios and the politicians who serve them: UKTube is one of many legitimate, British businesses that you have murdered with the stroke of your pen this month. In your haste to deliver larger profits to a few entertainment giants, you've let them design a set of rules that outlaws anyone who competes with them: any place where normal, everyday people can simply communicate with one another.

We've been a place where dying people can share their final thoughts with their loved ones; where people in trouble can raise funds or support; where political movements were born and organized and sustained. All of that is collateral damage in your war on piracy—a crime that you seem to have defined as "anything we don't like or that eats into our bottom line."

Lucky for humanity, not every country will be as quick to sell out as Britain. Unlucky for Britain, though: our government has sacrificed our competitiveness and our future. Britain's best and brightest will not stay here long. Other countries will welcome them with open arms, and each one that leaves will be a loss for this backward-looking land.

That actually made the news, and they cornered some MPs who'd supported the legislation about it, who sneered about histrionics and hysteria and theft, and they got some of the people who'd enjoyed using UKTube to talk about their favorite videos, and that was that.

But not for me. When UKTube shut down, half a dozen more

followed. More and more proxies were blocked off by the ISP that supplied the council estate next to the Zeroday. It felt like there was a noose tightening around my neck, and it was getting harder to breathe every day.

26 thumped my mattress, and said, "Come to bed, Cecil, bloody hell, it's been *hours*. I'm going to have to get up for school soon."

I jumped guiltily. I'd been sitting on the floor, back to the wall, knees drawn up and laptop balanced on them, reading the debates online, reading about how much money the different parties had taken in from the big film and record and publishing companies in contributions.

I scrubbed at my eyes with my fists. "It's hopeless," I said. "Bloody hopeless. We got all those people to go to their MPs. It didn't matter. We might as well have done *nothing*. What a waste."

26 propped herself up on one elbow, the sheet slipping away from her chest, which got my pulse going. "Cecil," she said. "*Trent*." I startled again. She'd never called me that before. "Just because it didn't work, that doesn't mean it's hopeless, or a waste. At least now people understand how corrupt the process is, how broken the whole *system* is. The film studios just keep repeating the word *theft* over and over again, the way the coppers do with *terrorism,* hoping that our brains will switch off when we hear it." She put on a squeaky cartoon voice. "*Stealing is wrong, kids!* It makes for a good, simplistic story that idiots can tell each other over their Egg McMuffins in the morning.

"But once they start passing these dirty laws through their dirty tricks, they show us all how corrupt they are. If it's just theft, then why do they need to get their laws passed in the dead of the night, without debate or discussion? Bloody hell, if it's just *theft,* then why aren't the penalties the same as for thieving? Nick a film from HMV and you'll pay a twenty-quid fine, if that. Download the same film from some Pirate Bay in Romania and they stick you in *jail*. Bugger that.

"Maybe now the average *Daily Mail* reader will start to ask himself, 'How come they never have to sneak around to get a law passed against actual theft? What if this isn't just stealing after all?'" I could tell what she was trying to do, make me feel better. I could have gone along with it, told her she was right and crawled into bed with her and tried to get some sleep. But I wasn't in the mood. I was feeling nasty and angry. "Why should they wake up this time? Your mate Annika, doesn't she say that there've been eleven other copyright laws in the past fifteen years? Are we supposed to wait for ten or fifteen more? When will this great uprising finally take place? How many kids will we see in prison before it happens?"

I was shaking and my hands were in fists. 26's eyes were wide-open now, the sleep gone. She looked momentarily angry and I was sure we were about to have our usual stupid barney, a bicker that went nowhere because we were both too stubborn to back down. But then her face softened and she shifted over to me and put a warm arm around my shoulders.

"Hey," she said. "What's got you so lathered up?"

"I just keep thinking that this could be me. It probably *will* be me, someday. Or it'll be my sister, Cora. She's careful, but what if she messes up? She needs to be perfectly careful every time. They just need to catch her once."

She cuddled me for a long moment. "So what do you want to do?"

I thumped the floor so hard my fist felt like I'd smashed it with a hammer. "I don't know. Fight. Fight back. Jesus, they're going to get me sooner or later. Why not go down swinging? Every time I go past a cinema and see a queue out the door, I think, look at those fools, every penny they spend is turned into profits that are used to pass laws imprisoning their own children. Can't they see?"

She didn't say anything.

"We should do something," I said. "We should do—I don't know. We should blow up all the cinemas."

"Oh, that'll make people sympathetic to your cause."

"Wait till they're empty," I said. "Of course."

"Keep thinking," she said.

"OK, fine. But I want to go to war now. No more complaining. No more campaigning. Time to do something *real*."

Chapter 4

A SHOT ACROSS THE BOW/FRIENDS FROM AFAR/
WHATEVER FLOATS YOUR BOAT/LET'S PUT ON A SHOW!

What's worse than making a great comic into a crap film? Making a great comic into *eighteen* crap films. Which is exactly what they did to *Milady de Winter*, which sold tons of books in Japan before it was translated into English and forty-five other languages, sweeping the globe with its modern retelling of *The Three Musketeers*. So naturally, it became one of the most anticipated films of the century by kids all over the planet. They signed the best-grossing adult actors in Hollywood to play the villains, and imported two Bollywood actors, Prita Kapoor and Rajiv Kumar, to play the beautiful visiting princess and the evil king of the thieves. The producer, who mostly made films where computer-generated spaceships fought deadly duels over poorly explained political differences, explained that these actors would "Open up the billion-strong Desi film-going market," in an interview that made it clear that his $400,000,000 film was an investment vehicle, not a piece of art.

They got the cutest child actors. The finest special-effects wizards. The best toy and video-game tie-ins, and advertisements that were slathered over every stationary surface and public vehicle in places as distant and unlikely as Bradford, and *Milady de Winter* was a success. Opening weekend box office smashed all records with a $225,000,000 tally, and all told, the first one alone was reckoned as a billion-dollar profit to Paramount studios and its investors.

Only one problem: it was an utter piece of *shit*. Seriously. I saw it when I was only twelve and even though I was barely a fan of the comics, even I was offended on behalf of every halfway intelligent kid in the world. Every actor in the film was brilliant, but the words they were asked to speak were not; it was like the film had been written with boxing gloves on. Whenever the dialog got too horrible to bear, the director threw in another high-speed and pointless action sequence, each wankier and stupider than the last, until by the end of the film, it was climaxing with a scene where swordfighters leapt hundreds of feet into the air, tossing their swords into enemy soldiers as they fell, skewering several at once like a kebab, then doing an acrobatic midair somersault, snatching the blades clean of the dead bad guys, and whirling them overhead like a helicopter rotor for a gentle landing. The critics hated it. The reviews were so uniformly negative that the quotes on the film posters were reduced to a single word, like:

"Action"—*The New York Times*

"Fast"—*The Guardian*

"Adventure"—*The Globe and Mail*

Of course, the actual reviews said things like, "Too much action, not enough thought," or "Scenes that move fast without managing to excite," or "Turning one of history's best-loved adventure stories into yet another trite Hollywood blockbuster."

So, what happened with this miserable, festering gush of cinematic puke? It was only the most profitable film in history. So profitable that they were already shooting the sequel before the opening weekend. Everybody I know saw them. Even me. And no one I knew liked them, but we all went anyway. And there was so much marketing tie-in, it was impossible to avoid: school gave out orange squash in *Milady de Winter* paper cups on fun-run days, sad men on the streets holding signs handed out *Milady de Winter* coupons for free chips at Yankee Fried Chicken and Fish (which didn't even let schoolkids eat there), the animated hoardings during the World Cup replayed the stupidest scenes in endless loops.

The standard joke was that *Milady de Winter* films were just barely tolerable if you downloaded the Italian dubbed version and pretended you were looking at an opera. I tried it. It didn't make the experience any better. And still, we kept going to see the sequels, and still, they kept making more, two or sometimes three per year.

Part 18 was scheduled for a grand London opening late in October. The openings rotated between Mumbai, New York, Los Angeles, and London, and lucky us, it was our turn. Everyone had a *Milady de Winter* joke, graffiti artists drew mustaches or boils or giant willies on the faces of the stars that went up on every billboard (the child actors had grown old and been replaced by new ones; the adult actors had found themselves forever unable to be cast in anything except a *Milady de Winter* film). But the polls in the freesheets reported that most Londoners were planning to go see Part 18, which was called *D'Artagnan's Blood-Oath*.

And so were the Jammie Dodgers.

Little known fact about pirate film downloads: most of 'em come from people who work for the film studios. A picture as big and complicated as *D'Artagnan's Blood-Oath* has hundreds, if not thousands, of workers and actors and cutters and sound-effects people who handle it before it gets released. And just like everyone else in the world, they take their work home with them (I once watched an interview with a SFX lady who said that when it came to the really big films, she often started working from the moment she got up, at 7:00 A.M., stopping only to shower and get on the bus to the studio). With that many copies floating around, it's inevitable that one or more will get sent to a mate for a sneaky peek, and from there, they slither out onto the net.

Hollywood acts like every film you download comes from some kid who sneaks a camera or a high-end phone into a cinema, and they've bought all kinds of laws allowing them to search you on your way into the screen, like you were boarding an airplane. But it's all rubbish: stop every kid with a camera and the number of early pirate films will drop by approximately zero percent. It's like the alcoholic dad in a gritty true-life film: he can't control his own life, so he tries to control everyone else's. The studios can't control their own people, so they come after us.

Which is how I got my hands on a copy of Part 18 a month

before it opened in London (I can't bring myself to keep calling it *D'Artagnan's Blood-Oath*, which sounds more like an educational film about a teenaged girl struggling with her first monthly visitor). It was all the rage on Cynical April, where we were all competing to see who could do the most outrageous recuts. They were good for laughs, but I had bigger plans.

It started when I went with Jem to visit Aziz. Jem was after some new networking gear for a project he was all hush-hush about, while I was thinking it'd be nice to get a couple of very large flat-panel displays, better than the beamers I was using at the Zeroday when I edited, because they'd work with the lights on full-go, letting me edit even when 26 was over doing her homework.

As we wound our way through Aziz's shelves, he pointed out his most recent finds, and stubbed his toe on a carton the size of a shoe box that rattled.

He cussed fluently at it, then gave it a shove toward an overflowing shelf.

"What is that, anyway?" I said.

"Thumb drives," he said. "A thousand of 'em, all told." He gestured at more small cartons.

I boggled. Sure, I had a dozen of them back at the Zeroday, ones we'd found at the charity shops and stuff. They were useful for carrying files you didn't want to keep on your mobile, or for loading onto older machines that didn't have working wireless links. Like most of the people I knew, I treated them as semi-disposable and never thought of them as very valuable. But a thousand of them—that was getting into serious money.

"Bugger," I said. "Are you going to sell 'em?"

He snorted. "These aren't the kind you sell. They're ancient. Only thirty-two gigabytes each. I only keep 'em here because I'm convinced someone will find something better to do with them than chucking them in a landfill."

"I might just take you up on that," I said, and my mind started to whirl.

I don't think I'd ever seen a 32 gig stick before then—the ones we got in first year were 128s, and they were obsolete and nearly filled with crap adverts for junk food and Disneyland Paris from the start. These ones were shaped like little footballs and emblazoned with the logo for something called Major League Soccer, which I looked up later (it was a sad, defunct American football league that had made an unsuccessful attempt to gain popularity in the UK before I was born, dating the sticks to nearly two decades before).

Thirty-two gigs was such a ludicrously tiny size, compared to the terabyte versions for sale in the little dry-cleaner/newsagent/phone unlocking place by Old Street Station—it would take thirty of the little footballs to equal just one of those. What the hell could you put on one of those?

"You're joking," Rabid Dog said, as I thought aloud about this in the pub room of the Zeroday, one dark September night as the wind howled and the rain lashed at the shutters over the windows. He'd got a lot less shy lately, and I hadn't caught him wanking in weeks. "Thirty-two gigs is tons of space. You could stick fifty 640 by 480 videos on one of those."

"Yeah, and I could get like a million films on there if I was willing to knock them down to ten by ten. You could pretend you were watching film on a screen ten miles away. Who cares about 640 by 480?"

"Fine," he said. "But what about one or two films?"

Durr. There it was, staring me in the face. If you wanted to distribute just a couple of films, at very high resolution, with four or five audio-tracks and some additional material, thirty-two gigs was *plenty*. They'd rattle around with all the space left over. And that's when the plan came together.

Aziz not only had a thousand thumb-drives; he also had a shelf full of bulk-writers for them, ones that would take fifty at a time and let you write a disk-image to all of them at once. We packaged up the leaked copy of Part 18 along with a couple hundred of the best piss-takes from Cynical April, along with a little video that we all worked on together, piecing it together using the dialog from the actual film and its earlier parts, cutting in one word at a time to have a blur of actors explain:

"When you go to see terrible shows like this one, you just give money to the people who are destroying our country with corrupt, evil laws. Your children are being sent to jail by laws bought with the money from your purchase. Don't give them your gold. If you must see this stupid film, do it at home and keep your money for better things. Make your own art. Originality is just combining things that no one ever thought to combine before." Some of the word choices were a bit odd—all eighteen parts combined had the vocabulary of a reader for a toddler—but it worked brilliantly.

Some of 26's anarchist pals were deep pros at making T-shirts; they lent us their silk-screening kit and showed us how to make a little grid of skull-crossbones logos with PLAYME written beneath. We lined up the loaded thumbs on the pub floor in a grid that matched the skulls on the screen and sprayed sloppy red and black identifiers on the footballs, straight over the naff old Major League Soccer marks.

Finally, we used one of Aziz's specialist printers to run off thousands of feet of scarlet nylon ribbon printed with the same manifesto that we'd loaded into the thumbs, and signed it THE JAMMIE DODGERS. I thought that Jem might mind—it was his and Dodger's thing, after all—but he just grinned and shrugged and said, "I'd have a lot of nerve to complain about you pirating from me, wouldn't I? I positively *insist,* mate."

So we threaded lengths of ribbon through all of the footballs and tied them off. We filled urethane shopping bags with them, and admired our handiwork.

"Now," said Chester, "how do you plan on getting them to people before they buy their tickets? Hand them out at some tube station or something?" If there was one thing that Jem's begging signs had taught us all, it was how to efficiently distribute small free items to commuters going into and coming out of the underground.

I shook my head and swilled some of the mulled wine that we'd made to warm up the night, spat a clove back into my cup. "Naw. Too inefficient. We want to get these to people who are actually planning on seeing the film, right before they stump up their money. Maximum impact." That was the whole idea: maximum impact. A film makes most of its gross on the all-important opening weekend. Attack the box-office take from that weekend and you attacked the studio at its weakest, most vulnerable point.

"I'm going to give them out in Leicester Square," I said. "On opening night."

They all gaped at me. 26 looked worried, then delighted, then worried again.

Jem put a thumb up. "All right," he said. "Why not? Go big or go home, right?"

Like any red-blooded English lad. I have seen approximately one million commando raids conducted with stopwatch precision, thanks to the all-popular military/terrorism thriller genre. I knew how to assemble the pieces: we needed cover, we needed countermeasures, we needed escape routes.

Cover: The enemy had given this one to us. Ever since the cinemas had introduced mandatory metal-detectors and coat-checks for phones and computers, every film opening looks more like an airport security queue, with a long snake of bored, angry people shuffling slowly toward a couple of shaved-head thugs who'll grope them, run them through a metal detector, and take their phone and laptop and that off them, just in case they're one of the mythological screen-cappers.

This is London. Where you have a queue of people with money, you have a small ecosystem of tramps, hawkers, and human spam—delivery systems passing out brochures, cards, and loot-bags advertising cheap curry, dodgy minicabs, Chinese

Tun-La massage (whatever that is), American pizza, Minneapolis Fried Chicken, strip clubs, and discount fashion outlets.

This would be our cover. Chester had found us an enormous bag filled with lurid purple T-shirts in a skip, advertising a defunct Internet café (most of them had gone bust since the Theft of Intellectual Property Act raids began). They were gigantic, designed to hang to your knees, turning the wearer into a walking billboard. To these, we added baseball caps from a stall in Petticoat Lane Market that was happy to part with them as they were worn and a bit scuffed.

Countermeasures: These caps were our countermeasures. Between the baggy shirts and the hats, it would be hard for the CCTVs to pick us up or track us (Chester had read a thriller novel that said that a handful of gravel in one shoe each, would add enough randomness to make our gaits unrecognizable to the automated systems working the cameras).

But just to be sure, Aziz hooked us up with strings of miniature infrared LEDs, little pinhead things that we painstakingly stitched around the brims with electrical thread that ran into a fingernail-sized power-pack that took a watch battery. These would strobe ultrabright infrared light that was invisible to the human eye, but was blinding to the CCTVs.

Or so Aziz said. He told us that the cameras were all sensitive into the infrared range so that they could take pictures in poor light, and that they automatically dialed up the sensitivity to max when the sun went down. As they strained to capture the glimmers of IR emitted by our faces, we would overwhelm them with the bright, invisible light. (Not that we told Aziz exactly what we were planning; as Jem said, the less he knew, the less he could be done for not reporting. Aziz didn't seem to mind.)

Aziz had a pile of CCTVs (Aziz had a pile of everything), and he had me put on the hat and walk around in front of it for a time, walking close and far, even looking straight at it, with the hat on. Then he showed us the video: there I was, but where my head was supposed to be, there was just a white indistinct blob, like my noggin had been replaced by a poltergeist that manifested itself as ball lightning.

Escape routes: Piss easy. Leicester Square is a rat-run of alleyways, roads, and pass-throughs that run through the lobbies of clubs, restaurants, and cinemas, leading down to the heaving crowds of Trafalgar Square, up into the mazed alleys of Chinatown, toward the throngs of Piccadilly to the west and the street performers and hawkers of Covent Garden to the east. In other words, getting from Leicester Square to the anonymous depths of central London was only a matter of going a few steps, finding a doorway to shuck your purple shirt and baseball hat in, and then you'd be whistling on your way to safety.

It was a mad rush to get it all sorted in time for the big night. We worked around the clock silk-screening, wiring, writing disk-images, planning routes. I saw Aziz's thumb-drives exactly ten days before opening night. I had the idea the next morning, leaving us with nine days.

By day eight, it was clear we weren't going to make it. I reckoned that to give out one thousand thumb-drives, we'd need at least fifteen people on distribution, which meant wiring up fifteen hats, and the hats were turning out to be a right beast. Aziz had shown me how to do it ten times, but soldering the flexible wire was harder than it looked, and I ruined two hats completely before I did even one.

26 promised me that she would be able to dig up ten more helpers through Cynical April. They had to be absolutely trustworthy, with nerves of steel. She knew which helpers had been the best when we were getting the word out on TIP, and which of them had been the nerviest when it came to sorting secret parties. We agreed that we'd bring them in at the last minute, to minimize the chance that one would blab our plan.

With forty-eight hours to go, I was a wreck. We only had three hats done, half the drives hadn't been flashed, and I hadn't slept for more than a few hours a day. I'd drunk so much coffee that my eyes wouldn't focus and my hands were shaking so hard I couldn't hold the soldering iron. Rabid Dog was trying to take over from me, but he didn't have a clue how to do it.

"No, shit, not like that!" I said as he burned the hat with the hot iron, filling the table with the stink of burnt plastic. "Shit man, you've *ruined* it. You retard—"

26 crossed the room in three quick steps and grabbed my flailing arms and pinned them to my sides. "Enough. That is quite enough of that. You. Are. Going. To. *Bed*." I started to object and she shook her head furiously, her mohican's ponytail flopping from side to side. "I don't want to hear it. You're going to make a complete balls-up of this adventure if you don't get some sleep—get us all arrested, if I don't kill you first. Now, apologize to Dog."

She was right. I hung my head. "Sorry, Dog. I was out of order."

He muttered something. I felt miserable. Dog was better about talking these days, sure, but when you were cruel to him, he went right back into his own head and pulled the door shut behind him. Jem glared at me. It seemed they were all furious with me. I recognized the paranoid, angry feeling for what it was: massive sleep deprivation and caffeine overdose. Time to go to bed.

I woke fourteen hours later, feeling like weights had been tied to my arms and legs by a merry prankster who finished the job by gluing my eyes shut with wheatpaste and then taking a foul, runny shit in my mouth. Yes, I know that this is a gratuitously disgusting way of describing it. Take comfort, dear reader, in the knowledge that it is not one half so disgusting as the taste in my mouth.

I staggered to the second-floor toilet and turned the tap on all the way. As always, there was a groaning and a sputtering and a coughing, and then it began to trickle cold water. The pressure up here was almost nil, and there were fittings for an old pump that was long gone that might have corrected it. As it was, it took forty-five minutes for the toilet cistern to fill up between flushes.

Every now and then we'd joke about complaining to the land-lord.

I slurped up as much of the water as I could get out of the tap, then changed into a brown corduroy bathrobe that 26 had surprised me with when the weather turned. I added a pair of rubber shower-sandals and made my way back down into the pub room, moving like I was underwater as the residual sleep and fatigue tugged at my flesh.

It was a hive of brightly lit, bustling activity, filled with happy chatter and speedy, efficient motion. Memory sticks were loaded, silk-screened and tied up with ribbon. Hats were stitched, soldered, powered, and tested. It looked like a proper assembly line. Only one problem: I didn't recognize any of the people doing the work.

They all stopped and looked at me when I walked into the room. Someone's phone was playing jangly dance music, DJ mixes that I'd heard on Cynical April. There were four of them, two boys and two girls, about my age or a bit older, with strange, pudding-bowl haircuts and multicolored dye-jobs that matched their multicolored, chipped nail-varnish (even the blokes). They had ragged tennis shoes that were held together with tape and safety pins, black cargo trousers with loads of little pockets, and cut-down business shirts with all the collars, sleeves, and pockets torn away.

"You'd be Cecil, then," said one of the girls. She had a funny accent. Not English or Scottish. Foreign.

"Y-e-s," I said slowly.

"Right," she said, and beamed at me, showing me the little skulls laser-etched into the enamel of her front teeth. "I'm Kooka, and these are Gertie, Tomas, and Hans the Viking." Hans didn't look anything like a viking. He looked like a stiff breeze might knock him down. What was it about wimpy blokes and big, macho nicknames? But he was smiling in a friendly way, as were the others, and waving, and I waved back, still not sure what to make of these strangers.

"Are you friends of—"

"We're friends of the Jammie Dodgers!" Tomas declared. He pronounced it "ze Chammie Dodtchers!"

"We're your reinforcements," Kooka said. "We've come from Berlin to help!"

"Berlin?"

"We'd have been here sooner, but the hitchhiking was awful," she said. "Not least coming up from bloody Dover after we got off the ferry. It's like English drivers have never seen someone hitching a ride before!"

I shook my head and sat down. "I see. Erm. Who the hell are you?"

"We're from Cynical April!" Kooka said. "It's not so complicated. We've been on the boards forever, from way back. We're the German wing." Hans cleared his throat. "German and Swedish," Kooka said. "We've been fighting off the same bastards at home for years and it seemed like a holiday was in order."

I felt my mouth open and shut of its own accord. Part of me was made up that we had this help, and so exotic and energetic, with their hitchhiking and that. Part of me was furious that 26 had brought in outsiders without asking me. But the enraged part couldn't work up much fury—I seemed to have burned out all my capacity to be furious, spending it on the weeklong binge of coffee and work.

26 appeared from the kitchen, teetering under a tray carrying our teapot, a stack of our chipped, mismatched cups, the sugar bowl, the cream jug, and a small mountain of posh little health-food seed-cakes that had turned up in the skip of a fancy delicatessen in Mayfair.

"The creature lives!" she said, handing me the tray and giving me a hard kiss on the neck. I handed the tray off to two of the Germans—or Swedes, or whatever—and gave her a cuddle.

"This is a surprise," I said.

"Surprise!" she said, and tickled my ribs. I danced back, squirming. She was grinning with pride. What was left of my anger evaporated. "I didn't want to say anything because I half believed they wouldn't make it. I mean, hitchhiking!"

"You must try it!" Kooka said. "It's the only way to travel. All the best people do it."

"But now they're here, we're in great shape! Kooka's done all sorts of stunts and raids, isn't that right?"

Kooka curtsied and the other nodded. "We're superheroes. Legends in our own minds. The scourge of Berlin!" She gestured at the works all around her. "And we're nearly done with all this rubbish."

It was true. What we'd struggled with for a week, they'd made short work of in a few hours. Of course, we'd spent a week getting all the kinks out of the production, making expensive mistakes and learning from them. The Germans had the benefit of all those lessons and, what's more, weren't crippled by sleep deprivation, squabbling, and caffeine shakes. So they had kicked quantities of ass and torn through the remaining work in no time.

"Ya," Hans said. "Then, the party begins!"

Which, indeed, it did. The next several hours were a blur. We started off heading down to Leicester Square, ostensibly to familiarize the Germans with the escape routes (the local volunteers wouldn't need any of that). It was sparkling, of course, even though it was only a Wednesday, buzzing with the chatter of thousands of people going into and out of the cinemas. I loved Leicester Square at night: the lights, the glamour, the grifters and tramps, the tourists and hen nights, the spliff and the brochure-ware spammers. It was like some other world where entertainment and fantasy ruled.

No one else seemed to have the same reaction. The Germans laughed at the slow, waddling coppers, climbed up on the wrought iron fence around the garden to get a view and then backtucked off it, landing on springheels like gymnasts. Rabid Dog cheered them in an uncharacteristic display of public enthusiasm. Jem joined in, and then the rest of us. Jem climbed up on the fence and gave it a try, though the rest of us told him he was insane and would split his skull. He surprised us all by doing a very credible backflip, though he landed heavily and staggered into a posh couple who shoved him off. He brushed himself off coolly and accepted our applause, then whistled the little two-note warning the drugs kids used that meant *coppers* and we saw the PCSOs heading our way and scarpered, up through Chinatown, up to Soho, threading through the crowds and stealing down alleys so skinny we had to turn sideways to pass.

26 said, "There's a big Confusing Peach get-together near here tonight." She pulled out her phone and made her most adorably cute face at it, poking at the screen until it gave up the address.

The parties that got listed on Confusing Peach of the Forest Green Beethoven were less exclusive and weird than the inner-circle events on Cynical April, but this one was held in an interlocking set of coal-cellars we reached through an unmarked staircase between two skips behind a posh Chinese restaurant. The cellars were narrow and low-ceilinged and they throbbed with music from cheap speakers that had been glue-gunned to the walls at regular intervals. There were so many people in that claustrophobic space that you were always touching someone, usually two or three people, and the music was so loud you could only be heard by pressing your face into someone's ear and shouting.

It was brilliant.

Twenty and I danced these weird, horny dances that were half-snogging, and I could feel people on all sides of me doing the same. Someone passed me a propelled inhaler full of sugar and I stared at it stupidly. I had never tried it, even though there was plenty for sale around the Zeroday of course. I guess I'd just heard all those scare stories at school and in brochures and on the sides of buses and so on, and I was halfway convinced that one hit would turn me into a raving addict who'd kill his own mother for another gasp of the sweet stuff.

Of course, I'd heard all the same stuff about spliff—the evil, evil skunk that would melt my mind and make me the perverted love-slave of some dealer who'd peddle my doped-up arse to twisted vicars and City boys until I was spoilt meat. I'd smoked spliff for years and the worst thing it did to me was make me lazy and slow the next day. And for all that they said that weed led to the hard stuff, I'd never found myself led anywhere.

They were wrong about spliff, so maybe they were wrong about sugar. I laughed: it wasn't grass that led me to the harder stuff, it was all the BS about grass. And then I realized that this meant I was about to take a puff off the inhaler, and my heart started hammering and the room seemed to zoom away from me as I brought it to my nose and touched the button on the bottom.

Blam! The gas-charge fired the sweet gas deep down my lungs, down to those little grape-clusters on the ends of the branches where the oxygen crossed over and entered my bloodstream. Only this wasn't oxygen: this was sugar, and my tongue felt like it had been drenched with honey even before I felt any other effects. Then I felt the other effects, just like you read about in the Sunday paper confessionals: "I was a gasper and it cost me everything." A feeling of supreme confidence. A feeling like time was stretching out, like I could reach out and catch a bullet. A feeling like I could see the connections between everyone and everything, all the little invisible strands that tied it all together, and like I could reach out and tug at the strands and make the universe dance like a marionette.

The feeling ebbed away as fast as it came, leaving me back in my boots, knees a bit weak, practically being held up by the sweaty bodies on every side of me. 26 was giving me a look that was half-worried, half-angry, and she plucked the inhaler out of my hand and passed it off to someone else. She put her lips up to my ear and shouted over the noise: "What was that about? Since when do you take sugar?"

I shrugged. I didn't know why I'd done it. And I wasn't feeling entirely back in my own skin just yet. Twenty's face screwed up lemon-sour and she walked off. I started to go after her, then gave up, feeling deliciously angry at her: who was she to tell me what to do with my life?

So I went back to dancing, dancing with the press of bodies and the thunder of music, and someone passed me another inhaler, but this time, I passed on it—the dancing was obliterating my worries and my insecurities perfectly, and I didn't want to take the risk that I might lose that peace and have to start thinking about what it meant that Twenty had gone off on her own in a right fury.

I moved from corridor to corridor, room to room, seeing people I vaguely recognized from different parties and events I'd been to since we all got on Confusing Peach. I stuck my head in one room and found that it was full of writhing, snogging couples. Embarrassed, I withdrew my head quickly, then I looked back in again. Had I just seen what I thought I'd seen?

I had.

There, back in the corner, two blokes kissing furiously. That wasn't unheard of at Confusing Peach events, plenty of the people on the boards were openly gay. But the two *specific* blokes who were kissing were Rabid Dog and Jem.

Rabid Dog seemed to feel my eyes on him and he looked up and met my gaze, then squirmed away from Jem, a look that was a cross between humiliation and terror in his eyes. Jem looked around, surprised, and saw me. He shrugged and turned back to Dog. I left the party.

As I made my way through Soho toward Trafalgar Square and the night buses, I wondered why I was so weirded out. I hadn't known many openly gay people in Bradford, though I'd once seen the gay pride parade and after an initial shock, I'd found it to be quite a lot of fun: clearly the people involved were having the time of their lives and they weren't hurting anyone, so why shouldn't I support them?

And after I came down to London, I saw *loads* of gay people, and not just on Confusing Peach. Loads of Twenty's anarchist friends called themselves "queer," though that seemed to mean different things. Soho was a gay district, filled with bars and restaurants that flew rainbow flags and had loads of same-sex couples hanging around. Like the people at the pride parade, they all seemed to be having a good time with each other and there were precious few good times around, so why should I begrudge them theirs?

But seeing Rabid Dog and Jem had done my head in, I admit it. Partly it was the feeling that I didn't really know them. How many times had we sat around before a night out, talking about girls and whether we'd meet any and what we'd do when we did? Had that all been lies? Had I pissed them off with what I'd said?

It wasn't just that. Partly, it was the picture of the two of them as a couple, maybe rolling around in bed the way that 26 and I did. The mental image made me squirm and feel all weird and discombobulated.

I found myself wishing that I had more sugar, and I found that I was also horrified to realize this. When I'd taken the sugar, the world had had a kind of clarity that I was already missing—I knew where everything belonged and how it fit, and knew that I was exactly where I needed to be, doing exactly what I needed to do. Of course, in my head, I knew that no one was ever exactly perfectly in the right place, and if you were, why would you do anything else, anyway? But I missed that feeling, even though it had been an illusion.

After all, my girlfriend wasn't talking to me, my two best friends were trying to dissolve each others' faces with saliva, and I was about to commit an act of artistic terrorism in the middle of one of the most policed, surveilled, and controlled cities in the world. A little comfort would have gone a long way.

I woke up the next morning alone and miserable. My head felt like it was two sizes too small for my brain, which I reckoned was the sugar, though it might have been all the cheap lager or the skunk or just the two hours I'd spent crying and wallowing in self-pity before dropping off to sleep finally.

The Germans were spark out and snoring in the pub room, two sleeping end-to-end on the sofa, two more on bedrolls on the floor. They didn't even notice when I switched on the light (and then quickly switched it off when I saw them), and I tiptoed into the kitchen to make myself a brew and get my lappie. I was sure that 26 had sent me email by now and if she hadn't, I was going to send her some, and though part of me yearned to tick her off for being such a pissy prude about my taking sugar, a bigger part of me wanted to grovel for her forgiveness.

When I got back upstairs to my room, there was Jem sitting at my edit-desk, feet up on the table, reading an old film magazine from the pile by my bed. He looked up when I came in the room, then nodded his head toward the bed.

"Have a seat," he said.

I sat, putting my brew and lappie down on the floor.

"Time we had a talk," he said.

I held up a hand. "No need," I said. "None of my business."

"You're right about that. No one's business but mine and his. But if you're his mate, you should know some things. So sharpen your ears, my old chum, and hearken to what Jem has to say.

"I never had no trouble with who I am or what I am. To me, it's always been natural that I'd spend some time with girls and some time with blokes." He winked. "Not ugly sods like you, of course, don't get no ideas. But as far back as I can remember, I've felt like either could be right for me."

I nodded, hoping that I was seeming cool about it, though again, it made me feel squirmy in a way I couldn't get my head around.

He blew out a sigh. "Look, I know it's not the usual, normal thing. Everyone expects you to grow up to be a big strapping lad and spend your whole life trying to get your end away with some girl, not some other big strapping lad. But everyone also expects you to live in a flat you're paying rent for, to buy your food at the grocer's, and to call yourself by your given name instead of some daft handle like 'Rabid Dog' or 'Cecil B. DeVil.' I say, bugger everyone, bugger their expectations, and bugger anyone who thinks less of me for who I fancy."

"Can't argue with that," I said with as much conviction as I could manage.

"Except you want to, old son, I can see that from here. You don't like it. It makes you go all skin-crawly, don't it? It's okay, you can admit it."

I shook my head. "Jem, I don't—I mean, look, you're still my mate and you're right, who you fancy, that's up to you. But yeah, I don't like to picture it."

He punched me in the shoulder. "You're afraid if you think about it too much you'll end up turning queer, yeah? That's what all this business is, blokes all being hyper-manly and calling each other *faggot* and so on. It's that fear that it might just be too nice to resist—getting together with another lad who wants it as much as you do, the way you do, who understands the way no bird can—"

"Enough," I said.

He laughed. "Look, don't worry about it. Take it from someone who's tried it both ways, it's not better, it's not worse, it's just different. And you'll know if you go that way, and when you do know, it won't be difficult to detect. It'll be as obvious to you as two plus two is four. You remember how you carried on about 26 when you first met her? That feeling? You'll not be mistaken about that feeling if you feel it again."

"Fine," I said. "I get it. And you're right, it's naught to do with me, what you and Dog do. Anything to keep him from locking himself in the loo for a wank, anyway."

"I'll do my part for the squad, cap'n. About Dog, though—" He looked uncomfortable. "Look, I should leave this for him to tell you, but he won't, and that's why I've got to say it. Dog ain't like me. He's exclusive to boys. Always has been, ever since he could remember. And one day he made the mistake of telling his older brother about it. His brother, who he looked up to like a hero.

"His brother beat six kinds of shit out of him, and then told their parents. His dad wasn't an understanding sort—which explains his brother's treachery—and he had all kinds of nicknames for Dog, 'the little fairy,' and so on. He wasn't shy about using these endearments in front of the other kids around the estate, and became clear to them that no one—not his dad, not his brother—would come to his defense, which was like bloody mince in shark-infested water. He was every bully's favorite punching bag, the punchline to every cruel joke. You've told me some of what you went through in Bradford. I went through my own this and that before I lighted out for Bloody London. But neither of us ever went through what Dog went through. Neither of us have half the guts that podgy little bastard has. He's quiet and he's broken in lots of ways, sure, but he's not anyone's victim anymore. Never will be.

"Which is why you need to make a point of telling him, as quickly and sincerely as you can, that everything you said about me goes triple for him. You're still his mate, you don't think any less of him, that sort of thing. He needs to hear that soonest so that he knows whether you and he are on the same side still, or whether he needs to figure out how to find some new people to hang about with. Understand me?"

"Yeah," I said. " 'Course. No problem."

"And when you're done with him, you'd better find 26 and make up to her for whatever had her so furious last night. I saw her leaving the party—looked like a bulldog chewing a wasp. We've got a major operation tomorrow night, sonny, and we can't afford to have any dissent in the ranks."

I left Twenty messages in all the usual places asking her to call me, hinting that I wanted to apologize for being such a dick.

Then it was a matter of waiting for her to get back to me and for Rabid Dog to wake up and make an appearance and for the Germans in our parlor to rouse themselves—wait, wait, wait.

26 called me first.

"Hi," I said.

She didn't say anything. The silence on the line was proper intense.

"I'm sorry, all right? I'd never done that before, and I don't plan on doing it again. I guess I just—you know, got overexcited. It was stupid of me. I'm sorry."

Still nothing.

"Look," I said. "Look, it was just one mistake. It wasn't even that good—" Except it was, it had been fantastic in a way that was kind of scary and not altogether unpleasant. "Okay, tell a lie. It *was* good. It made me feel like I could rule the world." I swallowed. My mouth was off on its own now, talking without any intervention on my part. "But I've felt that good before. When I'm with you." It was easily the soppiest thing I'd ever said and until I said it, I had no idea that I was about to say it. And then I said it and I knew it was true.

"You're an idiot," she said. I could tell that she wasn't angry anymore.

"I am," I said. "Can I be your idiot?"

"Come over to my flat tonight. I've got to revise for a maths quiz tomorrow. Calculus. Ugh."

"I'll help you revise," I said.

"By doing your usual impression of Cecil the Human Boob-Juggling Octopus? You will come and sit in the corner and contemplate your sins, young man. If you're very good, you might get a crust of bread and a tiny snog before I send you home. I expect you to be very grateful for this."

"I will be," I said around the grin that was threatening to split my head in two. What a lass.

I felt like a huge weight had been lifted from my chest, like

I'd been holding my breath overnight and could finally exhale properly. I could hear the Germans stirring downstairs and muttering in their language. I skipped down the stairs and said good morning and played host, making tea, bringing out some of the nicest treats in my larder. They were remarkably easy to chat with, and fun besides, and had had plenty of adventures in Berlin. Berlin was apparently the land of a thousand squats and they were well up for me going out and visiting them there.

I was daydreaming about how I could swing it—I'd have to wait until I could apply for a passport on my own in a few months at least—when Rabid Dog poked his head in the pub room. He scanned the room, blushed to the tips of his ears, and retreated up the stairs.

" 'Scuse me," I said, and set off after him.

I ran him to ground on the top-floor landing, headed into the big loft room where we stashed the spare bits of furnishing that we scrounged off London's curbs and in its skips.

"Dog," I said, "got a sec?"

He wouldn't meet my eye, but he didn't say no (nor yes, of course), and I took this for assent. I perched on a wobbly tabletop and thought hard about what to say next.

"Look," I said. "Jem was in to chat with me this morning. About your situation, like. Your dad and brother and that. I guess I just wanted to say that I think it's shit what they done to you, and it was, like, uncalled for." The opposite of what had happened earlier with Twenty was unfolding now, my mouth running away with dire stupidity while my brain looked on in horror. "I mean, Christ, I don't care who you shag. Shag anything. It's none of my business, is it? Whatever makes you happy. 'Course, not if it's like a kid or an animal or whatever, that's wrong. Not that being gay is like wanting to stick it in a dog!" I closed my mouth and stared at him.

He was staring back at me with a look of such unbelieving horror on his face that he'd forgot to be shy. I understood where he was coming from. I couldn't believe the miserable, bizarre stuff I was spouting. I clamped my mouth shut tighter and did the only thing I could think of.

I punched myself, as hard as I could, across the jaw. It turns out that despite the awkward angle, you can really hit yourself *very* hard in the face. I hit myself so hard that I knocked myself off the table and onto the floor.

Hitting yourself in the face as hard as you can is an experience I actually recommend, having done it. Not because it feels good, but because it feels bad in a bad way that nothing else you'll ever experience feels bad. I've actually been punched very hard in the face by someone else, when I wasn't expecting it, and that was terrible, but not nearly as terrible as this (though I think he actually hit me harder than I did). I think it was the knowledge that I had inflicted this pain on myself, deliberately. The stupid, it burns. Or throbs, really.

I rolled around on the floor for a moment, waiting for the stars to stop detonating behind my scrunched-tight eyelids.

"Holy God, that *hurt*," I said, and got to my feet. Dog was watching me with his jaw literally resting on his chest. "Oh, excuse me, Mr. Horror Film Gorefest. You've never seen someone break free of an intense attack of the stupids by beating the piss out of himself?"

He laughed aloud. "That was literally the dumbest thing I've ever seen," he said. "Well done, mate."

"Yeah," I said, and rubbed at my jaw. I could already feel the swelling there. "Well, someone had to do it and you're clearly too much of a pussy to punch me when I deserve it."

He laughed and as I was laughing, he managed to flick a finger, hard, square into the bruise that I was developing on my chin. "Pussy, huh?"

"Right," I said. "Let me try this again. First, let me say this: who you fancy or shag or whatever? That is none of my business. Next: also, I have nothing but the utmost respect and admiration for your sexual proclivities and congratulate you on them with-out reservation."

He gave me a golf–clap, but it was a friendly one, and he was smiling. "You're an idiot, Cecil," he said.

"So I've been told. But at least my heart's in the right place, right?"

"You are forgiven," he said. "Look, just so you know, I don't fancy you, okay? So you don't have to worry."

"Are you saying I'm not fancyable?"

He rolled his eyes. "No, Cecil. I'm sure that there are many boys who weep for the fact that you go for the ladies. But I'm not one of them. Ego satisfied?"

"Yes," I said. "That will do nicely."

He came over shy again, looking at his toes. "Cec," he said so quietly I could barely hear him.

"Yeah?"

"Just, well, it was nice of you to say that. Means something, okay?"

"Okay," I said, and found that I had a lump in my throat.

True to her word, 26 showed up with six of her friends in tow at exactly 7:15. We met in the shadow of Nelson's Column in Trafalgar Square, the 169-foot-tall pillar topped with a bird-spattered statue of Lord Admiral Nelson, a bloke who apparently did something important involving boats at some point in the past several hundred years.

It was a good place to gather. By day, Trafalgar Square was a favorite with the tourists, and there were always people coming and going. Human spammers were common, and you often saw them taking their lunch breaks on the steps or benches or in the shadow of the National Portrait Gallery at the top of the square.

We huddled up tight and went over the plan together, 26 leading the lesson, making each person recite his or her part of the plan, along with three escape routes. It was simple enough: "I pull down my shirt and put on the hat and turn on the lights and make my way to Leicester Square. I pick a spot in the Odeon queue and work my way down it, saying 'Free films, free films,' handing out the thumb-drives as fast as I can. Don't argue with anyone. Don't stop to talk. Keep my face down. After seven minutes or when I run out—whichever comes first—I walk quickly away. My first escape route is down through Trafalgar Square. My second is up to Chinatown. My third is east to Covent Garden. I step into the second doorway I pass and take off the hat and shirt and put them in my bag, then head *back* the way I came, toward Leicester Square, and go around it to my next escape route. We regroup in Soho on Greek Street at 7:25. Any trouble, call 0587534525 and enter my serial number, which is 4."

The phone number was one of those free voice-boxes. It came with a touch-tone or voice-menu, and I could access it using my prepaid mobile if someone didn't turn up within ten minutes of the appointed time.

"If I think I'm being followed, I go to the nearest tube station and board the first train, ride five stops, get out, and check to see if I can still see my tails. If they're there, I sit down on a bench and read a book for half an hour and see what they do. If not, I get back on the tube and go home, after leaving my serial number, which is 4, at 0587534526." We'd got another voice mail drop for this eventuality.

Once we'd each said it, quickly and perfectly, we put on our shirts and hats, openly, just as we would if we were any other gang of human spammers who'd just been given the night's briefing by our manager. Then we trooped in a loose line up to Leicester Square, the purple shirts hanging down to our knees, the hatbrims obscuring our faces. Other peoples' attention slid away from us as they avoided eye contact with a potential handbill-shover. I wished I'd thought to get some handbills from some real human spammer for us to carry into battle. Nothing made Londoners get out of the way faster than the sight of someone trying to give them an advertisement for some takeaway curry house or discount fitness club.

The mission went *perfectly*. We hit the queue in an orderly mass, half of us on its left, half on its right. It was drizzling out, which was normal for autumn in London, and the early September twilight mixed with the water made the whole square dark and gloomy. The forest of unfurled umbrellas provided excellent cover from the CCTVs and PCSOs and coppers with their hat-brim cameras. We efficiently went up and down the line, barking "Free films!" and handing out our little footballs. I could hear little surprised noises rippling through the queue as some people read the ribbon's message and worked out what they'd just been given, but by then I'd given out my lot of sixty-seven footballs. I checked my phone: less than seven minutes had elapsed.

I wadded up the nylon carrier bag I'd brought the boodle in and shoved it into my pocket, then turned on my heel and struck out back to Trafalgar Square. Again, I wished I had some fliers I could hold to make the crowd part—it was getting thick. I kept checking my reflection in the drizzle-fogged windows of the restaurants and office buildings on the way out of the square, looking for a tail, but I didn't see any. I concluded, tentatively, that I'd made it out of the square without being followed.

Back to the rendezvous, Greek Street, with its pretheater Soho throng and the office people who'd gone home and changed into their woo-party! outfits trickling back in, and we were just a bunch of teenagers, giggly and bouncy. Everyone made it. We got on the tube and headed back to the Zeroday, absolutely drunk on delight.

Chapter 5

We all had theories about what would happen next. I thought that the cinema people would go totally mental and announce a fatwa on all of us, releasing weird, blurry CCTV footage of our costumed army with our fuzzed-out heads; cut to apoplectic industry spokesdroid who'd call us terrorists and declare us to be the greatest-ever threat to the film industry, while solemnly intoning the millions we'd cost them with our stunt.

All the rest of the night, and then the rest of the weekend, we reloaded as many news sources as we could find, searched on every search term. All we found were a few bemused tweets and that from people who'd been in the queue; almost everyone, it seemed, had discarded the booty we'd distributed or not bothered to plug it in.

In hindsight, I could see that this made perfect sense. No one cared about what a human spammer shoved into your hands, it was assumed that anything you got that way was junk. That's why they had to hand out so many brochures to get a single person to sign up for a gym membership or whatnot. Add to that the antique media—you couldn't even do a rub-transfer, you had to fit it to a USB connector, and half the PCs I saw these days didn't even have one—and the risks of sticking dodgy files on your computer and it was perfectly reasonable that nearly all of our little footballs went in the bin.

What a misery.

"I'm a flop," I said, lying awake and rigid on Sunday night, while Twenty sat up and worked on her chem homework for the next morning. "I might as well go back to Bradford. What a child I was to think that I could beat them. They're bloody *huge*.

They practically run the government. They're going to shut down every channel for showing around video except the ones they control, and no one will be able to be a filmmaker except through them. It's just like music—the way they went after every music download site they couldn't control."

26 gave no sign of even hearing me, just working through her problem-set, tapping on the screen and at the keyboard.

"The worst part is that I got all those people out there, used up all their time, put them all at risk, and it was for nothing. They must think I'm an absolute tosser. I want to stick my head in the ground for a million years. Maybe then, everyone will have forgot my stupidity and shame."

Twenty set down her laptop and blew at the fringe of her mohican that fell across her forehead. She'd died it candy-apple red that week. "Cecil, you're wallowing. It is a deeply unattractive sight. What's more: it is a piece of enormous ego for you to decide that we all were led into this by you, like lambs led by a shepherd. We went into Leicester Square on Friday because we *all* thought it would work. You didn't make the plan, you got it started. We all made the plan. We all cocked up. But do you see RD or Chester or Jem moping? Look at the bloody Germans! They're out in Hackney tonight, trying to sneak into all-hours clubs and planning on drinking their faces off no matter what! So leave it out, all right?"

She was right, of course. Not that I felt any better about it. "All right, you're right. It's not just about me. But it's still awful and rotten and miserable. What do we do? They buy the laws, attack our families, put us in prison—"

26 picked up her laptop again. "Cecil, I don't want to talk to you when you're like this. You know the answer as well as I do: you're doing something that they want you to stop. They fear what you do. They fear what we all do. So long as you keep doing it, you're winning. You don't need to go on a commando raid to beat them: you just need to keep on making your own films."

I don't think anyone ever said anything more important to me than those ten words: "you just need to keep on making your own films."

I threw myself into the project, stopping work only long enough to eat and snatch a few hours sleep, or to go out for a little fishing in the skips to find some food. I hardly left my room apart from that. My skin grew pale from the hours indoors, and I noticed that when I went up and down the stairs, I felt all sorts of awkward pulling and pinching sensations from deep in my muscles, especially around my bum and back and neck. 26 said I was sitting too much and made me download some yoga videos, which we did together in my room when she could force me off the box.

But she wasn't pissed at me. No one was, that was the amazing thing. I was editing furiously, putting together films in ways that just seemed to appear behind my eyes and in my fingers—first a scene with Scot fighting vampires that pulled together all kinds of vampires from more than a century's worth of filmmaking, including the magnificently creepy Max Schreck, upsampled for some retrospective festival that the BFI had done. Rabid Dog spent an afternoon watching over my shoulder as I worked, and he was *amazing*—I'd never dreamt that anyone could know that much about vampire films. By the time the scene was done, I had a new appreciation for vampire films, and I decided that I would expand my scene into an entire short film, in which Scot is a distressed older gentleman, alone in the world, who befriends a young boy (also Scot, which worked surprisingly well), and discovers that vampires are on the loose in his town. Unlike the other videos I'd done, I didn't really play this one for laughs: it was straight up action-horror, and it took the combined might of my encyclopedic knowledge of Scot's thousands of hours' of footage and Dog's insane horror obsession to pull it off.

We worked on it for three weeks straight, editing and editing, subjecting our housemates to rough cuts. The idea was to polish out all the seams, all the places where it became clear that these were footage from different films. I dropped them all into black and white to correct for the different color balances in the different sources, then I punched up the shadows on a frame-by-frame basis, giving it the dramatic contrast of some of the older, scarier horror films that Dog made me sit through. Some days I spent hours just shaving out individual pixels, rubbing out the edges, until one day, I watched all twenty-two minutes of it and realized it was *perfect*.

"This is as good as anything I've ever seen at the cinema," 26 said from her perch on the sofa arm. "Honestly."

"But no one'd show this at any cinema," Jem said. "Not in a million years. Too weird. Wrong length. Black and white. Sorry, mate, but I think the best you'll do is a couple bazillion hits on ZeroKTube or similar."

I didn't say anything. Some old ideas I'd had were knocking together in a new way. I restarted the video and we all watched it through again. It was bloody scary. The kind of thing that made the hairs on your neck stand up—partly that was the way the organ music worked. That was another Dog find—it had come from a fifth-rate monster film, but the director had scored it in a huge old cathedral with the original organ, and you could really hear the reverberations of the low notes in a way that was flat-out *spooky*.

"Imagine seeing this somewhere *really* spooky," I said. "Someplace that actually feels haunted. Not on some tetchy laptop screen—somewhere *dangerous*."

"Like the graveyard," Chester said. "That night we all met up. That was brilliant. But it's too cold and wet for that sort of nonsense right now, mate. It'd have to wait for next summer."

"Someplace *like* the graveyard, but someplace indoors. Underground." I snatched up my laptop and went back to my favorite infiltration site. There was a whole subculture of mentalists who spent their nights breaking into boarded-up tube stations, forgotten sewers, abandoned buildings, and other places you just aren't meant to be. They lovingly documented their infiltrations with video uploads and maps, carefully masking their faces and voices. It was fantastic watching, all this brilliant mountaineer's rope-work, expert lockpicking, and the thrill of discovery as these modern explorers invaded modern ruins that human eyes hadn't seen for generations.

The video I called up was one I'd watched several times: it showed an infiltration gang making its way into an abandoned sewer under the Embankment, built as a spillover sewer when the river Thames was locked in the nineteenth century. They accessed it by means of an anonymous doorway that guarded a narrow stairway that led down into a maintenance room.

The door was locked, but not very well. The Greater London Authority standard for this kind of door was an old Yale lock, vulnerable to a "bump" attack, which even I could do: you just slid a filed-down key-blank into the lock, then rapped it smartly with a little hammer. The energy from the hammer-blow traveled along the key's shaft and was transmitted into the lock's pins, which flew up into the lock-mechanism for a brief moment, during which you could simply turn the doorknob and open the door. All told, bumping a Yale took less time than opening it with the actual key.

A series of locked (but bumpable) doors leading off the maintenance room took them deeper and deeper into the under-ground works, including a revolting stretch of catwalk that ran over an active sewer. The explorers wrapped cloth around their faces for this part, but even so, they made audible retching noises as they passed over the river of crap.

Two more locked doors and they were in: a huge, vaulted chamber, like the inside of a cathedral, all Victorian red brick-work with elaborate archways and close-fitted tiles on the floor and running up the walls. As the explorers' torches played over the magnificent room, we all breathed in together.

"There's my cinema," I said.

"Oh yes, I think so," Jem said. "That's the place all right."

―――――

We went that night. straight down to the Embankment with reversible hi-viz vests that we'd hung with realistic-looking laminated badges and passes for various municipal entities. They wouldn't hold up if we got hauled into a police station, but in the dark, they'd be convincing enough. We bumped the locks and retraced the spelunkers' route. We'd brought along some paper painter's facemasks and these did the trick well enough when we crossed the active sewer, and when we reached the big room, we strung up a load of white LED lanterns we used during the frequent breaker-overloads at the Zeroday. They lit it up with a spooky light that turned buttery with all the dust motes floating in the air.

Twenty paced the chamber's length, thinking aloud: "We'd get, what, two hundred or three hundred chairs in here. Put a bar over there. We'll have to clear out the dust; that'll be a ten-person job at least. Need lanterns strung along the route, too. The screen'll go, erm, there, I think, and we'll need to do something about a toilet—"

"It's a sewer, love," Jem said, prodding her in the ribs with a friendly finger as she paced past him.

"Yes, all right, sure, but we can't ask people to crap right here by the bar, can we, now?"

"There's no bar," Jem said.

"Not yet. But there will be. And three hundred people—that's a lot of wee and poo and that. We need a ladies' and a gents'."

Jem slipped his mask over his face and headed out into the active sewer. He came back a moment later, waving his torch.

"There's a little ledge to either side of the walkway there, just beside the door. Wide enough to build a couple of outhouses, they'd just have to have a hole in the floor leading straight down into the sewer, right?"

We all made faces. "That's disgusting," 26 said.

"What? It's where it all goes in the end. Not like we're going to be able to rig up proper plumbing down here, right? The smell'll stop people from lingering in the toilets, too. We'll put some hand sanitizer here, by the door.

"What about a band?" said Chester, finger on his chin.

"What about it?" I said.

"Well, something to get the crowd worked up, before the films, like?"

"Who ever heard of a band before a film?"

"Who ever heard of a film in a sewer?"

"Touché," I said.

"This is going to be brilliant," 26 said. She gave me an enormous hug, and it was all wonderful.

I'd learned a lot about construction and renovations from the work we'd done on the Zeroday, but that was nothing compared to the size of the job we faced in the Sewer Cinema, as we quickly took to calling it. First, of course, was the problem of how to move all the materials in without getting arrested.

Aziz looked at us like we were mad when we asked him about it, but after we talked about how wonderful it could be, and showed him the videos, he nodded. "Yeah," he said, "that could work. But you're going to need some things."

"Some things" turned out to be a portable chain-link fence with opaque plastic mesh, emblazoned TEMPORARY WORKS–J SMITH AND SONS–CONSIDERATE BUILDER SCHEME–RING 08003334343.

"Just bung that up around your doorway after dark, turn up with a bunch of hi-viz vests and hard hats and keep the brims low—"

"We could put those infrared LEDs in 'em," Jem said.

"Yeah," Aziz said. "That, too. And you'll need a vehicle."

He took us out behind his warehouse where there were a half dozen cars in various states of disassembly. One of them was a typical white-panel van, gray with city muck, hubcaps rusted, bonnet with the scars of an old, cack-handed conversion to hybrid. You saw one just like it every ten seconds or so on London's streets, night or day. The number-plate was artfully spattered with mud and filth, so you could only make out a few digits on it.

"That's my beauty," Aziz said. "The White Whale. She's a workhorse, she is. Go anywhere, carry any load, never complain. And a motor like that commands respect on the streets of London, my boy. Practically screams, 'I have nothing to lose'—any crash with an estate-banger like this is going to do more harm to the other geezer than you."

Jem grinned and smacked his hands together. "She's perfect, Aziz."

Twenty gave him a playful cuff on the back of the head. "It's a van, Jem, not a girl. Behave."

Jem pretended he hadn't heard. "How long can we have her for?"

Aziz shrugged. "I have far too much inventory these days. The skips have been too good to me. I was planning on having a week off from them, though it breaks my heart to think of all the lovely junk I'll miss. I'm just too full up now. So, a week? You *can* drive, can't you Jem?"

"I used to drive the tractor on the farm," Jem said. "Can't be much different, can it?"

I tried to picture Jem living on a farm somewhere, mucking out the pigpen and scattering feed for the hens. I couldn't do it. Jem almost never talked about his background, and when he did, he often told ridiculous stories, all of which contradicted one another. I didn't push it. If he said he could drive, I expected he could.

"Fine, fine," Aziz said. "But if you wreck her or get stopped by the law, I'm going to report it as stolen, you understand me?"

"I wouldn't have it any other way, my old," Jem said. "Just so, just so."

And that was how we got the car.

Aziz helped us fill the car with many of the bits and pieces we'd need from his enormous stock—practically everything we'd need to kit out the cinema: beamers, sound system, lights, loads of power supplies and that. We'd have to get the chairs and bar from somewhere—there were several dozen chairs in the Zeroday, of course, and folding chairs were an easy scrounge, the kind of thing that often turned up on the curb on rubbish day. 26 reckoned that if we put the word out to the Confusing Peach lot to snag any they saw, we'd have more than enough come the day. Chester, meanwhile, had quite an eye for building sites where there was extra lumber lying around unloved and unregarded, and he reckoned he'd have an easy time getting enough to build a few outhouses, especially as we planned on using wood for the floors and seats, and do the walls with tarpaulin, which we'd found miles of in the Zeroday's cellars.

And Chester had found a band: The Honey Roasted Landlords were an odd bunch, playing a huge number of instruments—big horns like the sousaphone, fiddles, and upright bass, a couple of squeezeboxes and a load of little drums—and all of them were acoustic, an enormous plus as it saved us working out how to get them all equalized into the cinema's sound system. The singers even sang into paper megaphones, using strange, nasal voices, a style Chester told me was actually called "megaphone singing," and it dated back to the time before electrical microphones. Their sound was dead weird: old-fashioned, of course, can't help but sound old-fashioned with all that brass and the megaphones and that, but there was something in the melodies, and the speed in which they played, that sounded not just contemporary, but somehow futuristic, like something out of a sci-fi flick. They had a big following in London already, and their own mailing list, and they'd do it for the chance to ring up some donations, as was their way. Chester told me that they could bring in a thousand quid or more in a night from the generosity of their audiences.

What's more, their fans were fantastic visual artists—collage types who'd whip up posters and handbills for their events that subtly reworked everything from commercial signage to iconic photos to fine art to film stills to make stuff that just *popped*. All illegal as hell, naturally, which was even better, far as I was concerned. Soon as I saw their stuff, I knew they were the right band and the right kind of people for our big night.

Chester was also working on his own film for the night, another short feature, this one a recut of all the MPs who'd said stupid, smarmy things in support of the Theft of IP Act, supered over infamous film courtroom scenes, and he replaced the prisoners in the dock with all the infamous kids who'd been bunged in jail since the law passed. It didn't have a spec of humor in it, but it wasn't really meant to, and watching it made my blood boil.

Rabid Dog had been secretly working on his own thing: an absolutely delightful remake of a popular zombie franchise, *The Walking Dead,* turned into a comedy, as was his thing, a series of six trailers, one after the other, for each part of the series. They got funnier and funnier, until you were roaring with laughter, practically wetting yourself. I figured it'd be a great warm-up for my feature.

There was no question that my feature would be the main event. It wasn't even *mine,* properly speaking. Everyone in the Zeroday had had a hand in it, arguing over the cuts and the pacing and the voice-over and that. It wouldn't have been nearly so good if it had merely been mine. We were all slavering to show it to the world—once we'd screened it, we would salt ZeroKTube and all the other video sites to get it shown around. I'd never been as proud of anything in my life.

We began to spend our nights at the Sewer Cinema, unloading kit from the White Whale, setting things up by battery-powered lanterns. We had a load of spare batteries for these and at the end of every night, we brought them back to the Zeroday to charge them. It was half-term for 26, and she simply told her parents she was working on a big, secret project with me and they left her alone. It made me doubly envious: first, to have parents that understanding; and second, to have parents at all. Whenever

I thought of my poor folks back in Bradford, it felt like sand had got in behind my eyes and a balloon was being inflated behind my heart, crushing it.

But I still couldn't bring myself to call them. At first, I'd been scared they'd order me home, make a scene. Then, as more time crept past without my ringing, I found that I was too ashamed to ring—ashamed that I'd let it go so long. I couldn't explain myself to them, had no way to account for putting my parents through their torture. But then, hadn't I always been torture for them? Hadn't I cost them everything already with my reckless behavior? I was the family's chief embarrassment and useless layabout—but here at the Zeroday, I was the mighty Cecil B. DeVil, with my glorious girlfriend, my brilliant videos, my excellent friends, and my grand plans to turn the sewers of London into cinemas.

I still checked in on the throwaway phone number I'd given Cora, ringing it every day or every second day if things were busy. She sometimes left me chatty little messages that barely masked the pain she was going through. Once or twice we arranged times for me to call her back and we had brittle little conversations that were lighthearted parodies of the real talkers we'd have back in the old days.

But on the third day of our preparations in Sewer Cinema, I got a different sort of message: "Hey, Trent. Well, hope you pick this one up soon. Very soon. Cos I'm on my way to London. Ha! Yes, I am. Gave myself French Leave, as they say. Things were just not working out with the crumblies and well, I shouldn't have to explain this to you, right? Of all people, right? So. Well. I'll be in about nine P.M. It'd be just great if you'd leave me a real number I could reach you on. You can't call my old number. Right after I finish this call, I'm dropping the SIM in the bin and getting a new one. Your little sister's no dummy, right? Well. Okay. That's it. Erm. Love you? Okay. Love you. Call me."

I was breathing so hard at this point that I was actually dizzy. I stood behind the J SMITH AND SONS hoarding in my hard hat a hi-viz, clutching my phone to my head, trying not to fall over. 26 was going past with an armload of chairs, but she stopped when she saw me.

"Cec? What is it?"

I unlocked my phone with shaking hands, checked the time: 11:00 P.M. Cora'd been wandering the streets of London for *two hours*. "Cora," I said, punching the redial button to call back into the voice-mail drop, talking as calmly as I could, "Cora, it's Trent," I said, and I caught sight of 26's face as I said my real name in front of her for the first time. It was all so much to be thinking about, I could barely keep track of it all. "Cora, it's me. Here's my number. Erm." I had an impulse to tick her off, tell her she was an idiot and irresponsible and did she know how much trouble she could get into here in London, a girl like her on her own? But even in my state, I knew what a hypocrite I'd be to say that sort of thing. I knew that I wouldn't tolerate it if our positions were reversed. "Call me, all right? Call me quick."

It wasn't until after I put the phone down that I realized I'd just given her my real number and that meant if she was still at home, helping my parents track me down, I was done for.

"What is it, Cecil?" 26 said again.

"My sister," I said. "She's in London on her own." I slid down the hoarding until I was sat on the pavement, my back propped against it. "On her own," I said again, my voice lost in the traffic noises from the other side of the hoarding. "Oh, God, Twenty, what will I do?"

The next hour was agony, I made 26 go back to work. I couldn't risk being down in the tunnel when Cora rang, and I waited and waited for the call, remembering all the creepy types in Victoria when I'd come off the bus that first night. It made me realize just how cruel and awful I'd been to my parents. That set me to crying. My friends trooped past me, carrying gear, silently, pretending that they couldn't see me standing in the dark, snuffling back my sobs, tears dripping off my face onto the pavement.

And then my mobile rang. "Cora?" I said, hitting the button.

"Hey, Trent," she said. Her voice sounded tiny, terrified, a one-molecule-thick layer of guts and bravery pasted over it.

"Where are you?"

"I'm in a call box," she said. "Near the station. Most of the phones were out of service, or were being used." I heard traffic behind her, heard some idiot boys hooting filthy things at her from out a car window. She gave a small, suppressed whimper.

"Is it safe to go back to the station? Tell me honestly. I need to know."

"Yes," she said. "I think so. It's a big road—I don't reckon anyone'd give me trouble with this much traffic about."

I'd been fully prepared to call the law if she'd said no, even if it meant turning myself in. But I knew my sister. If she said it was safe, it was safe. "Go back to the taxi rank," I said. Victoria Station served the Gatwick Express—the train to Gatwick airport—and there was a big rank with hundreds of black cabs all night, and several porters directing the travelers. She'd be as safe there as anywhere. "I'll meet you there in fifteen minutes." I'd already got thirty pounds off my mates to supplement the fifteen I had in my pocket. That'd be plenty for a cab there and back, with plenty left over for contingencies and unforeseen circumstances.

"Yeah, all right. Thanks, Trent."

I swallowed. "That's what big brothers are for, innit?" I put the phone down.

I kissed 26 hard, and said, "I'll be back quick." I stepped out into the road, leaving behind my hi-viz and hat, stood off a few yards from the White Whale, and stuck my hand out at the next black cab that went past. The driver pulled up to the curb and eyed me with suspicion.

"Can you take me to Victoria Station?"

The driver squinted at me. He was about a million years old, a proper ancient London black-cab driver, the sort that looks like he's some kind of wizened gnarled tree that's grown out of the seat of his taxi. "It's third tariff after ten," he said. "You know that, right, sir?"

I felt a sear of anger at this old bastard, giving me a hard time when I was trying to rescue my sister. Six months ago, I would have cursed him out and kicked the wheel of his cab, and sent him off, but now I knew I couldn't afford to indulge my anger.

"Sir," I said, drawing the money out of my pocket and fanning it out, "I have the money. I've just had a call to tell me that my little sister has run away from home and turned up at Victoria. She's fifteen, she's alone, and I'm trying to get to her as quickly as I can. Can you take me there?"

He grunted and squinted at me, then jerked a thumb over his shoulder. "Get in, mate, we'll go get this wayward sister of yours, all right?"

I jumped in, settling myself on the big backseat, belting myself in as the driver pulled away into the road, putting his foot down and turning London into a black blur dashed with streaks of white light that we tore past. The red intercom light was on, and the driver said, "She a clever girl, your sister? Good head on her shoulders?"

He was looking at me in the rearview mirror. "A lot smarter than me," I said. "But she's too young to be on her own, and I'm nowhere near responsible enough to look after her."

He laughed, a sound like a series of coughs, and winked at me in the mirror. "You sound like you're sensible enough to know that you're not sensible, which is a pretty good trick. Let's get this young lady with all due haste, then, shall we? Victoria's no place for a child to be out on her own after dark." So saying, he revved the engine and yanked at the gearshift, overtaking a night bus and pressing me back into the squeaking seat.

London had been a blur before—now it was a screech of lights and movement that I went past so fast I couldn't make out any details, just jumbled impressions of lights and motion.

Abruptly he geared down and braked hard at a red light and I saw that we were about to turn into the Victoria Station taxi rank. I put my thumb over the seat-belt release and dug for my money. He saw the notes in my hand in his rearview and said,

"Naw, naw, hold onto it. I'll wait for ya and take you back. We'll call it a tenner, even, and that'll be my good deed for the night, and don't say I never done nuffing for you."

I stopped with the money in my hand, trying to think of something to say that would express my gratitude, but no words rose to my lips. "Thanks" was the best I could manage, but the cabbie looked like he understood, and he swung into the turn-about and set the brake, unlocking my door. In a flash, I was out and searching, a fresh rain making everything go swimmy and glittery. I hunted the length of the long queue in the taxi rank twice before I spotted her, huddled, face down, hunched behind the luggage trolleys, her hair hanging over her face.

"Cora?" I said.

She looked up and for a moment, I was staring at my little sister again—not the young woman she'd become, but the little girl who used to follow me around, copy everything I did, look up to me, and look to me for approval. I nearly bawled there and then.

Her expression changed a bit and now I was looking at the Cora I knew, the teenager who was indeed much smarter than I ever was or would be, beautiful and sharp-tongued, who didn't really need her cock-up of a big brother anymore. Except that now she did, and she opened her arms and gave me a cuddle that was so hard the breath whooshed out of me. She smelled of home, of Bradford and our flat and the family I'd left behind, and that smell was a new shock as big as the earlier ones, and I was glad she was holding me so hard or I might have fallen to my knees.

"I've got a cab waiting," I managed. "Come on." I picked up her rucksack—it weighed a ton—and lugged it to the taxi, Cora clinging tight to my hand. We climbed inside, her eyes wide and staring in the buttery light from the tiny bulb in the cab's ceiling. I sat her down on the bench and folded down one of the jump-seats, so that we could face each other.

The cabbie looked over his shoulder, his face inches from mine, separated by the clear perspex, and he cocked a crooked grin at Cora. "You'd be the young lady, then," he said. "Your brother here's been having kittens over you being out there all on your own, you know?"

My stomach sank. Saying something like this to Cora was bound to get her back up, make her feel like she was being patronized, which would only make my self-appointed task of sending her home again even harder.

But she didn't snap at the driver. Instead, she actually looked sheepish, ducking her face behind her fringe, and said, "I expect he was."

The driver grunted with satisfaction. "Back to where I picked you up in the Embankment, yeah?"

"That's right," I said. "Thanks."

"Hold on, guv," he said, and hit the intercom switch, leaving us in privacy as the cab lurched into traffic, and I was glad I'd put on my seat belt or I would have ended up sitting in Cora's lap.

She grinned at me and I grinned back at her. "Welcome to London, I suppose," I said.

She made a point of looking out the windows. "I like what you've done with the place," she said.

Somehow. we managed not to talk about the fact that she had run away as we sped back to my friends. It seemed she knew the city better than I did, and she excitedly called out the name of each bridge as we passed it (I knew Tower Bridge and Millennium Bridge, because the former had a couple of bloody great towers in the middle of it and the latter looked like it had been built out of futuristic ice-lolly sticks and steel cabling), and I found myself sharing in her excitement. Something about all that steel and fairy archways, lit up in the night, over the lapping black water, everything prismed by the rain spattering the windows.

We got out by the hoarding and I gave the driver a tenner and then passed him another fiver through the window. He grabbed my hand as I gave him the fiver and gave it a single hard, dry shake. "You take care of that sister of yours, and of yourself, you hear me, young man?"

"I will," I said, and it came out like a promise.

He drove away, leaving us standing by the hoarding with the rain drizzling around us.

"Trent?"

"Yes?"

"Why are we in the middle of this pavement?"

I had thought this one through, a bit of showmanship. I laid my finger alongside my nose and led her behind the hoarding, opening the door and ushering her into it, closing it behind us, leaving us in the warm gloom of the lantern we'd left in the corner of the vestibule.

She cocked her head at me. "Trent, what's going on?"

I laid my finger alongside my nose again, changing sides this time. "Oh, all shall be revealed in good time, my dear. Come along, now."

I led her down the stairs, then said, "You'll want to hold your nose for this next bit."

"Trent, what the hell is this about?" She was looking rather put out, which was good. At least she'd lost all her fright and timidity.

"Trust me, little sister," I said. "All shall be revealed anon."

"Stop talking like Shakespeare and *explain* yourself, or I'm not taking another step."

I blew a wet raspberry at her. "Oh, come on, Cora, play along. It's a surprise, all right? Indulge me."

"Fine," she said. She handed me her rucksack, heavy as a corpse. "You carry this, though. I'm not going to lug it around while you play silly buggers."

I shouldered it with a grunt. "Right you are. Now, nose, please." I pinched mine. She followed suit. I opened the door that led into the room before the bridge. Even with my nose pinched, the smell was like a physical thing—I could *taste* it every time I breathed through my mouth. We would definitely need disposable face masks for the audience to wear. I had a brainstorm that we could decorate them with animal snouts, so that we'd be leading in a single-file army of tigers and zebras and dogs and donkeys. What fun!

I waited until she was right on my heels before opening the final door that led into the sewer itself. She recoiled from the sight, lit by lanterns spaced along the bridge and around the makeshift toilets at its far end. "Trent—" she began, then shut her mouth. It wasn't pleasant even *talking* in the presence of all that filth.

"Come along," I said, quickly, taking her hand and leading her to the door on the other side, then quickly through again and out to the screening room itself, releasing my nose and taking in big gulps of air.

My coconspirators were all busy in the cinema, having unloaded the night's haul from Aziz's van. They were setting up chairs, arranging the bar and the coolers and the cheap fizzy drinks and booze we'd bought in bulk from a dirt-cheap off-license near the Zeroday, setting up the speakers and stringing out the speaker wire along hooks set high into the brickwork, using handheld hammer-drills we'd borrowed from Aziz.

We stood in the doorway, contemplating the wonderful industry of the scene, and one by one my friends stopped work and looked back at us.

"Everyone," I said, once they were all waiting expectantly, "this is my sister Cora. Cora, these are the Jammie Dodgers."

"Like the biccies?" she said.

"Like the *delicious* biccies," I said.

"Not exactly," Jem said. "More like the criminal conspiracy."

"Oh," she said. "Well, that's all right then." So saying, she grabbed a chair from the pile of unsorted stock beside the door, plunked it down on the close-fit brickwork of the floor, and plopped into it. "Would someone care to elaborate?"

26 had poured out a shandy—half beer, half fizzy lemonade—in one of the little half-pint mugs we'd rescued from the Zeroday, and she pressed it into Cora's hands. "Take your coat off, love, it's going to take some telling."

Twenty and Cora hit it off immediately, and they worked together patching up the chairs we'd harvested, which were in pretty poor nick. 26 had a mate who'd given her a whole mountain of this brightly colored polymer compound called Sugru; you took it out of the wrapper, kneaded it like plasticine, then pressed it into the cracks in the wood, or the holes in the seat, or the snapped corners, and worked it in there. In twenty-four hours, it dried to something like epoxy-hard. They chatted quietly to each other, and when I eavesdropped, I caught fragments of their conversation and discovered that they were talking heavy politics, dropping the names of MPs like they were the headmasters at their schools.

"What do you know about MPs?" I said to Cora.

She held up two fingers at me and made a sour face. "I've been down to our MP's surgery every fortnight since you left, idiot boy. Practically lived there during the runup to the Theft of Intellectual Property Bill vote. Wanted him to know that his own constituents were losing their jobs and their education and their families to stupid laws like this, and if he didn't vote against it, we'd end up in jail."

I tried to keep the astonishment off my face. In my mind, my family had been frozen in time the moment I stepped on that bus, impossibly distant. I couldn't believe that Cora and I had been working on the same campaign in two different cities. "That's amazing," I managed. I realized that I was busting with pride. I found a chair without too much wobble in it and sat down with them. "Can you believe my little sister?" I said to 26.

26 rolled her eyes. "Not so little, mate. She really knows her stuff. Getting good grades, apparently."

"Really? I thought you said you were in trouble at school?"

She giggled. "I started checking out library books and bringing 'em down to the MP's surgery, and did all my studying in his waiting room. At first I just did it to prove a point, but now the library's only open four days a week, it worked out to be a brilliant place to get work done. Hardly anyone ever goes down there. His receptionist kind of adopted me and ticked him off any time he tried to get me to leave."

I remembered the heft of her rucksack. "You didn't bring a load of library books to London with you?"

She looked horrified. "Of course not. That'd be stealing. My bag's full of discards—it's shocking what they're getting rid of. No funding, you see. Taking 'em off the shelves is cheaper than reshelving them, so the collections keep on shrinking. There's always some gobshite at the council meetings saying, 'what do we need libraries for if everyone's got the Internet?' I keep wanting to shake them by the hair and shout something like, 'Everyone except me! And what about all the stuff librarians have to teach us about using the net?'"

"You go to council meetings?"

She rolled her eyes. "26 has been telling me all about this film night you're planning. Sounds like it'll be fun. But what do you hope to accomplish with it?"

I felt a flush in my cheeks. "What do you mean? We're going to put on a show!"

"Yeah, I get that. But *why*?"

The flush crept higher. "Cos I made a film, all right? And I want to show it. And there's no way I could show it in the real world, cos I broke every law in the world making the picture. That means I've got to find some other way around things."

She nodded. "Okay, that's fine. But wouldn't it be better to change things so that you didn't have to show your films in the sewer?"

I felt myself shaking my head, felt my ears burning. Of course, she was just saying the things I'd been thinking to myself all along, trying to shove down into the bottom of my conscience so I could get on with making Sewer Cinema ready for the opening show. Hearing Cora speak the forbidden words aloud made me want to stuff my fingers in my ears.

"Don't worry about me," I said, waving my hands. "I've got plans. Big plans. What about *you*, Cora? What did you tell Mum and Dad? Have you called them?"

Now it was her turn to squirm, as I'd known it would be. It felt good to have the heat on someone else for a change. "I didn't tell them anything. Why should I? You didn't. You just vanished."

One thing about Cora, she was smart. Smart enough to make me squirm some more, anyway. "We're not talking about me, Cora, we're talking about you."

Twenty chose this moment to weigh in: "Cecil, your sister has a good point. You did a runner without talking things over with your parents at all—you've got no call to tick off your sister for doing the same thing."

Cora nodded with satisfaction. "Thank you," she said. "So shut it, *Cecil*." I'd once told Cora over the phone that I was going by Cecil B. DeVil so that she'd know how to search for my videos. She'd told me it was a hilarious name and that I was pathetic to be using it.

Twenty wheeled on her. "However," she said, not missing a beat, "*I* have call to tick you off for doing it. Which I am about to do."

Cora's smile vanished. "Who are you to—"

Twenty just kept talking. "I've heard loads about your parents and from everything I've heard, they're basically good sorts. Not much money, maybe a bit short-tempered, but they love you to bits, don't they?"

"So?" Cora folded her arms.

"So you owe them more than this." She held up a hand. "And so does *he*. But you're meant to be the smart one. They've got to be worrying their guts out by now. So the first thing I want you to do is call them and tell them you've found your brother, that you've got a roof over your head tonight, and that you'll be in touch with them while you work out what to do next. Get a phone number like the one Cecil's been using with you and let them leave you messages there. Okay?"

Cora unfolded and refolded her arms. "Listen, I just met you. You have no right to tell me what to do—"

26 nodded vigorously. "You're right. Please consider all the previous material to be a strongly worded suggestion, not a demand. Better?"

That cracked us both up. "Fine," Cora said. "Fine, you're right. I'll call them as soon as I can get online, leave them a voice mail with a number they can reach me at." She rubbed her eyes. "Cripes, what are they going to say to me? They'll be furious."

"It only gets worse the longer you wait," I said. "Believe me."

When 1 finally woke the next day, 26 had already left, and so had Cora. Jem was in the kitchen making coffee, and he said something vague about them stepping out for some sort of errand. I gave up on getting more info out of him: when Jem was making coffee, you could set a bomb off next to him without distracting him. He had three notebooks' worth of handwritten "field histories" from his experiments in extracting the perfect shot of espresso, and he'd been playing with stovetop pots for months now, voraciously consuming message-board debates about "oxidization," "crema," "bitter oils," and ideal temperatures.

He'd hit on the idea that he needed to heat the bottom chamber until just enough coffee had perked up into the top pot, and then he had to cool it off instantly. His first experiments had involved plunging the pot into a bowl of ice water, but he'd cracked the pot in two with a sound like a cannon shot. Lucky for him, the charity shops were *full* of these things. He had a shelf of them, along with a whole mountain of rusted cast-iron pots and pans that he was slowly rehabilitating, buffing them up with a disc-sander attachment on his drill, then oiling them and curing them in high-heat ovens.

I paced the pub room and helped taste-test Jem's coffee until the girls came back, breezing in through the back door in a gust of raucous laughter. They set down heavy bags on a table and plunked themselves on the sofa, looking indecently pleased with themselves.

"And you've been . . . ?" I said, peering down my nose at them. I had caffeine jitters from all the experimental assistance I'd been lending, and it had put me in an intense mood.

"We've been at the bloody library, haven't we?" Cora said. She seemed giddy with glee.

"Well, it's certainly put you in a lovely mood, hasn't it? Been looking at the dirty books?"

Cora waggled a finger at me. "Oh ye of little faith," she said. "We've been thinking about your great project, and how to make it rise to true, epic greatness. And we have got part of the solution. Show him," she said, waving 26 on.

26 dug through the bags—which were bulging with books— and drew out a small, battered paperback. "*Beneath the City Streets,*" she said, and sniffed. "The fourth edition. Published in 1983. Written by one Peter Laurie, an investigative journalist of the last century with a special interest in nuclear bunkers, bomb shelters, underground tunnels, and whatnot. He dug up all these elderly maps and purchase orders and that, and walked the streets of London looking for suspicious buildings and big green spaces bordered by mysterious battened-down steel security doors and the like. Then his readers sent him all kinds of corrections and clues that he chased up for new editions, until you get to the fourth edition. Plenty of Internet debate about it, of course—but it's got these lovely maps, see, places where they built tube stations that never got used, or shut down stations and abandoned them. Basically, there's an entire bloody city down below London, not just some old sewers."

I could feel their excitement, and I paged through the book, feeling the old yellowing paper and the corners of the cover gone soft as mouse-fur from decades of handling. "Well," I said. "Well. That's certainly very interesting, but what about it? Just last night you were telling me that it didn't matter because it wasn't going to make a difference, right?"

"*One* film won't make a difference," Cora said. "But what about a hundred films? What about films all over the country, all over the world? You know you're not the only one making illegal films—there's enough out there on the net to show new ones every night forever. But out there in message boards and on ZeroKTube, nobody seems to get much worked up about the fact that the stuff they love is illegal, that their friends are going to jail for making art. I reckon that from a keyboard, it all seems like something imaginary and very far away."

26 leapt to her feet and nodded furiously. "It's like they're ashamed of it, they've seen all those adverts telling them that downloading is stealing, that remixing isn't creation. They think they're getting away with something, and when a bunch of billionaire corporations buy the government off and start locking up their mates, they just shrug their shoulders and try to make themselves as small as possible to avoid being noticed."

Cora took *Beneath the City Streets* out of my hand and waved it like a preacher with a Bible. "You get people coming out by the hundreds and thousands, you tell them that they've got to work together to make a difference, you get them to refuse to be ashamed to make and love art. Show them that they should be *proud* of this stuff. They can't arrest us all."

My heart was thudding in my chest. It was an amazing vision—films being shown openly all over the land, bringing the glories of the net to the real world.

But Jem was in the doorway kitchen, shaking with caffeine, looking grumpy. He waited until we were all staring at him, then said, "Come on, would you? You're not striking a revolutionary blow, children—you're just showing a couple of pictures in a sewer. It's a lovely bit of fun and all, but let's not go mad here, all right?"

We all stared at him. "Jem—" I said. I didn't know where to start. "Jem, mate, how can you say that? What they're doing, it's so *wrong*—"

He snorted. " 'Course it's wrong. So what? Lots of wrong

things out there. What you're doing could get you tossed in jail. That's pretty wrong, believe me." He pointed to the scar under his eye. "Pray you never have to find out how wrong it all is. What we're doing is a lark. I love larks, I'm all for 'em. But don't mistake a lark for a cause. All this high and mighty talk about 'creativity,' what's it get you? You're nicking stuff off other people and calling it your own. I don't have any problem with that, but at least call it what it is: good, honest thieving."

Something burst in me. I got to my feet and pointed at him. "Jem, chum, you don't know what the hell you're talking about, mate. You might know more about jail than I do, but you haven't a clue when it comes to creativity." This was something I'd thought about a lot. It was something I cared about. I couldn't believe that my old pal and mentor didn't understand it, but I was going to explain it to him, wipe that smirk right off his mug. "Look, let's think about what creativity is, all right?"

He snorted. "This could take a couple of months."

"No," I said. "No, it only takes a long time because there are so many people who would like to come up with a definition of creativity that includes everything they do and nothing anyone else does. But if we're being honest, it's easy to define creativity: it's doing something that isn't obvious."

Everyone was looking at me. I stuck my chin out.

"That's it?" Jem said. "That's creativity? 'Doing something that isn't obvious?' You've had too much coffee, chum. That's the daftest thing I ever heard."

I shook my head. "Only because you haven't thought about it at all. Take the film I just made with Rabid Dog. All that footage of Scot Colford, from dozens of films, and all that footage of monsters, from dozens more. If I handed you any of those films, there's nothing obvious about them that says, 'You could combine this in some exact way with all those other films and make a new one.' That idea came from me. I created it. It wasn't lying around, waiting to be picked up like a bunch of pebbles on the beach. It was something that didn't exist until I made it, and probably wouldn't have existed unless I did. That's what 'to create' means: to make something new."

Jem opened his mouth, then shut it. He got a thoughtful look. 26 was grinning at me. Cora was looking at me with some of the old big-brother adoration I hadn't seen for years and years. I felt a hundred feet tall.

At last, Jem nodded. "Okay, fine. But all that means is that there's lots of different *kinds* of creativity. Look, I like your film just fine, but you've got to admit there's something different about making a film out of other peoples' films and getting a camera out and making your own movie."

I could feel my head wanting to shake as soon as Jem started to talk, but I restrained myself and made myself wait for him to finish. "Sure, it's different—but when you say, 'making your own film,' you really mean that the way I make films is less creative, that they're not my own, right?"

He looked down. "I didn't say that, but yeah, okay, that's what I think."

"I understand," I said, making myself be calm, even though he was only saying the thing I feared myself. "But look at it this way. Once there weren't any films, right? Then someone invented the film. *He* was creative, right? In some way, every film that's been made since isn't really *creative* because the people who made them didn't invent films at the same time."

He shook his head. "You're playing word games. Inventing films isn't the same as making films."

"But someone made the first film. And then someone made the first film with two cameras. The first film that was edited. The first film that had sound. The first color film. The first comedy. The first monster film. The first porno film. The first film with a surprise ending. Jem, films are only about a hundred years old. There are people alive today who are older than any of those ideas. It's not like they're ancient inventions—they're not fire or the wheel or anything. They were created by people whose names we know."

"You don't know their names," Jem said, grinning. I could tell I was getting through to him.

Cora laughed like a drain. "Trent doesn't know anything unless he can google it. But *I* do. The novel was invented by Cervantes five hundred years ago: *Don Quixote*. And the detective story was invented in 1844 by Poe: *The Purloined Letter*. A fella named Hugo Gernsback came up with science fiction, except he called it scientifiction."

I nodded at her, said, "Thanks—"

But she cut me off. "There's only one problem, Trent: The novel was *also* invented by Murasaki Shikibu, halfway around the world, hundreds of years earlier. Mary Shelley wrote science fiction long before Hugo Gernsback: *Frankenstein* was written in 1817. And so on. The film camera had about five different inventors, all working on their own. The problem with your theory is that these creators are creating something that comes out of their heads and doesn't exist anywhere else, but again and again, all through history, lots of things are invented by lots of people, over and over again. It's more like there are ideas out there in the universe, waiting for us to discover them, and if one person doesn't manage to make an idea popular, someone else will. So when you say that if you don't create something, no one will, well, you're probably not right."

"Wait, what? That's rubbish. When I make a film, it comes out of my imagination. No one else is going to think up the same stuff as me."

"Now you sound like me," Jem said, and rubbed his hands together.

Cora patted my hand. "It's okay, it's just like you said. Everyone wants a definition of creativity that makes what they do into something special and what everyone else does into nothing special. But the fact is, we're *all* creative. We come up with weird and interesting ideas all the time. The biggest difference between 'creators' isn't their imagination—it's how hard they work. Ideas are easy. Doing stuff is hard. There's probably a million geezers out there who love Scot Colford films, but none of them can be arsed to make something fantastic out of them, the way you do. The fact is, creativity is cheap, hard work is hard, and everyone wants to think his ideas are precious unique snowflakes, but ideas are like assholes, we've all got 'em."

I sat down. 26 gave me a cuddle. "She's right, you know."

I made a rude noise. "Of course she's right. She's the brains in the family, isn't she?"

Cora curtsied, and Jem clapped once or twice. "Well, that was invigorating. Who wants coffee?"

Cora called Mum and Dad later that afternoon, shutting herself in my bedroom for what seemed an eternity. 26 and I amused ourselves by googling the locations mentioned in *Beneath the City Streets,* checking out satellite and streetview images, as well as infiltration reports from intrepid urban spelunkers. A surprising number of the abandoned deep tube stations had virtually no information on them, which was exciting news—if no one had been going down there, perhaps *we* could. Rabid Dog and Chester wandered in at some point and demanded to know what we were doing with our stacks of library books, then they, too, caught the excitement and began to google along with us. We were booked to take the White Whale down to the Sewer Cinema at nine that night, once the foot traffic had basically vanished, and they suggested that we visit some of the more promising sites beforehand, just to scout them in person.

We were all so engrossed that we didn't even notice when Cora came down the stairs and sat down on the sofa. And then I looked up and saw her sitting there, her eyes sunken and red-rimmed. I nudged 26—she had been emailing her day's lessons to her teachers so that she wouldn't be reported as truant. She looked at Cora for a moment, then elbowed me in the ribs. "Go talk with her," she hissed.

I got up and held my hand out to Cora. Her hand was clammy and cold. I helped her to her feet. "Let's go for a walk, okay?"

She let me lead her up to the top floor, out the fire door, and down the back stairs. We circled around the Zeroday and crossed the empty lot, striking out for the Bow high street.

"How'd that go, then?" I said, finally.

I saw her shake her head in my peripheral vision. "They're furious," she said. "They think you lured me away. They think you're a drug addict or a prostitute or something."

I felt like I'd been punched in the chest. I found that I was bunching my shirt in my fist. When I didn't say anything, Cora went on.

"I told them they were being stupid, that you had a place to live and that you were doing good stuff, but they weren't hearing any of it. As far as they're concerned, there was only one reason you could possibly have cut them off, and that's because you're ashamed of what you're doing here. And now they think I'm going to end up selling my body or something daft."

I chewed on air, trying to find words. I choked them out. "All right, the fact is, I *am* ashamed to call them. I'm living in a squat, eating garbage, begging to make cash. But it's not like they think it is. I'm doing something I care about. I don't know, maybe we should charge admission to our films, or I should ask for donations for my online videos or something."

Cora shrugged. "You know what? I think that whatever you're doing here, it's not one millionth as scary as Mum and Dad assume it is. The silence is worse than anything else. You were right about that—now that I've called them, they're not nearly so freaked out about me."

"It wasn't me that told you to call them, it was 26."

"Yeah, well, she's a lot smarter than you," Cora said. "I like her."

"Me too," I said.

We walked some more, passing boarded-up storefronts, kebab shops, cafés advertising cheap meals. One of them had a telly in the window, and something on it caught my eye. It was a scene from *D'Artagnan's Blood-Oath*, a film I knew down to the last frame. But it wasn't the film as it was being shown in cinemas.

It was a scene from my remix: D'Artagnan's big, stupid sword-fight remade as a big Bollywood dance number through the judicious use of loops and cuts to *Sun-King!*, a Bollywood film set in old-time France I'd found. And it was showing behind a Sky newsreader who then cut away to a serious-looking old bastard in a suit who was talking very quickly and angrily. A moment later, a caption appeared beneath him: SAM BRASS, MOTION PICTURE ASSOCIATION (UK).

We'd finally made the news.

As we hurried back to the Zeroday, Cora kept talking about her conversation with our parents. "I just couldn't stand it anymore. They were always in a panic—no money, on me about my grades, worried about my SAT scores, demanding to know where I was all the time. Since you'd gone, they've gone all paranoid, convinced that I was up to something horrible. And the fact that I had to spend all this time out of the house to do my homework only made it worse. I just couldn't take it anymore, you know?"

As miserable as this made me feel, I was also feeling elation, excitement. That snatch of SkyTV had lofted me to the clouds. After nothing had come of our raid on Leicester Square, I'd been shattered. Working on Sewer Cinema had been a welcome distraction, but it hadn't really offset the awful feeling that nothing I did really mattered. Now I found myself daring to hope that I could make a difference.

We pelted up the fire stairs and then back down into the pub room. I grabbed my lappie and began to google.

"What is it?" 26 demanded.

I shook my head and kept searching, then showed her my screen. It was the same newsreader, announcing that our little films had gone viral. Our remixes were being downloaded at speed from all corners of the globe, along with our message:

Buying film tickets only encourages them. Every penny
you spend goes to buying more crap copyright laws.
Your children are being sent to prison to protect
rubbish like this.

This seemed to have tipped the scales for Mr. Motion Picture
Association, an American who seemed to be based in London, or
maybe Brussels. He called us every name in the book: terrorists,
thieves, pirates, then compared what we'd done to murder, rape,
and pedophilia. By the time he was done, we were all grinning
like loonies.

"Well, better late than never," Jem said. "Did you see the
vein in his forehead throbbing? Poor bastard's going to have an
aneurysm if he's not careful. Needs to take up Tai Chi or something. You should send him a letter, Cecil."

We cackled like a coop full of stoned hens—and then Jem
started to spin up some of his monster spliffs and the cackling got
even more henlike. Getting high with my baby sister felt weird
and awkward at first—I veered from being embarrassed to smoke
in front of her to wanting to tell her off for taking a turn when
the joint came around to her. But after a few puffs, we were all
too blotted to care, and very little happened for a couple of hours
while we moved in a slow-motion daze. As I started to sober up,
I thought to myself (for the millionth time) that smoking weed
always turned out to be a lot more time-consuming than I'd anticipated.

As it was, we were too late to reconnoiter the ghost tube
stations we'd planned on visiting, and rushed into town in the
White Whale to finish up the Sewer Cinema. Our grand opening was only two days away, and we all reckoned that with the
publicity from the enraged film industry fatcats, we'd have a full
house and then some.

Chapter 6

THE WAR HOTS UP/HOMECOMING/
DROWNING IN FAMILIARITY

Opening night was upon us before I knew it. Right up to the time that we opened the house, I was convinced we'd never pull it off. Aziz's beloved White Whale had packed in the day before, leaving us without wheels with which to move in the last of the goods. Instead, we ferried massive armloads of junk down to the cinema on the buses in enormous black rubbish sacks, getting filthy looks from the other riders. Without the White Whale, we couldn't erect our temporary hoardings and we didn't have our hi-viz vests and safety hat disguises, so we just scurried through the door and hoped that no one called the filth. We got away with it, though no one left again until it was truly the middle of the night.

But Aziz came through with new transmission gubbins for his van—it turned out he had two more vans just like it up on blocks that he cannibalized for parts, drafting us all as unskilled manual labor. So we were able to ferry our audience down to the Sewer Cinema entrance in groups of twelve, picking them up at prearranged spots all over town, sticking them in the back of the van (we'd papered over the windows so that no one could see where we were going), then pulling right up to the hoarding and ushering them out in hi-viz and helmets that we stripped off and tossed back into the van so it could go for the next ferryload of passengers.

I'd left Jem in charge of making people feel welcome while we filled up. Most of the attendees knew one another from Confusing Peach parties or other social events, but we'd asked our friends to put the word out to their friends and friends of friends and had got a rush of RSVPs in the last few minutes. The Honey

Roasted Landlords played three sets, Chester and Dog tended bar—we set out a donation cup to cover the drink we'd brought in, and plenty of people showed up with bottles of something or other that went into the communal pool—Cora and 26 made sure nobody fell into the open sewer.

Aziz and I dropped off the last load at 11:00 P.M., four hours after we'd started, exhausted but grinning like holy fools. Aziz revealed two musty, wrinkled tuxedos he'd dredged up from one of his boxes and we both changed. Mine was way too big, but I rolled up the sleeves and turned up the trousers, then shrugged into my hi-viz and helmet and ducked inside to the most roaring, exciting, ridiculous, outrageous party I'd ever seen.

As I took it all in from the doorway, nervousness took possession of my belly, gnawing at my guts. The tux was redonkulous in the extreme, I looked like an idiot, my film was stupid, they were all going to hate it and me, I'd dragged them all into a sewer—

I knew that I had to grab the mic and start talking *right then* or I never would. So I did.

"Erm, hullo?" I said, holding the mic in a death grip. "Hello?" No one seemed to notice my amplified voice around the edges of the conversation-blast.

Jem grabbed the mic from me and pointed it into the nearest amplifier. Immediately, a feedback squeal that rattled my teeth. All conversation ceased instantly, as people shouted and clapped their hands over their ears. Jem handed me back the mic, and said, "You're welcome."

"Thanks," I said, my amplified voice loud in the sudden silence. I'd had a whole flowery speech worked out, thanking people for coming and introducing our project and so on, but I couldn't think of any of it just then. All those faces turned toward me, all those eyes staring. The whispers.

"Erm," I said. "My name's Cecil B. DeVil. My friends and I made some films. Let's watch them, okay?"

Of course, 26 wasn't expecting this, so she wasn't ready, and the lights stayed on and no films played on the screen. Everyone was still staring. Someone giggled. "Well," I said, "Well. Erm, while we're waiting, erm." I felt for something to say. Then, the words came. "You know TIP, right? Theft of Intellectual Property Act?" People booed good-naturedly. My heart thudded and my fingertips tingled. "The thing is—" The words were right there, tip of my tongue. Faces stared at me. Smiling, nodding, wanting to hear what I had to say. Twenty was frowning at her screen, trying to get the beamer working.

"I left home a year ago, when they took away my family's Internet access because I wouldn't stop downloading. I *couldn't* stop downloading. I know that sounds stupid, but I was making films, and to make films, I had to download films. I don't use a camera. I use other films and editing software. But I think my films are good." I swallowed. "Forget that. I don't care if my films are good or not. They're *mine*. They say something I want and need to say. And I don't hurt anyone when I say it. They say we have a free country, and in a free country, you should be able to say what's in your heart, even if you have to use other peoples' words to say it." The words were tumbling out now. "We *all* use other peoples' words! We didn't invent English, we inherited it! All the shots ever shot were shot before. All the dialog ever written is inspired by other peoples' dialog. I make new words out of them, my words, but they're not like, mine-mine, not like my underpants are mine! They're mine, but they're yours to make into your words, too!

"So they took away my family's Internet, and my Mum couldn't sign on for benefits anymore, and Dad couldn't work on the phone-bank anymore, and my sister—" A lump rose in my throat as I looked at Cora. I swallowed hard and looked away, but my voice was breaking now. "My little sister couldn't do her schoolwork anymore. It destroyed my family. I haven't spoken to my parents for a year. I—" I swallowed again. "I miss them."

I had to stop and swallow several times. The room was dead quiet, every face on me, solemn. "Now they've passed this new law, and kids like me are going to *jail* for creating things in a way that the big media companies don't like. They passed this law even though no one wanted it, even though it will destroy more families.

"It's got to stop. *It's got to stop.* We have to stop being ashamed of downloading. We have to stop letting them call us thieves and crooks. What we do is *creative* and has at least as much right to exist as *D'Artagnan's Blood-Oath!*" People chuckled. "So let's do it. Me and my mates made these films. Some of you make films. Some of you have films inside you, waiting to get out. *Just make them!* Sod the law, sod the corporate bullies. They can't put us all in jail. Let's tell them what we do, go public with it. It's time to stop hiding and spit right in their eyes."

The beamers sprang to life and blinding light hit me in the face. 26 was ready to show the films. I shielded my eyes and looked at the faces behind the swimming blobs of light that oozed across my blinded eyes. "Okay," I said. "Looks like we're ready. I hope you like our films. Thanks for coming."

The applause was so loud in the bricked-in vault that it made my ears ring, and as I stepped off the little stage, people started to shake my hand and hug me, strangers and friends, faces I couldn't make out behind the tears that wouldn't stop leaking out of my eyes. Finally I was holding Cora and Cora was holding me, and we were both crying like we hadn't done since we were little kids.

Behind us, the movie had started, and we dried our eyes and watched along, watched the audience watching the films, laughing, gasping, nudging one another and whispering. I don't think I'd ever felt prouder in my life. It swelled me up like a balloon in my chest and the big, stupid grin on my face was so wide it made my cheeks ache, but I couldn't stop it.

They applauded even louder when my film finished, and 26

kept the final frame paused until the applause died down before starting Chester's film. We had an hour's worth of footage lined up, and hundreds of strangers and friends watched with rapt attention, right to the last second, and then there were drinks and dozens of shouted, indistinct conversations. Everyone had something to say, something they loved, something they wanted to make, and it all blurred into a jumble of hands pounding my shoulders, lips shouting encouragement in my ears while the Honey Roasted Landlords played through the night.

Our Leicester Square caper had taken weeks to be noticed by the rest of the world. But Sewer Cinema was an instant hit. It turned out that there were reporters from *Time Out* and *The Guardian* in the audience, and we were on the front door of both websites the next morning—including a close-up photo of my face. Dozens of reviews of our films appeared, mostly very complimentary (though some people *hated* them, but even those people were taking them seriously enough to write long rants about why they were rubbish, and I found that even these made me proud).

The Guardian mentioned that all the video was up for download on ZeroKTube and the comment sections on the download page filled up with hundreds of messages from all over the world, sometimes with links to other mixes of the same footage that other people had made, seemingly overnight. Just a few hours before, I'd felt all alone in the world, an idiot kid fighting a stupid war. Now I felt like I was part of a whole world of people who knew what I knew, felt what I felt. It was the best feeling in the world.

Everyone at the Zeroday was in a fantastic mood. Jem made us coffee that was the strongest, most delicious thing to come out of his kitchen yet. Chester and Rabid Dog announced that they were making breakfast and disappeared into the kitchen. I trailed after them and they put me to work as sous-chef, chopping this, stirring that, googling recipes and scrubbing pots and rooting through our larder for ingredients.

We brought out breakfast to a round of applause that intensified as Chester announced each dish: buckwheat porridge baked in milk with black currants and honey; grilled mushrooms with dill; buttered scones with raspberry jam; streaky bacon and wild boar sausage; and more. It was all the bounty of various skips around town. Chester turned out to have a real passion for them, and had just lucked into a load of half-frozen organic meat that a Waitrose chucked out when its freezer broke down. Knowing the food had all come for free and been prepared with our own hands made it all the more delicious.

And so did Rabid Dog's special homemade chili sauce, which he had made and put up in little jars the month before, filling the house with choking, pepper-spray clouds made from the lethal Scotch Bonnet seeds he'd minced and flash-cooked before pickling them with spice and tomato puree. We sat there, stuffing our gobs and marveling at our own cleverness. After a year in London, I had found a home, a community, and a purpose in life. I was only seventeen years old, but I'd already made more of a mark on the world than either of my parents, already found something extraordinary to be and do. I felt like a god, or at least a godling.

So, of course, that's just when it all went to shit.

After breakfast, we did the washing up and drifted away to our laptops. It was gone two in the afternoon, and we'd wrangled two more days' use of the van out of Aziz to clear out the best junk from Sewer Cinema so that we could store it in the Zeroday for our next performance, whenever that was. But we couldn't do that until after dark, and so we drifted off to our laptops and began to read the reviews and that.

I lay down for a nap, my arms and legs leaden with food and hangover, Jem's coffee having lifted me up and then dropped me like a sack of potatoes. But I'd hardly closed my eyes when someone knocked at my door. I swam up from sleep, trying to make sense of the knocking and my surroundings.

"I'm sleeping," I grunted at the shut door and whomever was behind it.

"It's Cora." She sounded upset.

I groaned. "Come in," I said, and sat up, gathering my quilt around me.

Cora flicked on the light when she came in and I shielded my eyes against the glare. When they adjusted, I saw that she was grim-faced and starey. Uh-oh.

She moved a pile of dirty clothes and magazines and assorted junk off my edit-suite chair and perched on it. "I just spoke to Mum and Dad." I facepalmed myself and groaned again. Mum and Dad didn't read *The Guardian*—they didn't read any newspapers, but *The Guardian* was a paper they especially didn't read. But now that I'd given it two seconds' thought, I realized that *someone* would have passed the paper onto them.

"They're upset?"

She sighed. "No. Yes. Sort of. I think they finally believe me now about you not being some kind of junkie prostitute rent-boy."

"Well, that's a relief."

She glared at me. "You *should* be relieved. They've been beside themselves since you left, convinced you'd be dead before they ever saw you again. They've been mourning you. Now they're just pissed at you."

I sighed. "That's an improvement, then!"

"Oh, yeah," she said. "They'll forgive you. You're the number one son, Trent. One night I came home late from the library and I heard Mum and Dad talking in the sitting room—they didn't know I was still awake—and they were talking about how clever you were, how you'd always been so creative and how they'd always thought you'd go so far."

I shook my head. "Cora, what the hell are you talking about? I was the family cock-up artist! Oh, sure, I know they loved me, but they weren't stupid enough to think I'd ever amount to anything. I know that much."

"You are pretty stupid for such a clever person, Trent." She sighed again. "I don't want to argue about it. The only person who thought you were a cock-up artist was you. The rest of us thought you were pretty good. And Mum and Dad thought the sun shone out your arse. Believe it or not, but it's true.

"I even think they're a little proud." She looked at the floor for a while. "I think I need to go back to them." I didn't say anything. She was chewing on the words, trying to get them out. "Mum and Dad need me there. They just don't understand how the world works. They're about to get their Internet back, you know?" That startled me. But of course—it had been a year. "But Dad's got to find new work, and he's been offline for a year and you know what he was like—he could barely make the computer work when he was using it every day. He's hopeless." She heaved a huge sigh. "Trent, all this stuff you're doing here, I mean to say, it's really fantastic, honestly. Makes me proud to bust, just to be related to you. I thought that I'd come to London and discover a life of mystery and excitement, and I did, but I also discovered that I'm just not cut out for it. You and your mates, you're magic, but you're also insane. The truth is—" She looked me straight in the eyes. "The truth is, I *am* a good girl, the kind of girl who gets top marks and loves to study and so on. I'm not nearly cool enough to hang around with you and your friends."

"Cora," I said. "You're the coolest girl I know." And it was true. Cora didn't have illustrious clothes or a shaved head or a bunch of piercings or whatever, but she'd seen through what I was doing with Sewer Cinema instantly, and challenged me to be a better version of myself. "I know you think you're not cool enough for us, but the truth is that you're so cool you don't need to live in a squat or break the law to be cool. You're cool just by being you—you're cool enough to go to the bloody *library*. If anyone should be proud, it should be *me*."

She chuckled a bit and kicked her feet. "Who knew my

brother was so soppy? Whatever, Trent. Listen, I've spent the
past year worrying myself stupid about you, and Mum and Dad
are twice as worried as I am. So I've got a proposal for you: come
home and see them with me. Show them what you've done with
yourself. Talk with them. You can come straight back to London
afterward. I'm not trying to convince you to go live in Bradford
or anything, but, Trent, you don't know what it's doing to them.
They may not be the brightest people in the world, but they love
us both like fire, and it's just not right—"

I held up my hands. "You're right." I was surprised to hear
myself saying it, but as soon as I did, some band of tightness and
sorrow that had cinched up my chest for so long I'd forgot it was
there released itself, and I found myself breathing into corners of
my lungs that hadn't felt air in a year. "You're right, Cora. I didn't
call because I hadn't called, and every day that went by made it
harder to call. It's been nearly a year now, and I can't stay away any
longer. You're right, you're right, you're right."

She got up and kissed me on the cheek. "I love you, Trent,"
she said, and gave me a ferocious hug that made my ribs creak. I
guess carrying all those library books had given her strong arms.

No one was surprised to hear that I was going home to see my
family. Chester had been to Manchester twice in the time I'd
known him, returning in a weird happy-sad mood, with a big bag
of food and a little stash of money from his parents. Even Rabid
Dog called his parents once a month, and endured their shouting
and abuse, and then went out and danced his ass off all night, returning exhausted and red-eyed and crawling into bed for a day.
Only Jem was like me, a man without a past, never contacting his
family or anyone else from his old days, whatever they might have
been. I asked him about Dodger from time to time, but he just
shrugged and changed the subject.

26 took Cora out before we left and they went clothes shopping at the vintage places Twenty liked, and they did Cora's hair
in her bathtub, dying it a weird reddy-brown like a fox and

cutting it so that it stood out in clumps that looked random but did flattering things for her round face. They returned from their day happy and giggly as ever, and swore they'd stay in touch. I sat on my laptop and lazily worked on my timeline of the life-and-times of Scot Colford, a huge file I kept that documented every appearance Scot had ever made and all the people who'd costarred with him. It was a big project that I'd been working on for years, though I'd had to start over when my lappie was stolen.

They were deep in conversation about the intricacies of copyright, talking about something called "plurilateral trade negotiations," "TRIPS," and "the Berne Convention." It made me feel a bit dumb, but also proud—the women in my life were so bloody brilliant, and they let me hang around with them.

Cora and I rode the tube to Victoria, and I helped her carry her big bag of library books and another bag of clothes 26 had helped her pick out. I had a cloth carrier-bag with my lappie and mains adapter, a couple clean pairs of underpants and socks, a toothbrush, and a spare T-shirt. I was going back to Bradford, but I wasn't staying more than one night.

As the bus pulled out of Victoria Station, my anxiety began to mount. What would I say to Mum and Dad? What would they say to me? Cora could tell that I was starting to work myself into a state, so she started to explain what she and 26 had been talking about. It was the history of copyright treaties, starting with something called the Berne Convention that a French writer named Victor Hugo had dreamed up in 1886, the first in a long line of international agreements on copyright that all built on one another. I didn't quite understand what Cora meant by this, but she explained: Every copyright treaty ever passed, for hundreds of years, has had in it something like, "By signing this treaty, you agree to all the other copyright treaties ever." The way Cora described it, it was a net that got tighter and tighter, every time a country signed on and promised to make its laws comply with all the copyright laws anyone ever managed to come up with.

Cora told me that lately, copyright treaties weren't even being made at the United Nations, not since the big film and record companies figured out that you could get a lot more done by holding the treaty discussions in secret, then announcing the results to the world's nations and demanding that they sign on, and refusing to trade with them if they didn't.

At first I didn't understand her, and then I didn't believe her, and then she made me get out my laptop and jump on the bus's WiFi network—I had a whole fistful of prepaid credit cards now that I used for this sort of thing, topping them up with cash only at newsagents that didn't have CCTV cameras—and look it up. It was sickening, really, thinking that our laws weren't really being passed by our MPs, but instead being made up in secret meetings run by executives from giant corporations. How the hell could we fight that?

All this business made the time fly past, so that I didn't even have time to worry about seeing Mum and Dad again, which was what Cora had intended all along. When we got off the bus in Bradford, my mind was still whirling with thoughts about secret treaties, so that I hardly noticed where we were until we were out on the road, smelling the smells and seeing the sights of my hometown.

It was so *familiar*—it seemed like I knew every crack in the pavement, every spiderweb in a shop doorway. The faces of the tramps asking for spare change outside of the station were like old friends: I must have seen them a million times in my life. Watching them begging for money I wanted to run over and explain about Jem's sign-theory, but mostly that was about avoiding Mum and Dad for as long as possible.

I wanted it to drizzle while we walked home, for the sky to be iron-gray and low and glowering, but it remained stubbournly cheerful and blue, with clouds that looked like fluffy sheep. Stupid sky. We were home far too soon, and if the bus station had seemed familiar, the chipped cement steps leading up into the estate were like seeing my own face in the mirror. They still had the same graffiti, even the same withered crisp packets and sneaky dried-out fossil dog shits that I remembered, like the place had been pickled the day I left.

Cora had her keys out before we got to the door, and she wanded them over the panel, punched in her PIN, and the door clicked open, and the smell of my parents' house slithered out the crack and up my nostrils and I was *home.*

Mum and Dad stood in the hallway, and Cora gave them each a kiss and a long hug, then slid past them into the sitting room, leaving me alone and facing them. They seemed to have aged ten years since I'd last seen them, skin sagging loose on their bones. Mum was leaning heavily on Dad, and when she took a step toward me, she wobbled so violently that both Dad and I leapt out to steady her. So there we were, all holding onto one another, and it seemed like we'd start blubbing any minute. So I said, "I'm sorry I didn't call. You must have been worried sick."

Mom said, "We were," and her voice cracked a bit.

"I'm sorry," I said again. "I'm so, so sorry. But I couldn't stay here, not after what I'd done to you all. And once I was gone . . . Well, I just couldn't bring myself to ring, I didn't know how I'd explain myself to you. And the longer I waited—"

"We thought you were dead!" Dad said, so loud that we both jumped. "We thought you were a prostitute, or taking drugs—"

Mum squeezed his arm hard. "Enough," she said. "We promised Cora." She put her arms around my neck and squeezed me so hard I thought my stuffing would come out. "It's so good to see you again, Trent. We love you."

"I love you too, Ma," I said, and I didn't want to cry in front of them, so I squirmed away and ran to my little room and threw myself down on my old bed and stuffed my face into my pillow and sobbed like a baby.

My room looked like I'd just stepped out. I could have sworn that the sheets on the bed were the ones that had been on it when I left for London, though they smelled of fresh detergent, so I guessed that Mum had come in and cleaned up, which also explained the lack of dust. There were my schoolbooks, and my old clothes, and the parts of laptops I'd taken apart to keep mine running. There were the scuffs on the wall from where I kicked off my trainers every day, and even spare trainers under the bed. Though it had been a year since I'd last been there, it felt like I'd only just left—but at the same time, it had been so long I couldn't even remember what or who I had been then.

Worst of all was the feeling that I was somehow going backward, or sinking down, into the life I'd had before London. I'd always had a sad, worshipful insecurity about being from the North, always wanted to trade the northern habit of saying little, of being wry and low-key, for the gabby, exuberant blathering of Londoners in the TV and films I'd grown up with. In my time at the Zeroday, I'd reinvented myself, made myself into a fast-talking and wordy sort. Back home in Bradford, all that felt like a cheap trick, a flimsy mask I'd made for myself, and now it was slipping off as I found myself speaking—even thinking—in the northern patterns I'd been reared on.

I dried my eyes and went into the sitting room. Cora had changed into more of her new clothes and to my surprise, both Mum and Dad were making approving noises about them. When did they get so cool? In my mind, Bradford had been a remote village with the cosmopolitan sophistication of a pigsty. Mum and Dad made space between them on the sofa, and I smelled Dad's cologne, Mum's perfume, like they'd made themselves up for a big night out, the way they did when we were little kids.

"We saw your film," Dad said. "On the telly. They showed it on the news. Sky only had bits of it, but ITV showed the lot."

Mum said, "They say that the film company's going to sue ITV for breaching copyright by showing it."

I snorted. "Brilliant: it's illegal to report the news now."

"It was a damned good film," Dad said. "All that Scot stuff.

I didn't know you were as clever as that, son." He smiled, a proud and soppy kind of smile that sliced right through my guts. Making my dad smile like that was better than a hundred Christmases.

"You liked it?" I said, blatantly fishing now.

"Made us proud," Mum said. "Laughed ourselves silly. It was so much better than the real film."

We sat there in awkward silence for a while.

"Is this what you've been doing since you got to London, then?" Dad said. The temperature in the room seemed to drop ten degrees.

"Erm," I said. I thought of all the adventures—the food from the skips, the squats, the giant bags of skunk, the hours spent begging in tube stations. "Mostly."

"How do you live?" Mum asked.

"I—" I swallowed. Then I told them all about Jem, and about the squat and the skips and the begging, though I danced quickly over it. I wasn't proud of that, even though I had made some major advances on Jem's science-of-panhandling project. I didn't tell them about the weed or the drink or the parties, either. Some things my parents didn't need to know. "So you see," I said, looking back and forth at their pop-eyed expressions, "You don't need to worry about me. I'm taking care of myself."

I was worried that they'd explode again, but now they were completely silent. I guess it was a lot to digest.

Finally, Mum said, "Trent, what on earth are you going to do with yourself? What sort of future is there in doing this . . . stuff? Are you going to spend the rest of your life squatting in abandoned buildings, eating garbage?"

It was like a slap across the face, and my first reaction was to shout and scream like a little kid, or run out of the room, or both. Instead, I swallowed a few times, and said, "What am I going to do with my future? I'm going to make art. That's all I've ever wanted to do. Look, I just want to make my films. I don't really care how I have to live in order to get that done."

"How about how *we* have to live while you get that done?" Dad said softly.

"That's why I left," I said. "It's not fair for me to put all of you at risk so I can do my thing. With me gone, you won't have to worry about my downloading."

"We just have to worry about *you*."

Of course, they were right, and there wasn't anything to say about that. I reached out and squeezed Mum's hand, then Dad's. "I don't have a good answer. I can put you at risk, or I can make you worried. But when I go back, I promise I'll be much better about keeping in touch. I'll call every day, come back for holidays some times. I promise."

"When you go back," Dad said.

"Well, yeah. Of course. You didn't think I was going to stay, did you?"

"Son, you're only seventeen. We have a responsibility—"

I jumped off the sofa like I'd been electrocuted. "Wait," I said. "This is a visit. I *can't* stay here. I've got a whole life now, people who are waiting for me, films to make, events we're putting on—" I began to back toward the door.

Mum said, "Sit down, Trent! Come on, now, sit down. We're not going to kidnap you. But wouldn't you like to sleep in your own bed for a few nights? Have a home-cooked meal?"

The first thing that popped into my head were the mouth-watering, epic feeds that we brewed up in the huge kitchen at the Zeroday from all the ingredients that turned up in the skips. I had the good sense not to tell Mum that her cooking was well awful in comparison to our rubbish cuisine. "I'd love dinner," I said, carefully not saying anything about "a few nights." Mum smiled bravely and got delicately to her feet, holding onto the sofa arm and wobbling gently. "Erm, can I help with the cooking?" I found that I quite fancied showing Mum all the elite cookery skills I'd acquired.

She waved me off, though. "Don't be stupid," she said. "I can

still cook a dinner for my own family in my own kitchen, son."
She limped off, back stiff.

"I didn't mean to offend her," I whispered to Dad.

He closed his eyes. "It's all right," he said. "She's just touchy about her legs, is all. All the rehab clinics and physiotherapy only accept appointments over the net, and it's too far for her to walk to the library, so Cora's been booking her in, but it's not a very good system and she hasn't been getting enough treatment. It's got her in a bad way."

Dinner was just as awkward, though Cora tried bravely to make conversation and talked up all the fun things we'd got up to in London, how excited all her mates were to see me on the telly. Mum had made noodles with tinned tuna and tomato sauce and limp broccoli and oven chips, and it was just as awful as I remembered it being. I longed to take Cora out to the grocers in town and find a skip to raid and cook up some brilliant feed, but I knew that Mum would certainly take this as an indictment of her womanhood or something.

I went to my room and I lay in my narrow bed, listening to the Albertsons' dogs barking through the thin wall. I heard Mum and Dad go to bed and mutter to one another for a long time, then the click of their bedside lamp. Sleep wouldn't come. That morning, before I'd got on the bus, I'd been an adult, living on my own in the world, master of my destiny. Within minutes of crossing the threshold to my parents' house, I was a boy again, and I felt about five years old and totally helpless. London felt a million miles away, and my life there felt like a silly kids' fantasy of what life could be like on my own with no parents or teachers to push me around.

I was seized with the sudden conviction that if I stayed in that bed overnight, I'd wake up a small child again in my pajamas and housecoat, demanding to play with my toys. The dogs next door barked. My dad's snores shook the walls, chased by my mum's slightly quieter ones. I sat up in bed, put my knees over the edge, grabbed my bag, and stuffed it full of the things I'd brought, along with a few extra pairs of underwear and socks from my drawer. Then I tied my bootlaces together and slung them around my neck and padded on cat feet out of my room and down the corridor toward the front door and freedom.

As I reached for the doorknob, a hand landed heavily on my shoulder. I gave a little jump and a squeak and nearly dropped my bag as I turned around, giving myself a crick in the neck. It was my dad, unshaven, his dental appliance out so that his missing front teeth showed, looking grim. He reached out and turned the doorknob and opened the door, then jerked his head at it. I stepped out and he followed me, pulling the door closed behind him, but leaving it open a crack so it didn't lock.

"Going away again, son?"

I hung my head. What was wrong with me? Why couldn't I say good-bye like a proper person?

"Just—"

"Forget it," Dad said. He looked like a huge, sad, broken bear. Without knowing why, I found myself wanting to hug him. I did. He hugged me back, and the strength in his arms was just as I remembered it from my childhood, when I believed my father could lift a car if he took a mind to. "We're proud of you, son. Keep in touch with us, and stay safe."

He fumbled for my hand and stuck something into it. I looked down and saw that it was a pair of fifty-pound notes.

"Dad," I said, "I can't take this. Honestly, I'm just fine. Really." I'd seen for myself how tight things were around the flat, the soap in the bathroom made by pressing together carefully hoarded slivers from other bars. My parents were so broke they could barely afford to eat. This was a fortune for them.

"Take it," he said, trying for a big, magnanimous style. "Your mother would worry otherwise."

We had a kind of silly arm wrestle there on the doorstep as I tried to give it back to him, but in the end, he won—he was my dad, of course he won. He was strong enough to lift a car, wasn't he?

He hugged me again, and I walked off to the coach-station, and with every step, I grew taller and older, so that by the time I bought my ticket (not using the fifties; those went into the little change-pocket in the corner of my jeans), I was a full-fledged adult.

Chapter 7

I bought more WiFi on the coach, but there was something wrong with it. I couldn't access Confusing Peach or any of the secret sites that lived inside it—they just timed out. And two of the web-mail accounts I used were also kaput, along with the voice-mail site I liked. I poked around and decided that the censorwall on the bus-company's Internet had been updated with a particularly large and indiscriminate blacklist, so I tried some proxies I knew, but they didn't help. I folded away my laptop and looked at the motorway zipping past, the dark night and the raindrops on the window, hoping for sleep or at least some kind of traveler's trance, but my mind kept going back to the soap in the bathroom, my dad's sad, missing teeth, my mum's sagging skin and hollow, wet eyes.

I had the seat to myself, so I took out my mobile and called 26. I'd sent her a steady stream of texts from my parents' place, until she'd sent me back a stern message telling me to stop worrying about her and pay attention to my family, damn it. But I'd missed her fearsomely, with a pang like a toothache, and now that I was headed home—ha! London was home now, there was a turn up for the books!—I found myself trembling with antici-pation of having her next to me, spooned up against her on my bed on the floor of the Zeroday, my face buried in the fragrant skin where her neck became her shoulder.

"Cecil?" she said. "Have you heard?" Her voice was tight, hushed.

"Heard what?"

"They've raided Confusing Peach. Took all the servers right out of the rack."

"What?"

"They went at it like cavemen with stone axes! Took two hundred machines down—there's thousands of sites offline!"

I felt the blood drain all the way to the soles of my feet. There were any number of reasons I could think of for the coppers to go after Confusing Peach—the drugs, the parties—but the timing of the raid made me think that this had more to do with our screening, and all the coverage it had garnered. Sam Brass from the MPA had looked like he was ready to blow a gasket before; now that I was on the front of the paper exhorting people to violate copyright, he must be in full-on volcano mode.

"Why'd they do it?"

26 sighed and didn't say anything and I knew that I was right.

"It should be okay," she said. I couldn't figure out what she meant—how could it be okay? The sites that we used as our hubs and gathering place were down, and so were all those other sites. "I mean, the Confusing Peach people always said they kept the logs encrypted, and flushed them every two days in any event. And the main databases were all encrypted—remember last year when there were all those server crashes because of the high load from the encryption, and they were doing all that begging for us to send them money for an upgrade?"

I did remember it. I hadn't thought much about it at the time, just been annoyed. But now I knew what 26 meant when she said it was okay. She meant that they wouldn't be able to use the Confusing Peach logs to figure out who we all were, where we all lived, what we were all up to.

I'd never given much thought to encryption, for all that I'd used it every day since I was a little kid putting together my first private laptop drives. Depending on how you looked at it, the theory was either very simple or incomprehensibly hard. The simple way of looking at it was that encryption systems were black boxes that took your files and turned them into perfectly unscrambleable gibberish that only you could gain access to.

But, of course, I knew that it was a lot more complicated than that: crypto wasn't a perfect and infallible black box, it was an insanely complicated set of mathematical proofs and implementation details that were incredibly hard to get right.

The news was always full of stories about banking security systems, smart cards, ATM records, and all manner of other sensitive information leaking out because someone had done the maths wrong, or forgot to turn off the debugging mode that dropped an unscrambled copy of everything into a maintenance file. After all, that's what Aziz relied on, wasn't it? Badly done crypto rendering beautiful bits of kit illegal or unusable?

And that was just the start of the problem when it came to crypto. Even assuming the programmers got it all right, then you had to deal with the *users,* idiots like me who just wanted to get on with the job and not get hassled by having to remember long, complicated passwords and that. So we used short passwords that were easy to guess—especially for a computer. We refused to run the critical software updates because we were too busy. We visited dodgy websites with our unpatched browsers and caught awful viruses that snooped on our crap passwords. It doesn't matter how great the bank safe is if the banker uses 000 for a combination and forgets to lock the door half the time.

So maybe it was okay for us. Maybe Confusing Peach didn't have any readable logs or databases of users and messages. Maybe all that happened is that the poor admins who ran it—a group of University of Nottingham physics students who'd been handing the admin duties on to younger students since before I was born—were now missing all their computers and answering hard questions in some police station basement.

But I didn't think we should count on it.

"When did this all happen?"

"Just now," she said. "Midnight raid. They didn't even wait for the building maintenance people to let them into the server cages: they just cut through them with torches. Brought in camera crews and everything. It's all over the news. The Motion Picture Association spokesman called it a 'major victory against piracy and theft.'"

I swallowed again. "I am a total cock-up," I said. "God, what have I done?"

"*Trent McCauley*," she said sharply. I sat to attention. She had never called me by my real full name. "Stop it, this instant. This is not the time to wallow in self-pity, idiot boy. *You* didn't do anything—*we* did it. I was putting on Pirate Cinemas before I even met you, remember? You're not our leader, you fool—you're one of us, and we're all in this together. So stop putting on airs and taking credit for everything that we've all done, right *now*."

I opened and shut my mouth like a fish. "Twenty," I said at last. "I'm not saying that—"

"Yes, you are, whether or not you mean to. You need to get over feeling responsible for everyone and everything that goes on and realize that we're all in this together."

"I hate it when you're right," I said.

"I know. Apologize now."

"I'm sorry."

"Right, doesn't that feel better?"

It did. "Okay, boss. Now what do we do?"

"Come back to London and we'll figure it out."

I took night buses from Victoria to 26's house, creeping across dark London, seeing it again with new eyes though I'd only been gone for a day. Everyone and everything seemed so strange—big, menacing, mysterious. I felt paranoid, didn't want to get my laptop out in case someone robbed me for it. London didn't feel like home anymore, but neither did Bradford—I guess that meant that I was genuinely homeless.

I texted 26 when I was outside her place and she silently opened the door for me. She led me up the dark stairs, past her parents' bedroom, and into her room. We kissed for a long time, like we'd been apart for a hundred years. Then I slid in between the sheets beside her and cuddled up to her from behind. Her hair tickled my nose, but I didn't mind. Had I thought that I had no home? Of course I did: wherever 26 was, that was home.

In the morning, I got up and unfolded my laptop. 26 was still spark out, snoring like the world's cutest band saw, and I did what I always did first, hit Confusing Peach and began to read through the message boards, ping my mates, clear my queue of Tweets and mails and that.

I was at it for ten minutes before I realized that I was using Confusing Peach, which meant that it wasn't down anymore! I skipped up to the front door of the site, to the announcements section I generally ignored, and found a proud message from one of Peach's overseas admins, who boasted about how she and the Nottingham physics students had prepared for a raid years ago, building in redundant mirrors in three different countries (though she didn't say which, and my IP trace did something funny I'd never seen before, bouncing back and forth between three routers—one in Sweden, one in Poland, and one in Macedonia—without seeming to resolve to any one machine).

I shook 26's shoulder, then shook it again when she swatted at my hand. "Wake up," I hissed. "Come on, wake up."

She sat up, pulling the sheet over her, and nestled her chin in my neck, peering over my shoulder. "What?"

"Look," I said, showing her the message.

"Holy cats," she said. "Genius! What a bunch of absolute nerds. They must have had such a fun time playing superspy and setting up all those fail overs and mirrors. I guess that means that we can probably trust their crypto, too." She kissed my earlobe. "See? A night's sleep fixes everything."

Downstairs, I could hear her parents finishing their breakfast.

"What time is your first class?" I said.

She yawned and looked at her phone, beside the bed. "I've got an hour," she said. "Plenty of time. Come on, let's eat."

I'd spent the night at her's a few times, but I'd always waited until her parents left for work before skulking downstairs. Something about confronting them across the breakfast table—even if 26 and I hadn't been having it off the night before, it was still too weird.

"Is it okay?" I said.

"Come on, chicken," she said, and tossed me my jeans and a T-shirt of mine she'd worn home one night. I tugged it over my head, reveling in how it smelled of her.

Her parents were dressed already, and they were wrestling each other for space for their newspapers at the book-crowded table, drinking cups of coffee from a big press-pot and eating toast out of a tarnished toast-rack. Pots of jam and Marmite and various other spreads teetered on the book-piles.

They looked at me when I came in, muttered "Morning," and went back to their papers. 26 gave them each a peck on the top of the head, poured us each an enormous cup of coffee (finishing the pot), and piled the remaining toast on a plate that she handed to me, then rummaged through the fridge for cheese and juice and three kinds of fruit and yogurt. Her mum quirked an eyebrow at her and muttered something about teenaged metabolisms and bottomless appetites and 26 stuck her tongue out.

"We're inside-out with hunger, Mum!"

Her dad laughed. "I see you've deployed the auxiliary breakfast stomachs," he said. "Go on, eat."

We pigged out, and 26's parents showed each other (and us) bits from the paper, and I made another pot of coffee—it wasn't bad, though it wasn't a patch on the stuff Jem made—and then 26 looked at her phone and yelped and announced she was late for class and dashed upstairs, leaving me alone with her parents. She was back down in a flash, dressed, a toothbrush in her mouth. She spat toothpaste in the kitchen sink, dropped the toothbrush in one of the coffee cups, and kissed us each before charging out the door.

I'd almost forgot I was eating breakfast with my girlfriend's parents, but now it was as awkward as an awkward thing. I got up and began to wash up the breakfast dishes, but 26's mum said, "We've got a dishwasher, Cecil, no need for that."

Durr. I began to stack the dishes in the dishwasher, trying to project an air of responsible goodness. 26's father cleared his throat and said, "What are your intentions for my daughter, young man?" in a stern voice.

I turned around, feeling like I'd been caught in a horror film. He was absolutely poker-faced, no trace at all of his affable, absent normal expression. I remembered that he was a high-powered barrister by day. Then he burst out laughing.

"Oh, son, you should *see* your face! Christ on a bike, you looked like you thought I was going to go and get my shotgun!"

26's mum rolled up her newspaper and hit him on the back of the head several times with it. "Rosh, that was *very* cruel."

He waved her off. "Oh, our Cecil here is a fighter. I'm sure he'd have survived." She swatted him again. "Oh, okay, fine. Sorry, Cecil. I just wanted to tell you that, well, we *like* you. You don't need to tiptoe around us when you're here. 26 has told us a little about you, and it sounds like you've had some bad breaks. We saw your picture in the papers, you know, and 26 showed us your film. It was bloody good stuff, too! 26 hasn't always had the best taste in boys, but you're doing very well for yourself, so far. In any event, you needn't skulk around like a thief when you stay over."

I was at a total loss for words. That might have just been the *nicest* thing anyone ever said to me. I smiled awkwardly and said, "Thank you," then fished around, and said, "you know, thank you. A lot." Not my finest moment, but it seemed to satisfy 26's father. I had a thought, as long as we were all getting along so well. "Can I ask you something?"

He made a go-ahead gesture.

"What's her *real* name?"

He snorted and 26's mum started to stay something, but he hushed her. "I'm afraid I've been sworn to confidentiality on that score. It's true that 26 isn't the name we gave her at birth, but she chose it for herself very early, and to be honest, it's what we've always called her. I expect she'll change it by deed poll sooner or later."

I escaped from the kitchen after shaking both their hands (her mum even gave me a little, but warm, hug), got dressed and showered and slipped out the door and went home to the Zeroday.

I climbed the fire escape and slipped through the window, dropped my bag off in my room, and headed downstairs. There were voices in the pub-room, some I didn't recognize, and one I hadn't heard in quite some time.

I came into the room to find Chester and Rabid Dog on the sofa with their arms folded, looking worried, Jem perched on the arm, and sitting on the bar was the speaker, whose voice I hadn't heard in months and months: it was Dodger!

I almost didn't recognize him at first. He'd cut his hair, and while he was still wearing jeans and work boots, they were clean and free from holes, and his boots actually gleamed in the pub lights.

Standing beside him was a young man in a smart jumper and a little narrow-brim pork-pie hat and expensive trainers—your basic Bow hipster—watching it all with an intent, keen look.

Everyone turned to look at me when I came in. I waved—"Hi, hi," I said. "Dodger, mate, where've you been? Nice hair!"

He grunted and waved at me. "Cecil," he said, "meet Mr. Thistlewaite," he said, gesturing at the hipster, who waved back and said, "Call me Rob."

"Hi, Rob."

Jem turned to me. "Dodger was just explaining how Mr. Thistlewaite has this incredible offer for us all."

"Oh, yes?"

Dodger shook his head. "Jem, listen to me, will you? Before you come to conclusions?"

Jem folded his arms again.

"Right," Dodger said. "Right. Okay. Here's the story. Rob here is a property developer, specialized in derelict buildings."

I started to see why everyone else was looking so upset.

"What he does, right, is he buys them off the council or whomever for cheap and does them up when he can, and sells 'em off. But when he gets one like this, in a neighborhood that's too crap to sell anything in, he likes to wait for a while, cos there's no sense in spending a lot of money doing a place up if no one wants to live in it."

"I figure if a place is cheap enough now, I'll have a flutter on it, put some money down, wait and see if the neighborhood improves." Rob didn't seem to be embarrassed to be talking about how much money he had, which was unusual. I knew lots of hipsters were rich, but I didn't think most of them could talk casually about buying and selling whole buildings.

"Right. So Rob here reckons that Bow is going to come up nice, and so he's bought this place."

That was quite an announcement. I could tell that he'd already got that far with the other lads, and this certainly explained why they were looking so murderous.

"You working for landlords now, Dodger?" Jem said. "You show him which places to buy, grass out your old mates, sell our homes out from under us?"

Dodger shook his head. "That's the part you're not getting, Jem. Listen, okay? Just listen. Yeah, I give Rob help finding good places to buy. All the best places are squatted, cos we're all so clever about finding them, yeah? But a place like this, Rob doesn't want to do it up any time soon—it's going to take *years* before this dump is worth anything. And in the meantime, *you get to live here.*"

That got our attention.

"Yeah," he said. "Right. Rob wants to know that there's someone responsible living here, that it's not being used as a sugar shack or for tarts to turn tricks, that no stupid kids are going to burn it down cooking rock. He wants you to be tenants."

Jem still looked suspicious. "Don't tenants pay rent?"

"I'm only after peppercorn rent," Rob said. "A pound a year."

"Yeah," Dodger said. "And in return, you keep the place up and go quietly when Rob asks you to, whenever that may be."

"What's in it for him?"

"I get a caretaker I can rely on. Dodger vouches for you. And who knows, when the time comes, there might be some other empty property I need someone for I can move you to. No promises, but there's plenty of empty buildings these days in London, in case you haven't noticed."

"Yeah," Dodger said. "And you keep it up—*we* keep it up, since I'll go over everything with you and make sure the wiring isn't going to burn the place down. And in return, you don't grass him out to the council for substandard living conditions and whatnot. It's a fair trade—you won't find a fairer one, right? Best of all, you get legit, which means you don't have to worry about getting tossed out on a moment's notice. Rob here will give you at least a month to get your stuff together, probably more. Honestly mate, this is it, the squatter's holy grail."

Jem nodded slowly. "It certainly sounds like it. You always hear about landlords who work out that the best thing for everyone is to let you stay until it's time to go. But I'd figured they were an urban legend—like the kindly copper or the hooker with a heart of gold."

"Just call me a living legend," Rob said. He seemed supremely cool and unruffled by all this. I guess if I had loads of money *and* proper villains like Dodger for mates, I'd be supercool, too.

I was starting to get my head around what this all meant. "We've missed your cooking 'round here, Dodger—you staying for lunch?" I thought it'd be good to get us all thinking about the fact that we were all mates, that Dodger was one of the original Jammie Dodgers.

He grinned. "Yeah," he said. "Rob, you want a feed?" Rob looked a little uncomfortable for the first time; my guess was he was a little squeamish about the idea of eating garbage, but to his credit, he rallied.

"Sure," he said, and just like that, the tension was broken. Dog and Chester—who, I think, had always felt a little like Johnnie-come-latelies and thus not entitled to speak up on matters of household management—visibly thawed, and Dodger produced a baggy of his insane weed, and someone had papers, and the afternoon got very warm and friendly. Dodger scoured our freezer for gourmet tidbits, and ended up doing marrow bones, cod cheeks, grilled eels, and heaps of veg and beans, all arranged so artfully on the plate you hardly wanted to eat it.

Dog hardly wanted to eat it anyway, having no taste for organ meats and that delicacies, but we made such a great show of smacking our lips and groaning in ecstasy that he stopped trying to hide his marrow bone under his lentils and instead dug out the rich, oily brown stuff from within and piled some on the little triangle of brown toast—day-old bread from the deep freeze—with butter and tentatively tasted it. Thereafter, he became some sort of mythic, organ-devouring beast, who scarfed it all up and asked for seconds and then thirds, and there was white wine, and then Jem did coffee things, and Rob told hilarious dirty jokes, and the afternoon raced past and before we knew it, it was evening and our tummies strained at our waistbands.

By the time we pushed back from the table, we were all fast friends. Rob's bottomless supply of dirty jokes, Dodger's cooking, and Jem's coffee-making-fu had bonded us as effectively as a two-part epoxy.

"You're the guy from the Pirate Cinema, yeah?" Rob said. I felt myself blush. Just how many people saw the cover of *Time Out* and *The Guardian*, anyway? A lot, it seemed.

"We all did it," I said. "I just did the talking at the beginning."

Chester blew a raspberry. "Cecil there's the genius auteur around here. The rest of us are dogsbodies and hacks."

"I was gutted that I'd missed it," Rob said, grinning. "I had so many mates that went along, but I thought it all sounded too dodgy, going off to the sewer and that. Figured that it would be some wanky art-student film and I'd be stuck in the shit-pit with it. Downloaded it, though, afterward. Good stuff! Really brilliant!"

I blushed harder.

"You shoulda been there," Chester said. "It was a hundred times better with the whole crowd and all."

"Well," Rob said. "You'll have to let me know the next time you do one."

Jem got a sneaky look. "You wouldn't happen to have any derelict buildings lying about that you wouldn't mind seeing used as a theater now and again, would you, Rob?"

I opened my mouth to tick Jem off—Rob was already giving us a free spot to live, what more did we want?—but before I could, Rob got a faraway look in his eye. "Gosh," he said. "Now that you mention it, I rather suspect I do."

Dodger let out an evil chuckle. "You've got a devious mind, Jem-o," he said.

"He does, doesn't he?" Rob said. "I can see I'm going to have to watch out for you, young master. But you know, I've always fancied being a patron of the arts. This sounds like it'd be miles better than getting your name on a sign in a dusty wing of a museum."

"Plus you wouldn't believe the girls that turn up at this sort of thing," Dodger said, though as far as I knew, he'd never been to a Confusing Peach night, but he spoke with the utter confidence of a lifelong bullshit artist. And anyway, Rob was *old,* twenty-five or thirty, and most of the people at a Confusing Peach party were my age. Whatever—if he could get off with some lady, who was I to look askance?

26 rang me from work: she'd been pulling the late shift at the anarchist bookstore more and more, as she tried to juggle all the crazy film stuff, her schoolwork, and, erm, me.

"Why don't you come pick me up?" she said. "Annika's

around and she's really interested in Sewer Cinema." My fame had no bounds, it seemed.

"I'll come straight over," I said. Any residual intoxication from the wine and the weed had been burned away by Jem's coffee, which had the ability to cook away booze remnants like a flamethrower crisping a butterfly.

I went to my room to dress and dumped out the bag of Bradford clothes I'd taken home from my room. I contemplated it, lying limp on my bed, and realized that before I came to London, I'd dressed like a total burk. Honestly—shiny wind-cheaters with the names of sports teams? I didn't even *like* sport! T-shirts with rude slogans? Transparent kicks with fat electroluminescent laces that strobed like the most pathetic disco ever? Seriously—how had my family allowed me to leave the house looking like such a, a . . . *hick*? Like someone who dressed himself by studying the Primark adverts on the bus stations? Well, at least the underpants and socks were salvageable, just.

So I put on my Bradford underwear and slipped on a pair of oversize green trousers, cut with that funny midleg wibble that made it look a little like you were wearing kneepads; a pair of cut-down black wellies trimmed to sneaker-height; a crewneck sweater embroidered with nylon fishing line hung with mismatched buttons and a huge, waxed-cotton coat that started out as a surplus butcher's smock, carefully waterproofed by rubbing it over and over again with soft wax. I looked at myself in the dirty mirror beside Jem's mural in the corridor and grinned: I looked like a proper Londoner now. No one in Bradford dressed like this.

The bookshop was just shutting when I got there. 26 was selling a hippie-looking old dude a thick book on African history. He chewed a lock of his hair while she rang it up, then paid her in pound coins that he carefully doled out of his pocket, counting them aloud. He was about par for the course at the bookshop—all the customers were a bit odd. That was okay: I'd decided I'd rather be where the odd people were. They had more fun.

Annika was checking the stock and dusting shelves and doing all the other closing-down things that 26 usually did at the end of the night. As soon as the hippie guy was gone, she helped 26 count out the till while I made tea and scrounged some organic multigrain agave-sweetened vegan biccies that tasted only about half as horrible as they sounded. Annika put the cashbox away in its hiding place—a nook in a shadow under the stairs to the cellar, a box that had once held the gas meter for the shop when it had been a flat. They deposited the previous day's cash every day at lunchtime, because no one wanted to carry around a couple hundred quid in late-night east London.

Then we all sat down and Annika sipped her tea and dipped her biccie and I watched the elaborate, tentacled tattoo writhe around her skinny throat and down her skinny arms. "Cecil," she said, "I'm really glad you came down tonight. You see, I've heard about the Sewer Cinema you and 26 and your friends put on, the films you showed, the things you said. I wanted to tell you what an absolutely *wonderful* job you did. I don't know what you could have done to make it any better, honestly—it's got everyone talking about the right thing."

26 kissed me below the ear and squeezed my shoulders and I felt my ears turning red. I could see why 26 liked Annika so much; she was so calm, so assured, and she was very beautiful (though not as beautiful as 26, I hastily told myself). "Thank you," I said. "It wasn't just me, you know."

"Oh, I know. It's never just one person. But you're the one who's got his face in the papers and on the news. Which means that you're the one they'll be looking for when the time comes."

I gulped. "When the time comes?"

She shook her head. "You know what I mean. We're kicking the hornets' nest. That's good. I'm all for kicking hornets' nests! But when you do that, the hornets come out and swarm. I think it's a good bet that the coppers'll be looking for you before long."

I sighed. "Of course," I said. This had been in the back of

my mind all along, ever since I'd seen the papers. "Do you think they'll try to put me in jail?"

She shrugged. "Depends on how chummy the coppers and the entertainment types are that day. They might charge you with criminal trespass on the sewer, or they might charge you with criminal copyright infringement. Or both. Impossible to say."

I nodded. "Yeah. But they tried to shut down Confusing Peach and they failed. We took the private Pirate Cinema and opened them to the public. So we lost the TIP vote—maybe that means we'll just have to beat them outside of Parliament."

She smiled broadly and radiated approval. I basked in it. "That's the stuff," she said. "Why not—we could get hit by a bus tomorrow, after all. But there's no sense in you going to jail if you don't have to, yeah? So here's what I was thinking: there's a lot of us around here who've been at this for a long time. Why don't you teach us how you do your cinema nights, and we'll help with the work. You can show up in disguise—some of us are good at that—and watch the proceedings, but we'll have it all done by people in masks and so on. No more faces. 26 told me you had some more locations you were scouting—"

I nodded, and told them about Rob, and his offer of more places to throw events.

Annika nodded sagely. "I've heard about this bloke—he bought up a squat in Brixton where some friends of mine were living. They got to stay on for six months, then he moved them to another place in Streatham. Good for his word, I think. A rare bird, this: a landlord with a good heart. Most of them would rather see their places sitting empty than occupied by dirty squatters who don't pay for their lodgings."

I nodded enthusiastically. "He really seemed nice. And between his other empty buildings and the underground sites that we found in that book—"

She nodded back. "We could throw a new cinema every week. Do you think you could make enough films for that, though?"

26 set down her teacup. "Oh, there's plenty of people out there making films. I don't think we need to worry on *that* score. I'd be more worried about getting raided or whatnot."

Annika chuckled. "Oh, we've been through this before; I used to put on raves, back when I was just a little girl. It's an art and a science, a balance between technology and staying below the threshold for too much scrutiny. You'll learn it quick, you two. You're dead clever, aren't you?"

I couldn't argue with that. We clinked teacups.

Chapter 8

Before Sewer Cinema, the Pirate Cinema nights had been easy—just larks put on by friends at semisecret/semipublic parties, organized on Confusing Peach by 26 and her mates, girls like Hester who lived to climb trees and string up the cameras. Sewer Cinema had been a deathmarch, a chaos of fixing chairs and dealing with out-of-town relatives and a million kinds of chaos.

But with Annika and her friends scouting locations and managing the logistics of getting people from rendezvous places to whatever civil defense bunker, sewer, graveyard, abandoned warehouse, or other romantic spot, it became a kind of assembly line.

Oh, 26, Chester, Dog, Jem, and I all helped with the setup still, sneaking in chairs, usually wearing the old standby disguise of a hi-viz vest and safety hat; Hester and her friends also threw their backs into the work with a great deal of enthusiasm. But for us at the Zeroday, the real work wasn't playing stevedore with bits of furniture; we were making films.

Every spare minute that occurred, every hour that could be stolen from sleep, we were buried in our edit suites, cutting and mixing. Confusing Peach had got bigger than ever, and there were more secret sub-boards that we were being invited to all the time. There were loads of people making and posting videos, and there were loads of kids who loved their 3D animation software, and working with them, we realized new possibilities. Rabid Dog found a crew of Italian kids from Turin who loved the monster films nearly as much as him, and by working with them, he was able to realize some of the funniest disembowelment and dismemberment scenes in the history of illegal horror.

And now I came to appreciate just how enormous the whole

remix world was. A little venturesome wandering online and I was smack in the middle of music mixers, visual mixers, text slicers and dicers. They were just as obsessed as I was, just as driven to make new out of old, to combine things that no one had ever thought of combining. Of course, they were just as threatened by TIP as we were, though they were much lower-profile targets than those who raided the entertainment industry's multimillion-pound crown jewels.

I discovered that I was far from the only Scot-obsessive in the world. A pack of kids in Rio were dead keen on him, and they were incredibly skilled with a bunch of free 3D animation packages; what's more, they'd been perfecting their own Scot 3D models for years, trading polygons with other 3D kids all over the world. They had hardly any English and I couldn't speak a word of Portuguese when we started but we had loads of automatic translation engines, and a shared love of Scot. Apparently, he'd been *huge* in Brazil. Working with Sergio, Gilberto, Sylvia, and them, I was able to make Scot do things he'd never done in the films, and now we were *really* cooking.

We had Pirate Cinema nights every Friday and sometimes also on Sunday afternoons, changing locations every time. Sometimes we'd be in a big, derelict Victorian down by Notting Hill, with different screens in every room showing films to rapt crowds. Sometimes it'd be long, sooty, abandoned tube tunnels with films splashed on the ceiling, and loungers wedged between the steel rails so you could recline and watch. Sometimes it was warehouses, and once we even took over an actual cinema, one that had been closed down for fifteen years but still had working popcorn machines. For that night, we made ourselves proper usher's uniforms, sewing gold brocade onto our shoulders and down the sides of our trousers, and we packed the house—six hundred masked faces watching as the films we'd made and found unspooled on the huge screen.

Masked? Oh yes. After Sewer Cinema and my unexpected personal fame, Annika hatched a plan to keep all our identities secret—we'd turn Pirate Cinema nights into a masked ball. Some people came in simple domino masks or surgical face masks, while others went in for Black Block balaclavas, but the best were the elaborate carnival masks that people made for themselves. You'd get people tottering in with enormous confections on their heads—fantastic animals, monsters, cruel papier-mâché caricatures of politicians. There was a pack of zombies that came regularly, much to RD's delight: they competed each week to see who could do the most gruesome makeup; they'd fake dangling eyeballs, gaping slit throats, latex holes in their cheeks exposing "teeth" and gums. It was magesterially stomach churning.

It all went by in a blur. No sooner would we tear down a show than we'd be setting up for the next one. And now that the press knew who I was, I was getting all kinds of requests for interviews—as Cecil B. DeVil, of course. Annika encouraged me to do these—"just don't take them too seriously."

The first three or four made me very nervous, but then I realized that the press always asked the same questions, so I'd just flop down on the sofa with my laptop and my headset and take the call while Jem fed me so much jet fuel it was a race to see whether I could finish the interview before I attained liftoff and sailed into gabbling, babbling coffee-orbit.

I don't think I ever worked harder in my life, before or since. I'd roll into bed at 2:00 or 3:00 A.M., having come off a night's binge-editing; it'd be even later if I'd been out at a Cinema night. I'd wake up five hours later, merciless alarm beating me into wakefulness. I'd attempt coffee in the kitchen, and the sound of my fumbling inevitably roused Jem, who *hated* to be woken, but hated the sound of someone murdering his precious beans even worse. He'd make me a pot of French press and I'd go back to work, devouring the night's emails, status updates, tweets, and IMs, many from other people running their own Pirate Cinemas in other cities around the world, others from filmmakers who were hoping to get screened at one of our nights. Plenty of messages from fans, too, people who'd been to one of the nights or had seen the videos on ZeroKTube or some other site and wanted to sing my praises, which felt insanely great.

It was so much stuff that I actually created two separate identities, one for press queries—I'd get half a dozen of these every day, many for email interviews, others for video or audio link-ups. Some even wanted to come and meet me, but I never said yes to these, because I was paranoid that they might bring the police—or *be* the police. But I did all the others. The email interviews were easiest, since they always asked the same five or six dumb questions, and I just kept a huge file of prewritten answers in the form of a FAQ on the Pirate Cinema site. I'd just cut and paste the answers straight into the email and be done with it.

Then there were all the organizational emails. Annika and her people were amazing location scouts, always finding new places for us to try. But then there was the problem of smuggling in the attendees—and getting them there without tipping off the cops about our location in advance. For this, they employed tactics from the golden age of rave parties: they'd announce a rallying point and then someone would meet them with instructions for another location, and then another. On the way, hidden scouts would check them out, looking for anyone suspicious. Finally, they'd put them in white builders' vans with no windows and ferry them to the actual spot. I could think of fifty ways for the cops to defeat this, but it lent the whole thing an air of mystery and excitement, and it seemed the cops were not trying that hard to intercept us just then, because we didn't get busted once.

So—organizational emails, then I'd shove some food in my gob without tasting it, and hit the editing suite again. I was turning out thirty to forty-five minutes of video a *week,* and it took me more than an hour to edit together every minute. And on top of that, I still had to do my runs to the skips to harvest food, and on top of that I was always on the lookout for scraps for the mask-making projects, which had sprawled all over the Zeroday, taking over every horizontal surface with sloppy papier-mâché remnants—torn strips of newspaper, wheatpaste, paints, beads, glitter, fur, scraps of fabric and bone, even a load of false teeth that Aziz had dug up from somewhere.

Someone was always making masks, and it had turned into a competition and a game. 26 had upped the ante by making a mask for me one week and demanding that I give her the mask I'd been planning on wearing—a giant muppet head made out of fake electric blue fur with hundreds of eyes sewn all around it (the real eyeholes were hidden behind a scrim of window-screening). Thereafter, we inaugurated a ritual of trading masks just before heading out on show nights, and we'd surprise one another with our bizarre and hilarious creations.

By the time the editing and the grocery shopping and the eating and the interviews were done, if I was lucky I'd get an hour or two with 26, who was doing almost everything I was doing, plus keeping up with her final year's worth of schoolwork, before heading out for the night—either to one of our cinema nights or to some meeting that Annika's people had put together to talk about how to make things better next time.

I'd get home exhausted but unable to sleep from all the coffee and adrenaline and excitement, and often as not I'd spin up a little pin-sized spliff and then smoke it while I did a few more edits and waited for it to kick in and tie weights to my eyelids and my arms and legs and drag me off the chair and onto the mattress on the floor, until the alarm woke me to start it all over again.

Week after week this continued, punctuated by increasingly common phone calls home to Cora and my parents. It looked like Cora would finish out her year okay, not the best grades she'd ever got, but not the worst, either. She was using the newly restored network connection to do a series of independent study projects on how corrupt the Theft of Intellectual Property Act's passage had been, and was making a bloody pest of herself calling up the offices of MPs who'd voted for it, asking them to talk to her for the projects.

It turned out that her teachers *adored* this sort of thing and had put her up for some kind of district-wide student-work competition, with the winning essay to be published on the BBC's website and presented nationally. Which would be quite a laugh, what with it making Parliament look like a bunch of corporate lickspittles. Well, I'd laugh, anyway. Mum and Dad were doing a bit better now that the network was back, and most times when I rang, we could get through ten or fifteen minutes without them recriminating against me and telling me that I should come home and asking me what I was doing with my life.

I didn't answer this last one. My face hadn't been in the papers for quite some time now, and to be honest, that's how I liked it. It had been ages since anyone on the street had recognized me, since anyone on a bus had squinted at me from across the aisle, as if trying to remember where they knew me from. All in all, that was for the best.

But without my picture on the front of the paper, Mum and Dad quickly forgot how proud they were of me and once again began to worry that a wee lad like myself might get led astray by bad company in dirty old London. Nothing I said could dissuade them from this, and to be honest, if they knew, actually knew what I was up to, they'd say that they were perfectly correct about what had happened to their beloved son in the terrible city.

But those calls didn't get me down for long. Nothing did. That sense of overwhelming, all-consuming busyness kept anything from making so much as a scratch on me. I had *too much to do* to mope or grump or moan. I was living life, not complaining about it, and Christ, didn't it feel wonderful?

Yeah, so that was my life there for quite some time. It was all our lives, thrown headlong into it, and every week there were more emails, more films, more press queries, more people who seemed to care about what we were up to. And there were more people coming to the cinema nights, and there were more cinemas—not just ours. They popped up all over town and I tried to go to as many as I could make it to—even if it meant skipping out for part of ours. I wanted to see what they were showing, and if it was any good, I wanted to poach it for one of our nights.

Plenty of it was good and some of it was so bloody fantastic, I wanted to find the makers and prostrate myself at their feet and beg to be taught by one so skilled.

Of course, it couldn't last.

26 let herself into the Zeroday one Wednesday afternoon, just like any other Wednesday afternoon. She had her own key, and she came over plenty of days after school—her parents didn't mind so long as she spent at least three nights per week at home and kept her grades up. I was on the sofa in the sitting room, using a hot-glue gun to attach feathers from a feather duster to a mad birdy crow mask with evil button eyes and a cruel beak made from a bit of curved umbrella-ribbing draped with black vinyl, every bit of it rescued from the rubbish.

She plonked herself down on the sofa next to me and gave me a giant, flying cuddle that nearly crushed the mask, biting hard on my earlobe and my neck so that I squirmed and pushed and screeched, "Gerorff!" and tickled at her with one hand while holding the mask away from the melee with the other.

"Oh, oh, oh," she said, chortling and holding her belly and kicking her legs in the air while leaning back against me. "It's so fantastic, wait'll you hear!"

"What?" I said. I couldn't think of what it was—a great video she'd found, a daring location for the next cinema, top grades in some subject at school?

"I've had a call from Letitia. She says that she's going to introduce a private member's bill to repeal TIP. It's been such a disaster—there's over two thousand people gone to prison now, and most of them are minors. She reckons that between that and all the civil disobedience in the pirate cinemas, there's never been a better time to get the MPs whipped up about the issue. Everyone says there'll be an election before the summer, and no one wants to be on the ballot after voting for a bill that put kids in jail for listening to music and watching telly."

I cocked my head. "I don't know much about this stuff, but

isn't this kind of a, you know, a gesture? Is there any chance they'll pick it up in Parliament? Why would they vote *for* this when they wouldn't vote *against* TIP in the first place?"

She waved her hands airily. "When they were debating TIP, the entertainment lobbyists were saying that we were all over-reacting, that it would only be used selectively against organized crime kingpins and the like. Now we can show that we were right all along. I rang Annika on the way over and she thinks it might be a goer, too. She says that the cinema nights have kept all the attention on what real creativity is, and on the injustice of TIP; what's more, they're a perfect place to beat the drum for people to get out and support it."

I allowed myself to feel a small glimmer of hope. This was better than I'd ever dreamed: the Pirate Cinema nights weren't just empty protest or a way of having a great party and showing off, they were going to make a *difference*. We would change the law, we'd beat back those corporate arseholes, take power back for the people.

I set down the mask and gave 26 a huge, wet kiss that went on and on for quite some time. I couldn't stop grinning—not that evening, and not that night, behind the elaborately painted surgical mask I'd swapped Rabid Dog for. The films had never been better, the crowd never more fascinating, the night never more magic.

Chapter 9

IS THAT LEGAL?/COWARDICE/
SHAME

Of course, it couldn't last. Those whom the gods would destroy utterly, they first give a taste of heaven to (it's the epigram from *Wasabi Heat,* the deservedly least-known of Scot's romcoms).

I really dressed up for Letitia's office this time. I'm not sure why. Maybe it's cos I spent so much time in weird-looking rags that were carefully calculated to half-offend people from the straight world, like Letitia Clarke-Gifford: middle-class, ultra-respectable, law-abiding. If I was going to be spending my life eating garbage, squatting in pubs, begging, and making illegal films, I wanted to be sure that the people I met knew what an ultra-alternative, cutting-edge type I was.

But now that Parliament was apparently on my side, I felt like I should at least turn up looking like I'd made an effort to meet them halfway. Lucky for me, slightly out-of-date formal clothes are common as muck in the charity shops, since fashions change so often. I was able to score a very smart blazer-and-slacks outfit with a canary-yellow banker's shirt made out of cotton with a thread-count so high you could use it to filter out flu viruses. The previous owner had scorched the back with an iron, so I reckoned I'd just keep the blazer on.

When I met 26 at the Maida Vale tube, she looked past me twice before recognizing me. Then she clapped both hands over her mouth, crinkled her eyes, and made a very large show out of not laughing at me.

"Come on, it's not that bad," I said. "She's an MP, after all!"

26's shoulders shook. She took several deep breaths into her palms, then straightened up and put them down at her sides. She gave me a kiss and squeezed my bum.

"Do I look that stupid?" I said.

She shook her head. "That's what's got me horrified! It *suits you*! In another life, you could have been a junior banker!"

"Now you're just being cruel," I said. I felt self-conscious all the way to the MP's surgery.

At first, Letitia didn't even want to talk about the bill. Mostly, she wanted to talk about the films.

"I can't stop watching them. They're like popcorn! I download one, then there's another one I want to see, and another, and another—before I know, *hours* have gone by. Did you make the one where that Scot Colford is driving a black cab around London, describing all the landmarks with out-of-context lines from his actual films?"

I nodded. "The video was dead easy. I just took a matte of the back of Scot's head and some videos shot out of the windows of the Google Streetview cars, and stuck 'em into a taxi interior I'd cut out. The tricky part was finding dialog that worked with all the neighborhoods. 'Course, I was able to cherry-pick the streets and landmarks I had good dialog for, so it was a bit of a cheat."

"God, I loved that bit about 'made of ale!'"

That had been inspired. The first time I'd ridden out to see 26 on the tube, I'd listen to the announcement as we pulled into Maida Vale, but heard it as "The next station is made of ale." Which got me off on a whole tangent about some lost Victorian art of ale-based construction out of thick brown bricks and so forth. Well, one night, I'd been watching Scot in *Barman's Holiday,* mixing up exotic drinks for thick Americans in a seaside bar in the Honduras, and one of them says, "What's this one made of?" waving a mug in his direction. Scot deadpans back, "That is made of ale." When the two clicked together, comedy was born.

From there, it was just a matter of picking out some other Scot lines—"That shop. That is made of ale. That bike. That is made of ale. That boy. That is made of ale." I was worried the joke would get less funny with repetition, and I think it did, somewhere around the 0:30 mark. But by 0:45, it had gone through stupid and out the other side, which is an entirely funnier kind of funny, and the first time I showed it live at a Pirate Cinema, they'd laughed like drains, howling. Even now, people liked to point at random things and say, "That is made of ale." It made me feel brilliant.

"It's a real favorite," I said. I felt really weird in my suit now. The MP was wearing a flowy kind of dress with a big scarf—it was cold in her drafty office—and had taken off her shoes and crossed her legs, showing off her heavy wool socks with multicolor stripes. The only other person in formal clothes was the security guard out front, who hadn't even bothered to ask us for ID or to go through the metal-detector, having recognized 26 straight off.

"So," Letitia said, leaning forward to get down to business. "26 has told you about the bill, yes?"

I shrugged. "I guess so. I don't really know much about Parliamentary procedure or anything—"

Letitia nodded. "Okay, well, a private member's bill is usually just a kind of empty protest. The way it works is, an MP like me introduces it, rather than the governing party as a whole. If the government doesn't want it to pass, it's easy enough to knock down again, you just talk it out until the time for debate expires, and it dies. But sometimes a private member's bill is a way for the government to get a law passed without having to actually propose it themselves. They get someone like me, from the opposition, to propose the bill, then the Speaker gives it enough time for a full debate, a hearing in the Lords, and a vote and hey, presto, we've got a law! It's sneaky, but it's how we got some of our most, ahem, controversial laws passed.

"So here's the idea. I'm going to introduce a bill to amend the Theft of Intellectual Property Act. It will rescind all criminal penalties and end the practice of terminating Internet connections on accusation of piracy. In return, it will explicitly permit rights-holder groups to offer what are called blanket licenses to ISPs. These are already widely used—for example, when the DJ at Radio 2 decides to play a song, she doesn't have to track down the record label's lawyer and negotiate the fee for the use. Instead, all the music ever recorded is available to her for one blanket fee, and the money the BBC pays gets divided up and paid to artists. Under this scheme, film studios, game companies, publishers, and music companies could offer ISPs a per-user/per-month fee in exchange for unlimited sharing of all music, books, and films."

I tried to make sense of that. "You mean, I sign up with Virgin and give them, whatever, fifteen pounds a month for my Internet. They give five pounds to these groups, and I get to download everything?"

She nodded. "Yes, that's it exactly. It's no different, really, to what already goes on in most places. For example, when you go to a shop and they're playing music, they pay a small fee every month to what's called a 'collecting society' that pays musicians for the usage. Collecting societies around the world have deals with one another, and some insanely complicated accounting for paying one anothers' members. They're big and often very corrupt, but it seems to me that making the collecting societies fairer is an easier job than convincing everyone to stop getting up to naughty Internet copying. We've put more than eight hundred people in jail now for copying. Just imagine! It costs the state more than £40,000 per year to keep them there—that's £40,000 we're not spending on education, or health, or roads—or arts funding for films and music! It's an absolute disgrace."

She seemed to notice that she was practically frothing at

the mouth and she calmed herself down with a visible effort. "I'm sorry," she said. "I know I shouldn't get emotional about this, but it's just so dreadful. We keep passing worse and worse laws, and they're not solving the problem. It's a disease you get in government—like passing a law against marijuana, then passing worse and worse laws against it, until the prisons are busting with people who really shouldn't be there, and by then, you're so committed to a ridiculous law that you can't back down without looking terminally foolish for having supported it in the first place." She heaved a sigh.

"*Anyway,* the reason I asked you to come in today is because I've had a nice quiet chat in private with the Speaker of the House, who wanted me to know that if I was to introduce such a bill, he'd be inclined to allow for a full debate and put it to a vote. And he strongly hinted that his party's whips would see to it that all the MPs turned up for work that day and voted in favor of it. And I've been in touch with my party's leader, and she's inclined to let my lot vote our conscience, and I'm pretty certain that we'd all vote for it, barring one or two nutters who want to have practically everyone banged in prison for the next two hundred years or so, just to teach 'em a lesson."

My eyes felt like they were bugging out of my head, and I realized I literally had my mouth open so far I was beginning to dribble. I was still reeling with the fact that this Member of bloody *Parliament* had just told me she thought spliff should be legal and part of my brain was jumping up and down trying to get my attention, because that same MP was also proposing to repeal TIP, and even more, repeal the ancient Digital Economy Act that had got me and my family knocked off the Internet.

26 slugged me in the shoulder and then threw her arms around me and squeezed me so hard I felt like my lunch was going to make a second appearance. "Isn't it *amazing?*" she said.

I nodded vigorously. "Yes, but, erm—"

Letitia looked at me. "Yes?"

"What are you telling us for?" I didn't say it, but I was think-ing, *we're just a couple of kids!*

She clapped her hands to her mouth. "Oh! Didn't I say? No? Well, of course you two are absolutely *crucial* to making this hap-pen. The fact is, as soon as any of the horrible grasping lobbyists from the other side get a whiff of this, they'll be all over us—getting famous actors and pop stars to drop in on MPs, calling up Members and reminding them of all the money they donated to their election campaigns, that sort of thing. If this is to have a hope of passing, there's got to be enormous *counterpressure* on every MP in the country. Even more than with TIP—you're going to have to get loads of voters to come out with real, passionate sup-port for the bill. What's more, you're going to have to be prepared for everyone calling you thieves and worse. It seems to me, though, that you and your friends have a damned good rebuttal to that sort of thing: you're making films that people purely love, that are be-ing watched all around the world, and you've not made a penny off them. It's plain to me that you lot aren't just cheapskates after a free film or two: you're filmmakers yourselves, exactly the sort of person our copyright's meant to be protecting, and here we are, putting you in jail."

I shook my head. Could it be possible? "So, you're saying we'll basically be the poster children for a complete overhaul of British copyright law?"

She laughed. "If you want to put it that way. The fact is that there's almost certainly going to be an election called in the next three months; the government can't wait more than four months in any event. They've been in office for nearly five years now, that's the maximum, and odds are good they'll hold the election in May in order to tie it in with regional and council elections, which saves loads of money and always looks good when you're running for reelection. The party in power knows that they're vulnerable on this issue, and all the other parties are eyeing up the possibility of going into the election having championed such a popular cause. So everyone's got a reason to want to see this pass, provided the other side doesn't outflank us. But I like our odds. You lot are adorable, talented, and clearly harmless. They'll have a hard time painting you to look like villains."

She sipped at her mug of tea. "Not that they won't try, of course."

Annika called another meeting in the basement of the Turkish restaurant in Brick Lane the next week. There were the same carob brownies, but there was lots more besides: Jem and Dodger had spent two days in the kitchen, turning out all kinds of little delicacies, like miniature eel pies, plum puddings, tiny plates of stewed rabbit, and fluffy scones. I thought they'd overdone it when we'd loaded it all into six huge boxes to take down to Brick Lane on the buses, but there were so many people in the restaurant's basement that the food was gone in seconds. I was used to the Pirate Cinema nights being crowded—there'd been one in an old civil defense tunnel that had been so claustrophobic I'd had to leg it up the endless stairs to the surface before I had a panic attack, and it was a good job nothing caught fire because no one could have got out. But this was nearly as bad as that worst-ever night. The restaurant's owner kept bringing down pitchers of beer and stacks of cups and platters of mezzes and whomever was closest to the bottom of the stairs would have a whip-round for the money to pay for it, then the grub and booze would disappear into the heaving mass.

Annika called the meeting to order by the simple expedient of climbing up onto a table, extending her hands before her, and clapping a simple, slow rhythm: *Clap. Clap. Clap.* The people around her joined in, then the people around them, and in a few minutes, no one could possibly carry on a conversation. It was quite the little magic trick: clearly, Annika had run a meeting or two in her day.

She stopped clapping and made a pushing-down gesture, like she was patting an invisible table at chest height and like magic, the clapping stopped and all fell silent in the steaming-hot basement. The rasp of all those breaths was like the sound of distant rain. Like I said: magic.

"Right then," Annika said. "Let's get Cecil up here."

This was the part of the plan I wasn't exactly certain about. I'd introduced many of the Pirate Cinema screenings, but after the first night, I'd always worn a mask. But everyone knew what I looked like, thanks to Sewer Cinema, and all my mates figured I'd be able to explain it.

I jumped onto the table, helped up by Annika, and looked into the sea of faces. I had a scrap of paper on which I'd scribbled some notes, but I couldn't focus on it. Annika's hand had been slippery with sweat, and I could feel my own sweat running down my neck and back.

"Erm," I said. I felt physically sick, like I was going to throw up. All these people, looking at me. What the hell did I know about it? A few days before, I hadn't even known what a Private Member's Bill *was*. I was just some kid who liked to cut up films. "Erm," I said again. My vision swam.

I shook my head. There were words on the sweaty bit of paper, but I literally couldn't make my mouth form any kind of coherent statement. And the faces! They were all *staring* and some of them were smirking and a few had started whispering to their neighbors, and all of a sudden it was all too much. I shook my head and muttered, "I'm sorry," and got off the table and pushed my way out of the crowd and up the stairs. Out on Brick Lane, it was shitting down drizzle, that wet stupid gray low-sky weather that London seemed to have from October to May.

I stalked away down the road, half expecting that at any second one of my mates or 26 would grab me and spin me around and tell me off for panicking and then give me a cuddle and tell me it was all okay, but no one did. I came out to Bethnal Green Road, among the Bangladeshi shops and the discount off-licenses and taxi touts and tramps selling picked-over rubbish off of blankets, and drunks reeling through the night with tins of lager held high. London had never seemed more miserable to me than at that moment. What had come over me? I'll tell you what: the sudden, terrible knowledge that I had no idea what I was doing, I was just a kid, and I was going to cock it all up. I wasn't a leader, I wasn't a spokesman. I was a school-leaver from Bradford who liked to make funny films.

In my imagination, my mates were all standing around the restaurant's basement, shaking their heads knowingly at one another, muttering things like, "Bloody Cecil, what a little drama queen, knew he never had it in him."

I went home, studying my shoes in excruciating detail on the long walk, bumping into people and poles and rubbish bins. I let myself in the front door, opened the fridge door, stared unseeingly at the interior. I wanted to obliterate my mind: get drunk, smoke spliff, take a little sugar. There was no booze in the house, no weed, but right outside the door, there was as much sugar as I could possibly want. The drugs lookouts knew us all, of course, and didn't bother to set up their birdcalls when we came in and out, and I knew plenty by sight. I didn't have a penny to my name, but I was willing to bet that someone would supply me with a sweet gasp on credit. They all knew where I lived.

I stood at the front door for a long time, hand on the knob, feet jammed into my unlaced boots. My calves and feet still ached from the long walk home, my mind was wrapped in a gauze of shame and self-pity. I seemed to be looking at myself from a long way away, outside of my body, watching as my hand began to turn the doorknob and I thought, *all right then, he's going to do it, he's going to go and score some sugar.* At that moment, the boy with his hand on the doorknob was someone else, not me. *I* was watching myself with bland interest, like it was all some video I'd shrunk down to a postage stamp and stuck on one corner of my screen.

Oh look, that silly lad's off to get stoned on something that might just be nail-varnish remover fumes. I thought, and then the little voice in the back of my head that had been shouting in fear and

anger came to the fore and I swam back to my body and let go of
the doorknob. I gasped and stepped back and scrubbed at my eyes
with my fists. I was crying.

I decided to go to bed. If I couldn't sleep, I could always go
outside and score later. The sugar shacks weren't going anywhere.

I slept.

When I woke. I lay in bed and stared at the messy floor and the
door for a long time. I checked my phone. It was only 11:00 A.M.
Everyone would be asleep for hours, assuming they got in at their
usual four or five in the morning. Just to be on the safe side, I
slunk downstairs on cat's feet, not wanting to run into any of my
housemates and face their anger—or worse, their pity. I had plenty
of pity for all of us.

I got dressed and picked up a sign bedecked with a hand-
sterilizer pump, a packet of tissues, a packet of deodorant wipes,
and a chewable toothbrush dispenser. I rolled it into a tube and
headed for Old Street Station, found an exit that no one else was
begging in, and began to rattle the sign hopefully at the passersby.

I guess I must have been a dead sorry sight, because I raked in
the dosh—seventy pounds in two hours, an unheard-of sum. I
was out of the sanitizer and the toothbrushes, and running low on
everything else. I went round to the other exits and found Lucy
and Fred and gave them half of it. Lucy gave me a long, slightly
smelly hug, and I was glad for it—someone in this world who was
even worse off than me thought I was brilliant, that counted for
something, didn't it?

It was 4:00 P.M. by the time I got back to the Zeroday. I went
in by the old entrance up at the top of the fire escape, the one
we'd stopped using after we got legit with Rob, hoping to avoid
everyone if possible. I snuck back into my room, noticing that all
the lights were still off—I supposed that everyone must have got
up and gone out. Good.

I stared at my phone for a long time. 26 hadn't called me. Of
course she hadn't. Why would she want to talk to a pathetic sack

like me? I lay on my bed, wishing I could go to sleep and shut out the world. I thought of sugar again, and of the thirty-five quid in my pocket. That would buy more than enough sugar to see me off for the night. My personal camera began to dolly out, zooming away from my body again, and I knew that if I didn't do something now, that person on the bed with the red-rimmed eyes was going to go out and do something bloody stupid.

So I grabbed my lappie and logged into Confusing Peach. Of course, it was all chatter about last night. I looked away, but I couldn't not read it. I read it.

Then I stood bolt upright, grabbed my jacket, and *ran* for the door, barely stopping to lock it behind me. I was dialing 26's number as I tore down Bow High Street, hitting the wrong speed-dial icon three times before I got through, only to reach her voice mail without a ring. I called Jem next, then Dog and Chester and even Dodger—all the numbers I had for the people who'd been in the cellar the night before. No one was answering. I thought I must have Aziz's number somewhere, so I stopped running, grabbed my laptop from my bag and crouched down against the window of a shop while I went through old messages looking for it. I found it and dialed the number with shaking fingers.

It rang six times and then Aziz answered, with a distracted, " 'Lo?"

"Aziz, mate, it's me, Cecil."

"Yeah, hullo, Cecil. Listen, son, I'm kinda busy—"

"They've all been arrested, Aziz, all of them—Jem and Chester and Dodger and Dog and my girlfriend all, well, all of them! It was on Confusing Peach this morning—the coppers raided a meeting last night about this copyright bill, said they were after the pirates who'd been running the cinemas."

There was a long silence.

"Aziz?"

"One sec," he said. I heard his fingers clattering over a keyboard, then the grinding hum of a shredder. "Do go on," he said, calmly.

I opened and shut my mouth a couple times. "I don't know what to say, Aziz! I'm going spare, mate. What do I do?"

He sighed. "Look, Cecil, you're a good young fellow, but you're young. And when you're young, you still haven't learned that getting all in a lather doesn't help anything. I can hear you panting from here. Take several deep breaths, clear your head, and have a good think. People go to jail all the time. They haven't been convicted of anything yet, and if they are, it, erm, won't be due to any evidence on my premises." I heard the shredder whir again. "Meantime, calm the hell down and see what kinds of solutions present themselves."

My first reaction was to shout at him for being such a hardhearted bastard. But he had a point: *I* was running down the street like a headless chicken. *He* was taking steps to ensure that if he was raided, nothing in his place would put his friends in jeopardy. Which one of us was doing more to help? "Okay, Aziz, You're right. I'll call you later."

"Better to use encrypted email, son. I'm afraid I'll be ditching this SIM once we're done."

Durr. Aziz was much better at this than I was. Of course, he'd lived his whole life outsmarting people who tried to use technology to control their enemies. I put away my laptop, stood up and looked around. I'd worked up a sweat running down the road, but now I was freezing, my jacket unbuttoned, my feet jammed into my unlaced boots without socks. Right. I did up my boots and coat, wiped the icy sweat off my face. I thought about ditching my SIM, but it was the main way that 26 and the others would be able to reach me from jail, assuming they didn't have access to a computer.

Now I made myself walk calmly toward the tube station. I had no idea where I'd go, but wherever I went, I'd probably need to take rapid transit to get there. Good. I was getting somewhere.

Who could I talk to? Well, Letitia would be good for starters. I didn't have her number, but she'd be in the directory. Oh, and of course, there were 26's parents. If she'd only been given one call, she'd call them, wouldn't she, especially seeing as her stepfather was a lawyer, right? Of course. Now that I was thinking of this all calmly, it was starting to come together—even though it made me feel slightly guilty, as though I was betraying 26 by not running around in a panic while she was in trouble.

Now, did I have her parents' numbers? Of course I did. There was that time 26 had gone away with her mum for a weekend in Devon and had dropped her phone in the sea, she'd sent me her mum's number so I could call her and we could make goo-goo noises at each other (as her mum insisted on describing it, as in, "Darling, it's for you, it's your young man calling to make goo-goo noises again!"). It was in my phone's memory. I stopped walking, moved under a newsagent's awning, and dialed.

"Hullo?"

"Ms. Kahn?" I'd been calling her "Amrita" for months, but I felt the occasion demanded formality, like maybe she wouldn't want me to be so familiar with her daughter now she'd been arrested.

"Who is it?"

"It's me, Cecil."

She made a kind of grunt. "They've let you out then?"

"I wasn't in," I said. "I wasn't there when they raided the place. I've only just found out about it. Have you heard from 26?"

"My husband's been down at the Magistrates' Court for hours, now," she said. "Trying to force them to bail 26 and her friends. The police say that with such a large number of people arrested, it could take some time." There was a click. "Hold on a moment." She put me on hold. After quite some time, she came back on. "That's 26's father," she said. I suddenly remembered 26 telling me that her biological dad was a cop—and that her mum hadn't spoken to him for years and years. I guess this was the kind of desperate situation that got people to overcome this sort of thing. "I have to go."

"Wait!" I said. "What should I do?"

She made another grunt. "You may as well come over here, they'll come here first when they get her out. I'll be staying in for the duration." Her voice was tight as a bowstring.

The tube ride took a dozen eternities, but eventually I heard the robot voice call out, "The next station is made of ale," and I jumped up. I'd spent the whole ride staring at my phone's face-plate, willing it to light up with an incoming call from 26 or any-one, debating whether I should pull the SIM out and stuff it between the cushions on the tube. In the end, I hung onto it, be-cause they had all my mates, and that meant they knew where I lived and where I might be going, and if they wanted to snatch me, they could and would, and cutting myself off from everyone I cared about in the whole world seemed an impossible heartbreak.

So I pelted up the stairs three at a time, stuck my ticket into the turnstile, and went through it so quick I did myself an injury on the crossbar, doubling over and limping out of the station, then running like a three-legged dog all the way to 26's place.

Standing on her doorstep, sweating buckets, half-dressed in whatever I grabbed on the way out the door, I forced myself to ring the bell. 26's mum had seen me in yesterday's T-shirt and a pair of gym trousers at breakfast before, she knew I wasn't a fash-ion model. And this was more important than making a good impression on my girlfriend's parents.

She swung open the door with her phone clamped to her head. She was dressed as oddly as I was, in old jeans and a loose cotton shirt with a misbuttoned cardigan over it and fuzzy slip-pers, her eyes red and hollow. She made a "come in," gesture and then turned and walked back into the house, nodding her head at whomever was talking on the other end of the call.

"Yes, yes. Yes. No. Yes. Yes."

She rolled her eyes at me. I mouthed, "Going to use the toilet," and she nodded and seemed to immediately forget about me. So I went up to 26's room and dug around in the mountains of junk on the floor until I found one of my T-shirts and a pair of my pants—she often borrowed them to slop around in when she was over at mine. I had a very quick shower and changed, and the smell of 26 on the shirt was like a punch in the chest, so I had to sit down on the floor with a thump and catch my breath. Then I padded back downstairs in my socks.

26's mum was sat in the sitting room, an open book on her lap, not looking at it, staring into space. When I made a little throat-clearing noise, she looked up at me with a little startlement, then smiled sadly. "Sorry," she said. "Miles away. My husband says he's making some progress at the magistrates', and 26's father is apparently doing eighty miles per hour down the length of the M1 while calling every copper he knows in London. I suppose that means everything's going to be okay, but I'm still worrying myself sick." She closed her book and fisted her eyes. "How are you holding up, lad?"

I looked at my feet and mumbled something. I didn't want to talk about how I felt, because it was complicated—relief that I wasn't locked away, fear for what was happening to my friends, shame that I'd only escaped because I'd been such a coward at the meeting. "Can I make you some tea?" I said.

She nodded and wiped her palms on her thighs. "That'd be lovely."

When I brought it to her—milk and no sugar, but strong as builder's tea, the way 26 took it, too—she said, "I suppose I should have expected this. After all, you and 26 have been banging on for months about how crazy the law is getting. But I couldn't get over the feeling that this was just harmless fun. After all, it's not as if you were having gang fights and robbing buildings! You're not planning to blow up Parliament! You were just—"

"—making films," I said. "And breaching copyright." I sighed. "I guess I didn't think they'd come after us like this, either. I thought that since they mostly seemed to target random people to sue or arrest, they wouldn't come after someone *specific*, you know what I mean? Guess that was pretty stupid."

To my surprise, she stood up and gave me an enormous hug

that seemed to go on and on, the kind of hug I remembered from when I was a little kid, the hug that made you feel like everything was going to be all right. Damned if it didn't almost make me start crying. When I looked into her face afterward, I saw that she was nearly in tears, too.

Chapter 10

FACING THE PARENTS/LASERS IN LONDON/
RABID DOG'S HORROR

26 got back to her house just as her father—her biological father—pulled up in a beat-up red Opel that was covered in mud-streaks. 26 and her stepfather met her father on the doorstep. He was a big man, Asian like 26's stepdad, but with his balding head shaved to stubble, and dressed in clothes that made him look like a copper, even though they weren't a uniform. Or maybe I was just seeing things because I knew that he was the law, and that 26 and her family didn't exactly get on with him.

Her dad and her stepdad shook hands warily on the door-step, and 26 busied herself with the key and the lock and her handbag so she didn't have to hug him. I watched it all from the sitting-room window, as 26's mum rushed to open the door even as 26 fiddled with it. They all spilled into the front hall with a stamping of boots and a rush of cold, wet air, and I skulked in the sitting-room doorway, looking at 26 with a feeling like a doggy that's just seen his mistress come home after giving up all hope of ever seeing her again. Our eyes met and for a second I thought she was going to smack me for having left the club so suddenly, damn me for a coward, and order me out of her life. But instead, she practically leapt into my arms, crossing the intervening dis-tance with one long stride. She threw both arms around my neck and one leg around my waist and if I hadn't had the doorjamb to catch me, we'd have gone over like a cricket bail. I was intensely aware that three of 26's parents were watching us, including her copper bio-dad whom I'd never met. But I was even more in-tensely aware of the warm skin on mine, the lips pressing to my neck, the arms crushing my chest. I held her until I heard her mum pointedly clear her throat.

26 let go of me and I saw through the tears in my eyes that she had tears in her eyes, too. I had an overpowering urge to drag her out of the house and just *go*, run away and never come back. But there was the small matter of the giant copper looming over us, giving me a look so filthy, it should have come in a plain brown wrapper. I gently pushed 26 a little farther away and smiled at everyone with my best and most harmless grin. Her stepfather nodded back at me and managed a tired smile, but her bio-dad continued to look at me as though he was deciding which charges would send me to prison for the longest sentence.

26's mum stepped between us and gave 26 a hug, which let me escape to the kitchen to put the kettle on and load up a tray with biccies and cups and that. By the time I loaded it with the teapot and carried it into the sitting room, everyone was arranged in a kind of civilized tableau, with 26 equidistant from everyone on the floor, arms around her knees. I set the tea tray down and began to sneak away. I reckoned I'd go hide upstairs in 26's room until things calmed down, but 26 called to me and patted the carpet next to her. I maneuvered around the stacks of books and sat down next to her, looking down.

"I just can't believe what you're letting her get up to, Amrita," her bio-dad said. "Hanging out with crazy radicals, risking arrest over this *nonsense*?"

Her mum kept her composure. "Deepak, it's nice to see you taking an interest in her life again, but you've forgot her past three birthdays, so I don't really think you've got much business criticizing how we're raising her. But this young woman is smart as anything, gets top grades, is probably going to go to University College London next year only because she can't be bothered with Oxford, and she cares about injustice in the world around her and is doing something meaningful to change it. I, for one, am proud as anything of my daughter. I think you might start by telling her the same thing."

I really, really wanted to go, but 26 had made a manacle out of her fingers and had cinched it tight around one of my forearms. I'd have to gnaw it off if I was to escape. So I breathed deeply.

"Proud? Fine, you be proud. Here's what I know: my daughter's been charged with Criminal Trespass, Criminal Infringement, Criminal Computer Intrusion, and those are just the major charges. She could wind up in prison for the rest of her life, and they don't let you go to Oxford *or* UCL when you're banged up in Askham Grange. So forgive me if I am a little skeptical of your pride here."

26's stepdad cleared his throat. "I happen to think that, in my professional judgment, none of these charges will make it past a preliminary hearing. They're without merit, the evidence is poor, and many of the laws themselves are pending High Court review." He folded his hands on his tummy, as though he was resting a case in front of a jury. Her bio-dad's jaws jumped under his skin. 26 cleared her throat.

"Can I say something?"

All the adults in the room turned to look at her. She took a deep breath and got to her feet. "First, I want to thank you both for getting me free. Deepak, Dad tells me that I would still be there if it wasn't for you. Thank you, really and honestly for that. Jail is awful. Bugger that: jail is *bloody awful*. I don't want to go back there and I'm grateful not to be there and I'm worried sick about all my mates who are still there, because I never dreamt that it could be so terrible—" She took another deep breath and composed herself. It was like watching someone catch hold of a hummingbird with her bare hands without crushing it. I loved her more than ever at that moment. "So thank you both. Next, I want to say, Deepak, this is my boyfriend, Cecil. Cecil, this is my biological father, Detective Inspector Deepak Kahn." I scrambled to my feet and held out my hand and he shook it with a funny kind of pressure, like he was testing my balance, sizing me up for a judo-throw over the sofa and through the front window. Or maybe I was just being paranoid, still. "Next item of business: I need a shower and a change of clothes. No one is going to come and arrest me in the next fifteen minutes. There is nothing that can't wait that long, right? So I'm going to go upstairs now. I'd prefer it if you all remembered that you are adults and kept things civil, all right?"

And without another word, she was gone and I was alone with the three adults. I was still standing and wished I could sit down or possibly go crouch behind a pile of books and disappear. 26's bio-dad skewered me on his eyeball lasers and said, "I suppose you're part of this business as well, Cecil?"

"I guess you could say so."

"So why weren't you arrested with that lot? More sense than them? Or are you a grass? Working for the coppers?"

I shook my head. "No, sir," I said. "I just—" I didn't really fancy telling him how I'd come to be somewhere else when the law came for my friends. "I'd just stepped away when it happened. Pure chance."

He snorted. "And what do you do, with all these people?"

I licked my lips, then made myself stop. "I make films," I said.

He grunted. "The kind of films involving nudity?"

I held my hands up. "No! God, no! No, I make films about Scot Colford, mostly. I cut up footage, add my own, remix it, like. Mostly piss-takes, but also some serious stuff."

He raised one eyebrow so high I thought his eye would fall out of the socket. "Scot *Colford*? The actor?"

"He's very good," 26's mum said. "They've shown his stuff on telly. Cecil, why don't you go downstairs and get the clean towels out of the machine and bring them up to the bathroom? I don't think there are any in there."

I nearly ran.

26 got out of the shower, toweled off, and went straight to bed. I didn't blame her—after all the adrenaline (and lack of sleep the night before) I was ready to collapse myself. But being as her cop father was downstairs, I wasn't going to stay there with her. Besides, she would probably want to know why I happened to leave right before the coppers raided them, and even if she didn't believe that I was a supergrass, she would probably be just as disappointed to know that I was a coward.

So I slunk back home, more time on public transit to recriminate with myself. Except that I was hugely distracted by a bizarre sight: there was a group of German tourists on the overland with me to Euston, wearing funny fedoras with wide brims crusted with some kind of funny electronics and a weird, silvery hat-band that glittered like a disco ball. They were gabbling in German to one another, and I couldn't understand a single word, but those were, hands down, the weirdest hats I'd ever seen. They didn't seem to be a fashion thing, either—the crumblie oldsters and the little kids were all wearing them, and I never heard of any weird fashion that people of all ages got into.

So what the hell were they? They got out at Euston with me. It was unseasonably hot now—it had been running hot and cold for days now, so that you never knew when you left the house whether you'd be sweating buckets or shivering by the end of the day, and the hats certainly looked like they'd be plenty warm. I trailed along behind them toward the buses upstairs and then one of those hats did the strangest bloody thing: it shot out a laser beam!

It was a bolt of green laser light, only flickering into existence for a brief instant, sizzling in the humid air, the width of a pencil-lead and bright in the gloom of the platform. The Germans all pointed at the one whose hat had gone off and made excited noises and looked around on the ground, and one of them pointed at something and they all made more noises and got out their mobiles and snapped piccies of whatever it was. The others on the platform watched with that weird British noninterest thing where you pretend you're not staring and stare anyway.

Once they'd moved on, I looked at the spot on the floor they'd been pointing at and saw that there was a dead mosquito there, slightly crispy. That bloke's hat had apparently shot it out of the sky with a freaking *laser*!

On the bus to Bow, I googled "laser hat mosquito" and learned more. Apparently all the news had been full of stories about something called West Nile Fever, which is a terrible disease spread by mosquitoes in tropical parts. But now that the whole world was getting warmer and that, diseases were moving around, and there'd been six confirmed cases of it in London. All the red-top tabloid papers were going bonkers over this, predicting a planet-killing pandemic and the end of life as we knew it, and tourists were being advised to avoid London.

I felt like a proper idiot for not knowing this, and when I thought about it, it seemed to me that there had been newsagents' signs with screaming headlines about mosquitoes and tropical diseases, but I'd been too wrapped up in this bill and my films and that to pay them any heed. Ninety-nine percent of the time, the newsagents' signs were about subjects that were completely irrelevant to me: celebrities getting caught shagging each others' spouses, Royals getting caught snorting coke, footballers winning or losing big matches I couldn't give a toss about. Every now and again, I'd snag a free-sheet while I was running around town, but after reading about the miraculous lives saved by brave doggies and the horrible parents who'd absentmindedly put their kids down the kitchen sink garbage disposal, I'd stick them in a bin and move on.

Anyway, the Chinese had been fighting West Nile mosquitoes for years apparently, and they did it all with these powerful green lasers that were as cheap as chips. They'd hook 'em up to a couple of microphones that used sonar to locate the little bastards, then they targeted the lasers by bouncing them off curved mirrors, and zip-zap, no more little flying vampires. They worked a treat in houses, where you could mount 'em with brackets in the corners of the rooms, but when you were out in the world, you needed another layer of protection. Bug spray was nice, but laser hats were scorchingly bad-arse because *they put lasers on your head* and you went *pew-pew-pew* when you walked down the street. I couldn't argue with that reasoning, even if I hadn't had a single mosquito bite that I'd noticed since coming to London. Though, naturally, by the time I'd finished googling, I was imagining mosquito whines in the barely audible edge of the bus motors, and feeling phantom itches from nonexistent bites. I resisted the temptation to google "West Nile Disease" for as long as I could, but after the fifth nonexistent mosquito bite, I gave in.

Oh, lovely, comas. Twitching, horrible, usually terminal comas. That was just *fantastic*. I'd have to get a hat.

I got home and no one was there. I was about to ring Jem when he rang *me*. "Hullo, chicken," he said in his bravest voice, but I could hear the edge in it. Jem was tired, and hurting.

"Jem! Where are you? Do you need me to come and get you?"

"They just sprung us. Sounds like your girlfriend's old man impressed the magistrate. After her hearing, the old darling started to ask the law some tough questions about just why we were being held. There was a fixer from the film industry there, some smart city boy lawyer, kept trying to say something, but the magistrate told him to sit down or he'd have him chucked out of the court. So we're sprung. Only one problem, son, Rabid Dog—" He breathed a deep breath, and I heard a ragged edge in it. "He's not in such good shape. I don't have money for a taxi, and I don't reckon Chester and me can get him home on our own on the bus."

I squeezed my eyes shut as hard as I could and counted under my breath. At ten, I said, "What happened to Dog?"

"Some of his cellies started calling him things, 'nancy boy' and that. He was separated from us, in with two tough lads who'd been done for brawling outside a pub. Couldn't see 'em, but I could hear it. Dog told them that he thought they were unintelligent fellows of questionable breeding with a proclivity for sticking their johnsons in things that shouldn't be stuck, in so many words, and there was a lot of thumping and shouting and that. I was proud of the little bastard, but scared, too. Screws took their time breaking it up. Saw them bring out the brawlers. Big sods.

Size of houses. One of 'em looked like he wouldn't be seeing out of one of his eyes for a long time, the other one was bleeding from the nose and one ear. Thought that Dog had, like, finally got in touch with his inner horror film, maybe he'd done okay. But then they brought him out. On a stretcher. Wanted to take him to a secure infirmary, but I talked them out of it. Think they were glad to see him go, cos otherwise it'd have to be paperwork and maybe complaints and that. But—" He heaved another one of those fluttery breaths. "Well, he ain't so good, Cecil."

I had thirty-five pounds left from my begging, which was enough to get a minicab there and back, just barely. It seemed to me that all I'd done that day was run around, back and forth. The minicab driver drove the whole way without a word, and when we pulled up to the station, I jumped out and held the door open so he couldn't drive off. I reckoned that if Dog looked as bad as I thought he might, the driver wouldn't want to stay.

But he was a good egg. He found a blanket in his boot and spread it over the backseat and helped Chester and Jem get Dog into the backseat, and Jem went round to the other side of the car and got in and put Dog's head in his lap. Chester got in on the other side and put Dog's feet on his lap, and then I got into the passenger seat in the front and the driver took his car back to the Zeroday so gentle, I swear he didn't hit a single sleeping policeman or pothole.

We got Dog inside and I fetched a big bowl of water and a pile of clean black T-shirts we could use as rags—black because the blood wouldn't show. There was a lot of blood. Both of his eyes were swollen shut, and his nose was a big puffy ball, and his knuckles were all skinned like he'd dragged bricks over them. We couldn't get his T-shirt over his head because his arms hurt too much—he made these horrible *squeaks* that were worse than screams when we tried—so Jem got a scissors from the kitchen and cut all Dog's clothes off, down to his underpants. Now we could all see the bruises on his ribs and arms and thighs. Looking at him, I couldn't imagine ever suffering through a beating like that.

But Dog managed something recognizable as a grin and said, "Will I ever play the piano again, doc?" around his swollen lips. And that was when I knew that I would never be as mean and tough and hard as Rabid Dog, and no matter that he looked like a harmless puffball and no matter that he was queer. He was the most *macho* sod I'd ever known.

No one wanted to try to carry him upstairs, so Jem brought down blankets and a pillow and set up his lappie and queued up all his favorite slasher films, and made him a Lemsip and had him take three sketchy-looking pain tablets he got from some secret place in his room. He took them with sips of water, and pulled the blanket up around his chin, and watched the films with one eye until he fell asleep. We moved around him with murmurs and tiptoes, and eventually the three of us found ourselves up in my room, me on my bed, Jem at my editing chair, Chester on the floor with his back to the wall.

"What a mess," Jem said finally. "Shoulda seen it, they came in with bullhorns and truncheons and that and told us we were all under arrest, read out a charge sheet as long as a very long thing, all the while grabbing people and chucking them into vans. And you know what, your bloke from the films was there, the fellow that was on telly after the Leicester Square caper talking about what a bad, bad boy you were. Smirking and that, standing by the van, practically rubbing his hands together with glee. If I didn't know better, I'd say you've made someone very sad and angry, boy."

I couldn't help it, I laughed. Here was Jem, who'd been stuck in bloody jail, seen his boyfriend beaten to shit and back, and he was cracking jokes. It was why he was the original, all-time, world-beating Jammie Dodger, and there wasn't anything any of us could do that would top him, ever.

I was waiting for him or Chester—who was so tired he

could barely keep his eyes open—to say something about my departure, but neither of 'em seemed ready to bring it up. So I had to. "Felt like an idiot for running out when I did, but I guess I dodged a bullet, hey?"

Chester said groggily, "Just figured you were feeling a bit peaky, Cec. Anyway, you gave old 26 a chance to shine, didn't ya?"

"What?"

Jem slapped his leg. "Shoulda seen her! She hopped straight up on the table and gave a speech the like of which I haven't seen, not never! 'They say it's about protecting property, but they *invented* this idea that creativity is property! How can you own an idea? They say their imaginary property is more important than our privacy, our creativity, and our freedom. I say bugger that. I say we've got a moral *duty* to pirate everything we can, until they're nothing more than bad memories. Christ, the way they carry on, you'd think that they expect us to come home from work and flop down in front of the telly and anaesthetize our brains for four hours forever, like this is the thing we spent millions of years evolving to do! I say bugger that! I say bugger and bugger who says that's what we're on this planet for!'"

"You're joking!"

"Naw, mate, not at all! That little girl of yours is the cleverest agitator I've ever had the sincere pleasure of getting rabble-roused by, and I've seen some dead good ones in my years. By the time she was done, I wanted to grab a spear and a torch and run down to Knightsbridge and string up some film producers! 'Course, that's just when the coppers made their appearance. Damned good timing. Reckon they had a grass in the crowd."

That made me swallow. "26's dad—her real dad, a copper from Scotland—came down and said he thought I must be a snitch, cos I got out at just the right moment and all."

Jem laughed again. I liked the sound of his laugh, made me glad to be alive. "You! Cecil, mate, you're a lot of things, but a liar, you ain't. You've got the most *pathologically* honest face of any gee-zer I know. You'd be the worst grass in the history of Scotland Yard."

Chester nodded vigorously. "'Strue," he said, with a yawn. "You're rubbish at lying, Cecil. Not one of your talents."

"Go to bed, Ches," Jem said. "You look like chiseled cat shit." Ches nodded and lumbered away and now it was just me and Jem, staring at each other across the room in the squat.

"Can't say I reckoned it would come to this, back when I found you down in the tube that day," he said. "Look at us, couple of Che Guevaras now, real freedom fighters. You know, most of those freedom fighters get a bullet in the head and an anonymous grave, by and large. I means, all the hipsters will turn your piccie into an icon and put it on their T-shirts and that, but I don't reckon that's much comfort when the worms are chewing on your brain stem."

I had a plummeting feeling. "Look, Jem, if you don't want to go on doing this stuff, I can't fault you," I said, mind racing. "I mean, we could find a different squat and—"

And again came that laugh, so epic that it made my heart pound. "Oh, Cecil, don't be bloody stupid. I'm not tossing you out, I'm telling you how much fun I'm having. That's the thing, here I am, doing this stuff that I never really had any interest in before I met all you, and it's become my life. That's down to you and your mates, and I'm *grateful* for it. There's more to life than finding the goods in skips, honing my begging pitch, squatting. Turns out there's a *lot* more. I'm glad I found it."

I couldn't help it. I got up and gave him a big, back-thumping hug, and he laughed some more, a sound that seemed to ring through the whole Zeroday, and when he toddled off to bed, it seemed to me that no matter what else happened, no matter how beat up poor Dog was, no matter how much trouble 26 was in with her parents, it was all going to be okay. Better than okay. It was going to be *illustrious*. It was going to be *magesterial*.

The next time we all met, we were much more public about it. There'd been some argument about this, of course. Some of Annika's people thought that we should go deep underground, use secret codes and encrypted mailing lists to hide the location of the next meeting. But 26 overruled them, and I backed her up. First off, we wanted to have as many people as possible come out to one of these things, because the whole point was to get voters to go round to their MPs' surgeries and tell them to support the private members' bill. Secondly, because it was clear to anyone who was willing to look that we were thoroughly infiltrated. It just wasn't that hard to spy on what we were doing, where we were going, and when we'd be there. I liked to imagine that some kid, somewhere, was getting enough money to keep himself in bubblegum and trainers in exchange for showing idiot entertainment execs in suits how to search our message boards, snickering to himself, going to the films, maybe even getting off with some girl who'd be horrified to know she was snogging a supergrass. But it was impossible to say, really: maybe they were a lot cleverer. Maybe looking for our little screenings had turned them into experts.

But it was clear that we couldn't keep a secret to save our lives, and hell with it, it was time to stop trying. We were helping to pass a law. That wasn't illegal, that was *democracy*! We should be able to do it all nice and aboveboard, without sneaking about like spies. That's what 26 and I reckoned, and in the end, the others agreed with it. Not least because it meant that we could invite in shedloads of press—and I'd been meticulously writing down the name of every reporter who'd asked me for a quote or an interview, and I was prepared to ring every single one them and make sure they knew that our meeting was coming.

So Annika sighed and said, fine, we were all going to end up in prison eventually, why not now? (But she smiled when she said it.) And then she helped us sweet talk the nice people at Shoreditch Town Hall into giving us use of the big room, which freaked me out even more than the thought of an arrest. You see, the big room at Shoreditch Town Hall was big enough for a thousand people, and they had video hookups with three more rooms in the place should the attendees not all fit in the hall. We were told that we'd have to rent chairs if we wanted them and Annika sneered at the phone and said, no, people could *stand,* cos it's easier to stamp your feet and shout when you were standing. Everyone seemed to take it for granted that we'd get more than enough people to fill the whole building, thousands of 'em, and have to turn away more at the door. And everyone took it for granted that I would speak to all these people.

Every time I thought about this, I got a feeling in my stomach that was kind of the opposite of butterflies: more like anvils. Or dynamite. A feeling like I was about to fall face-first off the roof of a tall building into a field of very, very sharp spikes.

"You don't have to speak if you don't want to, you know," 26 said to me over the breakfast table one morning. It was the hundredth time she'd said it, which was why I knew she was lying, and it was the first time she'd said it in front of her parents.

"If you're worrying about an arrest," her stepdad said, not looking up from his job of meticulously spreading a single-molecule-thick layer of Marmite over every millimeter of the top surface of his toast, "I think you'll be okay on that score. I've got a friend at the magistrate's office and he's promised to let me know if anyone issues any sort of warrant for your arrest. There's plenty of people in the courthouses who think that this business is an abuse of the law, especially now that they're bringing in busloads of people whose only crime is going to a public meeting to reform a bad law. No one likes the idea that he goes to work at the court every morning for the purpose of increasing the profits of a small group of offshore companies. If they wanted to be corporate lackeys, they'd go to work for a big City firm and make a fortune as real corporate lickspittles. But these poor lads aren't being paid enough to sell out."

I swallowed my own toast, which I'd piled high with cheese and fake meat slices and HP sauce and then slathered with a chili sauce from her dad's private, homemade reserve supply (a little bottle of pure evil that made my eyes water when I cracked the lid, and which tasted so good I kept eating it despite the desperate pain signals it caused my digestive tract to send to my brain). "That's reassuring," I said after I'd wiped the tears away from my eyes and blown out my streaming sinuses on a tissue. Her stepdad had basically adopted me as soon as he worked out that I fancied chili as much as he did, and he nodded approvingly. "It's funny, when you and Letitia talk about it, you'd think that we've practically won the fight already. But when the TIP act was up for debate, practically everyone told us not to bother fighting because we were doomed to fail."

He shrugged, and 26's mum said, "Well, that's politics for you. There's plenty that the other side can do if they don't care about being able to repeat the trick. Call in your favors, tell a bunch of whoppers about how the sky will fall if you don't get your way, smear your opposition, arm-twist the MPs. Problem is, you can only do this so much before you run out of political capital. I mean, you can only declare that art is about to die so many times before people notice that it has conspicuously failed to die." I loved it when 26's mum talked like this. She'd been in government for years before quitting to be some kind of consultant—she'd even been a junior minister for a brief time, but she'd resigned over something her party had done, said she was through with being political forever. As if! When she talked politics, it was like she was sketching out the dark secrets of the world's inner workings. "I think the problem is that this lot doesn't really have a strategy. I can't imagine that most of them dream that they're going to reduce the amount of copying going on in the world, but there are enough people convinced that they *should* be able to. So they go on making these bizarre laws, then not having any idea how to turn them into money once they've got them. How many lawsuits did you say they'd had, dear?" She turned to 26, who was stuffing her mouth with slices of mango drowned in thick homemade yogurt. 26 rolled her eyes and pointed at me while she chewed.

"Eight hundred thousand in the U.S.; two hundred and fifty thousand in the UK." I'd been revising on all the facts and figures of the copyright wars, reading the FAQs from all the pressure groups like Open Rights Group and Electronic Frontier Foundation. I could reel them off like my date of birth and the timecode for the juiciest rude words in Scot Colford films.

She sucked air over her teeth. "Fantastic," she said. "Insane. This lot are like a dog that finally catches the car it's chasing. They've got the Internet, it's clear that they can get practically any law or regulation passed that they want. But having won the battle, they have no idea what to do next. They keep on ordering the world to behave itself, and then giving it a thump when it doesn't mend its ways. What a bunch of utter prats."

"But they keep on beating us," I said.

26 pinched my leg under the table, hard. She'd finally swallowed her mouthful. "Stop with the defeat talk. Christ on a bike, you're not going to get up in front of all those people in sackcloth and say 'doomed doomed we're all doomed,' are you?"

"'Course not." I swallowed. "It's just so easy to lose heart sometimes—"

"Be of stout heart and fear not, young sir, for you have right on your side," her dad said, declaiming like a Shakespearean. 26 rolled her eyes again. He thumbed his nose at her. "It's true, you know. For all that these are big and powerful interests, they are, at heart *wrong*. Take it from someone who's spent a lot of time in front of a lot of juries: being right counts. It's not an automatic win, but it's not nothing, either."

They all nodded as though that settled it, and I thought of how nice it must be to be someone like that—someone who could simply make up his mind that he was right, the world was wrong, and fearlessly stride forth to fix things. That was the crazy thing about 26's family: they believed that they could actually change things. They believed *I* could change things. I only wished that I believed it, too.

Chapter <u>11</u>

Writing a speech is stupid. You write it and speak the words aloud—I'd started off saying them into a webcam so that I could see what I looked like when I was talking, but I was so self-conscious about the horrible spectacle of all those stupid contrived words coming out of my spotty, awkward face—and they sounded as convincing as a cereal advert. The thing was, I'd heard plenty of speeches—Scot Colford had done more than a few brilliant ones in his films—and felt my heart soaring in response to the words entering my ears, so I knew it was possible to say things that moved people and maybe even changed their minds.

But I didn't know what words to say, or how to say them. I sat in my room, filling screen after screen with stupid, stupid words, discarding them, starting over, and finally, I called Cora.

I'd been chatting to her all the time lately. She loved the idea of reforming TIP, and said that all her schoolmates were geared up to help. They'd descend on every MP's surgery in Bradford with their parents in tow, and grab the lawmakers by the lapels and demand that they listen to reason and refuse to leave until they did. Cora was so much smarter than me. She was like 26 in that regard (and 26 probably called her even more than I did—she'd adopted her as big sister and coconspirator and the two were thick as thieves), just another one of the brilliant women in my life who were much, much cleverer than I'd ever be. Why weren't *they* giving the speech? Well cos 26 had already filled in for my speech, and cos Sewer Cinema had been my idea, and because, weird as it was, millions of people actually cared what films Cecil B. DeVil gave his seal of approval to.

Cora would understand what it was like to grow up in the

kind of family where no one believed you could change anything, ever. She'd know exactly what to say to me. I dialed her and listened to it ring two, three times. I checked my watch. Bugger, she was in class. I was about to hang up when it was picked up.

"Cora?" I said.

"Cora's at school," my mum said. "She forgot her phone—I found it between the sofa cushions. Is that Trent?"

I groaned inwardly. Mum and Dad and I had been on speaking terms since I'd gone back, and I rang them every fortnight or so to have a kind of ritualistic conversation about how many veggies I was eating and whether I was taking drugs or getting into trouble. The kind of conversation where everyone knows that the answers are lies, but pretends not to, in other words. I loved my parents and even missed them in a weird sort of way, but I hadn't gone to them for advice since I was a little nipper. I certainly wasn't planning on getting public speaking advice from my mum. The closest thing she'd ever come to giving a public speech was making the Christmas toast every year, and she was famously long-winded at that, too.

"How are you, Mum?"

"Can't complain, actually. Been looking up the drugs and that they have me taking for my legs, and you know what I discovered? Turns out the pills one doctor had given me, way back when I had *you*, were very bad to take if you were on the other pills, the ones I've been on for about five years. So I stopped taking the old ones and I can't tell you how much of an improvement it made!"

"Wow," I said. "That's fantastic news!" My mum's legs have given her trouble all my life, and on the bad days, she could barely stand. It had all been getting much worse lately, too. This really was brilliant news.

"It's better than fantastic, you know. Now that I can get about a little more, I've been doing the physiotherapy and getting some more walks in, and I've found a ladies' walking group that goes out three evenings a week. It came up as an automatic

suggestion when I was looking up the physio things, you understand. It's made such a difference, I can hardly believe it."

"Aw, Mum, I'm so happy for you! Honestly, that's just brilliant."

"Shall I tell Cora you called?"

I was about to thank her and ring off, but I stopped. She didn't
sound like my mum somehow—didn't have that note of deep,
grinding misery from years and years of chronic pain. Didn't
sound like she just wanted to make the world all go away. It was
the sound of my mum on her rare good days, the few I remembered growing up, when we'd go to the park or even to a fun fair
or a bonfire and she'd smile and we'd all smile back at her. When
Mum was happy, the whole family shone.

"Mum? Can I ask you something?"

"Of course, sweetie, any time."

"Well, you know. I'm giving a speech soon, and—" I told her
about the meeting and the talk I was supposed to give. "It's only
meant to be fifteen minutes or so, but everything I write sounds so
stupid. I'm going bonkers here."

She was quiet for a long time. "Trent," she said, "we haven't
really talked much about this, I know. All this business with
copyright and that. I think you probably think I disapprove of it
all. But the truth is, you convinced me." My heart sped up. "I
don't know how else to put it. When you started it all, the downloading and making your films, I thought it was a kind of hobby,
and I guess it was, though if you say it's art, I'll say it's art. It's not
like I'm any kind of authority on art, you know. Never had much
use for it, to tell the truth. But the thing that convinced me isn't
art or anything like it, it's the idea that protecting copyright is
more important than our network connection. I mean, look at
me. I was a complete disaster until I was able to use the Internet
to look up my troubles. It helped me find people around the
world who had the same problems as I did, and even helped me
find ladies from right here on my own manor who could help
me get out and about. It seems to me that everyone must have a

story like this—look at your sister's education, or your father's job, or the new people next door, the Kofis. They just had a baby, a darling little girl, and their poor old parents in Ghana can't come for a visit. So they have a visit over the video, every night. Take away their Internet, you take away that little girl's chance to know her granny and grandad. Seems to me that's just not right. If the only way the films and music and that can get made is by giving them the power to just cut off all our connections to each other and work and school and health, I think we should just let 'em die."

My mouth literally hung open. My mum hadn't said anything that profound to me since . . . well, forever. Or maybe she'd never said anything that profound at a time I was ready to hear it. I know that I'm often ready to ignore anything my parents say. But this came straight from Mum's heart, and she had clearly thought very, very hard about it. Had I ever wondered how I'd make any of this matter to my parents? What an idiot I was.

"Mum," I said, "that was genius. Really."

"Don't pull my leg, Sunshine. It was just what I feel. I thought that knowing you could convince a silly old woman might help you do your talk."

"Ma, seriously—" I felt for the words. "What you just said, it put it all into perspective for me. It's like—" And then I had it. "Never mind. Thanks, Mum! Love you!"

"Love you, too, Trent." She sounded bemused now. I rang off and put my fingers back on the keyboard.

It's easy to think nothing we do matters. After all, didn't we mob our MPs when they were debating—or rather, *not debating* the Theft of Intellectual Property Bill? And they passed it anyway. Most of 'em didn't even turn up for work that day, couldn't be arsed to show up and defend the voters. And now they're throwing kids in jail at speed for downloading, cutting off families from the Internet as though losing your net access was like being sent to bed without supper."

I looked out over the crowd. They'd said it would be huge, but I hadn't really anticipated what *huge* really meant until I'd got up on the little podium at the end of the hall. The people looked like some kind of impossible "Where's Wally" drawing, like a kid's drawing of a football stadium where all the faces are represented by a kind of frogspawn cluster of little circles all touching one another. Many of the heads were crowned with odd, mirror-brimmed hats—mossie-zappers, with green lasers ready to fight back the West Nile scourge. Even though no one was talking, there was an enormous wall of sound rising off the crowd—whispers, shifting feet on floorboards, rasping of fabric from arms and legs. Part of me noted this in the abstract, wished I had a really good multichannel recording setup pointed out at the crowd to use for Foley sound the next time I wanted to edit a crowd into a film project.

I took a breath, the sound enormously magnified by the PA speakers beside the podium and set up around the room.

"Here's why I think we're going to win. Because we *all* need the net. Every day that goes by, more and more of us realize it." I looked again into the crowd, found Cora, who'd come down for the day to see me talk. She was in a little knot of her school chums, all come down together on the bus after much wheedling of parents who thought London would swallow them whole. "My mum just explained to me that when we lost our net connection, she wasn't able to get the health information she needed to help with her legs. She was sentenced to a year of agony, trapped in her flat, because I'd been accused of downloading. It cost my dad his job: up in Bradford, practically all the work there is comes over the net. He worked as a temp phone-banker, answering calls for a washing machine warranty program one day and taking orders for pizza the next day. It didn't pay much, but it was the best job he could get. And my sister—" I looked at Cora again. She was blushing, but she was grinning like a maniac, too. "She was in school, and you just imagine what it was like for her, trying to do her GCSEs without the net, when every other kid in her class had Google, all the books ever published, all those films and sound files and so on.

"My mum and dad aren't geeky kids who want to remix films. They're just plain northerners. I love them to bits, but they'd be the first to tell you they don't know anything about technology and all that business. But last week, my mum explained to me, better than I ever could, why the net matters to them, and why laws like TIP, which make the net's existence contingent on it not messing up the big entertainment companies' ancient business models, are bad for normal people like them.

"That's when I realized why we were going to win in the long run: every day, someone else in this country wakes up and discovers that his life depends on the net. It may be how he gets his wages, or how he stays healthy, or how he gets support from his family, or how he looks in on his old parents. Which means that, every day, someone in this country joins our side. All we need to do is make sure that they know we exist when that happens, and lucky for us, we've only got the entire bloody Internet to use to make that happen. It's why there are so many people joining up with pressure groups like Open Rights Group and all that lot.

"So we're going to win someday. It's just a matter of how many innocent people's lives get destroyed before that happens. I'd like that number to be as small as possible, and I'm sure you would, too. So that's why I think it's worth trying to win this, today, now, here. Last year, our MPs didn't believe that enough voters cared about the net to make voting against TIP worth it. This year, they know different. Let's remind them of that, now that there's an election coming up. All of you who went out last time, it's time to pay a little 'I told you so' visit on your MP. And those of you who didn't care or didn't believe it was worth it last time: this time you need to care. This time it's worth it."

I drank some water. Something weird was happening: despite my dry throat and my thundering pulse, I was *enjoying* this! I could feel the talk's rhythm like I could feel the rhythm of a film when I was cutting it, and I knew that I was doing a good job. Not just because people were smiling and that, but because *I* could feel the rightness.

"They tell us that without these insane laws, our creativity will dry up and blow away. But I make films. You've seen them, I think—" A few people cheered in a friendly way, and I waved at them. "And I think they're plenty creative. But according to laws like TIP, they're not art, they're a crime." People booed. I grinned and waved them quiet again. "Now, maybe there used to be only one way to make a film, and maybe that way of making films meant that you needed certain kinds of laws. But there are plenty of ways to make films today, and yesterday's laws are getting in the way of today's filmmaking. Maybe from now on, creativity means combining two things in a way that no one has ever thought of combining them before." I shrugged. "Maybe that's all it ever was. But I think my films should be allowed to exist, and that you should be allowed to watch them. I think that a law that protects creativity should protect all creativity, not just the kind of creativity that was successful fifty years ago."

I looked down at the face of my phone, resting on the podium. My countdown timer had nearly run out. I'd timed this talk to exactly ten minutes, and here I was, right at the end, after ten minutes exactly. I smiled and raised my voice.

"They've been passing laws to make people like you and me more and more guilty for years. All it's done is crushed creativity and ruined lives. We've had the Web for decades now, isn't it about time we made peace with it? You can do that—tell your MP, and remind him that it's election season. We're going to win someday—let's make it today."

I swallowed, smiled, said, "Thank you," and grabbed my phone and my papers and stepped away from the podium. The applause and cheers rang in my ears and people were saying things to me, leaning in to shout congratulations and good job and that, and it was all more than I could take in, so it blended into a kind of hand-clasping, shoulder-shaking *hurrah*. My head was light and my hands were shaking and I felt unaccountably hot. I knew I'd done well, and I'd managed to keep all my nervousness at bay while I was speaking, but now I felt like I might actually faint—keel right over on the spot.

I pushed my way clear of the well-wishers and through the crowd (more people shaking my hands, whispering that I'd done a good job, while the next speaker—a Green MP I'd met once before at one of Annika's meetings—began her talk) and out into the cool of the entry hall. I leaned against the wall and put my head back and closed my eyes and concentrated on breathing heavily. Then I heard the door to the hall open again (the MP's voice growing louder for a moment) and two sets of footsteps approaching. They came closer and I smelled 26's hair stuff. She kissed me softly on the lips, pressing her body to mine, and I kept my eyes closed while my world shrank down to the lips gently pressing against mine.

"You okay?" she said, whispering into my mouth.

"Yeah," I said. "Just wrung out."

"Okay," she said. "Got to get back to it, I'm next."

"I'll be right in," I said.

She moved away and I opened my eyes to see who else had come out with her. It was Cora, of course, her eyes shining, and she flung her arms around my neck and hugged me so hard I thought I'd fall over. "You were brilliant! I'm *so proud*! My friends all think you're a god!"

I laughed. This was *exactly* what I needed. My sister and my girlfriend, both telling me I'd done it all right, hadn't cocked up, and an island of isolation from the crowd and the speeches and the rushing around and the pressure.

A man crossed the lobby. He was dressed like a hoodie from the estate I grew up on, but he was older, and really, too old to be dressed like a teenager. Thirty or forty, maybe.

"You Cecil B. DeVil, yeah?" he said. He was smiling, sticking his hand out.

I took it, embarrassed and proud to be cornered by a fan in

front of my sister. She'd probably assume that I got this kind of thing all the time, and that made me proud, too.

"Yeah," I said. "Nice to meet you." I took his hand, and he brought out his other hand so quick that I flinched back, sure he had a cosh or a knife in there, and he squeezed my hand even harder, pulling me in. I saw that he was holding an envelope, not a weapon, and he shoved it into my hand.

"Lawsuit for yer," he said, and laughed nastily, and let go of my hand, pushing me a little in the direction I'd been tugging, nearly sending me back onto my ass. I clutched the envelope and windmilled my arms, and Cora turned and shouted, "Sod off, you prick! Get a proper job!"

He just laughed harder and more nastily, and held up two fingers as he banged out the hall's front doors and into Old Street.

I held Cora back and shoved the envelope in my pocket. "Come on," I said, "26 is about to start."

It turned out that four film studios had filed a lawsuit with 15,232 separate charges against me.

Seriously.

One for every single clip I'd ever used in every video with Cecil B. DeVil in the credits. 26's stepdad seemed to think that this was some kind of marvel.

"You should put out a press release," he said. "Or call the Guinness World's Records people. I think this may be the thickest claims-sheet in British legal history. You could probably get a prize or something."

"Yeah," I said. "Like a £78 million bill." That was the damages being sought by the studios. They were seeking maximum statutory damages for each separate infringement (and I was rather bemused to see that they got some of the clips wrong—for example, in that virginity-losing scene that started this whole mess, they mixed up *Bikini Trouble in Little Blackpool* with *Summerfun Lollypop*, which I'd never heard of. I rushed straight out and downloaded it, then kicked myself because Monalisa was so much better in it and there was all kinds of audio I could have lifted—if I ever did a recut, I'd have to use that one, for sure).

He waggled his fingers at me. "Young man, unless I am very far wrong, you don't actually have £78 million."

"Not *quite* that much, no."

"I hope you won't take offense when I say that I believe that your net worth—exclusive of your not inconsiderable talents and charm—is more like zero million pounds."

"I don't even have zero *hundred* pounds."

"Quite so. We have a name for people like you: we call you 'judgment proof.' Doesn't matter how much the judge orders you to pay, you won't be able to pay it."

"What about my parents?"

"Do they own property, or a car, or have substantial savings or shares or bonds? Rare works of art?"

I shook my head.

"There you are, then. There is always the possibility that they'll try to bring a criminal charge against you. But as I've said, I'm reasonably certain that the director of public prosecutions isn't going to try to make a case for breaking and entering, and that leaves criminal infringement, but I don't think even the Theft of Intellectual Property Act is going to help them there. You weren't making full copies of commercial films available, so they can't get you under the piracy section. Your biggest risk is that they'll seek to permanently bar you from using computers or the Internet, but that won't stand up to a spirited defense. So, basically I think this is intended to serve as a nuisance. You're going to have to scrounge up a solicitor and a barrister to get up for you in court. I can recommend some good sorts who'd do the instructing for me, assuming you'd be happy to have me speak for you in court?"

I shook my head. "Of course I'd want you to be my lawyer, but I don't really understand all this stuff. Solicitor, barrister—it's just another way of saying 'lawyer,' right?"

He shook his head with mock sorrow. "You've clearly been

raised on American courtroom dramas. You should go dig up some Rumpole programs, they're good fun, and not a bad look in at the profession." He held up a hand. "On second thought, let me make a gift of the DVDs, right? We've got a set around here somewhere. Let's not have you downloading anything naughty while this business is going on, at least not on my account."

I smiled back, but I was thinking, *Not download? You're having a laugh, right?* I didn't really stop to count up how much downloading I was likely to do in a given day, but of course, it was an immense load. I probably broke the law a few thousand times a day.

"Anyroad, let me explain this for you quickly. It's all very archaic, but that's British justice for you—or, rather, justice in England and Wales, because it would all be too simple if it worked the same way in Scotland and Northern Ireland, right? Right. Okay, so there's two kinds of lawyer you need to occupy yourself with at this stage. There are solicitors, and barristers. A solicitor writes up threatening legal letters, prepares cases, files motions, advises clients on the finer points of law and so forth. A barrister is a low, brawling sort of fellow who actually goes to court— sometimes dressed in the most bizarre clown costume you can imagine, horsehair wig and great black robe like you were getting up to play the angel of death in a cheap melodrama—and tries to persuade a judge or a magistrate or a jury that you're innocent. We question witnesses, make arguments, the sort of thing you'll see in the third act of a courtroom drama.

"Wasn't too long ago that a barrister couldn't get a client for himself—we'd be brought on by the solicitor, who'd be hired by the defendant. These days, it's merely frowned upon, but I've never let that worry me. Nevertheless, I can't represent you on my own—I need to be instructed by a solicitor, and so we need to find you one of those upstanding chaps. Since you haven't any money, we'll either have to raise some, or find someone who'll be your solicitor *pro bono*—that is, for free."

I squirmed. "I suppose I could ask people for money, but I'd much rather they gave it to the campaign to repeal TIP."

He nodded. "Yes, I expect the people who cooked up this preposterousness figured that it would suck your time and other peoples' money and divert it from being used to fight their pet law. It's not a bad move, truth be told. Filing lawsuits like this can't be too expensive for them, as they've been doing them in onesie-twosies for years, it's just a matter of ganging them all up into one massive docket. All in all, a reasonably cheap way of taking you out of commission. You should be proud—they think you're important enough to neutralize. A mere stripling of seventeen! Dearie me, next thing they'll be fleeing in terror before an army of adolescents with bum-fluff mustaches a cat could lick off!"

We were sat in his basement workshop, and as he talked, he kept busy flitting between his kegs and jars and that, adjusting pressures, sipping, adulterating. Now he drew me off a cracked enamel cupful of something the color of honey. "Try that one," he said.

I sipped. It was astounding—a bit of sweet, a bit of lemon, and the beery sourness, all mingled together in a fizzy, cool drink that felt like it was dancing on my tongue. "Woah," I gasped after swallowing. "That's *fantastic* stuff."

He touched the brim of his laser-ringed hat. "Always thought I'd have been a brewer if I hadn't gone in for the law. Nice to have something to fall back on, anyway."

Chapter <u>12</u>

TIP-EH!/DON'T BE CLEVER/
A SYMPATHETIC DESCENDANT

The campaign was picking up steam now. Rabid Dog—who had healed up faster than any of us would have credited, though there was still something wrong with his nose and he seemed to have trouble breathing through it—came up with the name for it: "TIP-Ex," after *Tipp-Ex,* the old correction fluid you used to cover up mistakes with ink. I dimly knew the stuff existed, though I didn't do too much writing with pen. It was iconic, something that had been part of every office and home for more than fifty years, and the little bottles with their red labels were instantly recognizable, and perfect for repurposing into logos for webpages and avatars for the social sites.

The amazing thing about it all was how many people I'd never heard of seemed to care about it. I'd look at the news on any given day and there'd be five or six articles on local TIP-Ex campaigners organizing mass meetings, a demonstration outside the local chain cinema, or descending en masse on their MPs' offices. All over England and Wales and Northern Ireland, even in Scotland, though their Parliament had refused to implement TIP in the first place. Then reporters would run around and stick mics in MPs' faces and ask them what they planned on doing about this, and they'd all harrumph and make very serious noises about having serious debates and taking things seriously, seriously.

Letitia told me that this was all good news, but that we couldn't count on anything until the day the vote came in. The Lords were scheduled to start their debate in ten days, and the mailing lists were alive with grown-up clever people who were writing position papers and that for them. I just tried to follow along. I mean, I could get my head around the idea that there was a Parliament full of Members who were elected, but then there was this other bunch of lawmakers who were all *Lords* and *Ladies*, which made me think of fairy tales.

I didn't even know that they weren't "proper" lords until 26 explained it to me. I'd just assumed that the House of Lords was full of poshos whose great-great-grandads had killed a bunch of Normans in 1066 and had therefore guaranteed their descendants a seat in government forever. It turned out that there were a few of those around, but most of the Lords were "life peers," who got appointed by the big political parties, though technically the King still had to wave his magic sword at them and make them into extraspecial lordly types. They got to hang around for life, and didn't have to worry about getting reelected, and apparently there were a load of very young ones ("very young" in this case meaning forty, which made me realize that the rest of them must be as old as Jesus) that were dead keen on technology and stuff.

The Lords would debate the TIP-Ex bill, and made changes and that, and then send it back to Parliament for more debate. Apparently, Parliament didn't *have* to listen to them, but they usually did. There was a lot of this sort of thing, it seemed to me— stuff that worked one way on paper and another way in practice. I tried to make sense of it, but ultimately I reckoned that the best I could do was what I'd been doing all along: make a big stink and a lot of noise and let other people take care of the bits they were good at.

Which would have been easier if it wasn't for all this lawsuit business. The solicitor that 26's stepdad found for me was a young and eager type, in his midtwenties, named Gregory. I thought he was Chinese, but it turned out he was Malaysian, though he spoke posher English than I did. He was busily filing all sorts of papers with the court, and he rang me up every day to explain it all to me, and let me tell you, if the Parliament and Lords business was complicated, it was nothing next to this rot. I'd get ahold of a thread and feel like it was making sense, and then I'd lose track of it all.

But there was one thing that absolutely got my attention: "They want to get an injunction barring you from using the Internet until the trial," Gregory said. He insisted on talking on the phone—no IM, no email—because apparently phone calls had some kind of special legal status when you were talking to a solicitor and if someone were to wiretap us, it would go very hard on them. I kept trying to explain that we could just use encrypted VoIP or IM or even email, which would be *impossible* to wiretap (and not just illegal), but he had his way of doing things and wouldn't change them for a kid like me. So I bought loads of pre-paid airtime minutes for my mobile and took notes on my lappie.

"That doesn't sound good," I said.

"It means you won't be able to use the net for at least a month. It'll keep you offline until the TIP-Ex vote's gone past."

"Bugger," I said. "Do you think they'll get it?" I was bothered, but not insanely so. So what if I couldn't post as Cecil B. DeVil or Trent McCauley? I'd just read the net through our little bootleg connection and have someone else type up replies from me. It'd be a pain, but nothing terminal.

He sighed. "I think they might. Now, Trent, I know you're thinking that you'll be able to sneak online but I want you to understand what that would mean. Right now, you're facing a civil suit. As you know, there's not much bad that can happen to you no matter how it turns out—you haven't got any money, so even if they win a giant judgment off you, they'll never collect. But if the court orders you to do something—like stay off the Internet—and you don't do it, you'll be in contempt of court. That's not a civil problem, it's a *criminal* one, and the judge can and will stick you in jail for it. What's more, once you've been done on a criminal charge, the coppers get all sort of license to go scrounging around on your hard drive to see what else they might find. I'm sure there's some clever bugger over at one of the motion picture studios who's gone, 'Hang on, this Cecil kid is absolutely mad for the net. Why don't we get the judge to suspend his network access, wait for him to do something stupid, and then bang him up for contempt, search his computer, and find a bunch more reasons to do him over. As a bonus, we'll crack open his email and find out which of his mates we can get at, too, see if there's anything that looks like a confession of wrongdoing. Maybe he's skint, but some of his chums'll have parents with lovely houses and cars and that that we can get off them. He'll have a lot fewer friends once his little games get all his friends' families turned into paupers.' Are you following me on this one?"

I shook my head. "Fine," I said, feeling glum and self-pitying. I comforted myself with the knowledge that they'd never get anything off my computer, not with my encrypted hard drive.

"You're thinking about your computer's encryption, yeah?" Gregory said. He was such a sharp one.

"You're a mind-reader, then?"

"Let's just say you're not the first young man of my acquaintance who's got himself into trouble with a computer. I'm perfectly willing to stipulate that you can lock up your hard drive with fiendishly clever ciphers that His Majesty's best will never crack open. Allow me to quote a brief passage from Section 53 of the Regulation of Investigatory Powers Act 2000, a gripping read from start to finish, by the way: 'A person to whom a section 49 notice'—that is, you, once the law tells you to hand over your password—'has been given is guilty of an offense if he knowingly fails, in accordance with the notice, to make the disclosure required by virtue of the giving of the notice.' Tumpty tumpty tumpty, for the purposes of, sufficient evidence, etc and so forth, yes, here it is! 'A person guilty of an offense under this section shall be liable on summary conviction, to imprisonment for a term not exceeding six months or to a fine not exceeding the statutory maximum, or to both.'

"You follow that, o client mine? The law can order you to turn over your passwords, crypto keys, and all the other clevernesses you've got stashed in that young, foolish head of yours. If you don't do so in a prompt and cooperative manner, well, they bang you up for six months. Fancy half a year in jail?"

"No," I muttered, feeling all boxed in.

"Thought not. So don't be clever. They haven't won the injunction yet, and I'm sure your barrister will fight it like the vicious bulldog I know him to be. But if he loses, you are to comply with the order with extreme punctiliousness. Not because I expect you to have much respect for the law. To be frank, the law is my life and some mornings I don't have much respect for it myself. No, because if you fail to comply, you will be putting your head in the jaws of a large, deadly bear trap that these smart fellows have laid in your path, and I'd much prefer you to live to a ripe old age without getting your noggin crushed within the law's inexorable maw. Are we both very clear on this?"

"Clear as perspex," I said.

He clucked his tongue. "It's not me you should be getting arsey with. I didn't put you in this position, and I'm doing my utmost to get you out of it, even though I'm not getting a groat for my time. If it's any comfort, at least know that someone very clever and expensive has been paid many, many thousand of pounds to think this one up, which means that you've really upset someone. Whatever you're doing, it's got some rich and powerful people scared."

That cheered me some. "That's not a bad way of looking at it."

"There you go. So keep your pecker up, stiff upper lip, all that business. I'll come back to you once we've got a court date for the injunction. Stay out of trouble until then, right?"

"Right," I said. He hung up before I could add, "Thanks." That was just like him—everything seemed to be part of some viciously competitive game he was playing against himself, or maybe against the whole world, and he wasn't really one for the niceties. I reckoned I understood that somewhat, as there were days when I felt a bit of it myself.

But seeing as I had some time before I was coming before

the court, and seeing as how I'd just had the fear put into me, I thought it prudent to do something to protect my pals if the worst happened. The thing was, locking up your hard drive wasn't that hard, but most of the time it was obvious that you'd fiddled things—anyone who knew what to look for could tell in a second that you'd encrypted the lot. For years I'd used some clever stuff called TrueCrypt that had a "plausible deniability" mode that was pretty fiendish.

TrueCrypt let you set up part or all of your hard drive as an encrypted file. After booting the computer, you needed to enter the password to mount the disk. But if someone knowledgeable looked at the disk, it'd be totally obvious that there was an encrypted TrueCrypt blob sitting on it.

But the clever bit was this: TrueCrypt let you set up a second, *hidden* file within that blob. If you entered one password, you'd just see the "outer" disk. But enter a second password at the same time and you'd get an entirely different disk. And *this* disk was practically invisible: there was no way to look at the encrypted outer file and say that there was another disk hiding in it. If you had a good "inner disk" password, no one would be able to prove that it was there. Which meant that if someone—say, a representative of His Majesty's government—decided to force me to give up my password, I could cheerfully give them the "outer" password and insist that no inner password existed and they'd never be able to prove otherwise.

But I figured that if it ever came to that, no one was going to believe that I didn't have an inner, hidden disk. I mean, *of course* I'd use one! Even if I had nothing to hide, I'd do it because it was so flipping, deadly *cool* to have a little spy-drive all to my own.

The TrueCrypt boffins had thought of this, of course. So they'd recently shipped a new version that had room for a *third* inner layer inside the "deniable" partition—so you'd have to enter a password, and then another password, and then another password. You could go all the way down if you wanted, five or six layers deep. My solicitor was a clever-clogs and he was quite right that it would go hard for me if I got into a position where I had to give up my password and refused to give it. But as usual, the technology was running half a mile ahead of the law. After all, what could the coppers do, bang you in jail because you'd given them password after password and they *hadn't* found anything, and therefore you must still be hiding something?

Well, come to think of it, I wouldn't put it past them. It was a bit like an old-fashioned witch hunt: they *knew* you were guilty, so if they couldn't find any evidence, it must mean you were *really* guilty, because you'd hidden your deeds away so smartly. But hell, if it came to that, I'd be burned for a witch in any event, and I'd been meaning to try out this new TrueCrypt business for ages. It meant backing up all my data and repartitioning the drive, which was bloody tedious work, since the little lappie I'd built at Aziz's had a four terabyte RAID striped across the drives in its two internal bays, and it took almost an hour to format that much storage, not to mention backing up the data to an old external box I had lying about, and then clean-wiping the backup disk by writing random noise to it twenty times over, while its pathetic little fans whined to whisk away all the heat from the write-head going *chugga-chugga-chugga* for hours and hours.

But when it was done, I had, essentially, three computers. The outmost layer was an obvious shell, with nothing more than a browser and some config tools. But unlock the inside disk and you had a browser profile with cookies to log in to a bunch of pretty-much public email/Twitter/social accounts, the kind of thing I'd use to participate in public conversations and correspond with my fixer. Inside *that* layer, I stashed my real workspace, with all my hard-cataloged Scot video clips, all the sliced-and-diced audio, and all the private messages with my mates and Cora (I used a different account to talk to my parents, of course). Even as I was putting the finishing touches on this, I was thinking of all kinds of ways that I could still be done with it—for example, my inner layer, supposedly my main workspace, had no Scot material on it at all. But everyone knew I made all those Scot videos, which meant that anyone who looked at it would have a bloody good reason to think I was hiding something.

Oh, well. If it came to that, I'd have to just brazen it out and say that I'd seen the light, deleted all my Colfordalia, and gone straight. I even knew what I'd say: I loved Scot Colford's films. This was true. The geezer'd been a true genius, and not just as an actor, as a writer and director, too. And by all accounts, he'd been a decent sort, two kids who never said a word against him, a wife he stuck by all his adult life, just recently passed on. If my imaginary interrogators wanted proof of my Scot Colford trufan status, they'd just have to look at the passwords they forced out of me: I'd made them up by taking the first letter of each word from some of Scot's best-ever speeches, then rotating them forward one letter through the alphabet.

For example, "You think that you're special, just cos you were born to some posh manor? All that means is that your grandad was the biggest bastard around. You're not special. You're common as muck, and if you came over to mine, I'd count the spoons before I let you leave." That was from *Hard Times,* and if you took just the first letter, you got:

Yttys,jcywbtspm?Atmitygwtbba.Yns.Ycam,aiycotm,
    IctsbIlyl.

Now, shift each letter forward one and you got:

Zuuzt,kdzxcutqn?Bunjuzhxuccb.Zmt.Zdbn,bfzdpun,
    JdutcJkzk.

Then I used some simple number substitution and got:

2uuz7,kd2xcu7qn?Bunju24xuccb.2mt.2dbn,bf2dpun,Jdu
    7cJk2k.

It wasn't exactly random, but I could remember it and I'd never have to write it down, and you'd have to be pretty sharp to guess which Scot speech I used and so forth. Just to make things interesting, I rotated the inner password one letter *backward* and the inner-inner password forward by two positions. I felt like a right James Bond, truly.

I'd just rebooted and tapped my way into the second layer when I saw that I had an email to one of the very public Cecil B. DeVil accounts, the one I put at the end of all the videos. Not many people sent me emails—usually they just dropped me IMs or little updates on my social networks. Email was almost always from someone who was a little on the stuffy side—cops, lawyers, MPs, reporters, that sort of thing. So I always got a little flutter in my tummy when the flag went up. But I clicked it, because you've got to, right?

> To: Cecil B. DeVil
> From: Katarina McGregor-Colford
> Re: My grandfather

My finger trembled over the DELETE key—"My grandfather" made me think of the kind of spam that promised you millions if you helped smuggle someone's dead relative's fortune out of some foreign country. But the name Katarina McGregor-Colford rang a bell. I scrolled down.

> Dear Mr. "DeVil,"
>   My name is Katarina McGregor-Colford, and Scot Colford was my grandfather.

Whoa. That's where I knew that name from!

>   For more than a year now, I've been watching your little remixes of Grandad's films. At first, I was a little off-put, to tell you the absolute truth. I grew up watching Scot Colford films

and they're something of a holy writ in my clan, as you might imagine.

But as time went by, I saw the clear and unmistakable love in your work: love for my grandfather's films, love for film itself. And it didn't hurt that you clearly know what you're about when it comes to editing videos. I'd assumed from the start that you must be in your late twenties, like me, but when I read about you in *The Guardian,* and I discovered that you were just a kid (no offense), I was perfectly gobsmacked. Frankly, your work is very good, and sometimes it's brilliant. You're a talented young man, and I foresee great things ahead of you.

What's more—and here I come to the meat of this note—I *know* Grandad would have approved of your work. How do I know this? Because my grandfather, Scot Colford, was a mashup artist long before anyone had heard of the word! That's right! Grandad was an inveterate tinkerer and a proper gadget hound, and he kept a shed at the bottom of his garden that was absolutely *bursting* with film-editing and sound-editing equipment, several generations' worth, from enormous, boxy film-cutters and projectors and lightboards to a series of PCs connected to so many hard drives it sounded like a jet engine when he switched them all on!

On top of that, Grandad had *loads* of video. He'd collected films when he was a boy, and later on he'd digitized them himself, hundreds and thousands of hours' worth, along with the raw dailies from many of his films and, later, digitized VHS cassettes and ripped DVDs. It was his most-favorite pastime to disappear into his shed and make up one of his "special films." These were usually quite comical. He had a whole series of *Star Wars* ones that he'd show to us kids at Christmas, a little film-festival's worth, with Chewbacca and the Ewoks break dancing, Luke flying his spaceship through a series of other films (mostly Grandad's own ones!), and so forth. It was the highlight of the family Christmases.

A few of my cousins actually learned some editing from
Grandad. I tried once, but to tell you the truth, he could be a
little impatient with slow learners, which I absolutely was, and
so I gave up. I ended up going into medicine, as it turns out,
but I do have one cousin who works as a very successful
editor in Bangalore. He's actually the one who sent me your
films in the first place. At the risk of swelling your head, he
thinks you're dead brilliant.

Oh. My. God. She was talking about Johnnie Colford,
who'd cut *4 Idiots,* and the Asha Bosle biopic, and, well, practically every Bollywood film I'd ever thrilled to. He was a *legend.*
And he thought I was "dead brilliant!" I practically fainted at this
point.

When I first found your films, I was a little offended, yes,
but more than that, I was reminded of my own grandfather,
and some of the happiest moments in my childhood. I see
now that they're suing you for 78 million pounds, though as
far as I can tell, you never made a penny off your works. Well,
I don't control the Scot Colford estate and I can't speak for it,
but speaking as one of the man's descendants, I felt I had to
write to you and tell you that a) We've made (and continue to
make) plenty of money off Grandad's works, notwithstanding
your so-called piracy and b) If Scot Colford had been born
when you were, he would have done exactly what you've
done.

And you can quote me on that, Mr. DeVil.

Warmly,

Katarina

PS: The Internet being what it is, you might be wondering if
this is a fake (I certainly might!). You'll find my office email on
the list of NHS doctors in London at nhsonline.org, and you
can reply to me at that address. What's more, if you supply a
postal address, I'd be delighted to send along a drive of some

of Grandad's favorite little films, as I have a mountain of them here.

It took all of two minutes to locate Katarina McGregor-Colford on the NHS registry. She had a practice in Islington, in a posh road, and I replied to the email address on her record.

Dear Katarina,

I can't thank you enough for your email. You've made my day—even my century! I mean, wow!

I honestly don't know what to tell you. I'm speechless. Your grandad was a legend for me. I make the films I do because of how he inspired me.

I'd be completely utterly thrilled to get some of his mashups! I mean honestly, they're like holy relics for me! I wish I was more clever with words, I don't know how to express what I'm feeling right now. I'm on the ceiling, over the moon and around the bend. I'd even come round and get them and save you the postage!

Cecil

I sat there, feeling the warm glow, and moments later, I got a reply.

Cecil

The pleasure's mutual. I can have a thumb-drive at the reception at my practice for you tomorrow morning.

She followed with the address I'd already looked up. I forwarded the message to practically everyone I knew, and then spent the next hour on the phone and on IM with people who wanted to congratulate me on it. Then I had more interviews to do about the TIP-Ex, and there was a video I was cutting that I wanted to finish so I could drop it by Katarina's practice the next day, and by the time I wound down and stuffed a fistful of

cheese and salami slices—we'd found a mountain of dried salami
in the Waitrose skip that week, and even after giving away fifty
of them to the folks round Old Street Station, we were still struggling to eat the remainders—into my gob, it was nearly midnight. I called 26 to tell her I loved her and she blew me a kiss and
told me she was nearly done with her final paper for the school
year, and then I sank into a happy sleep.

I leapt out of bed the next morning like I'd been fired from
a cannon. I had dropped my latest Scot film (Scot gets strip-
searched on his way into the premiere of *Brown Wire,* one of his
top-grossing films; the cops find five cameras, three phones, and a
laptop on him, and he faces them down with withering sarcasm—I
was dead proud of it) onto one of the leftover thumb-drives from
the Leicester Square caper, and I slipped it in my pocket before
heading out the door. I practically ran all the way to Islington, not
even bothering with the bus—my enthusiasm, plus a triple espresso
from Jem's own hand, had filled me with more energy than I
knew what to do with.

I reached Katarina McGregor-Colford's surgery—a smart,
narrow storefront in Upper Street between a health-food store
and a posh baby-clothes shop—a little after ten. The secretary
behind the counter was an older Asian lady in a hijab, and when
I told her I'd come for a drive that the doctor had left for me, she
smiled and asked me to wait because the doctor has asked to be
notified when I was in.

I sat in the waiting room between various sick people, old
people, and restless kids for fifteen minutes, jiggling my leg and
looking up every time someone went in or out of one of the consulting rooms. Then a tall woman in a cardigan and jeans came
out of one of the little rooms. She conferred with the receptionist,
who pointed at me, and then she smiled and crossed the waiting
room in three long strides and stuck her hand out.

"You must be Cecil," she said. Her voice was uncannily like
Scot's, though shifted up an octave. Something about the inflec-

tions or the accent—whatever it was, I could have picked her out as Scot Colford's granddaughter by ear alone. I jumped to my feet and wiped my sweaty palms on my thighs and then took her offered hand. "I'm Katarina. It's such a pleasure!"

She looked like him, too, had the same famous eyes, the same trademark lopsided dimple, the same little gap between her top front teeth. She caught me staring at her face and stuck her tongue out and crossed her eyes. "You can stop making a checklist of all the ways I look like Grandad, now. It runs in the family—we've all got it." She had such a warm manner, and I knew that she must be a brilliant doctor to have.

"I can't thank you enough, doctor—" I said.

"Katarina," she said. " 'Doctor' is for my patients."

"Katarina," I said. "I, uh, I made a new film and I wanted you to see it first. It's got your grandad in it."

She looked over her shoulder at her receptionist. "How much time have I got, Sarina?"

The receptionist looked at her screen. "Ten minutes," she said. "Maybe twelve, if the usual gentleman is late as usual."

Katarina jerked her head at her consulting room door and led me in, closing it behind me. "I've got a regular Monday morning appointment with a fellow who is habitually late. Sarina always juggles things so he can get in to see me, though. Now, you said something about a video?"

I handed her the drive and she pulled a little media player out of her handbag and stuck it in. "Not allowed to plug anything into that, of course," she said, indicating the screen on her desk.

" 'Course," I said.

The video was only a minute and a half long—I'd based it off footage from an antipiracy ad they made you sit through before every film—and Katarina spent the next ninety seconds laughing her head off at the video. Before I could say anything, she ran it through again.

"It's very, very good," she said. "I mean, absolutely marvelous.

I know Grandad would have loved this—it's so up his street. Speaking of which—" She opened her desk drawer and pulled out a couple of old thumb-drives emblazoned with the logos of an office supply store. "I loaded one of these up with a bunch of Grandad's remixes, and the other one with some of my favorite family films. Stuff the public never saw—Grandad just being himself, not 'Scot Colford.' Thought you'd appreciate it."

My hands shook as I took them. "Katarina, I—" I took a deep breath and made myself calm down. "Listen, you can't know how much this means to someone like me. You know there's a whole legion of people like me who are mad for your grandad's work—when someone discovers a rarity, like one of the Japanese adverts he did or some outtakes from a film, it's like gold. It's cos every clip opens up the chance to make a whole world of new creations, films and stuff. It's like we're chemists discovering a new element or something." I grinned. "You know, I only know about chemists and elements because of Scot's Mendeleev film, *Elemental Discovery*."

She raised her eyebrows. "Even I don't know that one."

"Oh," I said, "well, it's quite rare. The Open Society Institute funded it as part of an educational series for the Caribbean. Most of them weren't very good, but *Elemental Discovery* is really brilliant. It's dead funny, too. I can get you a copy, if you'd like."

"Sure," she said. "I'd love to see it. You know, I really struggled with chemistry at uni. I had no idea Grandad knew anything about the subject."

"I don't think he did, really. He did an interview with Sky where he said he needed to do dozens of retakes because he couldn't keep the element names straight in his head."

"How do you know all this stuff?"

I shrugged. "You can't really make films by remixing them unless you know a lot about them. Whenever I watch a video, I'm looking for dialog or shots or effects or cuts that I can use in one of mine. It feels like I'm picking up pieces of a jigsaw puzzle that's been scattered all over the shop, and maybe it's three or four puzzles, or dozens of them, even, and I don't have the box and I don't know what piece goes with which puzzle. But every now and again, I'll find an edge or even a corner and a big piece of it snaps together into a video. Then I sit down and cut and edit and hunt down missing bits and reconsider things, and if I'm lucky, I end up with a bit of video that looks like the film I've got in my head."

"Gosh, it sounds like a lot of work. Don't take this the wrong way, but wouldn't it be simpler to pick up a camera and shoot the stuff that you want?"

I squirmed a little. I hated this question. "I don't know. Maybe I will, someday. But when I started, I was just a little kid, and I didn't know any grown-ups who would act for me, even if I had sets and all that. So I cut up what I could find, trying to get at that thing I could see in my mind's eye. Now I've been doing it for so long, it feels like cheating if I make my own thing. You know what it's like? There's this arsey, posh estate agent's near Old Street Station, Foxton's. They have this enormous sculpture in the window, a kind of huge moving thing made out of old silver spoons and other bits of Victorian cutlery and plates and china, and it's all geared up with old bike chains, and they make it all whirl around in this kind of crazy dance. The first time I saw it, I was completely taken away by it—not just because it's beautiful, but because I was so impressed with the idea that someone had found the beauty that was in all these bits of junk that they'd found lying around. It was like they'd unlocked something wonderful and hidden away, like the most wonderful diamond in history pulled out of the muck.

"Every time I passed by, I stopped to look at it and appreciate it. Then, one day, one of the estate agents came out, a big mucker in a camel-hair coat and shiny shoes and a silk scarf, and he said, 'You're always staring at that, hey? It's nice. You can hardly tell that all that stuff isn't real.'

"As soon as he said it, I could see it—every plate, every spoon and fork, they were all made of plastic. No one had excavated all this junk from a charity shop and made something brilliant out of it. They'd just sent off to China for a bunch of premade, injection-molded rubbish, just like you would if you wanted a load of plastic Christmas trees or artificial flowers. And though it was still pretty, it wasn't anything like the miracle I'd thought it was. It was just a clever little toy, not a work of art.

"When I make a film by finding real parts lying around, waiting to be shifted and shunted and twisted into place to make something new, it *feels real*. Like I've done something that no one else could quite make. When I started using a bit of computer generated stuff to fill in around the edges, it felt like a real cheat and it took me ages to get comfortable with it. Every now and again, I think about maybe making a film with a camera and that, but it just seems like if I did that, I'd have to get so many other people to cooperate with me, get the actors to say the lines the way I want them to, get the set designers to make the sets that I want them to make. . . . Well, it just feels like it'd be so much bother, if that makes sense."

"I can't say I ever thought of it that way, but I suppose it makes some sense after all," she said. She looked at the time on her computer screen. "Whoops! That's time. It was a real pleasure to meet you, Mr. DeVil. Now, did I understand that you were thinking that you might use some of those clips of Grandad in some new films?"

"Oh!" I said hastily, "yes, well, only if you don't mind, I mean—"

"Stop," she said. "No, I don't mind in the slightest. It just never occurred to me that you'd think of those clips as *footage*. They're just, well, memories for me. I think it'd be marvelous if you gave them a second life in one of your creations. Yes, please do."

I almost hugged her. I settled for shaking her hand and tripping out of the office on a cloud. I didn't even mind when an errant green laser from some tourist's mosquito-zapper caught me just below my eye, giving me a little scorch. The tourist—an

American girl who was quite pretty, though badly dressed—was very apologetic and made a little show of fawning over me, which was rather nice, and well worth the minor burn.

Gregory the solicitor had put the fear of the law in me, and so I refrained from posting my new Scot clip—the one I'd shared with his actual granddaughter, who'd shook my actual hand!—even though I was busting to show it around. Instead, I spent the week going to TIP-Ex rallies, taking coaches and trains all over England and Wales to attend the local rallies and shake hands and make little speeches. A TIP-Ex campaigner from the Green Party had heard me griping about not being able to afford the travel to get to these events and he'd bought me a month-long rail pass out of his own pocket, and I was determined to make it worth his while by going to as many of the bloody things as I could get to.

It was well worth it, too. I'd be in Milton Keynes one day, and I'd meet some little gang of media hackers who needed help getting inside the Open University to campaign there, and the next day I'd meet an OU prof at a demo in Loughborough and I'd pass on her details to the Milton Keynes crowd. I found that I was building up a mental database of people who needed to meet other people and so I created a message board on Confusing Peach, which had gone public and turned into a hub for the movement. But even with the message board, I was still always finding people who didn't know that they needed to meet someone, or hadn't thought of it. It got so I'd be dozing on a long coach ride and I'd be jolted awake by the realization that *this guy* really needed to talk to *that guy* right away and I'd whip out my lappie and start sending round emails.

I missed 26 like fire, of course, but it was better this way: she was revising like mad for her A levels, and finishing off her last papers, and arguing with her parents about what uni she should go to next year. (She was lobbying to take a year or two off to work and save money and generally arse around and figure out what she wanted from life, which sounded eminently sensible to me. Her parents disagreed.)

I came back to London at 2:00 A.M. the night before the hearing on my injunction. I'd found a passable suit—five years out of date, but approximately my size, and not entirely horrible—in the £1 bin at the Age Concern charity shop next to the Manchester train station, and I figured I could hang it up in the Zeroday's bathroom while I showered to steam out the worst of the wrinkles before I went to the court.

Jem and Rabid Dog were watching a video on Dog's laptop in the front room when I got in, all bundled up in blankets and cuddling. A couple months before, I'd have been embarrassed for them—or for me—but I'd stayed on so many sofas and floors in the past couple weeks that I was beyond embarrassment. Besides, these were my chums and they were making each other damned happy, so what kind of bastard would I have to be to object to that?

"The prodigal son," Jem said, as I stumbled in, rucksack on my back, clutching the carrier bag holding my court suit. "How were the crusades, then?"

I flopped down on the other sofa, which, for all its smelly horribleness, was still an absolute delight of familiar homeyness. "I'm beat, lads. Got to be in court in eight hours, too. It was an amazing time, but Christ, I feel like I've been beaten with sticks. Big ones, with nails through them."

Dog snorted. "No you don't," he said.

I waved at him. "Yeah, no I don't. Poetic license. No offense meant." As far as I knew, he was all healed from his beating, but his nose would never look the same again, and he had some new scars I'd noticed when he was making a dash from the shower to his bedroom. But the beat-down had changed him, made him a little less playful, a little more militant. Jem had told me that Dog figured if he was going to get gay-bashed, he might as well stop pretending he wasn't gay. That made a certain sense to me.

"Well, there's some concentrated cold-brew coffee in the

fridge," Jem said. "Experimental batch. Strong stuff. Help your-self tomorrow, but go easy. It's the kind of stuff that might make your heart explode if you get too much in you."

"You, sir, are a scientist and an angel of mercy," I said, hauling myself off the sofa and starting up the stairs, noticing that they were dusty and dirty. It had been my month to do the floors, ac-cording to the chores rota. Just one more thing to do after this stupid court business.

I set two alarms—one on my lappie and one on my phone—and set them halfway across the room so I'd have to get up to get to them. Then I slept like the dead.

Jem hadn't been kidding about the cold-brew coffee. I'd had a milk-glass full of the stuff, eight or ten ounces, and had briefly entertained having a second, but I decided to just get a move on and dash for the bus. By the time we entered Shoreditch, I felt like all the small muscles in my feet and hands were contracting and releasing in waves, and it felt like my ears were sweating. I was very glad I hadn't had a second coffee!

Gregory met me outside the courthouse. He was wearing a much smarter suit than mine, and he shook my hand warmly, then led me inside, through a metal detector and security check, and then into a crowded room filled with various coppers, fixers, and crims like me, looking uncomfortable in their suits or miserable with their weeping families. There were also loads of men and women in long black robes and ridiculous wigs. At first I thought they were all judges, and then I realized that one of them was 26's stepfather, and he was headed straight for us.

He shook my hand distractedly, then caught me staring at his wig and smiled wryly. "You see what we have to do, we poor bar-risters? Don't worry, I won't be wearing it for your hearing; I've just come from a full-dress drama, a bit of housebreaking. Proper villains. Not like your sort, Cecil. It's such a waste of everyone's time to send you through the system for a bit of downloading, when there's people accused of real crimes waiting to be tried."

I wondered if I should defend my honor by insisting that I was every bit the hardened bad guy, just as much as any of these arsonists, robbers, housebreakers, and murderers, but decided on balance that I preferred "harmless" over "convict."

"Right, this should be very simple and straightforward," Roshan took off his wig and robe and handed them to a porter behind a counter. "It's Dutta," he said to the porter. "Second from the left." Then he turned back to me without waiting for a response. "Simple. We go in, we explain that it's altogether too onerous to order you to stay offline because you can't possibly prepare a defense or work on your lobbying efforts without a network connection. You've got your list of recent appearances, yes?"

I nodded and waved my phone at him. "I don't have a printer at home, but I've got it here. News clippings, too, just like you asked."

He said, "Fine, we'll go to a client room and use a printer there. Got to have paper, so the clerk can then scan it all in again." He clucked his tongue and hustled away, while we followed in his wake. It was wonderful to see him in his element—it gave me real confidence in his skill as a barrister. At home, Roshan was just 26's stepfather, kindly, funny, a little vague sometimes. But here, he was utterly switched on, radiating competence and cleverness. I was damned glad to have him on my side.

I followed the networking instructions on a curling piece of paper taped to the printer and got my phone hooked up to it and my papers printed seconds before a bailiff gave a thump on the doorframe, and said, "You're up, Mr. Dutta," before hurrying off to another errand. I realized that the business with the old printer had completely taken my mind off the upcoming hearing and calmed me right down. I pushed away the anxiety that wanted to come back now that it was on my mind again, and took a deep breath as I stepped into the courtroom.

There was already a hearing in progress, something about a dispute between a landlord and a motorcycle courier firm that had been evicted from a building. The landlord had kidnapped all the company's effects and that and changed the locks. The judge asked each barrister a few pointed questions, shut them up when they tried to blather on about stuff he hadn't asked about, and then told the landlord to let the couriers come get their stuff, then ordered the couriers to pay their rent owing or they'd have to answer to him. He was ginger-haired beneath his wig—I could tell by the eyebrows and freckles—and about fifty. He had big droopy bags under his eyes, like a sad cartoon dog, and a long straight nose that he wiggled around when he talked. I decided I liked him.

Then it was our turn. Roshan got to his feet, and said basically the same thing we'd discussed before: it was unfair and prejudicial to my case to bar me from using the net, and it would dramatically curtail my ability to campaign for the repeal of a law that had given a great commercial advantage to the claimants—just what I thought he'd say. The judge listened intently, made a few notes, then settled his chin in his hand and listened some more. At one point, he looked me up and down and up again, and I felt like he was wearing X-ray specs. It was all I could do not to squirm under the gaze of his big, watery eyes, but I held still and met his stare and gave him a little smile. That seemed to satisfy him, because he went back to staring at 26's stepdad.

Then it was the other side's turn. Their lawyer made a big deal out of the number of legal claims that had been laid against me and called me a "compulsive thief" who "could not seem to stop downloading, no matter what the stakes." It was for this reason that he wanted the judge to shut me down, because unless I was cut off from the Internet, I'd carry on with my single-handed epidemic of downloading and copying. If I hadn't felt enough of a villain before, now I felt too much of one. They made me sound like a maniac who pirated everything and anything. It would have been funny if it didn't make me want to crap my pants with terror.

I kept my face neutral, but Roshan scowled with theatric ferocity as the studios' lawyer maligned me at great length. When it was his turn to rebut, he climbed to his feet and shook his head slowly.

"That was some performance," Roshan said. "And it was a rather fine example of the flights of fancy for which my learned friend's clients are so justly famed. But it had as much to do with reality, or, indeed, the law, as a courtroom drama. My client is a young man who stands accused of *selectively* downloading short clips for the purpose of making acclaimed transformational works that act as commentary and parody, and which constitute rather impressive creative works in their own rights. He is, fundamentally, a *competitor* of the claimants. They may paint him as an uncontrollable menace to society, but what business magnate would characterize his competition any differently? Indeed, my client has voluntarily suspended all of his filmmaking activities for the duration of this proceeding, which means a court order would be redundant in any event—and only serve to cut my client off from activities that are unequivocally lawful, such as lobbying (rather effectively) for the repeal of legislation that is particularly favorable to the claimants. I believe it is improper for the claimants to ask this court to remove their legislative opponents from the field by means of hysterical and stilted characterizations of his activities."

He sat down. I wanted to cheer, but I knew better. But he'd been brilliant, and I could tell that the judge thought so, too—he was controlling his grin, but you could see the tightness in the corners of his eyes and mouth where he was holding it in.

But the prosecution lawyer was grinning, too, and as he got to his feet, I could see that he wasn't the least bit worried, which suggested that he was still confident. He said, "Your Honor, can you please ask the court clerk to retrieve a video file I have just attached to the docket?"

Roshan shot to his feet. "Excuse me," he said firmly. "Your Honor, as my learned friend has not seen fit to make this evidence available prior to this proceeding—"

The prosecution lawyer nodded. "Terribly sorry," he said, "but it couldn't be helped. Only just came into our possession, you see. It's quite germane, as I think you'll see."

The judge cocked his head, then nodded at a woman sitting to one side and below him, in her own little wooden box. She moused around a bit, and a flat-panel screen beside the bench lit up and began to play a video.

My video.

The Scot video I'd made but not released, the piss-take on the anti-piracy warnings at the start of the films. The video I'd only given to one person: Dr. Katarina McGregor-Colford. The video I wasn't supposed to have made at all. The video, in fact, that my legal team had specifically instructed me not to make.

It played through and ended with two and a half seconds of credits, prominently ascribing authorship to Cecil B. DeVil.

All the blood in my upper torso had plunged into my stomach, and all the blood below there had filled my feet, rooting me to the spot, leaving me swaying lightly like an inflatable clown punching bag. Roshan and Gregory were both staring at me, one on either side. I couldn't meet their stares, so I looked straight ahead at the judge, who wasn't even bothering to hide his snigger. He dabbed at his eyes with the billowing black sleeves of his robe and composed himself.

"Did you make this, young man?"

It was the first remark anyone in the courtroom had directed at me. I cleared my throat, and croaked, "Yes, Your Honor."

He nodded. "When did you make it?"

"I finished that cut about ten days ago, Your Honor."

The judge consulted the papers before him. "That was, well, two weeks after you were served with notice of this suit?"

"Yes, Your Honor."

"I see." He drummed his fingers. "Could we see that again, please?"

A giggle rippled through the courtroom, and turned into a little cheer. The judge raised a finger once without looking away from the screen, and there was instant silence. The clerk clicked her mouse and the video ran once more. This time, there was audible laughter from the observers in the court. I snuck a look at the studios' barrister and saw his sour expression, like he'd just bit into something rotten. He clearly didn't see the humor.

The video finished and the judge put his chin back in his hand for a moment. Then he straightened up. "Mr. Dutta?"

"Your Honor, I would like a moment to confer with my client, if you would be so kind."

"I expect you would. Go on, then."

Roshan leaned in and whispered to me, "What is this, Cecil?" He sounded mad.

"I didn't release it," I said. "It leaked. It was just something I was working on in private." I shrugged. It sounded stupid and reckless when I said it aloud. I shut my mouth before I said anything stupider.

The judge studied his notes for a good long while, as the moments oozed past and my blood hammered at my eardrums. Then he nodded, and said, "Right, well, I suppose that about says it all, doesn't it? Young man, I don't mind telling you that I believe you to be a very talented filmmaker. It also sounds to me like you've got a legitimate grievance with this Theft of Intellectual Property Act, and you and your colleagues are certainly doing a good job of pressing your case."

I almost jumped on the spot. He was going to let me off. He *had* to let me off.

"Nevertheless, the existence of this video and your own admissions relating to the timeline of its creation are a clear indication that the claimants aren't simply going for dramatic effect when they characterize your somewhat compulsive relationship with their copyrights. In light of that, I'm afraid you're going to have to get used to life without the Internet until this case has been heard in detail. This court orders you to abstain from use of the Internet for any purpose for a period of two weeks, or until your suits are ruled upon, whichever comes first."

Roshan put his hand up. "Your Honor?"

"Yes?"

"May I bring to your attention the fact that most mobile

phone calls, chip-and-PIN purchases, and public transit ticket sales make use of the Internet? A prohibition on using the Internet for any purpose amounts to house arrest. Was that the court's intention?"

The judge snorted. "Fine, fine. This court orders you to abstain from *directly* using the Internet for the purposes of browsing the World Wide Web, making a nontelephonic voice or video call, partaking in an email, instant message, or social network exchange, playing a networked game, or substantively similar purposes." He made a little "so there" nod, and said, "I'm not a complete Luddite, you know. I'll have you know I once played Counterstrike for England on the national team." The court spectators buzzed with excitement. The judge stared at them until they fell silent. "For your benefit, young sir, I'll explain that Counterstrike was a paleolithic video game that we oldsters played before we got wiped out by MMOs and Xbox Live. I'm not unsympathetic to your plight, but the law is the law, and you'll need to find a way to change it that doesn't violate it."

He wiped his glasses, then said, "Ms. Murdstone, if you wouldn't mind running that video one more time?" It rolled along for ninety seconds, and even in my horrified state, I took in the fact that the judge was really enjoying it, and that the studio lawyers were furious to have it shown three times. When it was done, he murmured, "Hilarious," and raised his finger again.

My lawyers each took an elbow and steered me out of the courthouse, my wooden legs thumping ahead of me lifelessly as I contemplated spending the next two weeks without the Internet without losing my mind or the fight. I was also trying to work out what role Katarina had played in all this. If she'd wanted to get me in trouble, there were lots more direct ways than by leaking my video. She was Scot Colford's granddaughter, for God's sake. And what about all that footage she'd given me? I'd been cataloging it nonstop since I'd got it, thinking about how I could fit it into my ongoing projects. Was it some kind of trap?

Roshan and Gregory were sad and angry with me, I could

tell. We sat down in a café across from the courthouse and Gregory brought us cups of milky tea and the two stared at me.

"I'm sorry," I said. "I know I was an idiot. I didn't think it'd get out. I only showed it to one person." I didn't mention who that person was, because I was sure they'd never believe that Scot Colford's granddaughter was on my side; they'd think I was a naive kid who'd got suckered.

Roshan shook his head at me (I could tell I was in for a lot of head-shaking) and said, "I'd kick you up the bum about this, but you're the one who's going to suffer the most for your mistake. And it could be worse. By capping the ban to two weeks, the judge was telling the other side that they'd better not try a bunch of expensive delaying tactics to get the case put off and off and leave you in limbo forever. But I hope you've learned that we're on your side, and when we tell you to do something, we mean it."

I nodded miserably.

Roshan said, "All right, go on then. 26 is sitting her last exam this morning and I expect she'll be wanting to see you this afternoon, yeah?"

I nodded again, and headed for the bus stop.

Chapter 13

SHOPPED!/ON THE ROAD/
FAMILY REUNION

26 was outraged on my behalf and was sure that Katarina had shopped me. I told her she didn't know what she was talking about, that the lady had been so supportive of me. 26 demanded Katarina's email address so she could send an angry message to her, but I said that wouldn't be fair.

"How about if I write her a message on a piece of paper and you take a picture of it and email it to her?" I said.

She shook her head at me (I was already getting sick of this). "You poor sod, you're really stuck, aren't you? Am I going to end up being your Seeing Internet Dog for the next two weeks, then?"

"Come on," I said. "I need to know whether she betrayed me or whether it just got out."

26 rolled her eyes at me. "Fine," she said. She dug through the piles of junk in her room and came up with an old school notebook. She tore a page out of the back of it, handed me a biro, and passed them to me. I shut my laptop lid and used it for a desk.

I started to write, got as far as "Dear Katarina, I was in court today" and balled up the paper and chucked it aside.

"Paper," I said.

"Maybe you should do it in pencil, Cecil," 26 said.

"Shaddit," I said, and she swatted me and handed me more paper. It took three tries, but this is what I got:

Dear Katarina, I had my hearing today, about the court case where all the film studios are suing me for millions of pounds for remixing your grandad's films. They wanted the court to take my Internet access away and they got what they wanted.

*The reason that happened is that they had a copy of the video
I gave to you, the one about the security checks at the cinema.
You were the only person besides me who had a copy. I don't
remember if I told you not to distribute it. I guess I just wanted
to know if you passed it on to those lawyers to get me in
trouble, or what?*

I included my phone number and signed it, and 26 shot it
with her phone and attached it to an email and sent it off.

"How'd the exams go?" I said. She'd been playing nonchalant
about them all along, but I knew that her guts'd been in knots
about it. 26 was *smart,* the kind of smart they love at school, and
she'd always got fantastic marks, but that seemed to make her *more*
anxious about succeeding, not less. Figure that one out.

"I can never tell. I *think* it all went well, except, well, maybe
I'm wrong, right? Like the calculus—it seemed too easy, like
maybe I was just not understanding the questions right." She
shook her head hard and went *Waaaaargh!* and jumped up and
down on the spot a while. "That's better. It's over in any event.
And it's just going to start again at uni next year, of course."

I didn't say anything. We both knew that she was going to go
off to university eventually. She was such a brain-box, and her
parents would flay her alive if she didn't. She kept talking about
taking a gap year and working, but the parental authorities were
very down on the idea, and besides, it was only delaying the inevitable.

26 caught it. She always caught it. "I've been reading up on
the law program at University College London. There's an Intellectual Property specialist course that looks perfectly awful, raw
propaganda for the entertainment industry. I was thinking it'd
be a fun place to go and shout at people for the next four years."

I smiled. "Really? UCL? As in, right here in London?"

She'd put in for Oxford and Cambridge, of course, and Shef-
field and Nottingham. But this was the first she'd said about
UCL.

"Right here," she said.

"But I thought you wanted to do public policy, right? Oxford?"

She looked away. "Oh, Oxford's overrated. It's all rah-rah punting and snobbishness. Besides, law's just another side to public policy. And with a law degree, I could defend people like you! Public policy's just a fast-track to being a career bureaucrat or a politician."

"I think you'd make a great MP," I said. "You'd be the first woman with a shaved head and facial piercings to sit in the Commons!"

She bit my earlobe. "Do you *want* me to go away?"

I shrugged. "Of course not. But I don't want you to waste four years doing a degree you're not interested in just to be around me. I don't have to live in London, you know. Doesn't really matter where I am. I just want to make films. I could do that anywhere."

"You going to find a squat in Oxford?"

"Why not? There's empty buildings everywhere. Or," I held her gaze, "you could squat with me."

"That's the most romantic proposal I've ever had, Cecil B. DeVil. I think it's a little early for us to be playing house, though, don't you think?"

It's weird. I'd said it as a joke, but her refusal skewered me. Which was stupid, because here she was ready to pick a second-choice university because it would mean being nearer to me. Love makes you into an idiot. Well, it makes *me* into an idiot, anyway.

Neither of us said anything. Her room, which was always a tip, had grown even more chaotic, what with all the work on TIP-Ex and all the time spent at mine or on her exams. I suddenly felt exhausted. I pushed aside some of the crap on the bed and crawled along it face down until I had a pillow under my head and I buried my nose in it—26's scalp smell, delicious and familiar—and squeezed my eyes shut.

26 belly-flopped on top of me and chewed my hair. "Poor Cecil. It's all a bit much, isn't it?"

It was. In a short year, I'd moved to London, been robbed, squatted, been chased, squatted again, taken every conceivable substance including sugar and lived to tell the tale, lost a legislative fight, made dozens of films and screened them all over the city, traveled up and down the countryside giving speeches, reconciled with my parents, broken into a sewer, learned to build a laptop, and been sued for tens of millions of pounds. And lost my virginity. "It's been a busy season, I'll give you that. Dizzying, really."

"I know what you mean," she said. For a moment, I felt irrationally irritated with her. This was *my* moment to be miserable, not hers. What had she gone through, anyway? But a few seconds later, I came up with the answer: political campaigning, arrest, falling in love (yay!), a boyfriend who ran out and left her to give a speech with no prep, the business with her biological dad, and her A levels and impending graduation.

"What a pair we are," I said.

"We're a good team," she said, and chewed my hair some more, pulling at the roots.

"We'll figure it out," I said.

"We always do."

Living without the net was impossible. At first, I tried to stay off my laptop altogether, because once it was on, the temptation to log in and just have a poke around was enormous. I'd promised Roshan and Gregory that I wouldn't log in, not even a little, not even if I was dead certain no one could catch me. I'd learned my lesson about leaky secrets with the video I'd given to Katarina.

But with no laptop and no Internet, I started to go absolutely mad. I really liked Jem's mural, and it had got smudged or wiped away in places, so I tried my hand at fixing it up, but this involved asking Jem for loads of advice, and he soon bored of it. So I switched to cooking, which was Chester's major lookout, and we made good progress on things like soups and stews before he got utterly sick with googling recipes for me and he went out and bought me an armload of ancient Jamie Oliver cookbooks from the one-pound bin at the Age Concern charity shop. I got bored of being alone in the kitchen, so I went and bothered Rabid Dog, who was going through a phase of trying to perfect the artificial wound. He worked with unflavored gelatin, paint, food coloring, and various breakfast cereals and sand to create the most revolting gashes, slashes, scars, and scabs you'd ever seen. He had a half-formed plan to shoot his own slasher pic in the Zeroday some time, but mostly he just loved mucking about with all the gore and goop. Dog was very good about tolerating my ham-fisted attempts to create a realistic entrail-squib, a flesh-colored belly pouch filled with revolting viscera that could be slit open, spilling them down your front. But I wasn't very good at it, to tell the truth, and what's more, I kept forgetting to wash the brushes and cap the paints, and so after a day of this, he told me I'd need to get my own supplies if I wanted to go on. I swore I would, but never got round to it.

So I went back to the one thing I was good at: editing video on my laptop. I had a bunch more long bus and train trips to kill time on—talks at rallies in Cardiff, Bath, and then one in good old Bradford, so I reckoned I could spend the time editing the one video I was reasonably sure I couldn't get into trouble for playing with: the footage of Scot Colford that Katarina had given me.

I set to work cataloging this the day before I hit the road, and I was deep into it when 26 showed up at my door. I'd talked her into spending the night since we were going to be apart for so long.

"I got an email back from your doctor," she said, after she'd kissed me hello. "You're going to love this."

> *Dear Cecil,*
>
> *Oh god, I'm mortified. I was so delighted by that video that I sent it around to some friends (well, many friends—practically everyone I know, in fact). I hadn't realized that it was meant to be confidential, though I suppose I should have worked that out. I can't apologize enough for having landed*

you in the soup. If there's anything I can do to help, please let
me know (I was serious when I told you you should feel free to
tell people that Scot Colford's granddaughter heartily approves
of your efforts). I just googled and saw you've got a talk coming
up in Bath; I grew up there and have emailed all my friends
and told them to go and see you. I know this won't solve your
legal woes, but I hope it helps a little.

> *Best of luck,*
> *Katarina*

That certainly put me in a better mood—and my mood got
better still when 26 dragged me up to my room for a serious and
steamy snog. Afterward, we lay on my bed, sharing a big glass of
ice water and occasionally sneaking cubes out of the glass and
pressing them to one another's exposed skin, which was 26's idea
of comedy.

"Do you think we're going to win?" I asked.

She didn't say anything for a long time. "I think we might,"
she said, finally.

"Oh, that's encouraging."

She sat up. "It's just that most MPs still don't see this as a big
deal. They're more concerned with health care and jobs and education and the economy. They just don't understand that today,
all those things depend on the Internet. My mum decided that
we needed a new garden shed last week and she discovered that
the council doesn't even have paper building-permit forms anymore! You can't get a recycling box, you can't complain about
your neighbors, you can't report a pothole, none of it unless
you've got the net."

"Do you remember you once said we should get every MP
cut off from the net for piracy? Grass on the whole lot of them?"

She snorted. "Yeah, but I don't know how we'd pull that off.
I'm sure that when an MP gets an infringement notice, she can
just make it all go away. One law for them, another law for us. I
bet that there's also plenty of chances for rich parents to pay a

little 'fine' and stop their Internet being taken away or their kids going to jail."

"I keep coming back to it, though. It's like you said: the reason they voted this in is that they just don't think of Internet access as being anything like a right. They think the whole Internet is just a glorified system for downloading films for free and getting music without paying for it. If we could just show them what it's like to lose access—"

"You're right, but it's just a dream. A pretty dream, but a dream nonetheless."

But I couldn't get it out of my head. When I got on the train to Bath the next day, I found myself roughing out a video in which Scot Colford loses his Internet access. There was so much stuff in the footage dump that Katarina'd given me that lent itself to this, I could already tell that I'd be able to show Scot flunking out of college, losing his housing benefit, failing to help his kids with their homework, and not being able to produce a film. He loved to make comic short films where he played a bumbler or sad-sack, and once I had the idea, the video practically put itself together.

I got about half the rough cut done on the bus, chortling evilly to myself as I went, and then I was at the demonstration and giving a speech, which seemed to go well, but I couldn't tell you what I'd said, because all I could think of was my video, my video, my video. I was being hosted that night by some people from the local hackspace, a kind of technology co-op where everyone paid subscriptions to use a bunch of really fantastic communal kit: laser cutters and 3D printers and computer-controlled mills and lathes. The hack-space was in an old industrial estate that reminded me of Aziz's place, and it was even more cluttered than Aziz's, because they had less space and more people using it. They made their own beer, and it was quite good, and I chatted politely for as long as I could.

Finally, I had to say, "Look, I don't mean to be rude, but I've got this thing I'm making and I can't get it out of my head and I just want to get stuck in with my lappie. I know it's horrible guest behavior, but—"

The assorted hackers immediately rushed to say, no, no, by all means, get stuck in mate, if you're in the creative fog, don't let us get in your way. Of course I should have guessed that they'd understand. (Later, I found myself reading the hack-space rules that someone had posted in the toilet, and the third rule was "If someone's in the groove, don't bother them.") (Rule two was "If you don't know how to use something, ask someone who does before you try." And rule number one was "Don't be on fire." Which struck me as eminently sensible.)

Work, work, work. I wished like fire that I could use the net and email some of the other Colford freaks I knew and get their advice, and I burned to drop in some of the official Scot clips from his classic films—some of which I'd used in dozens of projects before, so that I knew exactly how many seconds they lasted and could even give you their timecode from memory.

But the constraint of having to work with nothing but the new footage meant that I couldn't use my familiar, lazy shortcuts. I had to think my way around each scene and cut, coming up with really inventive solutions. It was the best kind of puzzle-solving, something I'd been training for all my life, really.

Being in that kind of creative fog was weird. I just couldn't put the machine down. Not having Internet access actually helped, since it meant that I couldn't alt-tab away from my edit suite to check on my mail or read tweets or social media walls or the Web. I had to just get my head down and edit, create, refine. My world contracted until it contained nothing except for me and my computer, and before I knew it, the sun was rising and my phone was beeping at me, telling me it was time to wake up and get to the bus station, so I got started on the way to Cardiff. Except I hadn't slept yet, and when I stood up, my back and hips made a noise like someone stepping on a bag of peanut shells. My wrists felt like they'd swollen to three times their normal size, and when

I went to the toilet to sponge off and brush my teeth, I saw that my eyes looked like they'd been doused in chili sauce.

I didn't feel bad, though. Tired, sure. But I felt *amazing*. The video was some of my best work, maybe my best ever. The most wonderful part was that it was looking exactly like it had in my head. After years and years of trying, I'd finally found a way to connect the thing I saw when I closed my eyes with the thing that showed up on my screen. It felt like I'd attained some kind of psychic superpower. It felt like I was a *god*. Sleep? Hah! I could sleep on the way to Cardiff.

ᴍʏ ꜰᴀᴍɪʟʏ ᴡᴀꜱ ᴡᴀɪᴛɪɴɢ ꜰᴏʀ me when I arrived in Bradford: Mum and Dad and Cora standing awkwardly by the train turnstiles, and I spotted them before they spotted me. My parents were older than I remembered; Dad's hair had gone from thinning to balding, and Mum's shoulders were rounded and her head drooped forward a little as though her neck couldn't support it. They both looked a little frail. Cora, on the other hand, looked like an adult, practically—give her the right clothes and she could have passed for twenty-five. But for all that, they were definitely my family and I felt a rush of affection for them as soon as I spotted them. For a moment I resisted the impulse to wave madly to them, then I gave in, though it made everyone else in the station stare at us, and I ran the last twenty meters to them and enjoyed an epic four-way cuddle. Something tight in my chest let go, and I felt something unfold there, a spreading warmth that I can only call "homecoming."

Cora had just finished her school year with her usual top marks—pulled up out of the slump during the year when she'd been knocked offline. Dad had been getting more hours than ever, mostly answering the phone for an appliance warranty company and booking engineers to go on service calls for misbehaving washing machines. It didn't pay anything like his factory job had, but it was more money than the family had seen in years, and not having to feed me also made a difference (though Mum thumped him in the shoulder when he mentioned it), so the flat was looking brilliant. There was a new sofa, a new telly, a new lappie for Dad with a top-of-the-range headset, and a chair that looked like it belonged in the cockpit of an airplane. And Mum had a new exercise machine that was part of the rehab for her legs—she'd done away with her cane, and unless you know to look for it, you wouldn't have spotted her limping.

"What're you going to say tomorrow, then, Trent?" Mum said as we rode the bus home together. The faces on the bus had a weird familiarity—they weren't people I knew, but chances were they were people I'd *seen* once or twice or even dozens of times over the years. It seemed like I could go days in London without seeing a face I knew outside of the Zeroday.

I shrugged. "The same as ever, I suppose. I used to try to say something different everywhere I went, cos I knew that all the talks were going up on YouTube and that, and I thought it'd look weird if I said the same thing each time. But really, there's only one thing to say: why TIP is terrible, why I think we can wipe it out, how you can help. And when I tried to say something different every time, I couldn't really practice properly, so I was making mistakes all the time instead of getting better. Now I just say pretty much the same thing, and if someone sees two similar talks on YouTube, I don't worry much about it. No one's complained, anyway."

Dad shook his head. "Son, don't take this the wrong way, but I never figured you for the speechifying type. Fancy the idea that you've got people who show up to hear you talk!" He shook his head again.

I hid my grin. "What about Cora, then? She's going to talk tomorrow, too." It hadn't been my idea—the local organizers who were putting on the rally had invited her separately, and truth be told, I was half afraid she'd show me up altogether with her brilliance. But mostly, I was delighted that my little sister was going to give a talk and I'd get to hear her.

Cora pretended she hadn't heard and looked out the window, but I could see she was blushing.

Dad waved his hand. "Oh, Cora. Well, of course we always figured Cora would be some kind of politician or professor or a famous inventor or something. But Trent—" He opened and closed his hands, as though he was trying to pluck the right words out of the overheated, slightly smelly bus air. "Well, I guess what I'm trying to say is that we're proud of you, son."

It wasn't a very northern thing for him to say. It was a sentimental, London kind of statement, really. And of course, that's why it meant so much more than it would have coming from any of my southern pals. My dad, my actual, cynical, hard-as-nails dad, was getting all soppy with me. What I felt then, well, it wasn't like anything I'd ever felt before.

Dinner was better than any I remembered from home, and we all watched some telly together afterward, and after *that*, I showed Cora my new Scot Colford video, and she gushed that it was my best work so far. Then I went out to the community center and played snooker with some of my old mates, who all seemed to have got younger even as my family had got older. They were full of talk about who was snogging who and who was pregnant and who'd been banged up for public drunkenness or stupid, petty crimes. I made a real effort not to seem aloof or condescending, but I musn't have done much of a job, because before long, they were passing sarky remarks about how I'd "gone London," and I was too big for little Bradford. I pretended these didn't bother me, but they made me miserable, and my triumphant day finished with me staring in frustration at the ceiling as I tried to find sleep in my old bed, thinking of clever, cutting things I should have said to my so-called pals.

Cora talked before me. and as I expected, she was dead good. She'd changed her makeup and hair and put on her school uniform, and she looked years younger than she had the night before. It made her speech come off all the better, as she spoke about being a student and trying to keep her marks up and how she'd learned that sharing knowledge was better for society than locking it up. She finished out with something that made the whole room laugh:

"Back in the old days, they didn't have science, they had alchemy. Alchemy was a lot like science, except that every alchemist kept what he learned to himself." She made a wry face. "Alchemists were always 'he's'—and particularly daft specimens of the type at that." That got a chuckle. "And that meant that no alchemist could benefit from what he'd learned. Which meant that every single alchemist discovered for himself—the hard way—that drinking mercury was an awful idea." That got a bigger laugh. "As you might imagine, alchemy didn't progress very far." That got a bigger laugh still. She was working them like a comedian, and her timing was spot on. I couldn't believe that my little sister was kicking quantities of arse.

"Until, one day, everything changed. Some alchemist decided that rather than keeping his results secret, he'd publish them and let his peers review his results. We have a word for that kind of publication: we call it 'science.' And we have a name for the time that followed from this innovation: we call it 'the Enlightenment.'

"For hundreds of years, the human race has dreamt of a world where knowledge could be shared universally, where every human being on the planet could have access to our storehouse of knowledge. Because knowledge is power, and shared knowledge is a superpower. Now, after centuries, we have it within our grasp to realize one of our most beautiful dreams.

"And wouldn't you know it, some people are so bloody stupid and greedy and blinkered and ignorant that they think that this is a *bad thing.* The greatest library of human knowledge and creativity ever seen, ever *dreamed of,* and all these fools can do is moan about how they can't figure out how to stay rich if kids go around downloading rubbishy pop music without paying for it.

They think that the Internet's power to make sharing easy is a bug—and they've set out to 'fix' it, no matter how many lives and futures they ruin on this stupid mission.

"I may just be a kid, I may not be rich or brilliant or powerful, but I *know* that copying is a *feature*, not a bug. It's brilliant, it's wonderful, it's only because it snuck up on us so gradually that we're not on our knees in wonder.

"I think they're going to fail in the long run. In the long run, though, we're all dead. The question for me is, how many lives will we destroy before we wake up and realize what we've got is worth saving—worth celebrating?

"We've got a chance to start making the kind of world that's safe for the Internet and the people who love it—the people who use it to work, use it to stay in touch with their families, the people who use it to create art or do science. I've spent the past six months down at my MP's surgery every week, telling John Mutanhed about all the wonderful things we can use the net for, and how many innocent people are facing jail or ruin because a small handful of greedy companies have bought miserable law after miserable law, until we're all guilty, and it's only a matter of time until we're all in for it.

"Now there's this bill, you know it, the one they call TIP-Ex. Loads of people who know more about government than I do tell me that it stands a real chance of passing, of undoing some of the harm Parliament caused when they voted in that daft Theft of Intellectual Property Act. It stands a chance, that is, if you and the people you know get off your bums and go down to your MPs' surgeries, call their offices, write them a letter, and tell them what this means to you.

"These people are supposed to be our representatives. They're supposed to be doing what's good for us, not for gigantic American film companies. We can make them do what's right, but only if we pay attention, all the time, every day, and let them know we're watching. There's an election coming, and if there's one time that people like us can make a difference, it's just before the election. Maybe your MP thinks he's in a 'safe seat' where he'll never get voted out, but the dirty secret of safe seats is that the winner in those seats is usually 'none of the above'—quantities of voters just stay home rather than hold their nose and vote for the lesser of two evils. If you're upset about your neighbors losing their Internet access and their jobs, if you're upset about kids going to jail, you tell them, 'I will turn up at the polls come the day, and I will vote for anyone, no matter how big a bastard he is, if he promises to do away with this rotten, stupid, filthy, dishonorable business we call the Theft of Intellectual Property Act!' "

She had them. They roared with one throat, a sound so ferocious it made my balls shrink. My *god,* my sister was a brilliant speaker! I'd had no idea. I knew she'd given little talks at school, and had been in her debate society, but this—this was like watching a master performer.

And I had to go on after her!

I stumbled through my talk as best as I could. I was thankful that I was giving a speech I'd given so many times before, because I'd have got lost otherwise. As it was, I could have recited the words in my sleep, and that familiarity let me focus on delivering them with all the fire I could muster, trying to live up to the standard Cora had set. They applauded me, but not like they had for Cora. After a moment's jealousy, I decided that I was more proud than jealous. My sister! Who knew she was so brilliant? (Well, I had, of course, but I hadn't known that she could speak like that!)

Mum and Dad took us out for curry that night, a posh place with a huge menu that went on for pages and pages and a long wine list. Dad had an expression on his face like he was some kind of millionaire out on the town, and Mum kept reaching over to pat us on the shoulder or the leg, or touch our cheeks. Cora and I were the stars of the night, and we felt it. Big grins all round, and I slept like a baby that night, getting up early for a bowl of cereal with Cora before I dashed out to catch my coach to London—back to 26, back to the Zeroday, and back to my new life.

It was a beautiful day in the Kensal Green cemetery, the grass so green it looked artificial, watered into a lush growth by a wet and miserable spring. There were fresh flowers on the newer graves, and families strolled through the grounds with broad-brimmed antimosquito hats, the sound of zapped mosquitoes a punctuation to the cars in Hornton Street.

I squeezed 26's hand, and said, "I don't understand, why is Letitia meeting us here?"

26 squeezed back. "Like I said, I have no idea. But she insisted and it sounded important. I'm not bothered, anyway—much nicer to be out here than in her office, right?"

"Yeah," I said. "But I've got a bad feeling about this. Why wouldn't she want to meet us in her office?"

We found out soon enough. Letitia was right where she said she'd be, on a bench near a slip road behind the crematorium. She was wearing a broad-brimmed sun hat and sunglasses and a sundress, but for all that, she didn't look very sunny. As we drew near to her, I could see the slump of her shoulders, and it was pure defeat.

She patted the bench beside her and we sat down. She didn't bother with any niceties, just started in with, "First of all, let me say that I think the two of you have been *magnificent*. When I first discussed this with you, I never *dreamed* that you and your friends would be able to drum up so much support for my bill. You have every right to be proud of yourselves."

"But?" I said. I could hear the *but* waiting to come out.

"But," she said. "But. But politics are an ugly business. I have had a series of increasingly desperate meetings and calls with various power brokers in my party, and, well, let me say that I was lucky not to have to withdraw the bill altogether. But they made it very, very clear that all the whips had been firmly told by the party bigwigs that my bill must not pass, under any circumstances. I think it's likely that I will be expelled from my party if I vote in favor of TIP-Ex. Despite that, I plan to do so, because—well, because, all jokes notwithstanding, a career in politics shouldn't mean a life without integrity."

We sat there in numb shock.

26 said, "I don't understand."

I said, "She's saying that we've lost. It doesn't matter what we do. It doesn't matter how many voters shout at their MPs. It's fixed, it's rigged. It's done. Parliament is going to vote against her bill. End of story."

"But I thought with the election coming up—"

Letitia looked grim. "The election only matters if some MPs vote for the bill. If all the parties vote against it, there'll be no one to vote against, because there'll be no one to vote *for*."

"Someone got to them," I said. "The big film studios, or maybe the record labels, or maybe the video-game companies."

"Lobbyists from all three, I rather suspect," Letitia said. "They can be very persuasive. My guess is that there've been a number of very good, lavish parties lately, the kind of thing that's just packed with film stars and pop stars and that, and MPs and their families were invited—maybe weekends in the country where your wife gets to go to the spa with a famous film star while your kids frolic in the pool with their favorite musicians and you go for cigars and golf with legendary film directors. The content people can be very persuasive at times. It's their stock in trade, really."

"We didn't stand a chance," I said. "Might as well have stayed at home. What a bloody waste."

Letitia slumped further. "I'm sorry," she said. "I thought you could win it. I really did. I thought that my party, at least, would welcome the chance to distance itself from unpopular legislation just before the election. But the simple fact is, I was outgunned and outmaneuvered. These people are very, very good at playing the politics game. Better, I'm afraid, than I can ever hope to be. I am so, so sorry for this. I know it must break your heart." She drew in a shuddering sigh. "It's certainly broken mine."

None of us said anything. Then 26 stood up, and said, "Well, there you go. Bugger it all. Government's for sale to the highest bidder. Always has been, always will be. No wonder someone always ends up throwing bombs. No matter who you vote for, the bloody government always gets in, doesn't it?"

Letitia looked like she wanted to die. I knew how she felt. I was torn between wanting to sit and comfort her and wanting to chase after 26, who was walking away as quickly as she could without breaking into a run. I went after 26. Of course I did. Letitia was a grown-up, she could take care of herself. 26 and I were a unit.

"Hey," I said as I caught up with her. She kept walking quickly, head down, arms swinging.

"Hey," I said again. "Hey, 26. Come on, it's going to be okay. You explained this to me, remember? We'll build momentum up. People will see how unfair this is and more of them will come out next time. It's awful, sure, but it'll get better eventually. They can't put us all in jail, right?"

She stopped and whirled to face me. I took a step back. Her lips were pulled back from her teeth, and she'd cried mascara down her cheeks in long black streaks. She had her hands clenched into fists and her arms were held straight down at her sides. For a second, I was sure she was going to hit me. "Forget it, Cecil. Just forget it. My stupid father was right. This is a ridiculous waste of time. We'll never, ever change anything. Rich, powerful people just run *everything* and the whole world is tilted to their favor. We were stupid to even think for a second that we had a chance of changing things. All those people who believed us and worked with us? Idiots. Just as bloody stupid as we are. I'm going to go to school, keep my stupid head down, get a stupid degree, get a stupid job, grow old, die, and rot. Might as well face it. None of us are special, none of us are geniuses. We're just little people and we're lucky that the giants let us go on living and breathing."

It was worse than being slapped. "Twenty—" I said.

But she was already stalking off. I turned back to where Letitia had been sitting, but she was gone now, too. I found my hands were shaking. I wanted to run after 26 and tell her she was wrong.

The problem was, I really felt like she might be right.

Chapter 14

I thought about calling Annika or one of the organizers or politicos I'd met along the way, but in my head, the conversation got as far as "We've lost, there's no point, we might as well chuck it in," and then trailed off.

So I went home, sulking the whole way, the now-familiar long journey across London to the Zeroday. It was Friday, and the TIP-Ex vote was due on Monday. On Tuesday, I was scheduled to go on trial for £78 million worth of copyright infringement.

For all that, London seemed unaware that it had only days to go before all hope would be lost. The streets were full of people who clearly didn't give a toss about copyright, about TIP, or about anything apart from getting rat-arsed and howling through the night, vomming up their fried chicken into the gutter or having sloppy knee-tremblers with interesting strangers in the doorways of shuttered shops.

26 *was* right. These people would wake up on Tuesday morning and see some hard-to-understand headline about the defeat of some bill they'd never heard of and they'd ignore it and go back to talking about who had the West Nile virus, who had been rubbish and who had been brilliant on *Celebrity Gymnastics,* and which clubs they'd get blotto at next weekend. And if some of their mates went to jail, if their parents lost their livelihoods, if their kids couldn't make art or get an education, well, what could you really do about it? Just a fact of life, innit, like earthquakes or tsunamis.

Rabid Dog and Chester had scored some truly amazing food down at Borough Market and Jem had decided it was time for a feast. He'd been in the kitchen all day with Dodger, who had invited Rob over. Chester had brought along Hester, 26's old mate from Confusing Peach, and Aziz had come by with three kids about our age who'd been staying at his and helping him with a massive haul he'd brought in, turning it into saleable merchandise and moving it out through a small network of car-boot sale retailers he'd put together. They were your basic gutterpunks, but clever and moderately sober.

I'd invited 26 and she'd agreed to come and naturally we'd both forgot about this, so I came home just as Dodger was serving up a massive humble pie, stuffed with livers and heart and tripes in a simmering, rich brown gravy that was as thick as custard. The crust was yellow-gold and crackled like parchment when he sliced into it, releasing first a waft of butter smell, and then the meaty smells from within.

"Sit down, Cecil," he said. "And shut your gob, you're letting the flies in and the dribble out."

Something about coming through my familiar door and into a candlelit room dominated by a huge table (okay, it was a bunch of little wobbly pub tables pushed together), ringed by friends and friends of friends, drinking wine, laughing, and this big, beautiful, ridiculous pie in the middle of it all—it made me think that maybe, just maybe, my problems might be solved. Why not? We were the Jammie Dodgers, and we could do anything!

I took off my jacket, went into the kitchen and maneuvered around Jem—resplendent in an apron, working madly at five bubbling pots on the massive cooker—and washed my hands in the sink. Back at the table, someone had poured me a glass of wine, and Dodger had dished me up an enormous slice of pie. Jem burst out of the kitchen carrying platters of roast parsnips, duck-fat potatoes, tureens of white sauce, and a massive loaf of thick-crusted brown bread studded with olives and capers. It steamed when he tore off hunks and chucked them at us, and the air was filled with baked-bread perfume. There were saucers of coarse salt and saucers of dark green olive oil, and we dipped the bread in the oil and then the salt and chewed it like gum, hot and fatty and salty and so fresh it almost burned your mouth.

Then we attacked the pie and the veg and there was wine-guzzling and arms reaching across the table to top up everyone's glasses whenever they ventured even a little below the full line. We didn't talk about copyright or film remixing or finding £78 million with which to pay off the nutters at the film studios. Instead, we gossiped about friends; Dodger told near-death electro-cution stories; Hester regaled us with stories of drug-fueled excess from a party we'd all missed; Rabid Dog had a new joke he'd made up about three children who go wandering in a woods filled with serial killers (it went on and on, getting funnier and funnier, until it came to the punchline: "I thought *you* were going to chop the firewood!" and we fell about laughing); Aziz and his minions explained a gnarly driver problem they were having with a load of deauthorized sound-cards and solved it for themselves as they described it and cheered and slapped one another on the back; Chester had just read a mountain of downloaded ancient comics called *Transmetropolitan* that he couldn't shut up about. . . . In other words, it was a brilliant table full of amazing, uproarious conversa-tion, piled high with delicious food.

It was just the tonic I needed, and two hours later, as we mopped up the last of the custard-drowned sweet suet pudding with our fingers and piled the plates up and shuttled them into the kitchen, I once again felt like, just maybe, the world wasn't an irredeemable shit-heap.

I volunteered to be Jem's coffee-slave as he hand-brewed us cups of gritty Turkish coffee, and once we were all fed, we loosed our belts and took off our shoes and lay on cushions on the floor or on the sofa and Hester got out her mandolin and played a few old Irish folk songs that Chester knew the words to, and one of Aziz's helpers had a tin whistle and she played along with Hester and they got us to sing along on a gaggingly hilarious version of "The Rattlin' Bog," which went on and on, until we stumbled through the final chorus: "And the grin was on the flea and the flea was on the wing and the wing was on the bird and the bird was on the egg and the egg was on the nest and the nest was on the leaf and the leaf was on the twig and the twig was on the branch and the branch was on the limb and the limb was on the tree and the tree was in the hole and the hole was in the dirt and the dirt was in the ground and the ground was in the bog—the bog down in the valley-o!"

And then it got quiet.

"So, Cecil," said Jem, "are you going to tell us what's got you looking so miserable, or are we going to have to beat it out of you?"

I shook my head. "Nothing's wrong, mate, it's all fine."

"You're not fooling anyone. You came in here looking like your whole family had just been killed in a traffic accident. So spill. What is it? 26 angry at you?"

I shook my head. "So much for my career as a cool, collected man of mystery."

Aziz patted my shoulder. "Cecil, you have many virtues, but you're as easy to read as a book. Never take up a career as a poker player, that's my advice."

I told them. It's not like Letitia had asked me to keep it a secret, but still, I didn't exactly mention how I knew that the fix was in. Chester and Rabid Dog knew that I had a personal connection with Letitia, so they'd probably guess at the connection, but I had some feeling that putting up Letitia's name would just be getting her in trouble.

Hester shook her head. "What a right bloody mess," she said. "No wonder you're so miserable."

"The worst part is that it makes me want to give up. I mean, I knew it was going to be hard when we started, but for so long as I thought it was *possible* that we could win, I wanted to keep at it. Now I can't even release my new video or I could end up in actual *jail* for violating the judge's order."

Jem fingered his scar. "Not worth it, chum. You want to stay out of His Majesty's clutches, trust me."

"Well, let's see it, then," said Dodger. He'd been spinning up a Dodger-style spliff, big as a cigar, stuffed with skunk so pungent I could smell it through my ears. "World premiere an' that."

"Go on, then," Aziz said. The rest nodded.

Funny, I felt embarrassed. I'd shown my films to audiences of hundreds, uploaded them for millions to see. But my new video, made with the Scot footage that no one else had ever worked with, felt like a piece of me. I overcame my shyness and got out a laptop and found a beamer among the box of electronic junk. We had cleared a wall and whitewashed it, and we used it whenever we had film nights. The beamer focused itself and I started the video.

Three minutes and eighteen seconds later, I switched off the beamer. No one said a word. I felt a sick, falling feeling, and I felt like I might toss up the incredible meal, bread and tripes and suet and custard and all. Then Jem said, " 'Ken hell, mate."

"Fwoar," agreed Chester. Then it was nods all round. Finally, Rob began to applaud: *Clap. Clap. Clap.* In a second, everyone had joined in, and they whistled and cheered and stamped their feet. Aziz thudded me between the shoulderblades and Hester gave me a hug and yeah, that was about as good as it got. Some people are great artists—I think all my mates were, of one kind or another—but it takes a special kind of person to be a great *audience*.

And they were.

Youʼve seen the video. I suppose. What happened next guaranteed that practically *everybody* had seen it; what's more, there's whole libraries' worth of remixes of it, and if you ask me, plenty of them are better than anything I could have come up with. Still, I made that first mix, and I'm going to be proud of it for my whole life. Even if I never do anything else anyone gives a wet slap for, I made *Pirate*.

And since I'm writing all these adventures down and trying to tell them as best and truthful as I can, I figure I should set down a few words about *Pirate*, too.

It opens with Scot at his prime, thirtysome years old. He's not a teen heartthrob anymore, nor a twentysomething actor being cast for increasingly improbable teen roles. Now he's done four summers of Shakespeare at the Globe and had his directorial debut with *Wicked. Cool.*, a brutal film about a British foreign service bureaucrat who cynically funnels money and weapons to the Lord's Resistance Army in Uganda, despite their horrible atrocities and use of child soldiers, because they promise access to a rich deposit of coltan mud for a firm listed on the London Stock Exchange in return. He's put on some wrinkles and a few pounds, but he's better-loved than ever. Girls—grown, married women—fling themselves at him. The tabloids are obsessed with who he's shagging. He is a stunner, and he knows it.

Oh, he clearly knows it, The opening shot is him, sitting behind his desk, a humble little table, much loved and clearly a working tool, not a status symbol. He's grinning at his screen with supreme confidence. Cut to his screen, where I matted in a little VLC window showing another clip of Scot, much younger, teen-aged, horsing around with half a dozen nameless starlets on the set of some film. I'd done a little jiggery-pokery so that you could see his face reflected in the monitor, an expression that wasn't quite a smirk and wasn't quite a smile on his face. It was one of those unguarded, unself-conscious expressions that Scot was so famous for, the face of someone who you would swear had *no idea* that a camera was pointed at him. Another trick shot, zooming back so that now we're looking over his shoulder.

As the video on his screen runs out, he leans forward and takes the mouse, and I'd matted in the distinctive anonabrowser that The Pirate Bay had introduced, with its pew-pew laser effects as it zapped every tracking bug and cookie; the groovy animations of it hopping through all its proxies before plundering the world's treasure-house of films, music, and games. Reflected in the screen, his expression changed to one of fierce concentration. In the search-box, the words "Scot Colford." The mouse glided to the SEARCH button. More clicking.

Scot's door interior—the door of the house in Soho he'd lived in for thirty years, a fixture there, now celebrated with a blue disc. Scot crosses to the door, looking fearful (footage from a spooky Halloween short he'd made), opens it. Someone outside. We don't see who. We just see Scot's reaction shot, the fear turning into horror, the horror to terror, the terror to abject, weeping pleading. He'd played it for laughs, but with the right music and a v-e-r-y subtle slowdown of the framerate, it looked like he was shattering inside. I knew how that felt. I'd been there. I knew exactly how I wanted Scot to look, and that's how he looked. Just like I'd felt.

Now we see a young Scot, not even a proper teenager, and he's alone, staring abjectly at the blank eyes of a brick school, a massive place that might as well be a fortress or a prison.

An old Scot next, carrying a box of office things out of a glass tower somewhere in the financial district, suit rumpled, shirt untucked.

Another Scot, lying in a hospital bed, emaciated, tube up his nose. In the seat next to him, the young Scot again. Fingers on a keyboard. A screen. NETWORK ACCESS SUSPENDED.

Now the original Scot, and a zoom out to reveal him sitting on the floor of a grim cell, tiny. He is sunken and sallow, and he slowly, slowly raises his hand to cover his face.

A long beat, the light changing, and it looks for a moment like it will grow dark, but that's just a fake-out. The scene lightens, brightness edging in from the edges of the screen until it is a searing white. A perfectly black, crisp-edged silhouette . . . *dances* on that white screen. No, it's not a dance, it's some kind of boxing training, but so graceful, until the savage kicks and punches. The light changes, and now the silhouette is Scot again, teenaged Scot, shadow-boxing, and the background fill-in with a film set, and Scot is whirling and punching and ducking and weaving.

Now, the first words spoken in the whole film: "It's. Not. Fair." More punching and kicking—there'd been about ten takes of this in the video Katarina gave me, and I'd used them all, playing with the lighting and the speed and cutting back and forth so that Scot became a dervish. There'd been a moment when I was cutting that sequence where it felt like Scot and I were working together, across time and space; I felt like I could *see* what Scot was trying to say with his body and his facial expressions, and I was bringing that out, *teasing* it out, bringing his intention to the fore.

Back to the Scot in the hospital bed. If you watched the whole clip, it was just some footage of him recovering from having a kidney stone out, but he really looked like death, and he'd got his wife to bring in a camera and set it up at the foot of the bed so he could experiment with expressions of grief and dying. It was what made Scot Scot, that constant practice of his craft. There'd been one frame where he'd just *nailed it*, so much so that when he caught a glimpse of himself in the monitor, he'd startled and made a *yeek* sound. It was the face of someone who was angry and scared and hopeless and in pain—it was the exact mixture of feelings I'd felt the day they'd come and taken away my family's Internet. The second I saw it, I *knew* it was my closer. I let it flicker in a series of short cuts from the rage-dance, *flick, flick, flick,* faster and faster like a zoetrope starting up, until it was jittering like an old fluorescent tube. Then I held it still for just less than a second, and cut to black.

That was it.

"Dude." Chester said. He'd been watching a lot of American animation lately and it was all "dude" all the time. "Duuuuude."

Rob giggled. He'd had a little too much of Dodger's special helper and was lying boneless on the rug in front of the sofa. "I think what's he's trying to say is, that video needs to get a wide viewing."

I shook my head. "Well, maybe after the trial. But it'll be too late then, of course. The vote'll have gone ahead. We'll have lost. And I daren't release it before the trial, or I'll end up in jail;

everyone's been very clear on that subject." I sipped at my wine. "Christ, I wish I could put this online tonight."

"What if we got someone *else* to put it online?" Jem said.

I shook my head. "I don't think it'd work," I said. "It wouldn't get the play, and no one would pay attention to it before Monday."

Jem looked up and down, thinking so hard I could hear his brain whirring. "What if we got every major news outlet to play it?"

I made a rude noise. "Well, so long as we're playing what-if make-believe, what if we could show it to every MP?"

Jem nodded. "Yeah, that was my plan all right," he said. "What if we screen this thing somewhere everyone will see it? Somewhere that makes every single newscast the next morning? Something that'll be on every freesheet and website?"

"Erm, yeah, that would be great. How do you propose to do this, Jem?" I was skeptical, but I felt a tickle inside. Jem was grinning like mad, and he hadn't been into the skunk yet, so there was *something* going on in that twisty mind of his. Something grand and wonderful.

"You remember that time Hester and your missus put on that brilliant show in Highgate Cemetery? The outdoor beamers and all?"

I nodded, and felt a little disappointed. Yeah, we could probably get a bunch of the Confusing Peach types out to some park and show this to them, but we knew by now that our message boards were full of supergrasses who'd fink us out to the law, and besides, what did it matter if our crowd saw this? They were already on our side.

Jem caught my expression and raised his hands. "Hear me out now! What if you had a fantastic beamer, a giant one, one that was powerful enough to, say, paint an image on the side of a building a good five hundred meters or more away?"

"Are you asking me 'what if' as in 'imagine that there was such a thing,' or as in 'I have such a thing?'" I asked, and my excitement was creeping back now, because I thought I knew what was coming next. For one thing, Aziz's helpers looked like they were about to bust and Aziz was nodding thoughtfully.

Jem waved his hands. "That's the wrong question. Just imagine it for a moment. Where would you screen your little *tour de force* if you could show it anywhere?"

"I don't know. Erm. Buckingham Palace?"

Jem snorted. "It'd only be seen by a load of tourists, mate."

"The Tate? From across the river? It's got nice, big blank walls."

Jem nodded. "Oh, that's good. Hadn't thought of that. But think bigger, son. What else is on the river? Some place were MPs are bound to see it?"

I could see other people in the room getting it, which was frustrating as anything. Hester laughed. Chester and Rabid Dog laughed harder. Rob and Dodger roared with laughter. Aziz and his gang pounded their fists on their thighs. Then, the light dawned for me.

"Bloody Christ, Jem—*Parliament*?"

"Now you've got it!"

The Jammie Dodgers pulled off some *insane* stunts over the years, but nothing half so grand as the night we took over the House of Commons.

It wouldn't have been possible without The Monster, which is what Aziz and Co called this fantastic, forty-thousand-lumen beamer they'd rescued from a skip behind a cinema that was being pulled down in Battersea. None of them could believe that this astounding piece of kit could possibly work—not until they googled it and discovered that it had been decertified from use ten years before, thanks to a firmware crack that let bent projectionists harvest pristine, lossless copies of new-release films. Of course, *I* could have told them all about it: the NEC DCI Mark III was notorious for being thoroughly compromised within days of each of its patch-cycles, twenty-eight times in all over two years, before it was finally decertified, and thereafter no self-respecting digital film would play through its powerful lens.

Though I'd hardly been a tadpole when all this had happened, the zeroday film-release scene I'd grown up with was still wistful about that golden age, when new films would turn up online an hour before the worldwide premiere, smuggled out of the projection booth by someone who knew someone who knew someone. Of course, there were always screeners before the cinematic leak—advanced copies that had been sent to reviewers or awards juries—not to mention all those prerelease versions that leaked out of the edit-suites. But those tended to have big, ugly NOT FOR EXHIBITION watermarks on them, or were rough and unfinished. The Mark III was piracy's best friend in those long-ago days, and I'd assumed that all those beasts had been busted up for parts or melted down or beheaded and stuck up on the wall of the MPAA's chief pirate hunter's study.

And yet here it was, a huge box with a lens as big as a pie plate and a massive, 240V safety plug.

"It draws more power than a roomful of Gro-Lites," Aziz said ruefully, watching the power meter on his mains outlet whir around.

"But *look* at that picture!" I said. I couldn't restrain myself from hopping from foot to foot. We'd brought it up on the roof of Aziz's warehouse and we'd focused the picture on a low tower-block over the road and across a field, a good kilometer away. At that distance, the picture was three stories tall, and even at this distance, it looked bleeding *amazing*. I zoomed in on it with my phone's camera, and with magnification at max, I could barely make out the tiniest amount of fuzz. The Mark III had been overbuilt, overengineered, and overpowered, and as Aziz swung the projector around on the dolly we'd lugged up to the roof, the huge image slid vertiginously over various walls and windows. I held my hand in front of it and made a shadow doggy. Over the road, a giant's hand loomed up on the wall: Woof! Woof! But more like WOOF! WOOF!

"Of course, this only works if we don't care about getting nicked," Dodger said. He'd sobered up quite a lot on the ride over in the back of Aziz's White Whale, and he'd made appreciative, electrician-type noises as we muscled it onto the roof, using a winch and crane that seemed to be made of rust and bird poop at first, but didn't even rock an inch as we hauled away like sailors at its ropes.

From the ground below, we heard 26 shouting: "Hey, you kids, stop splashing your pirate photons all over the shop!"

"How's it look from down there?" I called.

"Like the Bat-Signal," she said. "But in a good way. Hang on, I'm coming up!"

And that, in a nutshell, was why I loved my girlfriend to tiny, adorable pieces: she'd gone home that afternoon in a miserable sulk, but when I'd called her and told her to drop *everything, right now,* and get her fabulous arse over to Aziz's place, she'd dried her tears, worked out the night-bus routes, and trekked halfway across England (well, all right, London), without a second thought.

Aziz killed the projector, leaving sudden blackness in its wake. We all blinked and waited for our eyes to adjust. I heard 26 downstairs, then on the steep aluminum ladder that went up through the skylight. She nodded hello to all of us, then came and slipped her arm around my waist and nuzzled my neck. "Sorry," she whispered into my ear.

"It's okay," I whispered back.

Dodger shook his head. "Look, you lot, this is pretty amazing and all, but I'm not up for going to jail. Maybe I can get you your power and then scarper before you turn it on, yeah?"

"What's the problem?" 26 said.

Dodger thumped the Mark III. "Only that this thing is an absolute beacon," he said. "These lunatics think they can shine it on Parliament tomorrow night, screen your man's home film on the House of Effing Commons, but we'll have the law on us in seconds. You said it yourself. That thing is like the Bat-Signal."

"Hrm," 26 said. It was the "hrm" she used when she was

really thinking about something. "Any of you lot know much about pirate radio?"

We mumbled words to the effect of, *Yeah, kinda. Heard of it, anyway.*

"It used to be *giant*," she said. "That was mostly before the net, of course. There were all these people, complete nutters really, and they'd climb up onto the roof of buildings and hide an all-weather broadcasting station up there. But then they'd add a second antenna, one that was meant to *receive* signals from anywhere that had line-of-sight to their rooftop."

I could see where this was going. "They bounced the signal off another building! It was a relay, right?"

She patted me on the head. "That way, when Ofcom's enforcers went all-out to trace their signal back to the transmitter, they'd just find a box on a roof that could be fed from any of thousands and thousands of flats. They'd take the antenna down, and the broadcasters would just aim their little transmitter at another antenna they'd already prepared."

"Oh," we all said at once.

"Listen to that penny dropping," she said, "it's a lovely, *luv-verly* sight. Now, I'm no expert on optics, but I *did* just write my A level on physics, and I don't imagine it'd be insanely hard to make this work, especially if you're not particular about the image quality and just want to make a big spectacle without getting banged in jail, yeah? What we want is some big mirrors, and a good monocle or better yet, a telescope."

Aziz was nodding so hard it looked like his head would come off. "I've got just the thing."

Jem drummed his hands on the top of the projector. "I'll get started on the coffee," he said. "Who wants some?"

As one, we each shot an arm into the air, and said, "I do," and Jem said, "Right," and scampered down the ladder.

Despite it being a short summer night, the time seemed to stretch out. Over the years, Aziz had accumulated all manner of monocles, SLR camera zoom lenses, telescopes, and other optics. There was also plenty of shiny stuff to be had, from outsized, clip-on rearview mirrors to satellite dishes lined with aluminum foil. The best results came from the smooth, bowl-shaped pot off the headlamp of a rusting old Range Rover Aziz had in back of his place. It had come out of the Rover a little dusty, but once we wiped it down with a lint-free cloth and then lined up the shot right, we could funnel the beam off the Mark III through a bugger-off huge Canon telephoto lens with a busted thread, then through a Minox tactical monocle, turning it into a pencil-beam of high-resolution light; thereafter, we could send it a good 100–200m into the headlamp pot, and bank it 90 degrees and into a building-side half a kilometer away. Sure, the final image was a lot more distorted, but—

"We could get four of these and spread ourselves out in hiding spots all along the south bank, set the projector up on the north side of the river, and hit Parliament over and over again, switching over every time we heard the sirens start," I said.

"There's only two pots on the Range Rover," Aziz said. "But there's a wrecker up the road we should be able to scout for more."

"Lining up the shots at that distance will be tricky," Chester said.

In answer, Rabid Dog pulled a laser-pointer out of his shirt pocket. "What about a laser-sight?" he said. He turned it on and aimed it at the pot we'd set up halfway down the road from Aziz's place. It neatly cornered and showed up on the building side where we'd been testing out the video.

The sun was rising now, and there was more traffic, and the projector light was harder to see. But it didn't matter. This would *work*.

"What about the CCTVs?" Dodger said.

"Hats," Jem said. "Pull 'em down low. Wear anonymous stuff—jeans and tees, that sort of thing."

Dodger made a face. "Forget it," he said. "They'll put your

piccie on the evening news, call you a terrorist, someone'll shop you by breakfast. Count me out," he said.

"When did you get to be such a scared little kitten? I thought you were meant to be all hard and fearless, Dodge." Jem and Dodger rarely fought anymore, but when they did, it was like watching brothers go at it, that same total abandon, that same fast and scary escalation.

Aziz raised his hands. "Calmness," he said. "Calmness, please. Jem, Dodger, there's something we'd like to show you." He nodded at one of his acolytes, Brenda, who went to a shelf and took down one of the familiar mosquito-zapping hats.

Dodger made a rude noise. "That thing barely has a brim! It wouldn't do you any good."

Aziz rolled his eyes. "It's not a disguise. Brenda?"

Brenda took off the flat-cap she wore. Her kinky black hair sprung out into a halo. She stuffed it back under the mosquito hat and smiled.

"Observe," Aziz said, and held up his phone so that the camera lens shone at her.

Zap.

An instantaneous line of green light snapped out of the hat and drilled directly into the lens. There was a light crackling sound from Aziz's phone, and then the screen went dark. He chucked it onto a workbench that I now noticed was covered in lightly charred, semiobsolete phones.

"I got the idea from those posh antipaparazzi handbags," he said. "The ones that detect a camera-focus and detonate a flash before it can shoot? Scourge of the tabloid photog, they are. I thought that I could probably use the optics in one of these things to find CCTVs, anything with a camera. You wear one of these going down the street and anything close enough to get a decent look at you will be fried before you come into range. What's more, you'll blend right in wearing these things—everyone's got 'em. Don't suppose they'll last long, once the law figures out what we're about, but I figure we might as well use them for something fabulous while we can. I've got eight ready—should be plenty for a projector crew and four runners to take on the reflectors. At this rate, we should be able to light up the House of Commons for a good two or three *hours* and still get away clean."

Dodger's mouth was slack, his eyes wide. Jem slapped him lightly across one cheek.

"Right," Jem said. "How's that suit you, Dodger my boy?"

When I'd first cut the "It's Not Fair," short, I'd automatically inserted my usual credit-reel, with my little Cecil B. DeVil pitchfork-and-horns logo and URLs. I excised this, then went over the file with a hexadecimal editor, looking for any serial numbers, user keys, or other metadata that might lead back to me. Just to be on the safe side, I ran the video through an online transcoder, upsampling the video and audio by a tiny amount, then downsampling it again. The resulting file was minutely fuzzier (which hardly mattered, given the projection method we were planning on using), but I felt better about the possibility that there might be some sort of sneaky serial numbers or other scary snitchware lurking in the file.

We built several quick-and-dirty pages to host it, embedding the video from five different sources, including ZeroKTube, but also using several YouTubes that punters would be able to access without having to install any software. But the really tricky thing was, we *also* embedded the TheyWorkForYou page that tracked the vote-record for each MP on the upcoming TIP-Ex vote. Because the vote hadn't happened yet, all this showed was N/A in each MP's voting column; but once they'd cast their vote, it would be there, searchable by post-code. A single link would place a phone call or send an email to the MP's office, and a second link went to a page with the platforms of all the MPs' competitors in the upcoming election.

The message wasn't subtle: "We're watching you. We will let every voter in the country know about how you voted in this one. You may think it'll be hard to get reelected if your party chucks you out for going against the whip, but it'll be just as hard to get your seat back if thousands of your constituents go door-to-door explaining to their neighbors how you sold them down the river."

Granted, it wasn't much different from the message that we'd been sending them all along, all the way back to the first TIP vote, but the numbers had been steadily growing, and with the media splash from our creative projector-graffiti, we were hoping they might take this a little more seriously.

26 and I caught a nap together that afternoon in the Zeroday while Chester and Hester and Jem and Dog scouted locations; they'd done fantastic work finding us underground sites for the original Pirate Cinemas, and reckoned that between Google satellite images of the rooftops and a little ground surveying, they'd be able to find plenty of rooftops on the South Bank with a view of the Commons. They were also going to scout out the North Bank for sites that might be able to get a clear shot of the east wall, which would be tricky, but a lot more dramatic. Aziz and his elves were working on gluing heavy fixings to the lampposts so that they could be attached to whatever was handy and then fast-cemented into place once they were correctly lined up. If we got it all right, each crew would show up in hi-viz vests with cones and that, get the reflector into place, make sure it was working, fix it with fiendish adhesive and scarper. The projector crew would hit each reflector until the law showed up and took it down—they could just drape someone's jacket over the reflector, of course, but it might take them a while to hit on that strategy, and once the pic went dark, we'd wait a random interval and then switch to another one. The law would never know if they'd got all the sites—and we'd save the last, a direct shot, for just before dawn, *hours* after the first hit, when the first of the morning commuters were coming across the bridges.

It was a risky strategy, but Jem insisted that it was our best one, the one that would make the biggest splash. And since he was going to work the projector, we couldn't really talk him out of it. He assured us that as soon as the picture was lined up, he'd do a runner and leave it running unattended until the lackwits and jobsworths at the Met took it down. We'd wear gloves and wipe everything down with bleach-wipes, and the laser-hats would take care of any CCTVs.

All this whirled through my mind as I tried to sleep in the middle of the hot, sunny afternoon, a wheezing fan blowing over me and 26. I tried to concentrate on my breath and the smell of her skin behind her ears and in the crook of her chin, but my stupid brain kept returning to the night's plan, and all the ways it could go wrong, and just how risky it was, and how much riskier it would be if I didn't get some sleep—I'd be so logy and stupid with sleep-deprivation, I'd be bound to make some ridiculous cock-up and get us all sent away. Which, of course, made me even more anxious and even *less* able to sleep, and so on.

But at a certain point, it just doesn't matter how tightly you're wound or how much your mind is racing, sleep comes and takes its toll from you, and so sleep I did, and dream terrible, anxious dreams in which I was looking all over for the Bradford motorcoach station, then looking for my knapsack and lappie in Hyde Park, then looking for Jem in all our haunts, then looking for the Zeroday, which seemed to have moved of its own volition, then looking for 26, then looking for the mirrored pots of the Land Rover lights—while a clashing brass band played on in the background, so loud it drowned out all thought, making it harder and harder to think straight. I was practically weeping with frustration when I realized that the brass band was my alarm, a little salute to Bradford and its brassy history, and it was time to get out of bed and commit some crimes by cover of dark.

I shook 26 awake, pulled on my clothes, then shook her awake again, for she had crawled back into bed and put a pillow over her head. "Come on, love," I said, "time to go and save Britain."

"Sod Britain," she said from under the pillow.

"Time to go and put the screws to Parliament, then," I said.

"That's a little better," she said.

"Time to go and pull off the most amazing feat of pirate cinematry that the world has ever seen—does that suit madam's taste?"

"*Much* better," she said. "Come on, then, enough slacking. Let's do it!"

Perhaps the simplest thing to do here is catalog all the ways that this plan went *wrong*. Because, of course, that's where all the excitement was—but also because the plan mostly went *right*. The building site that the scouting party found was just *perfect* for the projector. Dodger was able to tap into the mains without even using any special kit, and the route they found up the scaffolding avoided all the vibration anticlimb sensors. Once up on top, they used one of the many winches to bring the projector up and got it settled in in a matter of minutes. Of the four other sites scouted for the reflector setups, two were ironclad: one was a roped-off section of multistory car park that was invisible from the street and from the parking area, but had a straight shot to Parliament and the building site. The other was a pedestrian stairwell descending from the Embankment Rail bridge—all it took was some safety yellow tape and a NO ENTRY-CONSTRUCTION-WE REGRET THE INCONVENIENCE sign at top and bottom to ensure that no company would be along.

The other two were . . . less ideal.

The first was up on the roof of the London Film Museum. The scouting party had discovered an emergency stairwell during a daylight hours visit, and they'd fiddled the lock with a lump of polymer clay wrapped in aluminum foil so that it remained opened, but still closed the circuit that told the system it was locked. The idea was to go up all the stairs to the rooftop, get the shot sorted, and head back out—but the door opened out on the touristy strip in front of the London Eye and the London Aquarium. Hard to say what would be worse: trying to sneak out of the door with heaps of witnesses around in daylight, or sneaking out at night when it was utterly deserted. Okay, not hard to say: it would definitely be worse at night.

For a shot at the east side of Parliament, the best they could do was a temporary sewer-works site with its own temporary toilet; the green Porta-Loo box had removable panels below the roofline where someone standing inside the toilets might pull off a bank-shot with the projector's light, but it would be an insanely tight shot, and the person inside would have no idea whether or how many coppers were looking on as the gig unfolded. Plus the scouts were uncertain as to whether there were any handy poles, shelves, or brackets that might be used to anchor the reflector once it was in place, allowing the conspirators to get away while the show played on.

Of course, 26 volunteered us for this one. "Wouldn't want anyone else stuck in such an awful spot," she said. "Not for my idea."

"Excuse me, loads of us came up with the idea," I said. "All together."

"The reflectors were my idea," she said. "Case closed."

Aziz and the White Whale rolled up to the Zeroday around 7:00 P.M., just as the summer sun was starting to drift down toward the horizon, sending fierce light stabbing into the eyes of anyone foolish enough to look west. We piled into the back of the van and sorted through the piles of kit. We'd dressed in our dustiest, dirtiest builders' trousers from the Pirate Cinema heydays, proper builders' clothes caked in plaster dust and all sorts of muck and grunge. Aziz's gang had other plans, though: "Strip off," ordered Brenda with an evil grin.

Before we could ask what she was about, she'd torn open a huge black bin liner and spilled out a small mountain of awful Souvenir of London clothing: T-shirts that said "Bladdy Lahn-din," and "I LOVE LONDON" and "Norf London," and pictures of Routemaster buses, Union Jacks, Lord Nelson on his column, and various jug-eared Royals. The shorts had "London" emblazoned across their bums, and sported enormous cargo-pockets for all your tourist dross.

Jem said, "Eugh, did you lot rob a tour bus?"

Brenda shook her head, and her mate, Lenny, said, "Found 'em in the skip behind the Day's Inn near Stansted, the day after some huge publishing conference pulled out. They were still in the conference bags. Such utter rubbish the cleaners didn't even nick 'em. You won't find anything less memorable to wear in the whole of London. Put 'em on under what you're wearing now, and when you get a chance, change into 'em. Put the outer layer into one of these conference bags." He nudged a slithery pile of cheap carrier bags emblazoned with THE FUTURE OF BOOKS/EARL'S COURT/LONDON and the logos of a load of publishers. "You'll look like a bunch of out-of-towners finishing one last night's revelry before going back to Des Moines or Athens or whatever."

"Or like we mugged a bunch of that lot," Jem said. "I don't really think we'll pass as out-of-towners. We're too sophisticated, mate."

Brenda and Lenny fell about laughing at this, and for a minute Jem looked so affronted I thought, *My god, he was actually serious,* and then he couldn't keep a straight face, either. We were all so nervous that we laughed much harder at all this than it deserved, and when we did strip off, and Aziz hit a pothole that sent us into a half-naked squirming pile, there was so much hilarity and shouting that it was a miracle that the van wasn't reported to the law by someone who mistook us for kidnap victims being spirited out of London.

The safety helmets were like old friends, and I managed to find the one that had been my favorite when we were doing the heaviest Pirate Cinema activity. There was a modified mosquito hat for each of us, with spare battery packs. It was impossible to tell that they'd been modded. "Firmware-only hack," Brenda explained. "Once you've got the bootloader cracked, all you need to do is flash the bastard with your own code and away you go."

Hester's ears grew points. "Where's the I/O?" she said, closely examining her hat for a USB port.

Brenda said, "You'll love this. It's optical. You *literally* flash it—with pulsed light, right there on this sensor in the back."

"You're joking."

"It makes a twisted kind of sense. This thing has so many optical sensors already, why not use them for input? After all, how many times are you going to flash them? The ROMs only hold a couple megs; you can reflash one in a minute or two under ideal conditions."

Hester said, "What about nonideal conditions? Say, when someone's walking down the street and you're following at a discreet distance?"

Brenda rubbed her hands together. "I really like the way you think. I don't think it'd work, though. You want to be really close, and in shadow. . . . It'd stand out like a sore thumb. Still, it'd be something, wouldn't it? Surreptitiously reprogram every one of these things in London to kill CCTVs?"

26 held up a finger. "Could you use the lasers in the hats to zap other hats, and rewrite their firmware? Like, a virus for mosquito-hats?"

Brenda got a thoughtful, faraway look. "Tell you what: if we're not all in jail next week, let's figure it out," she said.

Jem covered his face with his hands. "You people are insane," he said. "Not in a bad way, you understand, but insane nevertheless. I thought squatting and perfecting scientific begging were odd hobbies, but little did I know that I would be the *least weird* one in this little group."

Rob cleared his throat. "I suspect that I might have that honor," he said.

Dodger put a huge hand on his shoulder. "We don't hold it against you, mate."

That ride in the back of the windowless van, swaying and making jokes, stands out as one of the most memorable moments of my life. We were balanced on the knife-edge of risk and success, a box full of possibility hurtling toward destiny. In the back of the White Whale, time seemed to stretch into infinity, and I was overwhelmed with feelings of real love for each and every one of my mates. Whatever happened after this, we'd already done something amazing, the minute we got into that van.

And then the van was pulling over at the first stop: the building site where the projector was to be mounted. First we stopped around the corner so that Brenda could hop out with a doctored mosquito hat on and wander around the site, killing any CCTVs. Then we donned our hardhats and hi-viz and set out hazard sawhorses and muscled the projector behind the hoardings. The scouts had already cut through the chain earlier in the day, working quickly and efficiently with the ease of long practice. In a moment, we were all back in the van except for Dodger and Jem, and barreling toward the bridge.

At each stop, we shed more passengers, until it was just 26 and me in the back. As we slowed to a stop, she grabbed me by the shoulders and gave me a ferocious snog that practically ripped my lips off. It was precisely the thing I needed at that moment. 26 is a clever, clever woman.

We opened the doors and ducked into the Porta-Loo box and pulled the door shut behind us. No one had been around to zap the CCTVs for us, but Aziz had pulled over right beside the toilet and we'd blocked ourselves off with the van doors, and we had our safety helmets pulled way down low. It would have to do.

Aziz's helpers had sorted out mobile phones from the enormous stash of semibroken old handsets in the pile: one for each pair and one more for the projector crew, with cash-only prepaid SIMs in each. Each one had been programmed with the others' numbers, listed in their address books as PROJECTOR, BRIDGE, CAR PARK, MUSEUM and TOILET. As soon as we got the door shut behind us and the ventilation grill unscrewed, we texted "1" to each of the phones. If we'd been nicked or run into some other problem, it would have been "0." The only other permissible code was "9," which meant "abort mission"—chuck away your gear, change clothes, *get out*.

No one sent out a 9 that night, but there were plenty of 0s.

0: The bridge. Chester and Rabid Dog were just getting this sorted—carrying a hazard barrier down to the stairwell's bottom—when they ran into a crew of graffiti kids, real hard lads with shaved heads and rucksacks full of multicolored spraypaint and painstakingly made stencils. They assumed (correctly) that Rabid Dog and Chester were as harmless as bunny rabbits and (incorrectly) that they were real building contractors sent to do something with the bridge's oh-so-convenient stairwell. Dog sent out the 0 while Chester negotiated with the four lads, explaining to them that he wouldn't be running to the law or nothing, but he couldn't just piss off, no matter how forcefully they pressed this point. Meanwhile:

0: The roof. This was an insane plan to begin with. Just because the alarm hadn't gone off when the scouts diddled the lock with their polymer clay did *not* mean that the alarm would not go off when Lenny and Hester opened the door. Which it did. They quickly retreated to a safe distance, setting up their barrier and then sitting down beside it and trying to look cool—or rather, look like builders who were standing around guarding a random patch of ground while they waited for someone to turn up with some vital part or instructions or whatnot—there's a lot of this around London. After twenty minutes of this, no guard had shown up to investigate the alarm. They decided that—incredibly—the alarm was just a bell that rang in that staircase, far from earshot of anyone who could do anything about it, the building equivalent of one of those car-alarms that hoots for twenty minutes solid at 3:00 A.M. without anyone who actually gives a shit whether the car is stolen turning up to investigate. At this point, they steeled themselves and *went back in* and walked up the stairs, attained the roof, verified their visual on the projector site, and sent a 1.

0: The car park. Yes, even the bloody car park, the safest, easiest, most secure spot our scouts had found. The spot was so safe that we left Rob there alone, because it was the *perfect* site, where nothing bad could possibly happen. So Rob only went and dropped the accursed reflector off the fourth-story ledge where he was getting set up, so that it plummeted soundlessly through the warm, black summer night, until it hit the pavement with a crash that was anything but silent. So, yeah. 0.

Are you keeping track? Zeros all round from the bridge, the roof and the car park, which left . . . the toilet.

That would be us.

Chapter <u>15</u>

In an ideal world, 26 would have stood out in the road and looked for the green dot of the laser-scope they'd fitted to the top of the Mark III's jerry-rigged optics, calling the projector team, giving them guidance. But it was still dead busy outside our little portable toilet hideaway; standing outside with a mobile clamped to your head, following a green dot and giving directions into the mouthpiece would have drawn attention. We didn't want any attention.

We had all agreed to keep phone calls to a minimum. No one knew exactly how long the old phones' batteries would hold out, and it just seemed like the more we left a digital record that could be traced back to us—by our voices, say, possibly captured by whatever superspy technology the MI5 or Met were using in London—the riskier it was. So we waited. 26 stood on the toilet, one foot braced on either side of the seat (I didn't want to think about what it would be like if she slipped and fell down the hole—but the lid was so flimsy neither of us wanted to risk our weight to it). I stood on the floor, craning my neck up to see if the green dot appeared on 26's face, which was level with the gap. We both hoped it didn't skewer her eyeball, because, well, that would be bad.

And there it was, on her nose. "Your nose!" I said. She whipped the reflector up and I clambered up on the seat beside her (nearly knocking her into the filthy stew of muck and wee and mysterious blue liquid sloshing around below us) and peered intently at the wall of the salmony-yellow brickwork of the Commons, now gray with the dim light of early night. I had a little pair of binox, but have you ever tried to spot a reflected, jiggling green dot on a wall a hundred yards away through a pair of tiny opera glasses? It's *thumpingly* hard.

But I caught it. "Right there," I said. We hadn't found anything to anchor the reflector to, but we'd figured on being the very last team to go, and from the opposite bank to all the other shots, which we hoped would have made the cops slower to respond. Ten, fifteen minutes, and off we'd go. Now we were first, and we'd have to stay up and running for as long as we could. I didn't know what was going on with my zeroed-out mates, but I was surely hoping that they got it sorted quickly.

I texted another "1" to the projector crew and held my breath.

Then I let it go in a whoosh as the opening frames of my beautiful, wonderful, *perfect* video started rolling on the crenelated walls of the Commons. We'd superimposed a QR code on the top right corner of the frame, and it rotated every 10 seconds; each 2D barcode translated into the URL of a different mirror of the video with the embedded TheyWorkForYou stats. The little battery-powered video player plugged into the projector was programmed to roll the video, wait a random interval between ten and two-hundred seconds, then roll it again.

The first time it ran, I craned my neck around 26's trembling biceps to see if I could see the crowd reacting. I heard some excited voices, and maybe a change in the timbre of the traffic noises, but I couldn't say for sure. Then the video stopped and we very, very carefully changed places, trying not to let the reflector budge by the tiniest amount. It wasn't that heavy at first, but after holding it in place while I counted *one hippopotamus, two hippopotamus* to forty-three, I felt my own arms start to tremble. Now it was my turn to be nearly knocked into the soup by 26 as she stood up on tiptoe to get a look out the grill. This being the second run, we expected a lot more people to notice, and they did; I could hear it from where I stood.

"They're stopping traffic," 26 said. "A whole gang of tourists, looks like, standing in the middle of the road where they get the best view."

"Any of them looking this way?"

"A few, but I'm pretty sure the beam is over their heads, the way you've got it aimed; they won't see the light unless they get up higher. Oh, wait, someone's moving one of the curtains on the high window. Shit!"

And that's when the second run finished.

We swapped again, both of us trembling. We'd been breathing floral-scented shit-fumes for ten minutes solid now, and between the lightheadedness, the excitement, and the weird, plasticky acoustics in the Porta-Loo, we were nervous as cats. Add to that the prospect of imminent discovery and arrest, and it's a wonder neither of us had a stroke.

"How many times are we going to do this?" I said. I hadn't wanted to be the first one to say it, but it was clear that 26 was a lot tougher than me.

She made the tiniest of shrugs, keeping the reflector still. "Until someone else is in position, I suppose. Can't stop until then."

Not unless we get caught. I didn't say it. Didn't have to. We were both thinking it.

The video started again. Now I didn't have to look out the window to know that it was drawing a crowd. I could hear them. Also, the unmistakable voice of authority, coppers telling people to move along, the crackle of police radios. Distant sirens. I was in the middle of switching with 26 when the phone buzzed. She dug it out of my pocket and fumbled it and we both snatched for it as it fell towards the festering crap-stroganoff below us. I managed to bat it so that it fell to the floor instead. 26 went for it as I tried to realign the reflector. It was from the bridge: 1. They were ready. I managed to get the reflector lined up again just as the video ended, and we changed quickly into our tourist outfits, stuffing the hi-viz and builder's clothes into the carrier bags and switching on our CCTV-killing laser-hats. We snuck out of the toilet hand in hand, our palms so sweaty that they practically dripped. As we slipped out the door, a beefy copper clapped a hand on each of our shoulders.

"Just a minute, please," he said, with that hard filth voice that made my heart stop beating. Four polite words, but they might as well have been, "And now you die."

I swallowed, then dredged up my thickest, most northern voice, widened my eyes and said, "Excuse us, officer! We're just here for the weekend and we told our Mam and Dad we'd meet them at the Parliament to take our coach and well, we were both caught a bit short and this was the only toilet we could find—I know it was wrong, but it was a desperate situation."

He got squinty and thoughtful and then, by microscopic increments, the hand on my shoulder loosened up.

"Mind if I see your arms, lad?" he said.

I understood then, but pretended I didn't. He thought we'd been injecting drugs in the toilet. I gladly held my arms out, and so did 26. "Like this?" I said, putting even more northernness in my voice, so I sounded like the comedy Yorkshireman in a pantomime. But the copper didn't twig. After a short look at my arms he said, "McDonald's is always a better bet for a public convenience if you really need to go. It's dangerous to sneak into a construction site, you never know what's lying around. Not to mention you could get done for trespassing. Don't let me catch you at it again, all right?"

He was almost smiling under his mustache, and he adjusted his anti-stab vest, running a finger around his sweaty collar. It was a hot night, which was good camouflage for our guilty flushes.

"Yes, sir," I said. 26 nodded vigorously.

"Go on now, go find your parents, and stay out of trouble."

We walked away as casually as we could, and 26 whispered to me, "I thought he'd get us as soon as your hat went off."

"My hat?" I touched the brim. I hadn't really paid much attention to it.

"You didn't notice?"

"Notice what, 26?"

"It killed the CCTVs in his helmet, breast pocket, and collar. *Zap, zap, zap,* the minute he grabbed us. Blink and you'd have missed it."

"I must have blinked," I said as my legs turned to water under me. I don't know what was scarier: the prospect of being recorded by the policeman's cameras, or the thought of what would have happened if the cop had noticed that my hat was shooting lasers at him.

"Let's go," I said.

It was only when we got to the Bridge Street corner that we dared to turn around. The crowd that had gathered had already started to disperse, but we could see it was in the hundreds. More importantly, when I powered up my own mobile and looked at the server logs for our video landing pages, I could see that we'd got fifteen thousand views in the past ten minutes—as people picked up the QR code and sent them around to their mates, and so on—and this was accelerating.

Now the mission phone buzzed again. It was the rooftop, also transmitting 1. I wondered what was happening to Rob in the garage.

As it turned out, he was being arrested.

Having dropped the reflector and smashed it to flinders, Rob found himself without much to do. So he fell back to plan Z: he rang Aziz on his own phone and told him what had happened. Aziz had grabbed a few spare reflectors from the wrecker's yard, just on general principles. He'd been parked on a dark street behind Borough Market, and it took him fifteen minutes to wend his way back to the car park. He was just about to swing into the ramp when he saw the motorcycle cop turn in and begin to ascend toward Rob.

Aziz kept driving. He thought of calling Rob but the last thing he wanted was for Rob to be on the phone with him if he got nicked. Besides, Rob wasn't an acrobat, he wasn't going to outrun a motorcycle or leap from the garage to a distant rooftop, so Aziz drove a ways off and parked up and drummed his fingers and swore under his breath for a good long while.

Meanwhile, the motorcycle cop had found our Rob, standing gormlessly in the No Trespassing zone on the fifth floor of the car park, sweating guilty buckets, waiting hopelessly for Aziz to turn up. Fortunately for Rob, he wasn't carrying anything more suspicious than a change of clothes and a laser-hat, but he was so utterly suspicious and out of place that he was nicked anyway. Aziz heard the sirens again as a police car hurtled up the garage ramps, and then left with the now-handcuffed Rob in the backseat, trying to remember if anyone he knew had a good solicitor as they took him off to the cells.

Speaking of guilty sweats: the projector team was in a considerable state, and why not? Dodger had been persuaded to leave all his ganja back at the Zeroday, just in case they got caught. No sense in handing the law an easy drugs offense for the charge-sheet. But they really could have used it. Dodger, especially—for all his gruff bluster, he confessed to Jem that he'd never been inside and he had terrors of being sent away. As touching as his confession was, Jem had other things to worry about, like swinging the huge projector around to line up with the marks they'd scratched on the girder for each of the sites.

It turned out that the random repeat-timer on the projector was a kind of torture for the poor lads. They'd line up the shot, hit "go," and then wait, jittery, for the video to start. Each run-through was spent watching the surroundings for pointing fingers, police helicopters, or converging squad cars—whilst also using binox to watch the reflector site to see if the cops were getting near it. Both the rooftop and the bridge crews managed to fix their reflectors in place and get lost, but Jem and Dodger were rightly worried that if they were still projecting when the cops got there, they'd be using the light-beam to get a fix on the projector's location.

It took the cops *forever* to get to the rooftop. For one thing, they clearly didn't know about the sneaky staircase trick and spent a hell of a long time monkeying around inside the building before they got to the roof, sixteen hard men in full riot gear, running around like commandos, chasing phantoms. That would have been worth a laugh from the projector crew, except they were alternating peeks through the binox with the gut-busting work of getting the projector lined up with the bridge. Having done so, they realized they had at least an hour to wait before they started up—it was only 10:30 P.M. and we'd planned on doing the final switch-on, from the projector itself, at 5:00 A.M., just before sunrise.

Given that there'd been nothing from the car park (we'd all stuck to the plan and not called Rob, though we spent the whole night wondering if he was being interrogated and whether he'd crack and give us up), they had to assume they'd only have the bridge, and then nothing until five. So they waited, and to kill time, they checked out Westminster with the binox and over their mobiles. It was *heaving* with people, a carpet of law enforcement, reporters, and late-night Londoners out for a spectacle.

In the seventy-eight minutes they'd been able to run the video off the rooftop reflector, hits to our landing pages totaled over a million, and the mysterious film was the front page of the BBC's site and creeping up on Sky, *The Guardian,* the *Mail* and even *Metro,* the free newssheet they gave away on the tube. Hilariously all of the news-sites had copied the video over to their server and then stuck it behind a DRM locker with a stern copyright warning. We'd have all had a laugh at that if we weren't shitting bricks at the thought of Rob and what he may or may not have been telling the law.

At 12:39, they hit the bridge. The graffiti kids were just putting the final touches on their mural, which was really a hell of a piece of work—running right up the whole side of the stairway and twining out over the archway, a jungle scene in psychedelic colors, all manner of slavering beasties peering out from between the foliage. When the green laser-dot began to quiver uncertainly over their mural, they were sure it was the cops, but then they caught sight of Dog, solemnly directing Chester and the reflector. Then Dog was looking at Parliament through his binox and calling out, "Higher, lower, right, right, left a bit, higher, stop."

The graffiti kids demanded to know what was going on. Dog and Chester ignored them utterly. Then, *wham,* the silvery bowl Chester was holding began to glow like a spotlight, and across the river, the video ran yet again on the walls of Parliament. Chester and Dog busied themselves with the adhesive and bits of wood and rock they'd gathered, cursing as they jiggled the reflector while trying to fix it in place.

Now the graffiti kids seemed to get what was going on, and they ran all around the embankment, picking up pieces of rubbish that might help fix the reflector into place, crowding around to give "helpful" suggestions in awed tones. With their help—or perhaps in spite of it—Dog and Chester got the reflector set before the first run-through.

"Now what?" one of the graffiti kids—sixteen, green hair, face mask, a paint-smeared white disposable boiler suit—asked.

"Now we scarper," Chester said. "And you never saw us, right?"

The painter laid a finger alongside his nose and shouted, "Skip it, lads!" and the graffiti kids vanished into the night.

"Right," Chester said, "let's shoot the crow, shall we?"

They changed into their tourist outfits and sauntered away, wet armpits and wet palms and fluttering hearts and all.

The plan said we'd all go back to the Zeroday when we got done with our part, but Rob never checked in, so for all we knew, the Zeroday was swarming with nabmen in blue. Plus—tell the truth—we couldn't any of us bear the thought of missing the show. So like dogs returning to their vomit, we stupid criminals returned to the scene of the crime. When Hester and Lenny sidled up alongside of us with their sheepish grins, we knew we weren't the only ones who lacked the discipline of hardcore urban paramilitary guerrillas. This was our greatest opening ever, and we wanted to be there. Luckily, there was a damned huge crowd to get lost in. Westminster Bridge was utterly rammed with gawpers, staring at the looping video on the side of Parliament, holding up their phones to video it or get the QR code and visit the site.

"How'd you go, then?" Hester said, her eyes shining.

"I think we did all right," I said.

"Brilliantly," 26 confirmed. "How about you?"

Hester assumed a mien of absolute nonchalance. "Nothing too collywobbly," she said. "Bit of running around, though, yeah?" She gestured at Lenny. "This one could bring home the gold for Great Britain in the half-mile men's depulsion. Right sprinter. Nearly left me behind."

Lenny affected not to hear and paid attention to his mobile instead. "Eleven million," he said.

"Cor," said Hester.

"Blimey, too." 26 agreed. *Eleven million* views! It wasn't even six in the morning yet! Who knew that many people were even *awake* at this hour!

We fell silent as another run of the video ended and the crowd shuffled around the stopped traffic. There were cops somewhere nearby, blowing whistles and telling people to move along. No one seemed to hear or care. People had snapped the QR code and landed on the website and were reading out the potted history of TIP-Ex to one another. An official car fought its way through the crowd. Someone started chanting "It's not fair!" at it, and the crowd picked it up. It was a kind of carnival atmosphere, not angry, but there was no mistaking the crowd's feeling on the matter of the morning's vote.

The car used its horn to push through a forest of arms holding mobile phones; half were taking snaps of the frosted windows and the grim-faced driver; the other half were showing the video to whatever luckless sod was in the backseat.

As the car swung into Parliament Square, the crowd cheered,

and another round of the video began. Traffic was picking up on the bridge, but there were too many people to fit on the pavement or even the lane closest to the video—both of the eastbound lanes were now shut down, and the horns began to honk. Over the river, we could see flashes of police lights and hear snatches of siren as they searched for the now-abandoned projector.

"So," I said, looking at the mission mobile, which showed the "1" the projector team had sent when they evacuated. "Nothing from Rob, then?"

Everyone looked at their shoes. "Nicked," Hester said. "Musta been."

That's when Chester and Rabid Dog reached us. It was hugs and backslaps all round as the video rolled again, and no, they hadn't heard from Rob, either.

It was another forty-five minutes before Jem and Dodger made it. They had eggs and fried mushrooms on their breath and down their fronts. When Jem gave me a hard hug, I said, "You bastard, you stopped for breakfast!"

He laughed and dug around his carrier bag and came up with a paper sack of drippy bacon sandwiches that we handed around. "Fantastic builder's caf just around the corner from there," he said.

"You are the coolest customer in all of London," I said.

"You're not so bad yourself, old son," he said, and put me in a friendly headlock that had me choking on my bacon buttie. I finished choking just as the video cut out, midplay. The crowd groaned and people started asking one another whether the video would start up again. A sizable portion apparently believed it wouldn't, and we took advantage of the general exodus to slope off and find a bus home to the Zeroday.

We made an odd group, with our shining eyes and trembling bodies, our touristy garb and hats. But London was full of odd groups just like us, and that was the point, wasn't it? I don't reckon anyone gave us a second look the whole way home.

"Nothing from Rob, then?" I said for the fiftieth time as we came through the door and began to collapse onto sofas and chairs and cushions and rugs. Jem chucked his balled up builder's trousers at my head.

"I'll make the tea," he said, and went into the kitchen before I could retaliate.

We stayed awake hitting "reload" and listening to Radio 4 streams for as long as we could. The hit counter went gradually berserk—by 9:30 A.M., it had hit eighty million, which was greater than the population of Great Britain, which meant that either people were watching more than once, or we had foreigners tuning in, or our hit counters were unreliable. It didn't matter, because a) the number was still rocketing up and; b) it was a *rattling* huge number.

What we *really* wanted to do was hear what was going on in Parliament, but, apart from a few tantalizing tweets from MPs on their way into work, it was a black hole. None of us had thought to sign up for seats in the gallery, and there had already been four tour-buses' worth of out-of-towners queued up to sit in when we left. We didn't dare call Letitia because we had already decided we wouldn't outright admit to her that it had been us. And we didn't dare call Rob in case some fat-fingered sergeant had Rob's phone rattling around in his trouser pocket, waiting to answer it and see who it was that was calling this gentleman in their cells.

Sleep demanded that we spend some time with it. We didn't even make it upstairs. The whole crew—even Aziz, who pulled up not long after we got in—ended up asleep in the parlor/pub room, the shutters closed against the blinding spring day outside. What woke us, of course, was Rob thumping on the door. He wheeled his bicycle in, looking remarkably well-slept and cocky for a man who'd been in police custody all night.

After we'd finished giving him backslapping hugs and someone'd pressed a cup of tea into his hands, he sat back on the sofa, crossed his ankles in front of him, and said, "Tell you what, I might be all butterfingers when it comes to the old reflectors, but I'm the very spit of perfection when it comes to playing dumb for the Bill. Soon as I was picked up, I started in like, what was the big deal, I was just trying to get up high to get a look at the lights on the Thames cos I wanted to maybe do a photoshoot up there some day. I laid it on proper posh, talking all this rubbish I half-remembered from the one year I spent at art school, and so on and so forth. They took my DNA and cloned my SIM—I assume you all had the good sense to ditch yours, yeah?—and forgot about me for the next eight hours. So I slept like a baby, didn't I? My solicitor came and got me out at nine sharp, and I went home for a shower and a change of clothes, which, frankly, the rest of you might consider, no offense. Looks like I might be in for a whopping fifty-pound fine, though my solicitor says he's sure I can beat it if I want to pay him ten times that to defend the claim." He laughed like it was the funniest thing in the world, and he was almost right, at that point.

Here's how we found out we'd won: a reporter from *The Guardian* rang me on my mobile to ask me how I felt about the surprise outcome of the vote. "How'd it come out?" I said. She laughed and said that she assumed someone would have told me, of course: "Only forty-six of them bothered to turn up, but twenty-four of them voted for TIP-Ex, and that makes it the law of the land!"

"Only forty-six of them turned up for work?" I said, and everyone in the pub room looked at me. I covered the mouthpiece. "We won!" I said, my fingertips and the tips of my ears tingling. The roar from my mates was deafening—Jem frisbeed the plate he was holding into the dead fireplace and shouted "Hopa!" as it shattered.

When I could hear the phone again, the lady from *The Guardian* was laughing hysterically. "Yes, seems like most of the MPs heard about those videos this morning—you *do* know about those?"

"I heard about them," I said. It was clear from the way she

asked that she was sure I was behind them, but I wasn't going to admit anything.

"Right, I'm sure you have. Anyroad, they heard about the business with the videos, and *then* they heard from their constituents, telling them that they'd better not vote against TIP-Ex. But, of course, the whips had told them they had to do this. So most of them solved the problem by pulling a sickie and staying home. So they barely had quorum when the question was called— the Speaker delayed the vote as long as she could, I suppose so that more MPs might straggle in, but at forty-six, they were quorate, and your Letitia Clarke-Gifford called the question; and oh, didn't she get the filthies from her party leader. But when it came to the vote, twenty-four MPs went for TIP-Ex—eight from the ruling party, ten from the opposition, and the six independents. And now, you've got the law you've been campaigning about. So now that you're all caught up, I wonder if I might ask you some questions?"

I have no idea what I told her, but apparently I was coherent enough that she was able to get a couple paragraphs' worth of quotes from me that didn't make me sound like I was boasting about the savage bollocking I'd just given to the horrible old content dinosaurs, which is precisely what I spent the rest of the afternoon doing.

Epilogue

The judge only deliberated for forty-five minutes. I wasn't surprised—the dinosaurs' case was ironclad. After all, I was guilty. All I could really say in my defense was that I thought it was real art, and that Scot would have approved. Katarina even went into the witness box and said so. But, of course, neither Scot nor his descendants were entitled to approve of my little films, and so guilty I was.

His Honor was kind, though: he reduced the damages to £152.32: one penny per charge. The entire courtroom laughed when that was announced, and I had to hide my grin. Roshan looked furious and patted me on the shoulder, but the dinosaurs' lawyer was even angrier as the giggles turned into roars of laughter. I didn't care. I wouldn't have cared if it was ten million quid.

We'd won the real fight.

That's why the crowd was laughing. Everyone—the judge, the claimants, and their expensive barristers—knew that the real fight had been settled two weeks before, in Parliament, not during the long, drawn-out, stupendously dull copyright trial. I'm sure that some clever lobbyist had decided, back when, that it would be incredibly effective: first, they'd defeat TIP-Ex; then they'd get a judgment against me for millions, then they'd bring criminal charges against me and put me in jail, and every horrible pirate in the land would tremble in terror at the awful fate awaiting anyone who crossed the almighty Content Barons.

But TIP-Ex was law, there would be no criminal prosecution, and the election was on in three weeks and not one single "rogue MP" had been chucked out of her or his party. Letitia had already promised another Private Member's Bill, if reelected, that would legalize remix videos. She told me that half the party power-brokers wanted to sack her and the other half wanted her to be the next Prime Minister. In any event, her constituents had turned up to her surgeries in hordes to tell her how happy they were with her.

I reckon I'll work on the election. Here in Bow, our MP was one of the ones who took the day off work, which is better than having voted against us. Maybe I'll campaign for her. Or maybe I'll go to Bradford and help Cora campaign for the poor bastard whose office she'd been haunting ever since I went to London.

"Are you coming out to Hester's cinema night?" I asked 26. I'd been texting her all day without a reply, so I finally broke down and called her. I knew she was working at the bookstore, but I needed to know so I could make plans with Chester and Dog, who each had a film in at the screens Hester had got permission to stick up in a community center in Brixton, where she lived.

"No," 26 said tensely.

"You okay?"

She covered the mouthpiece and I heard her have a muffled conversation with someone. "Just a sec," she said, and I heard her go into the back room of the store and up the little stairs that led to the tiny storeroom and loo.

"Cecil," she said.

I could tell from her tone of voice that this was going to be bad. I got that tingly feeling again, but this time there was nothing at all pleasant about it. "26?"

"I've decided on where I'm going to go for uni," she said in a tiny voice.

"Oh," I said.

"The thing is, I had this talk with my dad—my biological dad—and he told me loads of stuff he'd never said before, about how terrible he felt about letting me down, and how not getting to know me was the biggest regret in his life, and—"

I could hear that she was crying. I wished I could be there to hold her.

She snuffled. "Sorry. Sorry. Okay, well, the thing is, I don't think I ever got over his going away, never got over feeling rejected. I mean, like, I *thought* I had, but when I spoke to him—"

"So you're going to go to Glasgow?"

"No," she said. "That would be a little *too* close. But Edinburgh has a brilliant law school. And I'd sent them an application, just as a kind of Plan B, and, well, they accepted me, and—"

"Scotland's not that far away," I said.

She made a choked sound. "It's far, Cec. I know loads of girls who graduated last year and went away to places that are close, Reading or Oxford, and none of them stayed with their boyfriends. It was a disaster for all of them."

"We're different—"

"Everyone thinks *they're* different."

"But you and I, all the things we did, they *are* different—did any of your mates get a bloody *law* passed before moving away to bollocky Reading?"

I was marshalling my arguments, laying them out in my head, getting ready to deliver them like it was a debate, and I was going to use logic to convince her.

She made the tiniest of laughs. "I know, I know. But Cecil, I have to do this, do you understand that? Dad called me when he heard the news about TIP-Ex, told me how proud he was of me, told me all these things I'd waited so long to hear, and—"

And I realized this wasn't a debate. It wasn't a discussion. It was an announcement. The world dropped away from me and my whole body started to shake.

She didn't say anything else. Inside, I wanted to shout, "He *abandoned* you! He's a *copper*! It's *cold* in Scotland!" I also wanted to whimper: *Don't leave me all alone.* But I said neither.

"'Course I understand," I said. "'Course I do." I swallowed hard a couple times. "You coming to Hester's, then?"

"You go without me," she said. "I've got to break it to my parents."

"See you soon then?"

"Sure," she said.

But we didn't. Something happened—growing up, winning, her dad—whatever, and for me, it was the summer of heartbreak. There was plenty of work to do, plenty to keep busy with, but I didn't make another film until the winter finally set in and the sun started to set at four in the afternoon and the rain shitted down your neck every time you left the house.

And then, I *did* make a film. And another. And another.

And now, I've got to go and make another.